Destiny put them on different paths...Could love now join them together...?

He was much too close.

She took a step back.

Yet she'd been brave once, hadn't she? She'd kissed him and remembered it for years.

Without giving herself a chance to talk herself out of it, she closed the distance between them. Placing her hands flat on his chest, she stood on tiptoe and placed her mouth on his.

His hands traveled from her elbows up to her shoulders and then down her back, settling at her waist.

Delight spread through her like a fast moving burn, carrying effervescent bubbles to every part of her body. She was lighter than air itself. She was laughter and joy and only his touch anchored her to the ground.

There was something elemental in kissing Lennox. His hands pressed against her back, slowly sliding up and down, making her conscious of two things: her skin tingled beneath his fingers and delight was being replaced by need.

Oh beloved.

She wrapped her arms around his neck and held on.

In Your Wildest
Scottish
Dreams

KAREN RANNEY

AVON

An Imprint of HarperCollinsPublishers

AVON BOOKS
An Imprint of HarperCollins*Publishers*
195 Broadway
New York, New York 10007

Copyright © 2015 by Karen Ranney LLC
Excerpt from *Scotsman of My Dreams* copyright © 2015 by Karen Ranney LLC
ISBN 978-0-06-233747-4
www.avonromance.com

First Avon Books mass market printing: February 2015

Avon Trademark Reg. U.S. Pat. Off. and in Other Countries, Marca Registrada, Hecho en U.S.A.
HarperCollins® is a registered trademark of HarperCollins Publishers.

Printed in the U.S.A.

10 9 8 7 6 5 4 3 2 1

To all the workers and road crews who labored so intensely on first the street outside my house and then the water drainage system in my subdivision. There were days when I despaired of ever hearing anything but beep, beep, beep, and the deafening cacophony of jackhammers.

But you taught me patience and dedication. Because of you I will cherish the peace of each day much more now.

In Your Wildest
Scottish
Dreams

My darling sons,

When you each came into the world, I marveled at the miracle that created you. I held you in my arms and knew I would cherish you until the breath left my body.

Now I must bid farewell to all three of you at once.

The Almighty has indeed challenged me this day.

I know you go on a great adventure and do so with eagerness and enthusiasm. The Highlands offer less opportunity to you of late. I know this and mourn the circumstances of your leaving even as I know you will do honor to the MacIain name.

When someone asks me about my sons, I'll speak proudly of you. My eldest son, I'll say, remained in Scotland, a few days' journey away. But one of my sons traveled to England to make peace with the conqueror, while the other set sail for America.

You will have children of your own, each of them carrying the MacIain blood and name. Tell them about our history, how we dreamed of an empire. Tell them about the place from which we came, a corner of Scotland known for its men of greatness and nobility.

Mention your mother, if you will, who bravely relinquished her sons to the future.

The Almighty has not given us the power of

foresight, but I cannot help but think years from now your children and your children's children will be proud MacIains, as formidable as their ancestors.

Love sometimes means sacrifice, and I feel that truly on this day. I sacrifice you to honor, to your heritage, and to a future only you can create.

Go with God, my darling sons. May your dreams be realized and may He always protect you.

Anne Summers MacIain
Scotland
June, 1746

Prologue

July, 1855
Glasgow, Scotland

*G*lynis had planned this encounter with such precision. Everything must go perfectly. All that was left was for Lennox to come into the anteroom.

A few minutes ago she'd given one of the maids a coin to take a message to him.

"I don't know, Miss MacIain. He's with those Russian people."

"He'll come," she said, certain of it.

The girl frowned at her.

"Really, it's all right. Go and get him, please."

She could understand the maid's reluctance. Lennox was an excellent host while his father was away in England. This ball was held in honor of the Camerons' Russian partner, a way to offer Count Bobrov, his wife, and daughter a taste of Scottish hospitality. Hillshead, Lennox's home, was lit from bottom to top, a beacon for all of Glasgow to witness.

She took a deep breath, pressed her hands against her midriff and tried to calm herself. She wasn't a child. She was nineteen, her birthday celebrated a week earlier. Lennox had been there, marking the occasion by kissing her on the cheek in front of everyone.

The anteroom was warm, or perhaps it was nerves causing her palms to feel damp. Her spine felt coated in ice and her stomach hurt.

When was he going to arrive?

She pressed both palms against the skirt of her gown, a beautiful pale pink confection her mother had given her for her birthday. Pink roses were braided through her hair. A pink and silver necklace of roses was draped around her neck, and she fingered it now.

The anteroom wasn't really a separate room but a small area off the ballroom and accessible to the terrace stretching the width of Hillshead. A curtain hung between the door and the ballroom.

They would have enough privacy here.

He'd be here in a few moments. Lennox was too polite and honorable to ignore her request.

Had she worn too much perfume? She loved Spring Morning, a perfume her mother purchased in London. The scent reminded her of flowers, rain, and the fresh rosebuds in her hair.

Her hands were trembling. She clasped them together, took deep breaths in a futile effort to calm herself. She clamped her eyes shut, rehearsing her speech again.

Her whole life came down to this moment. She woke thinking of Lennox. She went to bed with one last glance up at Hillshead. When he called on Duncan at their house, she made sure to bring him refreshments, amusing Lily and their cook, Mabel, with her eagerness. When they met in the city, she asked about his latest ship, his father, his sister, anything to keep him there for a few more minutes. At balls she sometimes danced with him, trying hard not to reveal how much she adored him when in his arms.

The tips of her ears burned and her cheeks flamed. She would melt before he reached her, she knew it. She pressed the fingers of both hands against her waist, blew out a breath, then closed her eyes and envisioned the scene soon to come.

She should be reticent and demure, but how could she be? It was Lennox. Lennox, who held her heart in his hands. Lennox, who smiled down at her with such charm it stole her breath.

Lennox was tall and strong, with broad shoulders and a way of walking that made her want to watch him. There was no more handsome man in all of Glasgow.

Suddenly he was there, stepping into the anteroom. Turning slowly to mitigate her hoop's swirling, she faced him.

He wore formal black, his snowy white shirt adorned with pin tucks down the front.

His black hair was brushed straight back from his forehead. Intelligence as well as humor shone in gray-green eyes the color of the River Clyde. A stranger might think life amused him. Yet from boyhood he'd been intent on his vocation, fascinated with anything to do with ships and the family firm.

His face was slender with high cheekbones and a square jaw. She could look at him for hours and never tire of the sight.

"Glynis? What is it?"

She took a deep breath, summoned all of her courage, and approached him. Standing on tiptoe, she placed her hands on his shoulders, reached up and kissed him.

He stiffened but after a second he kissed her back.

She wrapped her arms around his neck, holding on as he deepened the kiss. She hadn't been wrong. She thought kissing Lennox would be heavenly, and it was. If angels started singing she wouldn't have been surprised.

Long moments later Lennox pulled back, ending the kiss. Slowly, he removed her arms from around his neck.

"Glynis," he said softly. "What are you doing?"

I love you. The words trembled on her lips. *Tell him. Tell him now.* All the rehearsing she'd done, however, didn't make it easier to say. He must feel the same. He must.

"Lennox? Where have you gone?"

The curtains parted and Lidia Bobrova entered the anteroom. She glanced at the two of them and immediately went to Lennox's side, grabbing and hanging onto his arm as if she'd fall if he didn't support her.

Lidia was as frail as a Clydesdale. Tall and big-boned, she had a long face with a wide mouth and Slavic cheekbones. Did Lennox think she was pretty?

The girl had been introduced to her as the daughter of Mr. Cameron's Russian partner only an hour earlier. Lidia had barely glanced at her, dismissing her with a quick, disinterested smile, the same treatment she was giving Glynis now.

"What is it, my Lennox?"

My Lennox?

"My father wishes to speak to you." She fluttered her lashes at him. "He mustn't be kept waiting. You know there's something important he wishes to discuss with you." She patted his sleeve. "The future, perhaps?"

Glynis pressed her hands against her midriff again and forced herself to breathe.

Lidia was clinging to Lennox, and all he did was glance down at her.

The Russian woman's gown of green velvet was too heavy for a Scottish summer. Gold ribbon adorned the split sleeves and overskirt and was threaded through Lidia's bright blond hair. Her hoop skirt was so large it nearly dwarfed the room, but she still managed to stand too close to Lennox.

Surely no unmarried girl should be wearing as many diamonds at her ears and around her neck. Were the Russians so afraid their wealth would be stolen that they wore it all at once?

"Come, Lennox." Lidia's voice wasn't seductive as much as plaintive.

The Lennox she'd known all her life wasn't charmed by whining and wheedling.

"Come and talk to my father and then we'll dance. Lennox, you promised. Please."

He glanced down at Lidia and smiled, an expression she'd always thought reserved for her. A particular Lennox smile made up of patience and of humor.

Until this moment he'd never treated her like a nuisance or a bother. Although she was Duncan's younger sister, he'd always seen her as herself, asking her opinions, talking to her about his future plans. Yet now he was as dismissive as Lidia.

She might not be there, for the attention either of them paid her.

Embarrassment spread from the pit of her stomach, bathing every limb in ice. She was frozen to the spot, anchored to the floor by shame.

"Please, my Lennox."

Grabbing her skirt with both hands, Glynis turned toward the curtains. She had to escape now. She didn't glance back as she raced from the anteroom, tears cooling her cheeks.

The last thing she heard was Lidia's laugh.

"OH, DO let the silly girl go, Lennox," she said. "We'll go meet with my father and then dance."

Lennox turned to Lidia Bobrova. He'd known the girl nearly as long as he'd known Glynis, having traveled to Russia since he was a boy.

She smiled back at him, a new and curious calculating expression that made the hairs on the back of his neck stand on end.

"Has the child always been so rude?" she asked.

"I've never found her to be so." Nor would he consider her a child, not the way she'd just kissed him.

Why hadn't her mother noticed the décolletage of Glynis's dress was far lower than normal? He wanted to pull it up himself to conceal the swell of her breasts. Wasn't her corset laced too tight? He'd never noticed her waist was that small.

He glanced toward the door, wondering how to detach himself from Lidia. She'd latched onto him at the beginning of the evening, and from her father's fond looks, her actions had familial approval.

Cameron and Company was in the process of selling their Russian shipyards to Count Bobrov. Negotiations were in the final stage and he didn't want to do anything to mar them. Yet allowing Lidia to signal to everyone that there was more to their relationship was going too far.

Lidia leaned toward him and a cloud of heavy French perfume wafted in his direction. Her face was dusted with powder and she'd applied something pink on her lips.

He needed to get out of the anteroom before anyone attached significance to his being alone with her. He needed to find Glynis and explain. Then they'd discuss that kiss.

He hadn't expected her to kiss him. His thoughts were in turmoil. He was just grateful Lidia—or anyone else—hadn't entered the anteroom a few minutes earlier.

What would he have said?

She startled me. Hardly a worthwhile explanation although it was the truth.

He should have pushed her away, not enjoyed kissing her. It was Glynis. Glynis of the merry laugh and the sparkling eyes and the pert quip. Glynis, who had managed to muddle his thoughts tonight as well as confuse him thoroughly.

Lidia said something, but he wasn't paying any attention. He began walking back to the ballroom. Since she'd gripped his arm with talonlike fingers, she had no choice but to come with him.

With any luck, Duncan would help him out, take the possessive Lidia off his arm and waltz with her, leaving him to find Glynis.

He didn't know as he left the anteroom that it would be seven years until he saw Glynis again.

Chapter 1

Glasgow, Scotland
July, 1862

"You've come home," Lennox said.

Glynis wanted to pull away but stood still. Precipitous gestures could be misunderstood. Better to allow him to hold her hand than cause a scene, especially when whispers swirled around them.

"It's the MacIain girl, home after all these years."

"Wasn't there some scandal about her?"

"Is this the first time she's been seen in public?"

Were people recalling those times she followed after Lennox as a child? At five years old she marked him as hers. As a young woman she was prepared to tell him she adored him.

Foolish Glynis.

He must not affect her. She wouldn't allow it. She was no longer nineteen and desperately in love.

"Why didn't you come home sooner?" he asked now, still holding her hand.

Instead of answering, she only smiled. The diplomatic ranks did not value honesty, and so she became adroit at sidestepping it.

He still smelled of wood and the ocean. Whenever anyone said the word "ship" or she tasted a brine-filled breeze, he would appear in her memory with a twinkle in his eye.

The hint of beard showing on this important occasion wasn't due to any sloth on his part. He had to shave more than once a day to eliminate a shadow appearing on his cheeks and chin.

"I think God wants me to have facial hair," he said to her. "But God and I are going to disagree."

He was a foot taller than she was, dressed in black evening wear accentuating his shoulders and height. All his life he'd worked hard, and it showed in the breadth of his chest and muscled legs. Something about him, though, hinted at power and always had. In a crowded room people sought him out the way they looked to leaders and confident men.

Lennox Cameron resembled a prince and a devastating Highlander and he'd been the hero of most of her childish dreams.

No longer, however. Too much had happened in the intervening years.

She'd grown up.

She needed to say something to ease his intent look. Some words to make him stop staring at her as if he were comparing this Glynis to the impetuous, reckless girl she'd been.

Did he think she appeared older? When she smiled, the skin at the corners of her blue eyes crinkled, the only sign that seven years had passed.

"Do you find Glasgow changed?"

Thank heavens he eased the silence with an innocuous question, one simply answered. She was capable of prattling on for hours about places, countries, people, or the recent weather. Ask her something personal, however, and words left her.

"Yes, I would say so. Your firm seems prosperous."

Was that an adequate word? Duncan said that a dozen docks along the River Clyde bore his company's name.

"We've been fortunate."

His shipyard was famous even in Washington. Members of the War Department said Cameron and Company affected the outcome of the war by aiding the enemy.

Lennox wouldn't care if the world talked about him; he'd continue to do what he wanted. Such bravado might be laughable in another man, but this was Lennox.

"Thank you for coming. My father will appreciate it."

"Duncan told me of his blindness. How horrible for him."

He nodded. "You'll find he's sanguine about the accident. He's just grateful to be alive."

A comment necessitating only a nod and a smile.

"Your husband died," he said, the words stark.

An odd way to offer condolences.

"Yes."

An accident, they said. What a terrible and senseless tragedy, and his wife so young.

He pressed her gloved hand with his. Her fingers were icy. Did he feel them through her gloves? Or suspect her lips were numb?

They were strangers and yet not. They never would be. They'd shared their childhood and too many memories.

He stared down at her. A woman could get lost in his eyes. Unless, of course, she was wiser, older, and tested by experience.

She pasted a formal smile on her mouth, a similar expression to one she'd worn when introduced to the matronly harpies in Washington. This occasion seemed no less important.

He dropped her hand. She almost sighed in relief, but restrained herself.

One must not attract attention.

"Thank you for inviting me," she said, the comment pulled from the bag of rote phrases she repeated without thought. "Now, if you'll excuse me, I'll go and greet your father."

He didn't say a word as she swiveled on her heel and turned toward the receiving line.

Pressing her fingers against her diaphragm, she drew in a deep breath. Her stomach gradually settled and her pulse slowed, yet a hollow feeling lingered in the center of her chest.

Perhaps if she didn't glance in his direction she'd eventually recover her composure.

She tried to focus on something else, anything else, the chandeliers, for example. William Cameron had them imported from France. Hundreds of candles in the six massive chandeliers illuminated the space. Crystal droplets hung from each of the tiers of branches bouncing rainbows throughout the ballroom.

The floors were marble and as slick as glass, forcing her to be cautious as she headed for the receiving line.

The arched windows were polished like crystal, mirroring all the brightly dressed women and the men in their formal black.

Catching sight of her reflection in her conservative mauve dress, she deliberately glanced away.

She passed the two buffet tables, each stacked with ornate brass structures holding a dozen types of cakes, biscuits, tarts, and candies. An army of maids carrying food in from the kitchen ensured that Hillshead's guests never lacked for any delicacy. Trays were filled with every sort of food from salmon to ices, and three different punch bowls offered beverages ranging from fruit punch to something more potent.

William Cameron had built the house after the shipyard in Russia began to show a profit twenty years ago. Over the years he'd added to the structure until Hillshead boasted a staggering sixty-seven rooms.

Two wings plus the main structure housed twenty-four bedrooms, twelve bathing chambers, an assortment of parlors, sitting rooms, music rooms, a dozen rooms set aside for the staff, a formal dining room, a breakfast room, and a family dining room.

"How do you decide where to eat?" she asked Mary once.

Lennox's sister smiled at the question. "Mostly in the family dining room," she said. "We use the formal dining room when we have guests."

Since Cameron and Company transacted business all over the world and Hillshead hosted many foreign visitors, she knew they must use the formal dining room often.

Tonight the crowd was much too large to be accommodated in any place other than the ballroom. The whole of Glasgow, it seemed, had been invited to honor William Cameron for receiving the Imperial Order of St. Stanislaus. The elder Cameron had been rewarded for his efforts in expanding Russia's ship-building industry.

The impressive gilded medal with its cerulean and scarlet ribbon hung in a display case in the foyer. Russian dignitaries tended to be dramatic people and their awards no less so.

The Camerons had changed the decor since she'd been here last, opting for cerulean draperies against paler blue walls. The alcove where she'd once waited for Lennox was no longer curtained. Instead, two settees upholstered in scarlet had been placed there with potted ferns on either side.

The colors reminded her of the ribbon on the medal.

Had Lennox opted for a Russian theme for his home?

Why hadn't he opted for a Russian wife? Why hadn't he married Lidia Bobrova?

He hadn't married anyone. A successful and handsome man would be the catch of Glasgow. Why was he still unmarried?

Richard's voice echoed in her memory. "Curiosity is an unwelcome character trait, Glynis."

A shriek warned her seconds before she was enveloped in a brown silk hug. Her breath left in a gasp as arms tightened around her.

"Glynis! Glynis! Glynis! Oh, my dear Glynis, here you are! I've missed you ever so much!"

"Charlotte?"

She took a cautious step back until her childhood friend reluctantly released her.

"You're just the same," Charlotte said, her broad smile as bright as the chandelier overhead. "I've gained six stone and you've not changed at all."

She'd changed in hidden ways. Once, she wouldn't have paid any attention to Charlotte's effusiveness. Now her old friend's praise and welcome, as well as the sidelong looks from others, embarrassed her.

"You're just the same as well," she said, skilled at lying. She'd had countless opportunities to practice the art of prevarication in Washington.

I've heard nothing about the course of the war, ma'am. I'm certain you're correct and the unpleasantries will end soon.

Yes, sir, your wife is a charming, pleasant woman. I enjoy being in her company and anticipate meeting her at future events.

No, husband, I won't complain. I'm among the most fortunate of women.

"Nonsense," Charlotte said. "I've four children and I've gained three stone with each of the last two." Her laugh bounced around the room until people turned to stare.

Must she call attention to them? Warmth traveled up from her feet to lodge at the back of her neck.

"You'll come to dinner," Charlotte said. "To meet all the MacNamaras."

"Yes, of course," she answered, trying to recall a man by the name of MacNamara.

Charlotte studied her mauve dress, her plump face crinkling into a mask of sympathy.

"Did you love him very much? You're too young to be a widow, Glynis. I'm so sorry. Did he die in the American war?"

"No, a carriage accident."

If Charlotte hadn't outgrown her love of gossip, any news she shared would soon spread like a winter breeze through Glasgow. All Glynis had to do was ensure her fellow Glaswegians knew nothing more about Richard.

Charlotte once again swathed her in a brown silk hug.

"God never gives you something you can't handle."

How many times had someone told her that in the last nineteen months? Often enough that she only nodded in response now.

"I must go and greet Mr. Cameron."

"You will come to dinner?"

"Of course," she said, hoping Charlotte forgot about the invitation.

She moved away with a smile. There, the second person she'd escaped from tonight.

Would the entire evening consist of her bouncing from one encounter to the next as the past reached out to swallow her?

She turned and caught sight of Lennox standing like a king surrounded by a group of admiring subjects, all young and female. Glynis didn't recognize any of the women, but she noted the rapt expression on their faces. She'd been the same once.

Nineteen and thinking she knew everything about life.

What a fool she'd been, what a naive fool.

Let them fawn over him. She wasn't going to act the simpleton. Washington had been filled with handsome, tall, narrow-waisted men with long legs and broad, straight shoulders.

Yet none of them possessed the power to make her heart gallop with a smile.

Glynis MacIain, flighty and outspoken, didn't exist any longer. Richard had trained her well, pressing her into the mold of a diplomat's wife.

A pity, since she preferred the girl to the woman she was now.

Chapter 2

$\mathcal{L}$ennox made his way through the crowd, speaking to those who'd gathered to honor his father.

Tonight was William's time, an occasion to celebrate the arduous years he'd worked in St. Petersburg.

Was a medal worth all the sacrifices?

Lennox wondered what memories the honor invoked. Did his father recall those years he labored in Russia and the strain doing so caused his marriage? Did he even think of his wife and her subsequent betrayal and abandonment? Or did he prefer to focus on each day as it came and abandon the past?

He should do the same.

Still, Glynis was on his mind when he answered a question for Miss Oldham. Yes, he was proud. Yes, it was an achievement. No, they had no plans to leave Scotland again.

He'd done his time in Russia, beginning as an apprentice to his father, learning how to design ships, then overseeing their construction. Once the shipyards had been sold to Count Bobrov, there was no reason to return to Russia.

Now Cameron and Company was concentrating on the shipyards in Scotland and involved in something lucrative and dangerous: building iron-hulled vessels for the Confederate States of America.

He scanned the crowd looking for Gavin Whittaker

and his wife. He saw Whittaker charming a group by the window, showing them his walking stick. Inside the handle was a razor-sharp stiletto, one he revealed with the delight of a child.

At least, he thought, Lucy Whittaker wasn't in sight.

He'd opened his home to the Whittakers because of his concerns about Gavin's safety. After three days he wished he'd directed them to a hotel.

As his houseguest, Gavin Whittaker normally affected the demeanor of a southern planter from the United States, complete with flat-brimmed hat and buff-colored suit. Tonight he was dressed in black. His blond hair, nearly white in the sun, was longer than fashionable. Brown eyes the color of spring topsoil held humor and self-deprecation. When he wasn't laughing, he was telling stories of his home in Georgia, to the delight of his easily acquired audiences.

In fact, Whittaker wasn't a southern planter but a ship's captain, and from what Lennox had discovered, a good one. He was probably a little too reckless and no doubt courageous. A blockade runner needed to be.

Whittaker had a blind spot: his wife. He didn't notice the woman's endless complaints. To Gavin, Lucy was delicate, shy, and fastidious.

Evidently, she was too shy and delicate to be worried about her husband. In a matter of weeks Gavin was going to be in danger, captaining a ship through the Union navy's blockade. If Lucy was worried about her husband, she didn't show it.

To Lucy, this trip to Scotland was a wedding journey of a sort, one proving to be a disappointment. Nothing about Scotland pleased her, from the food to the weather to the way the Scots spoke.

Lennox recognized her contempt for Scotland. It was similar to the derision the English had displayed toward his country for centuries. He could understand his ancestors' irritation and desire to go to battle. He felt the same every evening after dinner.

He took Whittaker to the shipyards with him each morning. To his surprise, the man gave him good advice on the changes on the *Raven*, plus he had ideas worth exploring on future blockade runners.

As for Lucy, he tried to avoid her when he could. Perhaps Eleanor MacIain might be persuaded to take the woman under her wing, show her Glasgow and find something to keep her occupied.

Only fourteen days separated him from peace. In two weeks Gavin would sail off with his English bride and a skeleton crew for Nassau. He could survive anything for two weeks.

"He's very tired," Mary said at his elbow.

He glanced down at his sister. She worried him, and had ever since their father's accident. Stress pinched her features and changed the whites of her green eyes to gray. Her black hair appeared dull and her expression listless. Despite being a young woman, she behaved like someone tired of the world.

She acted more the widow than Glynis, a thought jarring him into violating the privacy each accorded the other.

"Are you feeling ill, Mary?"

She blinked up at him, obviously surprised at the question.

"Is there something wrong you haven't told me?"

She opened her mouth to speak, shut it again, then shook her head.

"Are you certain?"

"Yes," she said.

Her tremulous smile was no doubt meant to reassure him, but failed.

"See to Father," she said before he could question her further. "He should rest."

An answer, then, and the only one he suspected he would get.

He glanced over at William. Although he smiled at his well-wishers, fatigue etched his face.

After making his way to his father's side, he bent down and whispered, "Are you ready for me to banish all of them, Father?"

William's smile deepened the vertical lines bracketing his mouth.

"Not yet, my boy," he said, his sightless green eyes staring out over the ballroom as if he could see the line of people waiting to greet him. "A man can't have too much admiration, do you think?"

Lennox clasped the older man on the shoulder, a little alarmed when he felt bone where there should be muscle. He smiled and moved away, determined to talk to Mary about taking their father to Rothesay on the Isle of Bute. The hydrotherapy retreat would do them both good.

"You throw quite a shindig, Lennox."

He turned. Gavin stood there, a full plate of food in one hand, a cup of punch in the other, and the ubiquitous walking stick on his arm.

"You should at least try some of the salmon," Gavin said, thrusting it at him. "Avoid the haggis."

Lennox held up his hand to block the plate. "Thank you, no."

"I tried to interest Lucy in the food, but she's not hungry, poor darling."

Whittaker motioned to the opposite side of the ballroom where a series of couches were arranged for the convenience of the older guests. "I thought she would be happy talking to the other women over there, but she's a shy little thing and all these people are over-whelming. I think she's gone back to our room."

At least she wouldn't be insulting the guests here to honor his father.

Lennox glanced around the room, caught sight of his best friend and excused himself.

The shoulders beneath Duncan's black evening attire were tense, his nervous energy expressed in the tapping of a shoe on the ballroom floor.

Lennox moved toward him, accepting well wishes, answering questions, smiling and thanking his guests as he made his way to Duncan's side.

"Is it going that bad?" he asked, reaching his friend.

"As bad as it can be," Duncan said, spearing a hand through his hair.

His features were drawn, his eyes haunted. He probably hadn't slept well for days.

The Glasgow mills were suffering for lack of raw materials. The same blockade of the southern United States proving so beneficial to Cameron and Company was slowly starving the Scottish textile industry.

He motioned Duncan into the hallway and down the two flights of stairs to his first floor library. No one would bother him there and they could speak in privacy.

"Will you let me help?" he asked, closing the door.

An infusion of cash would keep the mill going until Duncan found a source of cotton.

Duncan's lips curved in a humorless smile. "By magically ending the war? If you can do that, yes. Otherwise? No."

They'd been friends since they were six, confided in each other like brothers. The day the first ship he'd designed was launched, Duncan was at his side. When Duncan took over the helm of the mill, he'd celebrated with him.

Now, their fortunes were on separate paths and he felt compelled to help, only to be blocked by Duncan's pride. He might have acted the same had the situation been reversed. Hopefully, though, he would have possessed more business sense and accepted the assistance.

He didn't like knowing the MacIain mill would close unless something miraculous happened.

Instead of building ships for the Confederate navy, maybe he should construct his own fleet to run the blockade.

"How many days until the new ship is finished?" Duncan asked, sitting in one of the chairs in front of the cold fireplace.

"About two weeks," Lennox said, taking the adjacent chair. "The changes in the hull design proved bothersome, but we finally finished the modifications."

They talked of business matters, shared news of the war. Both the Union and the Confederacy had their fervent supporters. Each side in the American Civil War had good points and bad. Lennox disliked slavery. He also despised bullying. Knowing what he did, he suspected the Confederacy would ultimately lose. They didn't have the manufacturing might of the northern states.

Duncan probably didn't give a flying farthing who won as long as the mill got cotton.

A great many Scots had volunteered in America's war. A few official letters had come to parents and wives of Glasgow indicating their beloved son, husband, brother, or father had fallen in another nation's cause and would forever be interred in American soil.

Just yesterday he learned one of his ships, the *Elizabeth*, had been grounded off the coast of North Carolina. She'd been burned to escape capture, but her crew hadn't been so fortunate. They were probably incarcerated in a Union prison now.

The majority opinion—that the conflict would be of short duration—looked to be wrong. The war might drag on for years—advantageous for his company and disastrous for Duncan's.

"Are you sure there's no way I can help?"

Duncan shook his head, his narrowed eyes warning him not to ask again.

There was no one as stubborn as a Scot, a comment his father uttered often. He managed not to laugh since William Cameron had to be the most stubborn and opinionated Scot that Lennox knew.

He'd already ventured into forbidden territory. He might as well compound his sins by asking about Glynis.

"I'm glad you were able to convince your sister to come."

One corner of Duncan's mouth turned up as if he appreciated Lennox's courage.

"I'm also happy you decided to emerge from your hermitage."

"I wouldn't miss it," Duncan said. "I consider your father partly mine. How is he?"

"I'm concerned about him," Lennox said. "He's getting increasingly frail."

One day he would lose his father just as Duncan had a few years ago. Working at his father's side was important to him. Not only was the older man's greater experience invaluable, but Lennox genuinely liked him.

"Do you find Glynis has changed much?" he asked Duncan.

"Do you?"

Her triangular face and soft blue eyes were arresting. That mouth of hers with the full bottom lip and pointy top lip fascinated him. Yet something was different about Glynis: a wariness, perhaps. Or the way she had of holding herself immobile.

The girl he'd known, the irrepressible Glynis, had constantly fidgeted, as if impatient to be living her life. This woman gave him the impression of a fragile statue on the verge of shattering.

"Yes, I do find she's changed," he said, giving Duncan the truth. "She's brittle. Very polite, excessively so. She smiles at you but her eyes are flat."

The woman he saw tonight had Glynis's face, her blue eyes, her light brown hair, her mannerisms, but not her personality. The bright, intelligent girl he'd known all his life had vanished, her spark tamped down until only a flicker remained.

"She's a widow. She's lost her husband."

Did she still grieve for the man? A question he shouldn't be asking. No doubt they'd been a compatible pair, a true joining of the minds and hearts.

What claptrap. He didn't believe it.

She'd been married a month after arriving in London. Hardly enough time to form a fondness for a stranger.

Why had she married so quickly? Had she done something to spark gossip? Had she kissed another man the way she'd kissed him, without warning but a great deal of enthusiasm?

The night he'd last seen her remained engraved in his mind.

She'd been nineteen and dressed in something pale and pink, making her complexion appear to be porcelain dusted with a faint blush.

"She isn't the same person you knew," Duncan said, intruding into his memories.

He glanced at his friend. "What do you mean?"

"She's been through a lot of experiences we don't know about."

She'd been married to someone else for seven years.

"She's beautiful," he said, then immediately wondered if he should have made that comment.

Here she was, not quite the Glynis of his past, but a mystery, a woman who intrigued him and made him want to know how, exactly, she'd changed.

Who was Glynis now?

Chapter 3

$\mathcal{G}$lynis slid in line, smiling at the two women complaining about something to her mother.

Eleanor MacIain was the kindest person she'd ever known, a fact she only truly appreciated after being exposed to Washington society. The harridans and doyennes of America's capital were Scottish eagles compared to her mother's soft, dovelike personality.

Unless, of course, one of her children was involved. Then Eleanor was fiercely protective.

Her mother never met a stranger, evident when so many people stopped and greeted her, studying Glynis as they did so.

She smiled in response, well aware she was the subject of speculation in the ballroom. Glynis MacIain, come home to Glasgow. Glynis widowed now. She lived in Washington, you know.

Had Charlotte already started talking about her?

Her hands still trembled. She clenched her reticule, forced herself to breathe deeply and felt her smile freeze into a rictus of expression.

She should congratulate herself for venturing out into Glasgow society. Nothing would have prepared her for the encounter with Lennox, but at least it was done now.

At five years old she'd marked him as hers, tucked him into a spot behind her heart where he'd always stayed. So much had changed in the intervening years. She pitied the child who loved so well and so fully.

"What is it, dear?" her mother asked.

She blinked, bringing herself back from the past with difficulty.

"Nothing."

"You have the saddest expression on your face. Are you thinking of Richard?"

The best answer would be to nod and allow herself to be caught up in her mother's sympathy. Instead, loath to lie to her, she said, "No, when I was five."

Eleanor smiled. "You were the most beautiful little girl. And woman," she added.

Her mother had always been her staunchest defender, even on that night seven years ago. After leaving the anteroom, she'd fled to their carriage, where her mother found her.

"I never want to see Lennox Cameron again in my entire life," she'd said.

Her mother had only leaned over and hugged her. "You don't truly mean that, my dear."

She described the scene in the anteroom, carefully omitting the kiss.

"She just hung on him and he let her."

"There's some talk of a marriage between him and the count's daughter," her mother said gently.

She'd felt her heart break in that moment.

"It would be a very good match. The families have known each other for years. The Camerons are selling the shipyard in St. Petersburg to the Russians."

She hadn't been able to hold back her tears.

"Oh, my dear, I'm so sorry," Eleanor had said.

Her mother surprised her with a trip to London the very next day. The thought of returning to Glasgow ten days later horrified her so much she'd begged to stay in England. Reluctantly, her mother left her with their English cousin. Three weeks later she sent a letter to her parents informing them she was going to be wed.

Richard seemed to be the answer to a prayer, but perhaps some prayers should not be answered. Or even uttered.

At the south end of the ballroom, twin archways led to the terrace. The night beckoned, promising a breeze and a little solitude.

After she'd spoken to Mr. Cameron, she'd escape.

People jostled each other good naturedly, the drone of conversation growing louder with every passing moment. Laughter brought brightness to the room, and it made her smile to hear it.

Finally, she stood in front of Mr. Cameron. He sat in a thronelike chair, his left hand resting on one of the lion's heads at the end of the arms. Ever since she was a little girl he'd had a shock of white hair like a patch of gorse on his head. Clean-shaven like Lennox, he flashed a bright, wide smile at her.

"It's Glynis, Mr. Cameron," she said, placing her fingers on the back of his brown spotted hand.

"Glynis MacIain, home again. How nice of you to come. Have you changed much, little Glynis?"

She smiled at the appellation. He'd often called her that, especially as she raced through Hillshead.

"Not in appearance," she said. "I'm a little older and wiser."

"Ah, but aren't we all? What is the perfume you're wearing? It's spicy and sweet at the same time."

"It's called Spring Morning."

One of the few things about her Richard hadn't been able to change.

She smiled up at Mary, who stood behind her father. After congratulating Mr. Cameron, Glynis kissed him on the cheek, then moved away.

Glancing around, she found her mother occupied in a discussion with Mrs. MacKenzie. Heading for the doors to the terrace, Glynis escaped into the night.

HILLSHEAD STOOD on a hill overlooking Glasgow, the River Clyde sparkling in the moonlight. To her left, down the slope but still on the West End, was her home, not far from the cotton mill bearing her family's name.

Plumes of white smoke against a night sky gave evidence the city never slept.

Edinburgh might have more charm and history, but Glasgow possessed power. The city was like a once dormant Scottish creature, a demon of myth and magic now coming alive, soon to rival London itself in industry and commerce. Its claws were stretching to Dumbarton and beyond. Its tongue lapped at the Clyde. Hidden among its scales were the desperate poor of Glasgow's tenements and the inhabitants of the more prosperous West End.

More importantly, Glasgow was home.

Here no mosquitoes waited to bite her exposed skin. No sulfurous air smelling of the swamp clung to her hair and clothes. The summer would be temperate, not oppressive and miserable like Washington.

Glasgow was industrial not political. Commerce thrummed through the air, not intrigue.

She leaned against the terrace wall, staring down at Hillshead's gardens. From here on the third floor she had a view of their intricate paths and the bench she remembered from her childhood. The gardener's hut had been moved and rebuilt to the size of a cottage. Once, Hillshead had boasted four gardeners to manage the vegetable and flower gardens and prune all the bushes and trees. Were there still four or had Lennox added to their number?

A movement to her left caught her eye. She jerked, startled, as a shadow slid toward her.

"I told myself a little patience would be rewarded."

She slowly turned, each second measured in hours. The night had been stressful, the only reason the man's voice sounded horribly familiar.

Please let me be wrong.

"Just wait, I said, and Glynis will come out for air. She hates crowds."

She turned back to the railing, holding herself tight. Perhaps the girl she'd once been would have screamed in frustration. Or pummeled the man who approached her soundlessly.

She imagined him on the ground writhing in agony. She would watch him with a detached air, much as he observed life around him.

Once, she'd accused him of being like a cat in his calm perusal of the world, unaffected by the pain he so effortlessly inflicted on others.

"But you're no bird, Glynis," he'd said, "frightened of me."

How wrong he'd been.

He was too close now, only feet away. She wanted to hold out her hands and keep him at a distance. Words would have to suffice.

"What are you doing here, Baumann?"

"Matthew. Haven't I told you to call me Matthew?"

"You're a little far from Washington," she said.

He chuckled, emerging from the darkness like a monster from his cave.

"Did you follow me?" she asked.

"On the contrary, Glynis. You followed me. I've been in your fair country a good six weeks."

That's why she hadn't seen him in those last months in Washington, why he hadn't bedeviled her before she left.

"Why are you here, Baumann?"

"I like your country," he said. "You Scots are fiercely independent, just like New Yorkers. You'd rather spit in someone's face than take orders and you're not above bending the law."

"Are you lecturing me on morality, Baumann?" she asked. "That's a little hypocritical, isn't it?"

"Oh, Glynis, you don't approve of my being here," he said in a mock aggrieved tone. "I'm hurt you don't want to extend a little Scottish hospitality to a visitor."

"There's nothing here for you, Baumann."

She faced the night, praying for . . . courage? Faith? Strength? Something to counteract the abrupt and penetrating horror of Baumann's presence. He couldn't be here. He mustn't be here.

"On the contrary," he said, his voice hardening. "I would say this place, this Glasgow of yours, might be the most important city in the world right now."

Slowly, she turned to face him.

"Our host is a shipbuilder, Glynis. What do you think he's working on? Some vessel to take a midnight sail? A paddle wheeler to cruise the Potomac? No, he's building a ship to run the blockade."

"Is that why the War Department sent you?"

He moved into the light from the ballroom. His thick hair, brown flecked with a lighter shade, curled around his collar. A mustache and a trimmed goatee enhanced his full lips. His eyes, a dark, intent brown, often appeared mocking.

His nose was pockmarked with scars resembling a row of stitches. When she'd first met him three years ago, she caught herself staring, flushed, and looked away.

"Barbed wire," he'd said, grinning at her.

She had glanced back. "I beg your pardon?"

"I landed on a bunch of barbed wire in a tumble,"

he said. "I was just a boy, but the scar is a reminder not to be so impulsive in the future."

"Are you very impulsive, Mr. Baumann?"

"I find, to my discredit, Mrs. Smythe," he had replied, "that I can be still, yes."

She'd never found him to be impulsive. Instead, he was calculating, his eyes always taking the measure of others.

Tonight, Baumann was dressed in black, like most of the men inside. He'd always been adept at social occasions, even waltzing well. More than once he'd swept her up in his arms so fast she lost her breath.

"Go away," she said, wishing she had the power to banish him with a wave of her hand. "You shouldn't be here."

"On the contrary, I think here is exactly where I should be."

"You're wrong to have come to Glasgow," she said. "And I wish you hadn't. Nothing good can come from your spying here, Baumann."

She gathered up her skirts and left him, heading toward the light with a feeling of terror.

LENNOX LEFT Duncan in his library and returned to the ballroom. He made his way across the room, greeting people he had not yet spoken to, including Eleanor MacIain.

"Thank you for coming," he said, reaching out and taking her gloved hands in his.

"Don't be ridiculous, Lennox, I wouldn't have missed it. I'm so glad dear William has been recognized at last. I just wish Hamish had been here to see it."

He nodded. Hamish MacIain and William had been long-standing friends. Hamish's death had been felt at Hillshead as well.

"It's a lovely celebration," Eleanor said, looking around. "You've done a magnificent job."

"That's Mary's doing more than mine," he said. His sister had spent weeks in planning for tonight. The last few days had been filled with frenetic activity. "I was looking for Glynis," he told her.

"Glynis has taken the air, I believe," Eleanor said, smiling. She put her hand on his arm, gave him a gentle shove. "You look as if you could do with some fresh air as well."

He was left without anything to say. He left Eleanor and made his way to the terrace door.

Any thought of continuing his conversation with Glynis abruptly vanished when he saw her talking to Matthew Baumann.

Did she know he was a Union spy? The man hadn't made any secret of it from the first. A month ago he'd come to the yard and introduced himself.

"I'm a representative of the United States government, Mr. Cameron," he'd said. "As such, I need to know if you've accepted any commissions from the Confederacy."

Baumann then produced a document, a letter of introduction that looked perfectly legal and absolutely useless. He didn't care who Baumann represented. If he thought he could march into Cameron and Company and demand to know confidential details of their business dealings, he was wrong.

"Mr. Baumann," he'd said, "I'm sure you can understand that I don't discuss my business with anyone." Even his designers didn't know about the ships currently under negotiation until all the points of the contract had been finalized.

The man's mustache twitched as he smiled. "In other words, you're not going to tell me."

"It's not any of your business, Mr. Baumann."

"That's where you're wrong, Mr. Cameron. It is my business. It's the War Department's business. It's my nation's business."

He could have sworn the man puffed up like a banty rooster.

"That might be so, but I'm a Scot, Mr. Baumann. Cameron and Company is a Scottish firm. We're neutral in your war."

On May thirteenth last year, Queen Victoria issued a proclamation of neutrality forbidding British subjects from taking part in the American Civil War.

Lennox prided himself on being a Scot and only minimally British. London didn't have to know everything he did.

Baumann studied him for a moment. "We'd be very appreciative, Mr. Cameron. Very appreciative."

He'd wanted to tell the man where he could put his appreciation but he smiled instead.

"I'm not amenable to either bribery or coercion, Mr. Baumann."

"I'm disturbed that you would consider my words either, Mr. Cameron."

"How are you liking your first visit to Glasgow?" he'd asked, changing the subject and hoping the man got the hint. He wasn't going to surrender any information to the Union operative. Not now and not in the future.

"An interesting city," Baumann had said.

He'd invited him here tonight for one reason only. He wanted to know what Baumann would do, with whom he would speak. Who, in Glasgow, was his friend?

He hadn't considered that the man would talk with Glynis. Or that they would know each other.

What was Glynis doing talking to a Union agent? For that matter, why had she come home now?

Chapter 4

"Go to bed," Lennox said to his sister.

She ignored him and directed one of the grooms to a tray piled with food. Tonight they'd feast in the stable and in the kitchen. What wasn't consumed by the servants would be dispensed to the poor.

The garlicky smell of mutton vied with roast beef and the fragrant, warm yeasty aroma of Cook's brioche, a recipe she swore was given to her not by a French relative but an Irish one. Above all the other scents was the odor of candle wax as servants extinguished the hundreds of candles in the chandeliers.

Mary moved to the other side of the room, giving orders to the maids as she went. His sister directed everyone with militaristic precision, a general with a full complement of troops at her disposal. Her voice, however, was husky with fatigue.

He grabbed a nearby tablecloth, wadded it into a ball and tossed it into the basket to be taken to the laundry. A maid grinned at his perfect aim.

When Mary returned to his side of the ballroom, he grabbed the stack of plates in her hand.

"Go to bed," he told her again.

Mary glanced at him in surprise. "Nonsense," she said. "There's still too much to do. The best dishes must be packed up and put away."

"Mrs. Hurst and the staff can do that."

She nodded. "Yes, but the carpets should be swept and the floor damp-mopped." She glared down at the floor. "There are spots where the wax dripped. Those must be repaired tonight."

"You don't need to do it. If the maids have any questions Mrs. Hurst can't answer, I'll tell them to come to me."

"When did you get so domesticated, Lennox?" she asked, glancing up at him with a smile.

"I've been watching you all these years," he said. "The chores can be ably managed by Mrs. Hurst. Isn't that why we employ a housekeeper? Or, if not her, they can wait until morning."

"It won't take long to finish."

"Do you mind caring for Father?"

She glanced at him in surprise.

"Why would I mind?" she asked. "Hasn't he always cared for us?"

He nodded. "But in the last two years you've changed," he said, the first time he put his concerns into words.

She walked to a side table, occupied with gathering up the silver.

"The accident was a terrible thing to happen," she said, glancing over at him. "I can't imagine how awful it must be to be able to see one moment, and the next to be blind."

"You didn't cause it, Mary," he said.

She just sent him a look, gathered up the soiled napkins and dropped them in the basket at the end of the table.

"I can finish the rest of this," he said. "You should go to bed."

She smiled at him. "I'm not tired. Tonight was a very successful evening, don't you think?"

"Thanks to you."

His sister acted as the heart of Hillshead. Everything ran perfectly because she was at the core of the house, planning, organizing, ensuring he and his father were comfortable.

Didn't she want her own home? A question he'd never asked and one startling him now. She had never given any hint of wanting a husband or a family, but shouldn't she?

Perhaps if she weren't so involved in running Hillshead she could devote herself to her own life.

"I want you to take Father to Bute for the waters."

She turned to him, her eyes widening. "Bute?"

He nodded. "People come from all over Scotland to stay at the hotel. The water comes from a mineral spring. It will be good for him."

She folded another napkin, the task evidently requiring her full attention.

"I don't think—" she began, but he cut her off.

"Please, Mary." He came and took the napkin from her. "It would do both of you good to get away."

She stared straight ahead. "Perhaps you're right."

"You'll meet new people."

She sent him a quick glance. "Do you think I need to broaden my social horizons, Lennox?"

"I think you need to stop catering to me and Father so much. What about you, Mary? Don't you want your own life? Your own family? Don't you want to find someone to marry?"

A shadow flitted over her face. "My life is fine," she said, walking to the final table to be stripped.

The clink of silver, the murmur of the maid's voices behind them, the soft sigh of wind through the open terrace doors supplied the only sounds for long moments.

Evidently, he shouldn't offer suggestions to Mary about her life.

"I was surprised that Glynis came," she said, gathering up the last of the silver from the table. "She's been home for a week and hardly anyone has seen her since she arrived. Of course, being a widow, she wouldn't socialize much."

He didn't say anything.

"Why do you think she came tonight?" she asked.

"A gesture of friendship? Our families are close."

"I always thought she was a beautiful girl. She's not a girl any longer but I think she's even more beautiful."

He would be wiser not saying anything.

"Don't you think so?"

He nodded.

"There's something about her, though." She stopped placing the silver in the box and turned to him. "I don't think she's very happy."

He braced himself against the wall, folded his arms and regarded his sister.

"She's a widow. She's not supposed to be happy."

She shook her head. "Glynis was always basically happy. That was her nature. Remember when the mare she loved died?"

He nodded again.

"She cried for days and she mourned for weeks, but grief didn't change who she was. I think the woman we met tonight isn't the Glynis we knew."

She'd been talking to Matthew Baumann. That encounter still troubled him.

"I've always wanted to be more like her, fearless and daring. But tonight she didn't seem the same, did she?"

"No," he said, compelled to answer. "She didn't."

"Do you think marriage changed her?"

He didn't respond.

"Perhaps she adored her husband and grief has made her listless."

He was not going to discuss Glynis's dead husband. He didn't want to talk about Glynis at all.

Thinking about her, however, was a different matter.

GLYNIS WAS different, and it was a change Baumann couldn't put his finger on, something disturbing and fascinating at the same time. Until tonight he thought he knew Glynis Smythe very well. Evidently coming back to her homeland had given her a dimension she previously lacked.

Tonight she stood her ground, leveled that pointed chin at him and insulted him, something she hadn't done in Washington. He felt like a boy being upbraided by his schoolmaster.

Being in Scotland had made her brave. It fascinated him to see her in a different environment. Glynis had always had her share of courage, but she'd never defied him.

She'd been wasted on that bastard she married. Richard Smythe had been an opportunist who knew how to take another's work and claim it as his own. He was a master at exploiting his wife's talents. Any success he had at the legation was due to Glynis. She had a natural ease with people and was well liked, something Smythe was not.

At least she was no longer wearing full mourning, but he still didn't like to see her showing respect for Smythe. The man didn't deserve it.

He'd asked for this assignment. Not only to follow Glynis back to Scotland, but to investigate what he could about Cameron and Company.

The War Department was correct. From every indication he'd had, Lennox Cameron was more than happy to build up the Confederate navy all on his own. Not only was Cameron building steamships, but they were iron-hulled behemoths that could turn the tide of war.

He was damned if he was going to let that happen.

ONCE THEY were home, Duncan bent to brush a kiss on her cheek.

"Lennox thought you looked beautiful," he said.

Before she could comment, he was ascending the stairs.

She watched him, wishing her heartbeat hadn't spiked at the news. She wasn't a child to be assuaged by compliments. Nor did she quite trust them anymore. In Washington, nothing was ever adequate, sufficient, or commonplace. No, a dress, a reticule, a hair style must be described as exquisite, magnificent, glorious, or superb. Anything less implied an insult.

Beautiful?

Who was Lennox Cameron to note her appearance at all? Seven years ago he hadn't known she was alive.

"Are you all right?" her mother asked, removing her shawl and hanging it on the hook beside the door.

Glynis nodded, turning to Eleanor. "I'm fine."

"Was tonight so difficult?"

She shook her head. "I had to see him again."

Now she could put a checkmark beside that duty: encounter Lennox. Smile and be pleasant to him. Express not one emotion in his presence. She'd done that, too, hadn't she? She'd been a sawdust figure with a sawdust smile.

"He looked well, I think."

"Yes." He hadn't changed. If anything he'd grown more arresting. The intervening years had given him authority; there was no doubt who was the head of Cameron and Company. She suspected that Lennox would have risen to the position early even if Mr. Cameron had not been injured.

"How very sad about Mr. Cameron," she said.

Her mother sighed. "William is the very best person. He hasn't complained or become querulous. Some men might have, I think."

"How did the accident happen?"

"An unbalanced load of timber, I think. Still, he's lucky to be alive. The blow to the head could have easily killed him."

"And Mary cares for him?"

Eleanor sighed. "To her detriment, I think." She reached over and hugged Glynis. "I think she's heartsick. I know the signs."

Glynis tried to smile but it was a feeble attempt.

"Come, I'll make us a cup of tea," her mother said. "We'll talk of other things."

"I think I'll retire," she said.

"Are you very sure you're all right?'

"I am. I had to see him and I have."

"Oh, Glynis."

Those two words contained a world of patience and kindness.

She blinked back tears and bent to kiss her mother on the cheek.

"I'm going to visit Father's grave tomorrow," she said. "Would you like to come with me?"

"No, I've been there enough. After he died, I visited the mausoleum every day for weeks and months. I realized, finally, that he wasn't there." Her mother tapped her chest over her heart. "He's here. But you go and say your farewells."

She nodded, bid her mother good-night, and mounted the steps.

The night of pretense was over.

She hadn't expected to encounter Baumann, however.

Why had he come to Scotland? The man was cunning, dangerous, and knew entirely too much about her.

She'd thought she could leave the war behind in America. Baumann had brought it back to her doorstep.

Chapter 5

The strange night, marked by her fitful sleep, finally ended. Glynis rose from her bed at dawn to see the view of Hillshead obscured by fog. At first only a wisp appeared, then a white, smoke-scented cloud settled over the house.

She waited until almost noon and the appearance of a bright, tardy sun to travel to the Necropolis.

The carriage wheels rumbled over the arched Bridge of Sighs, the crossing over the Molendinar Ravine from Cathedral Square, and crept up to the cemetery. The Necropolis, a spectacular city of monuments and crypts, sat on a hill above the Clyde and overlooked the Glasgow Cathedral.

Her father had been buried here five years ago. She'd been en route from Cairo to the United States and hadn't known of his death until well after the funeral.

She untied her bonnet and left it sitting on the seat. As she opened the carriage door, the soft wind keened, the sun tucking itself behind a suddenly appearing gray cloud. A greeting, then, from the dead to the living.

She shivered.

Following the instructions Duncan had given her, she took the narrow path to the MacIain crypt. The sculpture erected atop the roof stopped her, tears coming to her eyes. The statue of the angel resembled her father, down to the small smile he always wore, as if a secret amused him.

Five years ago the MacIain coffers had been large enough to afford such a costly mausoleum. Now the mill teetered toward ruin and Duncan's haunted eyes weren't the only evidence. Economies were everywhere in the household.

She couldn't even help her own family.

Richard hadn't left her an inheritance or any funds other than his salary. At his death she had the contents of her modest jewelry chest, her more extensive wardrobe, and the best wishes of the diplomatic service to which she was now a liability.

A penurious widow embarrassed the legation.

She took a few steps toward the crypt, studying it with awe. The builder had constructed it to resemble their manor house. Hedges grew around the walls and rosebushes were in beds on either side of the door. She smiled. Had her mother arranged to have them planted there?

Even as a little child she'd known her parents loved each other. The knowledge shone in the flash of eyes across a room, in gentle smiles and soft laughter. Love cemented their family, had given her and Duncan a foundation of security and joy.

How strange she'd married as a business proposition and without thoughts of love.

The door opened easily on oiled hinges. Inside, two brass sconces on each wall sat above stone benches, no doubt placed there for solemn contemplation. Leaving the door ajar so the muted sunlight could illuminate the space, she walked to the catafalque in the middle of the room, pressing her hand against the cold stone.

"Hello, Papa."

How did she apologize for not being here? For not knowing of his death until word had reached her?

He'd been the most wonderful of fathers, gentle and filled with humor, telling stories of his days and the men and women who worked at the mill. He'd been an amateur historian, proud of his heritage as a MacIain, and determined to pass on a love of Scotland to his children.

Duncan had his stubborn chin and a fixed expression in his eyes that spoke of determination. Perhaps she had a bit of obstinacy as well. Or maybe pride had fueled the last seven years.

Bowing her head, she said a prayer, the one he'd taught her as a little girl kneeling beside her bed.

O Lord, see our souls as we slumber.
Give us rest that we may do thy work.
Look over us and guard us with thy love.
And forgive us our sins that we may be better people.

Did her father look down on her from heaven? If so, did he judge her? Would he pity her for the decisions she made or would he understand?

"Forgive me, Papa."

Her entreaty wasn't entirely for being absent all these years, but incorporated all the other mistakes she'd made. Things she'd done that had caused the deaths of others and for which she couldn't forgive herself.

After a few moments reality seeped in along with the chill. Her mother was right. Her father wasn't here. There was nothing here but cold stone and the musty scent of a closed and empty space.

She turned and left the mausoleum softly so as not to disturb death's slumber.

GLYNIS STOPPED when she saw him, her eyes widening. She remained at the door of the mausoleum a few moments before stepping down and closing the door behind her.

Lennox didn't apologize for startling her. He wasn't the one who needed to explain himself. He simply stood beside his carriage and watched her.

Finally, she began to walk toward him, choosing to look at the path rather than in his direction.

Once she neared him, he asked, "What were you doing talking to Baumann last night?"

The sun slid out from behind a cloud, bathing the gray stone of the mausoleum. Glynis, with her lavender dress and auburn hair, was the brightest object in the monochrome Necropolis. She tilted her chin back, firmed her lips and stared at him with flat eyes.

"Who are you to question me, Lennox Cameron?"

"Is he a recent acquaintance?"

"Is that any of your concern?" she asked.

"You had an animated discussion with him."

"Were you watching me?"

"Yes," he said, the one word causing her eyes to narrow.

He'd spent most of the night thinking about her meeting with Baumann, and when dawn arrived he'd shot beyond annoyance into full blown anger.

He'd gone to the MacIain home, only to be told she'd come to the cemetery. The Necropolis was a good enough place to have a confrontation with her.

She gathered up her skirt with one hand and would have walked past him if he hadn't reached out and grabbed her arm.

She swung around, her face inches from his. They hadn't been so close in years. The last time was when she'd kissed him, a memory suddenly at the forefront of his mind.

She'd asked him to come to the anteroom. Once there, she'd kissed him. By the time he could search her out she'd disappeared. He'd learned that she and her mother had left the ball. Only later did he realize she'd left Glasgow, too.

"Why did you never come home after going to London?" he asked, lowering his voice. "Why did you marry a stranger?"

"Why didn't you marry Lidia Bobrova?"

He stared at her. "What?"

"Lidia Bobrova. You were supposed to marry her."

"Where did you get that idea?"

She didn't answer him, only jerked away.

Her face, half gamine, half seductress, fascinated him. He wanted to place his hands on either side of her head and keep her still to study her. Perhaps he'd brush his lips across the contours of her cheeks just to learn them, and kiss her throat to measure her pulse. Desires he'd never had before but that felt natural now.

He stepped back, his thoughts tumbling one over the other.

"You thought I was going to marry Lidia?"

"All of Glasgow thought it."

He tucked that information away to study at another time.

"How do you know Baumann?"

"Why should I tell you?"

"Because he's a spy," he said.

She surprised him by nodding. "Yes, he is. How do you know that?"

"He told me he worked for the War Department."

"If Baumann gave you any information," she said, "it was for a reason. He never divulges anything unless it serves a purpose."

"You met him in Washington," he said, guessing.

She nodded.

"One of your many admirers?"

His question was rewarded with a smile, her expression lighting something up inside him.

"You're evidently not aware of Washington society," she said. "A married woman isn't allowed admirers, especially if her husband is attached to the British Legation. If so, she's on the next ship home with a reputation for being scandalous."

"Why weren't you?"

She frowned at him. "What, scandalous?"

"On the next ship home. You didn't come home for over a year and a half after your husband died."

She huffed out a breath. "There's a war on, Lennox. Passage wasn't easy to arrange." She glanced at the MacIain mausoleum. "I wish I'd come back sooner," she said. "Before my father died."

Shame flooded him. He shouldn't have followed her here. He shouldn't have intruded on what was a private moment.

"Avoid Baumann."

"Gladly," she said. She tilted her head and studied him. "I despise the man. Why did you invite him to Hillshead last night? Especially if you already knew the War Department sent him?"

"I find it easier to keep people I don't trust close to me."

"Was that the reason you invited me?"

"No," he said, amused.

"Then why?"

"I invited Duncan and your mother."

"So I was just an afterthought."

"You've never been an afterthought, Glynis."

She looked surprised by his comment. He'd not intended to say that, but the minute he did he realized it was the truth.

Turning, he walked back to her carriage, opened the door for her and stepped aside.

"Avoid Baumann," he repeated.

She pursed her lips and looked as if she'd like to argue. He almost wished she would. They'd have a good rollicking fight and air out all the emotions pulsing between them.

But this new Glynis only nodded and entered her carriage. Without another word she gave the order to her driver and he returned to his own vehicle.

His concern for his father and sister distracted him, along with the arrival of a Union spy and having a Confederate captain with an annoying wife as a houseguest.

He didn't have time to worry about Glynis or to be confused by her. He sensed her story wasn't a simple one of a widow coming home to Scotland. Did she know about the blockade runners he'd been commissioned to build for the Confederacy? Which side did she favor? More importantly, what were she and Baumann discussing?

She'd come home at the worst time, bringing too many questions with her.

Chapter 6

*H*e'd been close enough to kiss.

A thought she shouldn't be having. A thought that had intruded a dozen times since seeing Lennox in the Necropolis a week ago.

When she was eleven, she'd kissed the sixteen-year-old Lennox. She'd hidden behind the shed and caught him and her brother smoking his father's cheroots. She'd threatened to tell if they didn't let her smoke, too. Duncan laughed so hard at the threat she'd stomped off into the woods.

Lennox found her sitting behind the trunk of an old oak.

"It's no good being mad," he said. "He's your brother and he'll always tease you."

"Do you tease Mary?"

"No," he said, grinning at her. "She isn't like you. She would never dare smoke a cheroot."

She jumped up, tucked her hand in his, allowing him to lead her back to the shed. Just before they got there she pulled him to a stop and threw herself at him. She wrapped her arms around his neck and kissed him.

His lips tasted of tobacco.

He'd thrust her away from him. "Glynis! Stop that!"

He hadn't objected to her kiss seven years ago. The memory of it had fueled her dreams for years. The lonely imaginings of a woman who was willfully foolish. Nothing had come of that kiss.

Nothing had come of the rumors, either. He hadn't married the Russian girl. In fact, he looked shocked when she asked.

Had she looked as surprised when he revealed what he knew of Baumann?

A touch on her shoulder brought her out of her reverie.

She glanced up to see her mother standing there, a cup in her outstretched hand.

"You haven't read a page of your book, my dear. Is something troubling you?"

She glanced down at the book in her lap, a silly novel about a haunted castle, a prince, and a woman without a bit of sense. Lennox became the prince in her imagination and she was the woman wandering through a dark and unknown place with only a candle to guide her. The author hinted at the woman's fascination with the hero of the story. If the prince proved to be half as intriguing as Lennox, she couldn't fault the poor heroine.

From now on she needed to avoid Lennox completely.

She closed the book, placed it on the table, and took the cup from her mother. Eleanor sat beside her and for a few moments they sat in a comfortable silence. Her mother was a restful woman, someone who seemed to calm a room simply by being in it.

The parlor where they sat was a warm and welcoming place in the summer months, but not nearly as pleasant in the winter. The fireplace was located at the far end of the room. Anyone entering had to run the gauntlet of some nasty drafts before reaching a warmer spot.

Although nowhere near as elegant or large as Hillshead, their own manor house was a hundred years older, built by Glynis's great grandfather. A Highlander by birth, he'd come to Glasgow to make his fortune, like many men. After working for the competition for a decade, he started the MacIain Mill. Once the mill showed a profit, he constructed his home.

She doubted he'd taken advice from anyone, let alone someone who might be preparing meals or maintaining a home. The result was a house that was a strange amalgam, as if the man couldn't decide whether to build a castle or a manor house. Built in the shape of a T, it showed a restrained face to the world, with a Grecian entrance complete with columns. Instead of being square, however, the front of the house had curved sides, as if the builder had wanted to create towers and changed his mind halfway through the building. The curved windows let in the drafts—fine in summer, but miserable in the winter.

Yet the pride of workmanship of those early carpenters was evident in the wood beams, the windowsills, sashes, and the mantel pieces carved with pictures of deer and thistles.

The sprawling floor plan made no sense, however. The bedrooms were odd sizes. The family parlor adjoined the dining room, which was on the other side of the house from the kitchen. The halls and staircases were too narrow, the treads so high it was treacherous descending them with a full hoop. One corridor on the third floor abruptly ended in a wall. Drafts swirled from room to room like restless ghosts.

At night the house groaned like an old lady with lumbago. Lily called rainy days Discovery Days because she always spotted another leak beside a window or near the roof.

Her mother, unfailingly kind and sweet-tempered, could be heard muttering imprecations about the house and her husband's ancestor, sentiments shared by Lily, the upstairs maid, and Mabel, the cook.

In the MacIain home there wasn't the demarcation between servant and employer as in the houses of Washington or even at Hillshead. Her mother often sat down at the kitchen table and took tea with Mabel, since the woman had been with her for years. In addition to Lily, they employed a scullery maid and a maid of all work. Her mother hadn't said, but she doubted they'd be able to afford all their wages for very much longer.

"Can I tell you what a joy it is to see you sitting there?" her mother said, turning to her. "I can't quite believe you're home after all these years."

She smiled at her mother, feeling the same.

"Richard didn't approve of Scotland. If I came home to visit, I might return with more of a Scottish accent, undoing all his work to make me sound English."

Eleanor shook her head. "I didn't know your husband well," she said.

An understatement: her mother hadn't known her husband at all.

Their courtship, if it could be called that, occurred over a period of weeks. The decision to marry had been a mutually beneficial one. She didn't want to return to Glasgow, and Richard needed an amenable wife, someone intelligent enough to become the perfect diplomat's protégée.

At first she respected Richard for his knowledge of the world and his devotion to his diplomatic calling. Later, she merely tolerated him, being all too aware that the life she'd made for herself wasn't the one she wanted to live.

The awe she felt at meeting the world's important people had faded after a few years. She'd seen the diplomatic community for what it was, a close knit association of individuals who overtly wished to further their country's aims while covertly supplementing their own.

Famous people were like everyone else. A president could have personal problems. The wife of a president might be afflicted with depression or excessive pride. Ministers, congressmen, doyennes, and matriarchs each had failings and faults—their positions didn't exempt them from being human.

Yet their positions or their prestige sometimes made them act as if they were elevated above the common man. The diplomatic service seemed to attract people like that, individuals who were adept at false smiles and parroted phrases.

Gradually, she'd become expert at both herself, becoming a product of the very society she'd once viewed with awe and later grew to loathe.

In Scotland, people spoke their minds, not what they thought someone wanted to hear. They said what was in their hearts whether wise or not. She craved the bluntness of Scottish speech and the unfettered thoughts of her fellow Scots. She wanted honesty, not fawning duplicity.

Scotland had been like a beacon for her. All she had to do, she'd told herself, was endure, and she'd return to Scotland one day.

With Richard's death the diplomatic service lost its power over her. She was neither the attaché's wife nor a member of the legation, but a private citizen. No one insisted she be discreet, demure, and ceaselessly polite.

Now she was plain Mrs. Richard Smythe of Glasgow, Scotland. A woman who'd met the important people in the world at one time but who now chose to live quietly and without attention.

Her mother stared down into the cup, cleared her throat, then looked at her. A sure sign that she had something of importance to discuss and was trying to find the way to broach it.

She finished her tea, placed the cup beside her book and sat back. Had she done something wrong? For the last week she'd been a hermit in their home. She hadn't gone out, even to shop. She hadn't seen anyone. Although she'd received an invitation to dinner from Charlotte, she hadn't yet answered it, unsure whether or not to attend.

The diplomatic service would invariably come up as a topic of conversation, and she didn't want to talk about America or Richard or Egypt. But short of those subjects, what did she have to say? Almost nothing, and wasn't that a pitiful admission?

She had no children, no hobbies, and no talent other than her affinity for numbers and details.

Figures made sense to her. She'd tried to explain it to Duncan once. Numbers sang to her, almost like music. She could see where someone had made a mistake or where sums didn't add up. She kept her own household books in Washington, practicing economies to stretch Richard's salary.

Her mother bit her lip, glanced at her and then away.

She waited, knowing that no amount of urging would make Eleanor speak faster. *For everything there is a season,* her father would often say. Sometimes he made the remark while waiting for his wife to speak.

"I've told Lennox I would do something and I need your help," her mother finally said.

"What have you agreed to do?" she asked, folding her hands and willing her heartbeat to slow. Would she always be affected like this? All she had to do was hear his name and her pulse raced.

Once, at a Washington dinner party, the discussion had centered around the newly instigated blockade of southern ports. Evidently, some politicians had discovered that Scottish shipbuilding enterprises were aiding the southerners. A threat had been lobbed that if England didn't stay out of the Civil War, the Americans would retaliate by invading Canada.

She hadn't been surprised at the volatile nature of the comments: it was war, and everyone's emotions were heightened. She hadn't been surprised, either, at Richard's sanguine response.

Nothing ever ruffled Richard.

She wished she could have said the same, especially when talk turned to particular shipbuilders thought to be aiding the Confederacy. Cameron and Company was mentioned along with several other firms on the Clyde.

She'd kept still, waiting for someone to say something more. She wanted to hear about Lennox. The discussion had veered to another topic, but that one hint of him was enough to make her ache for weeks.

No, she was not nineteen any longer. Not a foolish girl so in love she'd dared scandal by kissing him.

He was not going to affect her like that any longer.

". . . Glasgow. The poor thing hasn't been away from Hillshead."

"Who?" she asked.

Eleanor frowned at her. "Weren't you listening to a word I was saying, Glynis? Lucy Whittaker. She and her husband are Lennox's houseguests. He's asked me to show her Glasgow and I thought you could accompany us."

Before she could demur, her mother added, "She might have questions about America." Her mother patted her arm. "I really do want you to come."

Before she could frame an excuse, Eleanor stood.

"I'll be ready in a few minutes."

"Now?"

Eleanor nodded. "I've already sent for the carriage."

What a pity her brother couldn't have made some economies there, too. Instead of two carriages, they only needed one to take him back and forth to the mill.

Yet if Eleanor didn't have a vehicle for her own use, she probably would have taken Lucy Whittaker on a walking tour of Glasgow—and insist that she come with them.

Glynis stared at the book she'd abandoned. Suddenly, she wanted to read the story of a silly woman a lot more than she wanted to entertain Lennox's houseguest.

Fifteen minutes later she was in the carriage attired in bonnet and gloves.

As they headed for Hillshead, she straightened her skirt, checked the toes of her shoes, loosened the cord of the reticule around her wrist, pulled at her gloves, and brushed an imaginary speck of dust from her bodice.

Anything but think of Lennox.

Her mother didn't seem to notice her discomfort.

"The poor girl doesn't know anyone in Scotland, save Lennox and her husband, of course. Mary is taking her father to Bute for the waters, so she will be alone all day. Why shouldn't we extend a little Scottish hospitality and make a friend in the meantime?"

Of course her mother would care for the girl. Eleanor was kind to everyone. She'd no more disappoint Lennox than she would anyone coming to the door looking for food.

Her father had been the same. He hired people for the mill that others had fired. He instituted meetings for men in the grip of alcoholism, took up collections among his business friends to help children of his employees. They weren't merely workers to him. Everyone at MacIain Mill was a member of a large extended family.

When her mother went inside to collect Mrs. Whittaker, Glynis remained in the carriage studying Hillshead.

The three-story house sprawled across the hilltop and was remarkable for the number of its white-framed windows. Despite the size of the house, there were only three people in the Cameron family: William, Lennox, and Mary. Speculation abounded as to the whereabouts of Olivia—Mrs. Cameron. All she knew was that Lennox and Mary's mother had left Scotland when they were both children and hadn't returned. Lennox never discussed his mother's absence. Nor did she ever question him.

Hillshead required a great many servants. Seven people were employed in the kitchen alone. An army must be required to keep Hillshead dusted and swept, mopped and polished. Their own small staff of four had enough to do every day, and the MacIain house was one-twelfth the size of Hillshead.

The house seemed to have a personality, one not the least modest or unassuming. The red brick, contrasting pleasantly with the white windowsills and green hedges, was sharp at the corners and bright in color, as if proud of its newness. *I'm not the clay of old cities and ancient homes,* it seemed to say. *I was newly kilned and set up only decades ago to reveal my owner's wealth.*

Only the front of Hillshead showed, not the two wings to the rear. A wooded area filled with huge oaks and tall pines bordered the property here and in the back of the house. As a girl she'd followed Duncan and Lennox into those deep woods to climb a few of the trees herself. The walkway wound from the road to the door, bordered by more hedges, trimmed so not one leaf was out of place.

How many times had she raced down that path, through Hillshead, and out to the gardens? The house was rife with memories of boisterous voices, laughter, and a childhood dusted with joy.

She turned away, refusing to allow the past to draw her closer.

Chapter 7

Lucy Whittaker was an attractive woman with an oval face and dark brown eyes. Her blond hair was tucked up in her bonnet, the green bow tied at a jaunty angle beneath her chin.

The woman began their relationship by insulting Eleanor.

"I can barely understand you," she said after both women settled into the carriage, skirts had been arranged and proper introductions made. "You people in Glasgow speak worse than most Scots."

Since she'd worked diligently to eradicate all trace of Glasgow from her voice, Glynis had to admit a Glaswegian accent was occasionally indecipherable.

But Lucy wasn't done with her complaints.

"Scotland is colder than I'm used to and the city smells of fish."

"We're on the Clyde," Eleanor said, her mouth curving in a thin smile. "You'll soon become familiar with the odor. Are you staying long in Glasgow?"

"I don't know," Lucy said. "Gavin says not too much longer, but it all depends on Mr. Cameron."

"Do you have any questions about America, Mrs. Whittaker? I'm certain my daughter can alleviate any anxieties you might be feeling about traveling to a new country."

"I doubt I'll be there anytime soon," Lucy said,

to Glynis's surprise. "I'm to be put ashore at Nassau while Gavin goes off to war. He says it's not safe for me to be aboard ship when they're running the blockade."

Did Lennox know how easily Lucy divulged her husband's secrets? In a matter of moments she'd told a stranger that Mr. Whittaker was in the Confederacy and soon to be engaged in outwitting the Union navy.

Glynis could just imagine what Baumann would do with that information.

"It's not fair, truly," she said.

Lucy turned from regarding the scenery through the carriage window. Tears swam in her brown eyes, causing Eleanor to reach over and pat the younger woman on the arm.

"I'm sorry," Eleanor said. "I didn't mean to cause you any distress."

"I'll be living in some hideous place while Gavin goes off to play at war. I'll never see my family or go home again."

Play at war? Did she think the thousands of casualties were part of a game? Wasn't she concerned about her husband's safety?

Evidently not, because the woman rarely mentioned her husband for the rest of the day, and when she did, it was in a quarrelsome tone. She wanted a maid and Gavin wouldn't hire one since they were due to leave Scotland soon. She needed new dresses and he was just being too frugal. She wanted a puppy but he had stated that he didn't feel comfortable bringing a pet into someone else's home.

Nor did her complaints end there.

Glasgow was thriving because of shipbuilding. But Lucy saw nothing impressive about the shipyards or the port with its docks and new quays.

In her eyes England was even better equipped.

They traveled down Trongate, past the Glasgow

Cross, the original center of medieval Glasgow. Neither it nor the Tolbooth steeple interested Lucy.

London, Lucy said, was filled with ancient landmarks and buildings.

When Eleanor pointed out the horse-drawn buses, Lucy shrugged and remarked that Glasgow had a reputation for being one of the filthiest cities in the Empire. Eleanor countered that Queen Victoria had opened up the Loch Katrine Scheme and now the entire city drew water from the Trossachs.

Nothing Eleanor said affected Lucy's opinion about Glasgow or Scotland. Sometimes, people neither wanted to learn nor change their minds.

To Lucy, London was the hub of the universe, the place to be admired above all others. Although they were careful not to show Lucy the wynds and closes of Saltmarket and Gallowgate in the East End, Glasgow still came off a poor second to Lucy's birthplace.

Glynis found it less irritating to retreat into silence. When you were silent, people couldn't argue with you. They didn't know what you thought unless you told them.

She had no intention of telling the woman she considered her petulant, privileged, and difficult.

At least the outing had reacquainted her with Glasgow. Her home was vibrant, the city teeming with people, and there were magnificent places such as the Botanic Gardens, Kelvingrove Park, and the St. Vincent Street Church. Built less than ten years ago, the Grecian style church was one of the city's most famous landmarks.

While Glynis admired it, Lucy's only comment was, "I'm not a Presbyterian."

Did Mr. Whittaker notice Lucy's complaints? Or was the woman different around her husband? If she wasn't mistaken, the dress Lucy wore—a silk stripe in green and beige—was expensive. Mr. Whittaker provided well for his wife, but Lucy didn't say one kind word about the poor man. In a few years Lucy's youth and beauty would fade, leaving the dregs of her character, in this case a thoroughly dislikable woman.

Even her mother's powers of persuasion could not transform Lucy Whittaker into a pleasant person.

"Perhaps another day we'll travel north," Eleanor said. "There's the remains of Dumbarton Castle. It's perched on a rock overlooking the Clyde. Or we might go to Bothwell Castle. Either are sights we should visit."

"There are many historic places in England," Lucy said. Her voice quavered. "My papa loved to take trips on Sunday."

She was very much afraid the girl was going to weep again. She didn't know what was worse, the constant denigrating of Scotland or the tears.

"Tell us about your family," Eleanor said, a comment causing Glynis to glance at her in disbelief. "I've found that talking about sorrow sometimes makes it easier to bear," her mother continued.

"I have three brothers and a dear sister, who is as close to me as anyone could be." Lucy blotted at her eyes with a handkerchief. "And my darling dog," she said. "Jasper."

A woman who liked animals had at least one good character attribute. Perhaps Lucy was simply desperately homesick and not as querulous as she appeared.

"He's a King Charles spaniel and the smartest animal in all of England. Or Scotland," she added.

For the next thirty minutes they were regaled with Jasper's antics from his trick of taking treats from between Lucy's lips to jumping up the steps to the carriage without being prompted.

"He, too, loved to take trips," she said, looking as if she might cry again.

"Perhaps he would have liked a sea voyage," Glynis said. She ignored her mother's look for the view from the window.

"I'm told that I will like America, but I don't see how I shall."

Richard hadn't liked America, either. He thought democracy made the government weaker than it should be, handing too much autonomy to the masses. Americans were, to his mind, not only ignorant, but excessively violent. She was forced to listen to a similar speech at least once a week.

She hadn't found the Americans to be either violent or ignorant. Instead, they were a fascinating group of people with distinct thoughts on liberty and freedom. The Civil War was stripping the soul from the country, and it was being felt on both sides.

The most common color for women was black, and before she left America each one of her acquaintances had been touched by the death of a soldier in some way.

But she never bothered to tell Richard her opinion. He wouldn't have listened. His inability to hear other people or to empathize had been his greatest drawbacks and why he wouldn't rise to the meteoric heights he envisioned for himself.

Once, he'd been so filled with images of his own success. "I've been told that my future is bright in the diplomatic service," he said on the day he asked her to marry him.

They'd been in Alexandra's garden, a tiny but perfect spot behind her English cousin's town house.

She couldn't imagine a more unassuming man. If the aim of the diplomatic service was to employ only males of a certain conformable appearance, Mr. Smythe was a perfect employee. Of short stature, he had auburn hair, brown eyes, and a narrow face he kept expressionless. One could not tell if Mr. Smythe was excited, amused, or irritated. Instead, he was an island of nothingness in a sea of emotion.

He was the antithesis of Lennox Cameron.

Mr. Smythe did not make her feel anything at all.

He'd begun to walk, his hands clasped behind him.

"It has been brought to my attention that my career would advance more quickly if I were married." He glanced at her. "I haven't the temperament to go court- ing, Miss MacIain."

He stopped in front of the bench where she sat and regarded her intently.

A slight frisson of curiosity pierced her misery.

"Nor do I have the time, having been sent my new assignment." He cleared his throat. "I have found you to be a very personable young woman. Although a Scot, you're related to Lady Alexandra."

"She's my cousin," Glynis had said, wondering where he was going with his speech.

"I would then like to propose something to you. A match between you and me. Not one of love, Miss MacIain, as much as expediency. A business arrange- ment, if you will. I can offer you a position as my wife. You will meet important people and be present when history is made. My wife, of course, would be called upon to represent the Empire as well as myself. If you agree, you will need to learn certain things, and I will avail myself of the finest teachers for you."

She didn't dissuade him from continuing. Instead, she listened.

"I can guarantee you my future is a bright one. It has been hinted that if I conduct myself well in Cairo, my next assignment will be to one of the British lega- tions."

He began to walk again, a jaunt of four feet one way, a turn and four feet the other.

"Would this arrangement suit you?"

"You want me to marry you, Mr. Smythe?"

"I do, Miss MacIain."

Her mother's letters had been filled with speculation about Lennox and Lidia Bobrova. Glasgow was rife with rumors about the joining of the two families that had been so close in business.

How could she bear returning to Glasgow? How could she tolerate seeing him every day? Or worse, having to socialize with his wife?

"If I marry you, would we be returning to Scotland?" she'd asked.

He frowned. "No, Miss MacIain. I see no reason to do so. Do you have an excessive fondness for your homeland, one that would prevent you from considering my offer?"

"I love my family, Mr. Smythe. I would miss them."

"Perhaps they could visit us occasionally," he said.

She wouldn't have to see Lennox again. Nor affect a nonchalance when he married.

"I realize we have only known each other a few weeks."

"Three weeks to be exact," she said.

"Which means this is a precipitous offer. I am due in Egypt in a month. Therefore, our wedding would have to take place within days."

Enough time to send for her parents and Duncan to attend the ceremony.

What did it matter who she married now, she'd asked herself, especially if Lennox was marrying that Russian girl? All she cared about was that she didn't have to return to Glasgow.

"Yes, Mr. Smythe," she said, standing. "I will marry you."

She allowed him to kiss her on the cheek. On their wedding night she allowed him into her bed. She didn't even try to pretend Lennox held her and kissed her perfunctorily.

Lennox wouldn't have made her want to bathe after her marriage was consummated.

Richard's career had been hampered by his personality. He didn't want to speak to women or servants, since each class—as he'd said on many occasions—was given to extreme emotionality. He never realized some men respected their wives and their judgment. Nor did he understand a diplomat's position was to listen more than speak.

A lesson Lucy Whittaker could learn as well.

Glynis couldn't wait until the day was over.

DUNCAN MACIAIN walked to the window and stared out at the mill buildings stretching before him. His great-grandfather had built this empire and it flourished until two years ago.

"You can never forget you hold the lives of these people in your hand, Duncan," his father once told him. "Every decision you make affects them. You may feel like king of the mountain here, but like leading a clan into battle, your actions have consequences."

He'd been a boy at the time, amused at his father's metaphor. Having been the head of MacIain Mill for the last five years, he now realized the comparison was apt. Every change he instituted affected not only himself and his family but the hundreds of people who worked for him.

Having to lay off a third of the employees had been difficult, but he'd originally hoped it would be enough to keep the mill open. They were still doomed, not because of the competition from Manchester or the loss of the contract for wicking. He couldn't get any raw material. He couldn't loom nonexistent cotton.

His father had had a way of looking at everything

in the best possible light. "Duncan, my boy," he'd say, "there's nothing so bad that you can't find some good in it."

He was trying to find something to celebrate in this situation but hadn't come up with anything. Nor did he have any solutions. Short of sailing to America himself, he was out of ideas. He'd rejected every idea but one because it didn't produce the one thing he needed: cotton.

For a while he'd seriously contemplated Lennox's offer of help. If he took money from the other man, it would forever alter their friendship, and he didn't have all that many friends left.

The idea of closing the mill and turning his back on his family's business, one he'd learned since boyhood, was anathema to him. He liked that, in busier times, the floor of his office vibrated with the clacking rhythm of hundreds of looms. Their cotton was the finest in Scotland, just as each employee at MacIain Mill, all seven hundred sixty-three of them, were the most dedicated and loyal in Glasgow.

Coming into the mill each day was an indictment, a demonstration of his failure. If he didn't do something, every single person would be gone, the mill shuttered, the windows boarded up, and the doors chained.

What would his father think of his plan, even now growing more substantial? Something Lennox said had started his thoughts in that direction.

Sometimes, bold action was required. He was a MacIain, a family heralded for their courage.

It was time he acted the part.

GAVIN WHITTAKER stood on the dock, staring at the ship soon to be his. The *Raven* was the most beautiful vessel he'd ever seen.

Her twin smokestacks were painted gray, her hull

the same color, with a black line indicating where the cladding began. An iron and steel paddle wheeler, she had a length of nearly three hundred feet and an eleven-foot draft. She could carry a crew of sixty-six, had five watertight compartments and four boilers. Fully loaded, she could still outrun anything sailing today.

Wait until they encountered the blockade. She'd fly right past the Union bastards. No one would forget her once they saw her lines or her speed.

Too bad they'd already named her *Raven*. Gavin would have christened her "Ghost," because he intended to slip past the Union blockade just like an ethereal being.

His life, his honor, his single-minded purpose, was wrapped up in this ship.

A damned shame so much deception had to be part of the initial voyage. When he sailed from Glasgow, his destination would officially be listed as Bermuda. A few Scots would accompany him to Wales, where he'd rendezvous with his Confederate crew. After their cargo was loaded they'd set off for Savannah, with a stop at Nassau to make sure Lucy was settled.

On his outgoing trip from Georgia he'd be carrying cotton and mail, bound for Nassau. After a few days with Lucy, he'd run the blockade again, intent on furnishing his fellow southerners with those commodities needed to survive the war.

He'd received word from his first mate that the weapons and ammunition had arrived, ready to load. His crew was waiting. The *Raven* would be handed over to him in a week, and the money transferred to Cameron and Company.

The plan, however, was marred by only one thing: Lucy.

In England, she'd been demure and accommodating, reminding him of the women he knew. She smiled often, was gracious to people and polite to a fault.

She'd been the sweetest thing in England. He'd found himself besotted on the spot. Never having believed in love at first sight, he found it strange he should be afflicted in such a manner. But she had bright sparkling eyes and the most enchanting smile. He knew his sisters and mother would adore her when they met.

Something happened on their arrival in Scotland. She'd become querulous and argumentative. She hated Scotland. She hated the idea of living in America.

He wasn't sure what she did like, but he knew for certain what annoyed her.

Lucy was providing the kind of problem he wasn't sure he could handle. Give him an entire fleet of Union ships trying to block his way and he'd sail right through them.

Give him a complaining woman, however, and he wasn't sure what to do.

Chapter 8

*W*hen they arrived back at Hillshead, a carriage was in the drive. Glynis suspected it belonged to Lennox since the side lamps had been replaced by brass anchor lanterns.

Her stomach shouldn't clench at the sight. Nor should her palms become damp.

In the last seven years she'd met the President of the United States, along with numerous dignitaries. She'd been forced to deal with cabinet secretaries and their wives. More than one British diplomat's wife, as well as Mrs. Lincoln, had attempted to intimidate her.

Lennox wasn't going to succeed where they'd failed.

"I won't be any time at all, Glynis," her mother said.

She nodded, grateful not to have to escort Lucy into Hillshead. The woman grated on her. But she smiled and made her farewells with a grace she'd been taught and had practiced over the years.

A few minutes later the door opened and she moved her skirt aside, thinking it was her mother returning as quickly as she'd promised. Instead of Eleanor, however, Lennox entered the carriage, his size making the space feel even more confined.

In Washington she could converse about a variety of inane subjects. The skill left her as he settled on the opposite seat, staring at her as if she were a creature from the depths of Loch Lomond.

He took his time perusing her, from the top of her hair, which wasn't as neat as it had been this morning, to her shoes, muddy from the excursion through the Botanic Gardens. She was certain she was wrinkled as well. The deep mauve fabric with the embroidered collar and cuffs was a pleasing dress, but it was designed for a woman to sit in the parlor and read, not an entire day of sightseeing and exploration.

Did he think her changed? Or would she be forever ten years old to him, dressed in a soiled pinafore and climbing a tree? Did he recall when she raced Rainbow, her pony, down the river road? Or what about the time she'd been tossed off another horse, only to land in the mud unhurt and furious that he'd witnessed the whole thing?

She firmed her lips so they didn't tremble, forcing herself to return his stare.

Even now, at the end of the day, he looked like he'd just left his chamber and was about to go to the yard, not returning from it. His shirt was white and crisp below his dark blue jacket. His trousers bore a crease but not one speck of dust. His black shoes gleamed with a shine.

"Have you finished inspecting me?" she asked, looking away.

"You've grown more beautiful in the last seven years."

Her heart stopped at those words. Her mind urged it forward. This was just Lennox being charming. Lennox being conciliatory. What else could he say? *Glynis, you're haggard in your mourning.*

"Thank you."

Seven years ago she might have preened or even flirted with him. She'd thought herself a beauty, known she was destined for great things.

Seven years ago she'd been an arrogant child.

In Washington she'd been a minor celebrity. Mrs. Richard Smythe, the wife of the British attaché. *My dear, you must simply attend one of her dinners. I don't know where she got her chef but the food and the discussions are unforgettable. Convince her, if you can, to invite you to one of her salons. They're the talk of Washington. Even Mr. Lincoln attends periodically.*

She'd overheard those remarks and more. For a time the approval from people she admired had been enough. A funny thing, however, about admiration, praise, or notoriety. It had no value without someone with whom to share it.

Richard expected her to be a great hostess. That's why he'd married her at nineteen and spent so much effort and money to train her in the role he wished her to assume. If he'd heard those comments, he never told her. He wouldn't have said something like, *Well done, darling. You're just what they need.* Instead, he would have congratulated himself on his ability to train a Glasgow girl.

She didn't expect behavior from Richard that he'd never promised. Theirs wasn't a love match but a business arrangement. He desired a conformable wife who would do him honor. She desperately wanted away from Scotland and the man who sat in front of her now.

What an utter fool she'd been.

Being around Lennox made her feel awkward. She felt nineteen again, desperately in love and foolish with it.

"I shouldn't have followed you to the Necropolis," he said. "It was wrong of me."

She glanced at him, trying to discern the motive behind his apology. One thing Washington had taught her: people almost always had a hidden reason for doing or saying something.

"Thank you," she said.

"But I meant what I said about Baumann."

She was willing to accept his apology, but his warning grated on her. She was no longer nineteen and naive.

"Baumann isn't a man to underestimate," she said. "Have you posted guards on your ships?"

He didn't answer, but his gaze never left her.

"If you haven't, I suggest you put them in place. Don't assume that Baumann is the only Union spy in Glasgow."

When he smiled, she frowned at him.

"I don't mean me," she said, shaking her head. "I heard you were building blockade runners in Washington. Baumann knows that as well. I wouldn't be surprised what he's discovered since coming to Scotland."

"You seem familiar with the war."

"You can't help knowing something, living in Washington."

"So they're talking about my ships there?"

Once more she nodded.

"What else have you heard?"

She smiled. "That you pose a danger to the Union. That you're single-handedly trying to outfit the Confederate navy. Are your blockade runners that good?"

"Better," he said. "The *Raven* is the fastest ship I've ever built."

"Something else Baumann probably knows."

"Which side are you on, Glynis?"

"I'm not on one side or another. It no longer matters. Too many good men have died on both sides. What does it matter to win a war when you've lost all your young men?"

She looked away, unable to hold his gaze. Clasping her hands together tightly, she took a deep breath and pretended a calm she didn't feel.

He was too close in the confines of the carriage. She could reach out and touch his trouser-covered knee. She could stroke his leg, shocking him. She might even launch herself at him and kiss him again.

That would take his mind off Baumann and the war.

The image was so real that she could almost feel his mouth beneath hers, his arms tightening around her waist. But in the next instant it was gone, the impulsive girl she'd been buried beneath the proper and demure Mrs. Smythe.

She cleared her throat. "You need to be concerned about Mrs. Whittaker," she said.

"What do you mean?"

"You should caution her not to go around telling everyone her husband is a Confederate. Knowing how well gossip travels in Glasgow, Baumann is probably aware of that, too."

"She said that?"

She nodded.

"The woman's a scunner," he said.

Lennox pronounced some words with an English inflection. Some sounded French, while others had a Russian flavor. Now he sounded definitely like a Scot.

"A nuisance?" she asked, biting back her smile. "Why are she and her husband staying with you?" Her question was intrusive and none of her concern so she half expected him not to answer.

"Three men were murdered in Glasgow recently," he said. "All Americans."

"So you're protecting them at your own peril? And your family's?"

He stared right through her. Did no one ever question Lennox? Had he grown so autocratic since she'd last seen him?

"They won't be staying much longer," he finally said.

"Is it safe? Are you in any danger?"

Was she revealing too much by asking that question? He studied her in those moments, the silence stretching between them like a web, binding them to this place and time.

She could feel the tension rise in her body the longer he regarded her. Her shoulders ached; her stomach clenched and her fingers trembled. What did he see in her? What was he looking for?

Unable to bear his scrutiny one more second, she turned and looked out the window, willing her mother to hurry or Lennox to leave. When she heard the carriage door open and close a moment later, she blew out a breath.

From now on she would be better off avoiding Lennox. Being around him was dangerous. She'd never lied to him, even when the truth pained her. Lying to Lennox would be like violating an oath.

But half-truths? Yes, she was guilty of those.

Chapter 9

"*T*hank you for a lovely day," Lucy said to Eleanor in the foyer of Hillshead. Her voice was dull and lacking any sincerity.

Eleanor pretended the girl's words were from the heart rather than simple good manners and reciprocated.

"An enjoyable experience," she said, lying. "We must do it again." Dear heavens, she hoped not.

"My love," Gavin said, entering the foyer. "Did you enjoy your day?"

Lucy nodded, giving her husband a thin smile. "Glasgow is nothing like London, however."

Eleanor said a quick prayer to be forgiven for wanting to strangle the woman and smiled at Gavin.

"Mr. Whittaker, I'm afraid we may have exhausted your wife. We've explored the whole of the city."

His smile was more genuine, but then, she'd found the man to be thoroughly charming. He had a delightful accent, one making it sound like each of his words was resting on a plump pillow. Not only was he courtly in his mannerisms, but he was solicitous of his wife.

The foolish woman didn't seem to notice, however. Mr. Whittaker asked if she wanted to retire straightaway. Could he bring dinner on a tray for her? What was her preference as to refreshments? Lucy brushed aside his words as if the man were an annoying insect.

Their marriage was none of her concern, but it was difficult witnessing Lucy's stupidity and unconscious cruelty. Mr. Whittaker deserved better from his wife, especially since he was going to war in a matter of days.

They chatted for a moment, the topics innocuous and acceptable: Scotland's weather, the ceremony for William, the size of the Cameron and Company shipyard. When enough time had passed and she couldn't be accused of rudeness, Eleanor said her farewells.

"If you would like to see the nearby castles," she said to Lucy before leaving, "we can certainly arrange that."

"I do not wish to see any more of Scotland," Lucy said. "I doubt I shall recover after seeing as much as I did."

She watched as Lucy excused herself and mounted the grand stairs. She could hear every one of the woman's footsteps in the soaring foyer of Hillshead. The stained-glass cupola was three floors above her and the entire space was perfect for echoes.

"I apologize," Gavin said when the footsteps were no longer audible. "Lucy hasn't settled into Scotland yet."

Her smile wasn't forced. She genuinely liked Mr. Whittaker and pitied him his wife.

"From what I understand," she said, "you won't be remaining here long."

"No," he said. "Not long." He gave her a charming bow and they parted.

She wouldn't have minded seeing more of Mr. Whittaker, but hoped Lennox wouldn't ask her to have anything more to do with Lucy.

What a tiresome woman.

LENNOX STOOD in his library, staring after the departing carriage.

The girl he'd known was there below the surface.

He saw flashes of the old Glynis in her gamin smile and quick glance. The woman, however, was different. Not only was she beautiful, but she was alluring, daring him to ferret out her secrets, compare who she was now to the girl she'd once been.

Glynis had always been part of his life, but he only realized it when seeing her again. Her coming home was like the final placement of a piece of iron cladding on a hull. It fit, finished the hull, rendering it whole. He felt whole, as if he'd been only partially himself until she smiled up at him.

Yesterday he'd been discussing the seaworthy trials for the *Raven* and he remembered the last time he and Glynis had rowed down the river. When he was eating breakfast, the smell of apples had brought her face to mind. As a girl she had a fondness for one of the mares in the stable and took her an apple each morning. He could almost tell the time by the sight of her traipsing up the hill and down the path to the stable.

He remembered once when he'd gone to get Duncan so they could watch the trial launch of a new Cameron ship.

She'd grinned at him, precocious at ten years old, her eyes shining with daring. She'd sat primly between the columns at the entrance to her house and announced that Duncan couldn't go with him.

"I'm to tell you Duncan is indisposed," she said, sounding out the word with great care. "But it's really because he's got the trots. Mother made him use the outdoor privy, he was smelling up the house so bad."

He hadn't known what to say then and he hadn't known what to say when he was a sophisticated twenty-four, newly returned from Russia and already the designer of two new ships in his father's fleet.

She'd come into the MacIain parlor where he was waiting for Duncan.

"You're back," she said. "I've waited a very long time."

"Have you?"

She nodded. "You went to school, then you went to Russia, then you went to France. Have you finished your travels, Lennox Cameron? Come home to Scotland finally?"

He felt a surge of humor at her chastisement. "I'm back for a while."

She startled him, then, by reaching out and patting his jacket with a personal, almost proprietary, touch.

He'd thought himself worldly and sophisticated, but standing there with Glynis smiling at him, he felt as callow as a boy.

"It's time," she said, "for you to settle down. No more exploring the world."

"Is it? And who would you be, Glynis MacIain, to tell me what I should or should not do?"

She only smiled at him and he'd been startled into silence by her beauty. He had the curious notion she was somehow older and wiser.

Now she was home, a widow.

Had she loved her husband? He hadn't asked her. Perhaps he should, but was he prepared to hear her answer? What if she'd adored the man? Hardly likely since she married Smythe only a month after meeting him. Maybe the years had added a fondness to the relationship that hadn't been there at the beginning. Had Richard Smythe been the epitome of a good and decent husband? Did she mourn him still?

He couldn't think of her in the man's bed or allow himself to visualize her passion. Some things were beyond him.

The Glynis of his past was a source of amusement and fondness. He smiled when he recalled her.

He was far from amusement when he thought of Glynis now.

Did she know how beautiful she was? Did she realize how much he wanted to kiss her?

He'd come damn close in the carriage. He wanted to pull her across the seat, settle her on his lap, and kiss her until the urge left him. He had the feeling, however, that it would only make the situation worse.

He didn't want to be a source of ridicule. He didn't want to amuse her by an inappropriate display of affection. Affection? Hell, he wasn't just feeling affection, he was fascinated with her, confused by her, and lusting after her.

No, the best thing would be to avoid Glynis when he could and keep those necessary and unavoidable encounters as short as possible.

Chapter 10

"Thank you for letting me do this," she said to Duncan, settling in at the bookkeeper's desk across the room.

Duncan had taken over her father's office, a spacious room large enough for both him and the bookkeeper to work as well.

"The mill is as much yours as it is mine, Glynis," he said, settling in behind the large desk their father had once occupied.

How right he looked there.

She smiled, but didn't comment.

Duncan, as the head of MacIain Mills, was the one who had the responsibility and worry.

The windows overlooking the mill buildings were dusty, as they'd never been in her father's time. Water damage stained the wooden sills, trailing down the plaster wall to the floor where the planks were discolored.

Wasn't there a custodian still on staff? Someone really needed to trim the wicks of the lamps and clean the globes. Plus, the floor needed to be swept and damp-mopped.

An indication, then, of how distracted Duncan was by other things, like penury.

He looked like he hadn't slept for a week. His trousers were wrinkled, his jacket hung off the back of his chair, and his shirt had ink spots on it.

Charlotte once told her she thought Duncan was the most handsome man she'd ever seen. His eyes were a brilliant blue, darker than hers, and they tilted down at the outside corners, making him look self-deprecating, amused at the plight of the world and everyone within it.

His mouth was full, his face lean. His brown hair was often mussed because he had a habit of raking his fingers through it when he was agitated.

Duncan had their mother's kindness. She had their father's nose and his fascination with numbers. She wished, however, one of them had inherited Hamish MacIain's optimism and his way of looking forward to each day.

Every Saturday she'd come to the mill with her father and sit here like now. Hamish MacIain thought practice in business would be advantageous for his only daughter.

"You'll find Mr. Smithson's work is not as neat as it should be," Duncan said, speaking now of the book-keeper. "The man is getting up in years and has a tendency to lose a thought and sit there with his pen dripping with ink. In the last few months I've convinced him to use a pencil."

The entries were hideously difficult to read. The expenses were nearly obliterated by dark blue blotches, some of which hadn't dried when Mr. Smithson closed the book, resulting in a mirror stain.

If the man hadn't been a loyal employee of their father's, Duncan would probably have pensioned him off years ago. But Mr. Smithson had been among the first of the employees their father had hired at MacIain Mill, and might well prove to be its last.

By the time she finished studying the ledger,

she knew they were in desperate straits. Soon there wouldn't be any money to pay anyone, even her brother.

The war in America had nearly decimated their fortunes, but she hadn't understood to what degree until now. Most of their best cotton fiber was imported from the southern states of America. Although some cotton made it through the blockade, it wasn't enough to keep the mill going full-time.

A third of their employees had been let go. While Duncan had tried to help where he could by decimating his savings, her brother couldn't manufacture money.

If they didn't get an infusion of cash, Duncan would have to make further cuts, resulting in more people losing their jobs.

"How was it?"

She blinked, pulled out of her dread by Duncan's question.

"How was what?"

"America. You've never said."

She wished he'd asked about Cairo instead.

"I quite liked America. The people were all different. Maybe because it's such a large country. People in New York aren't like people in Washington, for example."

"How was it being married?"

She turned in the chair and regarded her brother.

"It wasn't bad, Duncan. It wasn't good. It simply was. I have ten fingers and toes. I had a husband."

He smiled, and it was one of Duncan's wry smiles, as if he wanted to come out and say something but was prevented from doing so by good manners.

"Evidently, he wasn't an appendage or you'd miss him more."

Plainly, he didn't care about good manners around

her, but she was his sister, and Duncan had always said what he thought to her. How very like him to pin her ears to the wall. Everyone else was so careful of her widowhood. They treated her as if she were a fragile vase capable of shattering if anyone looked at her wrong.

She sat back in her chair and spoke without looking at him, her attention on the columns of numbers in front of her.

"I should say I was sorry he died, shouldn't I? I should sound devastated by his loss." She glanced over her shoulder at him. "I can't lie to you, Duncan. I think I was relieved, most of all. My first thought was: he's dead. I won't have to put up with him any longer. I won't have to put up with his petty tyrannies. I won't have to be the focus of his anger when someone at the legation was rude or dismissive of him. I won't have to be afraid for the servants. Most of all, I won't have to worry about Richard's hobbies."

"You need to explain most of that."

She looked up to find Duncan approaching the bookkeeper's desk. He sat on the corner, one leg drawn up, his arms folded. Anyone else might have thought he was relaxed, but she knew her brother. He was poised to attack.

"What do you mean, his hobbies? Was he unfaithful, Glynis?"

In Duncan's voice was the same incredulity her father might have expressed. The MacIain men were Scots to the core, and a Scotsman was faithful to his code of honor, his country, and, not the least, his wife.

"I didn't mind," she said, another bit of truth she offered to him. Until she knew exactly what his proclivities were, she'd been grateful Richard was visiting some other bed.

Perhaps everyone needed to learn some difficult

lessons. She was more fortunate than most, having learned them so young. She would never again allow someone to rescue her, especially not because she'd been stupid. If she acted in a foolish manner, she'd face the humiliation. If she erred, she'd stay her ground and accept the consequences of her own behavior.

"He had such great visions of his career," she said. "After that first year in Cairo, I knew Richard would always be a second tier attaché. He'd be sent to those legations people didn't want to go to, given duties no one else wanted to assume. He wouldn't rise in the ranks partly because he was too obsequious, too much a toady."

That was only one side to his character. There was another side she wouldn't comment upon to her brother. Richard had a core of cruelty. The more he was overlooked by men he admired, the greater his cruelty.

Duncan stood. For a moment she thought he was going to speak, utter some castigation of Richard's behavior. But Duncan had never been foolish. Why criticize a man who had been dead for nearly two years?

"Are you glad you came home, Glynis?"

She looked up at him, not speaking for a moment, realizing the question was a deeper one than it seemed. He wasn't asking about the joy in seeing him or their mother again.

"Why didn't Lennox ever marry?" she asked. "Why didn't you?"

"Time," he said with a small smile. "That's my excuse."

"And Lennox?"

Was he going to be loyal to Lennox? He always had been. The two of them had been inseparable since they were boys. Whenever one of them got into trouble, the other was there to either take the blame or try to explain.

One summer, the fathers agreed to let both boys go to Russia for several months. When Duncan returned, he was changed. He was no longer a boy, but a man who set about learning the trade providing the family's income. He began in the looms, worked his way through various jobs at the mill. When their father died, he had been ready to step into his place, only for circumstances beyond his control to threaten the mill.

"He was engaged once, Glynis."

She nodded. "I know, to Lidia Bobrova. But it wasn't really an engagement, was it? Just a lot of gossip."

He frowned at her. "Who are you talking about?"

"The Russian girl," she said. "You met her."

He shook his head. "The girl wasn't Russian," he said.

Her mouth was suddenly dry. "Then who was it?"

"A Glasgow girl. Rose something or other. I can't remember her last name."

"Why didn't he marry her?"

He shrugged. "One moment he was engaged. The next he wasn't. You'll have to ask him for the details."

From what she knew about men, experience she'd gleaned from diplomatic circles, they didn't pry about each other's personal life. She doubted any of Richard's superiors had known about his perversions. Or the sad state of his marriage.

They discussed a man's dislike of alcohol, his affinity for cheap cigars, his way of avoiding looking a servant in the eye, or staring down at the floor when talking to a woman. They talked about how a man cared for his horses, his dogs, and his servants, but they rarely broached the subject of how he mistreated a wife.

In Washington, she'd been almost masculine in her friendships. She didn't confide the details of her personal life to another woman. Firstly, because the atmosphere at the Washington British Legation was poisonous. The stress of trying to remain neutral in an emotionally charged country meant people used information as ammunition.

Secondly, if the poor state of his marriage—and the reason for it—was known, Richard might have been forced home early. A man was judged by his ability to control his impulses. In the last two years in Washington, it seemed like he was doing the utmost to ruin his life, while she was attempting to make everything look normal and ordinary.

The patterns of Washington came to her aid now as she shook her head. She wouldn't ask Lennox about his engagement. It was enough to know he'd found someone, a woman he'd cared enough about to ask to be his wife.

What had happened? Why hadn't he married after all?

"What are you going to do?" she asked Duncan, determined to push Lennox to the back of her mind. "You can't keep the mill running with no cotton."

He nodded. "I know," he said, spearing his hand through his hair. "Give more people the sack."

"Would it make a difference?"

"Not against the greater hemorrhage of cash," he said. "I've sold the Edinburgh house, and I've got the land in England for sale. There are a few more parcels outside of Inverness, but after they're gone, there's nothing else to sell."

He walked to the window looking out over the mill buildings. Once, the noise from all the looms made it difficult to hear someone speak, even in this office. Now it was eerily quiet.

"I wish I could help," she said. "But by coming home I've only given you one more mouth to feed."

He glanced at her and smiled. "You don't eat much,

Glynis." His smile slipped. "The bastard didn't leave you anything?"

"A stipend," she said. "It ran out in Washington. Wouldn't Lennox help?"

He gave her such a fulminating look she almost withdrew the question.

"I'll not take charity from my friends, Glynis."

If they didn't find a way out of this mess, they would be forced to beg for food, another comment she didn't make to her brother.

She tilted her head and studied him. "You have an idea, though, don't you?"

He shrugged again.

"Tell me."

"I will, when it's time," he said.

And that was that. She knew herself to be stubborn at times, but Duncan was intractable. He would speak only when his plan was complete and not before.

Chapter 11

Glynis entered her room, slowly untied the ribbon of her bonnet and sat heavily on the end of the bed, clasping her hands on her knees.

On her return to Glasgow she'd been speechless at the sanctuary her mother had created of her room. Not one thing was changed. On the bureau were the miniatures of animals she collected as a child. A few treasures had been here for years: a smooth rock with her initials carved into it by Duncan, a tiny sailboat Lennox had given her when she was eleven, a threadbare stuffed rabbit she'd had since she was a baby. Her dolls, including one poor creature with a missing eye, sat on top of another chest as if waiting for the child she'd been to come and claim it.

The view from the window was of the hill and the house topping it. How many hours had she spent sitting there, her attention on Hillshead, wondering what Lennox was doing? Had he returned home from Russia? Was he going to France? Every single day seemed to be marked with some thought of Lennox.

Perhaps she could be forgiven her obsession because of youth. She'd been naive and headstrong, stubborn and stupid. Foolish was not the right word to use to describe herself because she'd been arrogant as well. So filled with her own knowledge of the world she didn't think anyone else could be right or she could possibly be wrong.

Poor sad girl, to learn so much in such a quick time and none of it casting her in a good light.

How long she sat there she didn't know. Something inside her opened up, a cavern filled with memories and moments captured forever in her mind.

Nothing was as she'd expected it to be. Everything had changed; life was like the Clyde, and it had flowed along without her. Her father had died. Duncan had matured. Her mother had aged. Lennox had found someone to marry.

What had she expected? That people would remain frozen in time? That no one would age or die? That she would be the beloved MacIain daughter when she returned? That the mill would still be prosperous? That nothing had changed?

The world was a grand and marvelous thing beyond the borders of her country. It was also scary and dangerous. Friends were not truly friends. Nor were enemies always enemies. She'd raced from an idyllic existence into one where smiles meant nothing, politeness hid a cruel heart, and a man wasn't what he seemed to be.

For the last seven years she'd been playacting, and that thought brought her up short. She had acted the part for which she'd been trained well enough to survive in Washington.

Who was she, beyond the role she played?

She could never return to being Glynis—the girl, albeit with a few more years of understanding. She knew too much. Guilt was a millstone around her neck.

She wanted her life back the way it had been before she left. She wanted the hope and the promise of it. She wanted to return to being as innocent, and wasn't that a foolish notion?

A wild goose never laid tame eggs—one of Mabel's favorite expressions. That's what she'd been: a wild goose. A wild child without any sense at all.

She pulled on her earlobe and caught herself.

Bad habits are an indication of the lower class, Glynis.

Richard was forever reminding her of her faults, which were numerous, according to him. Even with him gone, she could relate them without any difficulty at all. She loved mornings and was consequently always sleepy at late night functions. She had no skills at needlework. She did not oversee servants well enough. She had a habit of laughing too loud when she was genuinely amused. That was one fault he'd not be able to chastise her about for the last two years of their marriage. She hadn't found anything amusing about being married to Richard.

He'd always seemed so blind to any of her assets. She learned quickly. She had enduring patience. She was exceptionally good at stretching money and could practice economies with a great deal of creativity. She was quite good at numbers, figures, and facts that bored other people.

Perhaps it was that reason she had been growing popular in Washington. She remembered the numbers and the facts of a man's career: when he was appointed to his current post, what he had done, his constituency. Such things charmed most men, she'd discovered.

She was also good at travel. She didn't mind the inconveniences or discomforts, being fascinated with the sights she saw. She was curious about her fellow travelers. Why were they going to their destination? Were they excited about the journey or did it fill them with trepidation?

She wanted to know about people, and that curiosity, too, was seen as another flaw.

Richard liked criticizing her, but she'd developed another quality: she learned to completely ignore him.

Eleanor appeared at the door.

"Do you really think I should have changed it?" her mother asked, coming into the room. She moved to the window to straighten the curtains before checking the top of the bureau for dust.

"I just couldn't, my dear. It gave me such a comfort to come here, and imagine you sitting here listening to me. You were always such a great companion, even as a child."

Her mother's smile warmed her heart. She'd always adored her mother. Why hadn't she considered the loss of her parents when she married? Another question for which there was only one answer: her own selfishness.

Her thoughts had been centered on Lennox to the exclusion of anything else. Hardly fair to him. One person could not occupy the whole of another's mind. No matter how much she had loved him, she'd been herself as well.

Lennox hadn't catapulted her from Scotland. Her pride had.

Eleanor walked to the bed, grabbed the corner of the counterpane and tucked it into place, then looked around at all the furniture. "Perhaps I should make this a guest room. Or a place to read, somewhere away from Duncan to give him some privacy."

She went to fix a drawer not aligned with the rest. Pulling it out, she once more inserted it into the bureau. A second later she opened the drawer again.

"Glynis," she said, "what is this?"

She held the object with two fingers, turning to stare at Glynis with wide eyes.

"It's a gun, Glynis. Why on earth do you have a gun?"

"It's Richard's Derringer," she said. "I found it among the possessions returned to me after he died."

Her mother's eyes widened. "Richard? What on earth could he have wanted with such a thing?"

"No doubt protection for some of the places he went," Glynis said. "The brothel he frequented wasn't in the best area of town."

She had the disconcerting notion of seeing her mother do something she'd never done. Eleanor dropped the gun back into the drawer, slapped her hand on her bosom and stared at her, mouth open.

"Do not say such a thing, child. What do you mean, brothel?"

Surely her mother wasn't that innocent?

"Richard had odd tastes, Mother. That's the most polite way to say it." She wasn't going to go into Richard's exact preferences. Her mother didn't need to know.

Eleanor blinked at her.

"I never liked the man," she said. "I didn't like him at your wedding. I didn't like him through your letters. He was a selfish, grasping, mean person."

"You never said anything." Glynis said, surprised.

Her mother sat on the bed next to her. "What was I supposed to say, Glynis? You had agreed to marry him. Nothing I said would've made any difference."

Had she truly been that headstrong? Yes, she had. Perhaps nothing anyone said could have dissuaded her from her decision. She'd desperately wanted to be away from Glasgow, Scotland, and, most of all, Lennox.

Still, in all these years, she'd never heard anything in her mother's letters remotely critical of Richard. When she said as much, her mother smiled.

"Marriage is forever, my darling child. I knew he was going to be your husband for the rest of your days. He was your choice."

A very bad choice, another remark she wouldn't make.

She made a mental note to retrieve the Derringer and tuck it into her reticule. As long as Baumann was around, it wouldn't hurt to have some protection.

Eleanor's expression clouded. "God forgive me, though, I'm glad the man is no longer in your life. Not that I would wish an early death on anyone, but it does seem providential, doesn't it?"

It had been an answer to a thousand prayers, yet another comment she wouldn't make.

"I do hope you at least chastised him verbally. Threw something at him. How dare the man frequent a brothel!"

Glynis smiled, amusement bubbling from deep inside. How very dear her mother was. In her world, people were either black or white, either good or evil. There was no gray for Eleanor MacIain.

"I can assure you I wanted to pitch something at him, Mother. But it was just easier to go along with the situation as it was. Nothing I said ever affected Richard in any way."

She didn't like seeing her mother angry, especially since it did no good in this case. Richard was far beyond any earthly punishments.

Eleanor reached over, tucked a tendril of hair behind Glynis's ear.

"Did he ever hurt you, my darling girl?"

She shook her head. Physically, Richard had never touched her. Did his constant barrage of criticism count? What about his conscious cruelties like refusing to allow her to come home for a visit? He hadn't even returned to England when his own mother died. Any emotion he felt was reserved for the diplomatic service.

"It's glad I am that it's over and you're home," Eleanor said. "What's done is done."

She turned her head and studied her mother. "Why didn't you tell me Lennox was engaged?"

Time stretched and pulled and twisted itself while she waited.

Finally, Eleanor said, "You still feel the same about him, don't you?"

She shook her head. "Too much has happened. I'm not the same girl I was back then."

Her mother glanced at her but didn't comment. Did she believe her?

"It was a very short engagement," Eleanor said. "Before I knew it, the wedding was canceled."

"Duncan said her name was Rose."

Her mother nodded. "Rose Hollis. I quite liked her."

Is she pretty? Accomplished? Had she kissed Lennox? Had he held her in his arms? From whom did she get those answers? No one. She would have to quash her curiosity. She didn't want her own past examined; it was hardly fair to want to know everything about Lennox.

She tilted her head back, studying the ceiling. She wasn't sad but she did feel empty, as if all her memories had been dumped from the trunk where they'd been carefully stored. Nothing was left of the impulsive girl she'd been.

She was Glynis Smythe, widow of the late British attaché Richard Smythe, accomplished Washington hostess, and master spy.

Chapter 12

$\mathcal{F}$or three days Glynis thought about what she discovered on the trip to the mill and how close they were to disaster.

Duncan was doing what he could. He'd left for London the day before, the stated purpose to sell some English property. She suspected he had other plans, but he didn't confide in her.

She stood up from her secretary, placing her hands on the small of her back and stretching. She stared at the figures she'd taken from the ledgers for hours but couldn't see a way out of their situation.

If they did nothing, the mill would slowly grind to a halt. As it was, Duncan hadn't paid some of his vendors and payroll was a huge outlay of dwindling cash. Even if they let the rest of the employees go, they'd still have expenses, unless they closed the doors and walked away.

The MacIain family would be among the gallantly and proudly poor.

Starving with grace had absolutely nothing to recommend it. She'd come close to doing exactly that in those last months in Washington. She had to dismiss the servants and leave the house Richard had rented. She took a room in a less genteel area of Washington in order to save money. She'd subsisted on the one meal allotted with her rent, sold all her gowns and jewelry, and contacted the legation weekly to try to arrange passage home. If they hadn't picked up the cost of the voyage, she wouldn't have been able to return to Scotland.

She analyzed her skills in those months, applying for positions without thought of pride or pretense. No one wanted a female bookkeeper or accountant. None of her experience at the mill was translatable to a paying position anywhere. She wasn't a talented seamstress. Nor did she know how to trim bonnets. Factory work wasn't an option since no manufacturing existed within walking distance.

At least when she lived in Washington she only had herself to support. Now there was an entire household.

Duncan had some investments not associated with the mill that would carry them for a few months, but what then? She didn't have an answer other than finding employment. They had to outlast the war. Yet even once the blockade was lifted, was there any guarantee they'd be able to acquire raw cotton again? Would the Confederates win? If they did, could they produce and export cotton in time to save the mill? If they lost the war, would the fields be razed by the Union?

Everything was dependent on the Civil War, an irony that didn't escape her. Yet the same war decimating the MacIain coffers was helping Lennox. He might even be the richest man in a city filled with wealthy men.

Did Lennox still treasure his friendships and care about people? If he did, why hadn't he realized Duncan needed help? Why hadn't he offered?

Duncan wouldn't go to Lennox. His pride would prevent him from asking for help. The question was: how much pride did she have?

She stood, walked to her vanity and leaned her

hands against the top, peering at her image in the mirror. Her cheeks were flushed. She brushed her hair into place, inserted a few more pins to keep the tendrils tamed, and applied a little salve to her lips.

She glanced toward Hillshead. Could she really go to Lennox and ask him for help?

Gloaming settled over Glasgow like a memory, making her recall a dozen times she left her house for Hillshead. Now she slipped out of the kitchen much as she had back then, smiling at Mabel and Lily before heading for the path Lennox and Duncan had worn into the grass as boys.

She hesitated at the arched bridge at the bottom of the hill. The structure had to be rebuilt every couple of years when the burn would outgrow its banks for a few weeks and become a river. Now the water gurgled and babbled as it fell over the smooth stones, as if telling her all the secrets since she'd last crossed.

She grabbed her skirts, trying to hold them away from the ground. She took the track winding through the pines, breathing in the pungent smell of the needles. Here it was almost dark, but she remembered the way.

The wind soughed through the trees, the branches clicking like a convocation of gossips.

Already a few lights had been lit, a sign this was not the proper hour for calling on anyone, let alone a woman on a man, even if she was a proper widow and Lennox was an old friend.

Should she simply wait until morning?

No, she might lose her courage by then. Better if she went and explained the whole sorry mess to Lennox so he understood. If there was any groveling that needed to be done, she'd do it. Hadn't she done even worse things in Washington?

The house was an open box with the back of Hillshead shielding the three gardens. On the third floor the terrace outside the ballroom ran the width of the building. On either end of the terrace, steps curved down and around to the Italian gardens filled with fountains, gravel paths, and marble statuary.

Instead of going to the front, which she might have if the hour had been decent and this errand anything but surreptitious, she headed toward Hillshead's back door. She'd come here often enough as a girl, either following Duncan, to his disgust, or acting as her brother's messenger.

Was the cook the same? She'd been a lovely woman with graying hair and a well-lined face, but she had a contagious smile that made Glynis smile as well. Whenever she came to Hillshead, the woman had always offered her a selection of pastries. Sometimes she'd eaten her fill and sometimes she wrapped a few into her handkerchief and tucked them into her pocket, a present to Duncan for sending her to Hillshead.

The last rays of sunlight danced on the lush plants of the kitchen garden. The onions and peppers, lettuce and cabbages, grew so thick the tilled earth could no longer be seen. In a separate bed, herbs waved merrily in the breeze, fronds of mint and rosemary perfuming the air.

The ghost of the girl she'd been walked alongside, her face sunnied with a bright smile, her eyes sparkling with anticipation about seeing Lennox.

Had she always been a fool about him?

Yes.

The stark answer stopped her on the path.

This errand was too important to be rashly contemplated. She should take her time, marshal her arguments, perhaps even prepare a balance sheet for Lennox to peruse.

She would call on him at the yard. She'd dress in her

best black dress with white cuffs and collar, with an attractive bonnet framing her face. She wouldn't appear before him with stickers adhering to the bottom of her skirt and the wind pulling her hair loose from its proper bun.

That was the best thing to do. She wouldn't go to him like a supplicant but an equal, a woman of the world. Her entreaty would be a businesslike matter, not a personal one.

The urge to come to him had been so basic she'd been impulsive again. The Glynis of her girlhood had simply come to Hillshead as she had so many times before.

A rough-hewn bench sat in front of the gardener's cottage. To her right the path branched in three directions. One led to the kitchen garden she'd already passed. The second went to Hillshead's flower garden. A third headed toward the formal Italian garden with its fountains and statuary. To her left was Glasgow itself, the house's elevation revealing a panoramic view of the city and the River Clyde.

She walked to the bench, her shoes crunching on the shells. She sat, contemplating the sight of the city and the river. Her fingers trailed over the knurled wood of the bench. Here was something that hadn't changed.

She tucked her feet beneath her skirts and remembered.

"I want to make the greatest ships on the ocean," Lennox once said as he sat here, holding her eleven-year-old self captive with his plans. "Ships people will recognize just by looking at them. They'll say, 'Lennox Cameron designed her and it was built at Cameron and Company.'"

She'd listened, enthralled, as he mapped out his future. To the best of her knowledge, he made each one of his dreams come true.

When he was seventeen he announced he was going to Russia and wouldn't be home for months. Sometimes she came and sat here, staring up at the window of his room and wishing him home.

On this bench he'd told her of school and his trip to the Continent, how he liked Paris but didn't think it as impressive as Edinburgh. She'd been fifteen to his twenty. How odd that she was the more well-traveled of the two of them now.

Most of the memories of her childhood involved Lennox in one way or another. He was part of her life and she could no more cut him out of it than she could Duncan or her parents.

She tipped her head back and stared up at the stars peeking coyly from behind the edges of the clouds.

Fertilizer, roses, clipped grass, and the damp of the evening rolled over her. She was as far from Washington as she could possibly be.

"What are you doing here, Glynis?"

For a moment she felt like she'd conjured him out of the mists of memory. She slowly turned her head to see him standing there in the shadows, no longer a boy. Instead, Lennox was a man, one who, despite her wishes, still had the power to make her heart race.

Why did he still fascinate her?

Could it be the way he walked, as if he commanded the deck of a ship? Or his physique, with his broad shoulders, long legs, and wide, muscular chest?

She'd seen him nearly naked once, down to his underclothes. He and Duncan had been swimming, and when he emerged from the river she'd been unable to look away. At sixteen she'd known what the throbbing in her own lower parts meant. Ever since that day she wanted to touch him, measure his chest with her hands and let her fingers dance over his body.

Even now he made her think of things no other

man ever had: wrinkled sheets, sweaty skin, and being kissed. She used to wonder what it would be like to be with Lennox, to feel his hands on her naked skin, to abandon herself to the pleasure of loving. With him it would be a world apart from anything she knew, anything she'd ever experienced.

She'd catch herself, make herself think of anything but Lennox. And she should do that now. She didn't come here to lust after Lennox. She should stand, right now, and go back to her revised plan of calling on him at the yard. But the past lured her, trapped her in a silken web. She didn't want to move or face the reality of the present.

For a few moments she wanted to be young again and innocent.

"I was thinking of all the times you and I sat on this bench," she said. "It feels like forever ago. Those were quieter times, weren't they?

"I'm not certain they were quieter," he said, coming closer. "We were children. We had few responsibilities. Everything looks easy when nothing is expected of you."

Expectations—she'd heard the word often enough in the last seven years. For a little while, she didn't want to be reminded. Let her be a child for a time, if only in her memories.

"Do you remember when I put the beehive in your boat?" she asked, smiling.

"And returned the same day with your mother's ointment. Your tricks would have been better if you hadn't always regretted them."

"I knew, almost immediately, that I shouldn't have done it. I spent a great deal of my childhood regretting the things I did."

"And not your adulthood?"

She wasn't going to answer that question.

"You never retaliated for the nettles in your jacket and I always wondered why."

"I was forbidden to," he said. "First of all you were a girl. Secondly, you were five years younger than me, and maybe the most important reason, Duncan was your brother. I was under an oath to Duncan."

She glanced at him, surprised. "Were you?"

He nodded. "I was to think of you like Mary," he said. "Since Duncan was always a gentleman around my sister, I was to remember it."

Had he remembered that oath in the anteroom? Did he still consider her Duncan's little sister?

"I might admit to being a hoyden," she said.

He nodded. "Yes," he said, "you were. A trial. A terror."

She sent him a chastising look. "You weren't perfect, Lennox."

"I was the epitome of patience when it came to you," he said.

She couldn't say anything to counter his words because he was right.

"I remember when we used to sit here and watch the stars," she said. "You told me about the great ships you'd build."

"You told me how you wanted to work at the mill, become your father's bookkeeper," he said, coming to sit beside her.

She smiled. "I miss those days," she said. "The future looked so promising."

"Have you spent the last seven years making up for your childhood, Glynis?"

There was more truth to the comment than he knew. From the day after her wedding, Richard had put her through her paces, almost like a thoroughbred. She had a succession of teachers, people who informed her husband she was woefully lacking in ladylike manners.

Pride made her adept at all her lessons from the social graces—most of which she'd thought she mastered well enough at home—to memorizing the titles and names of everyone at the British Legation.

There wasn't time to be a hoyden. Or to be rebellious, either. She learned because it was expected of her. Richard was the only person she knew on their voyage to Cairo, and he disapproved of her making friends among the passengers.

She had nothing to do all those miserable days but study. Yet the greatest lessons had nothing to do with Cairo, the diplomatic service, or the proper way to address heads of state. The most vital things she learned in that first year were personal: how selfish she'd been, how petty, spoiled, and insular.

The discoveries she made, however, had come much too late for anything but regret.

Chapter 13

"You haven't said why you're here, Glynis."

There were certain times when nothing but truth would serve, as bluntly as possible.

"We need help," she said. "The mill will close without an infusion of cash. We've no cotton and we can't spin cloth out of straw."

When he didn't say anything, she stared off into the garden. The air was heavy with mint and onions, a curious combination.

"Give Duncan a loan." She turned to him. "Aren't you friends, Lennox? He'd help you if you needed it."

"I've already offered. Duncan won't take the money."

She should have known he wouldn't have turned his back on Duncan. Her brother's pride was becoming an irritant.

"Then give it to me. I'll say it's an unexpected bequest from Richard's estate. Something no one realized was there."

He didn't say anything. Had she been too abrupt?

"I wouldn't ask, Lennox, but the mill isn't just about us. Hundreds of people are employed there. If they lose their jobs, where will they go for their next meal? How will they pay their rent?"

"It's a test of character you're giving me, is that it, Glynis? Either I let the mill close or hide my benevolence behind your sainted husband?"

His comment startled her so much she retreated into silence.

"Richard wasn't sainted," she finally said. She took a deep breath. "I have no assets, Lennox, or I'd sell them." She stood. "If you don't want to help, then hire me as an accountant. My father trained me. I'm very good."

He still sat there, one arm draped over the end of the bench. It was too dark to see his expression. She really should have gone to his office at the yard.

"Did he leave you nothing, Glynis?"

"Only regrets," she said. Marry in haste, repent at leisure.

"Did you love him?"

"Is that important?" Did he want the truth in exchange for a loan? How much was she willing to sacrifice for the mill?

"Why did you marry him?"

She was not going to tell him she'd married because of a rumor, one that had sent her from Glasgow in tears.

"Does it matter?" she said. "I was his wife."

He stood, approaching her with a grace he'd always had. She remained where she was, only tilting her head back when he stopped less than an arm's length away. He'd been tall since he was sixteen, a man still in a boy's body. Now he was all man.

"Duncan said you were engaged," she said. "Why didn't you marry?"

He didn't respond. Lennox had always been exceedingly loyal. Perhaps he still felt that way about his once fiancée.

"I can't imagine why a woman with any sense would break her engagement to you."

"She didn't break the engagement," he said. "I did."

"Whatever did she do?" she asked.

He studied her, making her wish she could read his expression again.

"Does it matter?" he asked, repeating her words.

She strode past him to stand at the juncture of the garden paths. In the past, the Camerons had put lanterns on poles on summer nights, illuminating the garden. Now the moon performed the same task.

"I missed you," she said. A comment she'd not expected to make. Once uttered, however, she could not call it back.

She turned and faced his shadow.

"When things were difficult I would imagine myself talking to you. I'd find myself asking, 'What would Lennox advise me to do?'"

"I remember your never taking my advice as a child."

She smiled. "I did, more often than you knew. I just never told you."

"What was difficult for you, Glynis?"

He really shouldn't use that tone of voice. Gentle, almost tender, as if he truly cared about her life in the last seven years. As if he cared about her.

Pride stiffened her spine and banished the hint of tears.

"I have to do something, Lennox. The mill is going to close. If that happens it will destroy Duncan."

"I've tried to help," he said, approaching her. "A half-dozen times at least."

He was much too close. She took a step back.

Yet she'd been brave once, hadn't she? She'd kissed him and remembered it for years.

Without giving herself a chance to talk herself out of it, she closed the distance between them. Placing her hands flat on his chest, she stood on tiptoe and placed her mouth on his.

His hands traveled from her elbows up to her shoulders and then down her back, settling at her waist.

Delight spread through her like a fast moving burn, carrying effervescent bubbles to every part of her body. She was lighter than air itself. She was laughter and joy and only his touch anchored her to the ground.

There was something elemental in kissing Lennox. His hands pressed against her back, slowly sliding up and down, making her conscious of two things: her skin tingled beneath his fingers and delight was being replaced by need.

Oh beloved.

She wrapped her arms around his neck and held on.

She wasn't that removed from her ancestors. A few generations earlier she would have been attired in a skirt made of plaid, her clan's brooch pinned on a fold of cloth. Strong, fearless, and proud, she would claim her mate with a glance. He would bow to no man, but he might well surrender to her.

But she wasn't a Highlander. Instead, she was a woman newly returned to a bustling, industrious city, stuffed into a corset and protected from touch by a swinging hoop and layers of clothing, most of it silk and none of it tartan. She was a civilized creature, for all she sometimes wished she weren't.

Lennox was as much a product of the nineteenth century as she was, but in this moment they allowed themselves to be wild and untamed.

His lips were hard yet soft. Her tongue stroked his bottom lip, coaxing a response. His arms pulled her closer, pressing her breasts against his chest. His mouth turned hot, his tongue brushing hers. Stars sparkled behind her eyelids.

Her body was turning molten, the sensation so indescribably delicious she wanted it to last.

She pressed both hands on his cheeks, his skin warm to her touch, the bristles of his almost-beard abrading her palms. It had been a lifetime since she kissed him, but that kiss had been a pale imitation to this one.

His fingers trailed along the back of her neck as he deepened the kiss. She angled her head, widened her mouth, tasting him. She inhaled his breath as his tongue darted with hers, his teeth nipping at her bottom lip.

Long moments later they separated.

She blinked open her eyes, startled to realize her hands were linked behind his neck, her fingers threading through his hair. He was breathing as hard as she was.

What had she done?

She'd revealed too much without a word spoken.

Dropping her hands, she stepped back.

A great deal had changed in the last seven years. She could mask her emotions quite well. She knew how to leave a charged situation with aplomb. She had practice in mustering her momentary devastation and fusing it into a smile.

She'd been married to a man with perverted tastes, placed in a city thrumming with intrigue and expected to fail. Instead, she'd succeeded. She'd charmed, pleased, and cajoled men and women of staggering power and influence.

Who was Lennox Cameron in comparison?

"I shouldn't have come," she said, grateful for the calm of her voice. She shouldn't have kissed him. She shouldn't have given in to the temptation.

Without a backward glance she turned and walked away.

I'M SURE I shall dislike Nassau intensely," Lucy said. "Is it absolutely necessary for me to travel with you?

After all, you're going to be busy doing what you want. Why can't I do what I want, stay home in London surrounded by my family and those things I hold dear?"

Gavin Whittaker turned from the armoire and faced his bride.

He had to find another way to try to explain that the future of his home was in jeopardy and that's why he was so set on running the blockade. If the Confederacy lost the war, the Union wouldn't hesitate in decimating the South. There wouldn't be anything left to the way of life he and his fellow southerners had always known.

Lucy's life had been spent in a stable monarchy. She had no concept of a country struggling to identify itself. Nor could she grasp why being the captain of the *Raven* was so important to him.

So far he'd failed in explaining his mission, but he wasn't giving up.

He approached her where she sat in the chair beside the window. If he was too bold, she would hold up both hands, give a little shudder, and plead with him. *No, Gavin, please. Must you always be touching me?*

But she was acting as a lady would, and he couldn't fault her. Men, he'd always been told, enjoyed passion, while their women folk merely endured it.

"You'll be safe enough in Nassau, honey," he said. "There are a lot of English people there. You'll make friends, and I'll visit you when I can. I couldn't do that if you were in London."

"You could come and get me when this awful war is over," she said.

He stopped a few feet from the chair. This time after dinner and before bed was always an awkward one. For the last week, Lucy had used these hours to argue with him.

"I could stay here in Scotland," she said.

"I thought you didn't like Scotland," he said, taking a few steps closer.

She was a lush little thing, with surprising curves underneath all her clothes. He liked cuddling with her and loving her. He only wished she liked it as much.

He took another step, only to be met with a frown.

"Leave me alone, Gavin," she said, turning and looking out the window. "Do what you men do when you're not playing at war or being ravening beasts."

He took a step back, staring down at his wife. He should go down to Cameron's library, find a book on ship design and avail himself of some of his host's excellent whiskey. After a few hours had passed he'd return to their suite to see if his wife was any more receptive to his touch.

If he took her to the *Raven*, maybe she'd understand. Once she saw the vessel and he explained how, exactly, he was going to outrun the Union ships, she'd understand that running the blockade wasn't for glory but for survival. The fate of women like his mother and sisters might depend on the supplies he got through to the South.

Lucy needed to comprehend the rightness of his cause. If she did, she wouldn't be so hesitant about sailing to Nassau. She might even be more welcoming to him. She'd send him off to war the way women had done since the beginning of time, with a kiss and memories to keep him warm.

Until then he'd leave her alone, intent on her view from the window.

SHE'D DONE it again, managed to confound him with a kiss. No, more than a kiss. By her words, by the soft, resigned tone in which she'd spoken of Washington.

He stood where he was for several minutes, then followed Glynis's path through the darkness.

Glasgow had changed in the last seven years. He wanted to make sure she was safe walking home. He stood on the hill watching, seeing the flash of her cuffs occasionally. When the door opened, he let out the breath he was holding.

Yet he didn't move.

A dozen minutes later the light went on in the room he knew was hers.

He still didn't move.

She'd kissed him again. Unlike seven years ago, he didn't have any trouble thinking of Glynis as a woman. He might have forgotten his honor, but he could still feel her in his arms.

She'd felt right being there.

Glynis was in his bones, like Scotland. She was a part of him. A laughing companion, a patient listener, a girl who'd become a woman without him noticing. Then, she blindsided him by leaving Glasgow before he had a chance to act on that knowledge.

He'd been damn lonely the past seven years, something he hadn't told anyone. The only person who might have guessed was Eleanor, who insisted on reading Glynis's letters to him. She was a compassionate woman, one who'd taken the place of his own mother. He might have confided in her if the situation had been different, if she hadn't been missing Glynis herself.

The light was abruptly extinguished. Was she standing there in the darkness watching him? Did she wonder why he hadn't moved, why his gaze was still fixed on her window?

He wanted an explanation, an answer to his confusion.

Why had she been so curious about Rose?

Rose was a lovely girl with a lilting laugh and a sweetness in her demeanor. Yet he'd realized he couldn't marry her a month before the wedding.

She listened to him talk about his ships, but she never once challenged his thoughts or asked about his designs. He'd kissed her twice but he never felt the top of his head lift off like he had a few minutes ago.

Rose wasn't Glynis.

She didn't dare him. She didn't intrigue him. Not once had she done anything to startle him. She'd never caused him any sleepless nights. Nor had she brought any tumult or confusion to his life.

He didn't love Rose.

It struck him with the force of a blow.

He'd been waiting for Glynis.

All this time, he'd been waiting for her.

Chapter 14

"That's it, sir. The ship's empty, ready for your walk."

Lennox nodded and thanked his foreman.

This last inspection of the *Raven* was a solitary one. The day before, he'd taken the foremen of the crews with him, the boilermakers, carpenters, ship fitters, and joiners, listening to their comments and concerns.

This was his time alone, a farewell to the vessel born in his consciousness, brought to life on paper, and created in wood and iron. For now, this space of an hour or so, he, the designer, the builder, and in a way that always amused him—the mother—would say goodbye to his creation.

He breathed deeply, inhaling the sharp scent of newly sawn wood, varnish, turpentine, and paint, all odors reminding him of his daily work, of Cameron and Company, and the magic of creating ships to cross the oceans of the world.

If he hadn't built ships for a living, he would've sailed them. But it was enough for him to envision the voyages of Cameron ships and, recently, to imagine the newest iron-clad ships as spirits on the ocean, blockade runners too fast to be captured.

He'd never see or sail the *Raven* again. Nor would he stand on her bow and greet the dawn. He'd never have the thrill of riding out a storm, knowing she was solidly built and more than a match for Mother Nature.

He'd spent hours poring over the plans, making changes, engineering details for this ship, as he'd done for no other. The cladding had proved difficult only because of the shape of her hull. The *Raven* was designed to fly over the waves, and when she'd finally taken shape, he realized he'd achieved his dream.

His emotions were tied up in this ship, foolishly so. He wanted the *Raven* to succeed for a variety of reasons. He wanted the world to know how fast and well built a Cameron and Company ship was. He wanted her to succeed in bringing cotton back to Glasgow so half the city wouldn't be hurting because of the Americans' war, and he wanted, too, for his father to be proud.

His father had an affinity for ships, the same love Lennox had always felt. Although William Cameron couldn't see the *Raven,* he'd felt her. He'd stroked his weathered and callused hands across the planed and sanded wood. He'd felt the archboard where the *Raven*'s name had been painted. Then, in a moment as breathless as the seconds before a gale, he smiled, turned in Lennox's direction and said simply, "You've done us proud."

Now all he had to do was turn over his ship to Gavin.

The man was like most of the blockade-running captains he'd met, filled with confidence and an almost idiotic bravado. Whittaker had already lost one ship, ground it rather than surrender to a Union vessel sliding out of the fog.

The man's rendition of the tale was meant for female ears or those without any experience aboard ship. Lennox interpreted what Whittaker didn't say, knew the man had been nearly suicidal, deliberating steering his ship onto the sandbar rather than allow the Union forces to capture her and use her against the Confederate navy.

He hoped Whittaker would treat the *Raven* better.

Lennox stood at the stern, watching the dismantling of the bridge connecting the two docks on either side of the ship. They'd constructed a new berth for the *Raven* because of her size. Now smaller ships—average ships—would take her place.

His joy in this accomplishment was tempered by the realization that he had no one to share it with. Duncan was a close friend, yet the occasion would be tantamount to boasting if he called for Duncan to join him, especially in light of the mill's troubles.

What would Glynis think? He could imagine her grabbing her skirts and racing up to the forecastle, or staring at the massive midship paddle wheel in wonder.

Would her face have turned to his, her eyes sparkling? "It's the most wonderful ship you've ever built," she might have exclaimed.

He wanted to show it to her. He wanted to prove he was so much more than he'd once been, that his experience had grown and his talent had developed.

He wanted her to be proud of him.

Smiling at himself, he finished his inspection. Already the *Raven* was part of his past.

Did Glynis realize she was part of his future?

CHAOS MARKED their morning, the normal pattern of their quiet days disrupted by weeping coming from the parlor, along with her mother's gentle voice.

Eleanor never allowed a person's status or job to interfere with her interest. If something changed in the cook's life or for one of the maids, her mother knew of it first. Glynis overheard enough tearful confessions and explanations to know people saw her mother as a gentle soul, someone who would understand more than condemn.

Once the tearful scene with the maid was over, she entered the parlor and hugged her mother. Eleanor looked surprised, then pleased, glancing up at her with wise blue eyes.

"She's finding herself in the family way, poor dear. And there's no one to help her out. Her young man has gone off to sea."

"And we'll have a pregnant maid until she gives birth," Glynis said. "And after that, will you set up a nursery in the attic?"

Her mother smiled. "I might consider it. Thank heavens I never had such a problem with you."

Not for lack of wanting. What would her mother say to the truth?

Her smile fixed, she glanced toward the window. The day promised to be a sunny and bright one, the hills of Glasgow visible with no fog or mist. If she looked left, she could see Hillshead standing like an eagle in its aerie.

Cook peered around the door. A strange sight to see Mabel's round and normally beaming face wrinkled in worry.

"It's all right, Mabel. We'll handle things as they come."

Cook nodded. "Right you are, missus. It's God's gift you are, Mrs. MacIain."

Eleanor smiled. "The girl just needs a kind word and a helping hand."

How had she done without her mother all these years?

Since returning from America, she discovered that she and her mother had a great deal in common. They had similar taste in books, sweets, and a matching sense of humor. Her mother loved tea, and half-empty cups could be found scattered around the house, as if she'd been distracted in the act of drinking them. Glynis had done it often enough herself that whenever she found a cup, she smiled and returned it to the kitchen.

"I truly missed you," she said now, smiling at her mother as she sat beside her.

"And I truly missed you," her mother said. "To have you home is one of the great joys of my life."

She should have found the money somehow, disobeyed Richard, and come home for a visit. She hadn't, though, and she'd always regret not seeing her father before he died.

"You look tired, Glynis. Did you not sleep well?"

She shook her head. "No, not really," she said.

Eleanor reached out and patted her hand. "We will manage somehow, my dear. We MacIains are a strong bunch."

She glanced at her mother and forced a smile to her face. She wasn't thinking of the mill. She hadn't been able to sleep well last night because of what she'd done.

She remembered her abandon with twin emotions of shock and despair. She certainly hadn't acted like a proper widow, had she? She felt like she was repeating the past, becoming the nineteen-year-old girl who'd fled Glasgow for London. Except in the intervening years she'd learned she couldn't escape from herself.

She had custody of her thoughts and guardianship over her mouth. She was no longer the hoyden, the girl-child with the adventurous spirit, the female who said what she thought, however inappropriate and ill-timed.

She'd entertained personages at her Washington home. She'd been renowned for her dinners. She'd discussed events of the day, ideas of the times. Not once did she ever utter a shocking or scandalous word. Nor did she humiliate herself.

What had happened to her?

After all, she was a sophisticated woman of the world. She had decorum and possessed a certain poise. Rarely was she incensed or pushed beyond the boundaries of proper behavior. She held what she felt inside. Otherwise people might use her thoughts and emotions as weapons against her.

Why, then, had she forgotten all those cautions around Lennox?

She'd been coached by Richard for years. Everything she did had to be perfect. If it wasn't, he made her rehearse it endlessly until he was certain she'd learned her lesson.

"You weren't attentive when the French ambassador was telling his story," he said on the night he died.

"Which story was this?" she'd asked.

"It doesn't matter. Your eyes must never roam. You must never look bored, Glynis. It doesn't reflect well on me. You must be perfect."

How many times had she heard that comment? *You must be perfect.* Often enough she should have embroidered it on a pillowcase or two. Perhaps a footstool on which she could kneel, asking for forgiveness.

She did three things perfectly, according to Richard. She dressed well and frugally, because she found a young seamstress with talent, someone who had dreams of being solicited by the women of Washington. For a minimum sum the woman copied the gowns of the day, and in return Glynis did everything she could to promote the woman's business.

Richard also approved of her table manners. All of the various bowls, plates, goblets, and silverware at state dinners or diplomatic functions never posed a problem for her.

In their bed she pleased him because she didn't move. Nor did she speak during the act. She managed to endure the experience simply by pretending to be a doll whose limbs he arranged to suit him.

Blessedly, they didn't have relations after the year in Cairo. Once in Washington, he stopped coming to her bed altogether.

"Do you not want to have children?" she asked him once.

He frowned, his mouth thinning with disapproval at her question.

"Children would be a detriment to my career, Glynis."

Everything Richard did was seen through the viewpoint of his career. His wardrobe, his reading material, his acquaintances, must at all times be aligned with the diplomatic service.

The pity of it was, he didn't realize that had he been less obsequious, he might've advanced further. People he admired called him names behind his back.

At home was a different matter, however. He wasn't the same person. Yet even there he wore a cloak around his true nature. Richard was an onion, never revealing himself completely to anyone.

Would his bosses have been impressed by how well he'd fooled them all?

Until she'd gone to Baumann, she, too, had been deceived.

Was that why he insisted on her being perfect, because he knew he wasn't? Did he regret who he was and what he was doing? Or did he even consider his own behavior?

As for being perfect, she was most definitely not. Look what she'd done last night; she'd humiliated herself in front of Lennox again. Warmth traveled up her spine to settle at the base of her neck, the better to fuel the flush she knew showed on her cheeks. Even her ears felt red.

She was adrift in embarrassment. She was scared about the future and frustrated at her inability to do anything to change it. A part of her wanted to be a child again. She wanted to be cradled in her mother's arms, rocked back and forth and told there were no monsters under the bed, her future was bright, and everything would be fine.

But she knew that wasn't right, didn't she? She'd been married to a monster. Her future stretched out before her, uncertain and unformed, and everything would be fine as long as she studiously avoided Lennox Cameron.

Somehow, she was going to have to gather up the dented, scattered bits of her pride, glue enough pieces together so that when she saw him again she'd smile, ask about his father and Mary, all without turning crimson.

She was not a young girl anymore but a widow with some experience of the world. Instead of fleeing for London she was going to remain here in Glasgow and take the advice of a seventeenth-century Englishman: living well was the best revenge.

She would simply settle into a hermitlike Glasgow life for a few months. Then perhaps she'd cast her eyes for a man with black hair and shining eyes, with a mouth that made her think wicked thoughts. She'd flirt and smile and dance and charm in the hopes that he might turn her attention away from the one man on the face of the earth who could reduce her to idiocy.

"Charlotte's dinner is this evening," her mother said, the comment pulling her out of her reverie.

She nodded, wishing she could find an excuse for declining the invitation at the last moment. Why on earth had she accepted it?

"I would give you a caution, if I may." Eleanor glanced away, then back at her. "I know she's a dear friend of yours, but she tells tales."

"She always has," Glynis said. "Ever since we were girls I knew not to say anything to Charlotte unless I wanted it spread through the whole of Glasgow by morning."

"I had no idea," Eleanor said.

"Most of the women in Washington were like Charlotte. On the outside they were very proper and rigidly polite, but they couldn't wait to spread the latest story about some mischief or faux pas. They'd ruin you with a smile."

"What a dreadful group of women."

"When I first arrived, I felt like a baby rabbit among hungry eagles. Each one of them was ready to tear me apart."

Eleanor's eyes widened. "You never said. Your letters were only filled with what you were doing, who you'd met. Was it so terrible?"

"Instructive," she said, sparing her mother the whole truth.

Washington had proven to be educational. She'd always be grateful for the lessons she learned there, not only about other people but also herself.

"After the women of Washington, I can face Charlotte."

Glasgow was her home and she was not going to hide or retreat again—ever.

Chapter 15

"Oh, I've anticipated this dinner for so very long. I'm so glad you're here." Closing the door behind her, Charlotte stood smiling toothily at her.

Glynis wondered if the dark blue dress with its silver buttons was too festive. Her mother had reassured her it was perfectly acceptable for a woman coming out of mourning. Although a little more formal than what she'd wear during the day, the garment revealed less than a ball gown. Fabric covered her shoulders and décolletage until she looked as proper as a woman attending church.

"This is Archibald," Charlotte said, pushing forward a portly middle-aged man. "He didn't get a chance to meet you at Hillshead."

"We've met before," Archibald said, bowing. "You were sixteen. My uncle had the confectioners on the corner of Trongate," he said. "I've taken it over."

"And made a success of it," Charlotte said, grabbing his arm and leaning close to her husband.

Charlotte's round face plumped with her smile. Only the unkind would ever mention her rotund figure.

"Archie has three more stores besides and is thinking of opening one in Edinburgh."

"I imagine people will always want something sweet," Glynis said.

Charlotte nodded vigorously. "Exactly that. Even in bad times, people will want to buy a bit of chocolate."

If bad times had come to Glasgow, they weren't evident in Charlotte's West End home. Furniture crowded into every room she passed, and an excess of curios on the tables in the hall made movement almost impossible. Glynis kept her hands pressed against her skirt, hoping to minimize the size of her hoop as she walked into the crowded parlor.

She stopped on the threshold, causing Archibald to walk into her. He apologized as she stared at the group facing her.

The two men in the room stood at her entrance.

"You know Lennox, of course," Charlotte said, glancing coyly at her.

She formed some kind of smile and nodded at him.

"And his houseguests, Mr. and Mrs. Whittaker."

She bit back her sigh and smiled at the couple.

"I haven't had the pleasure," Mr. Whittaker said, grinning at her.

"You are from Georgia, Mr. Whittaker?" she asked.

"I am, Mrs. Smythe," he said. "But how would you know something like that?"

"I lived in Washington for a time, but I had many acquaintances from the South," she said, moving to the corner of the settee, and as far away from Lucy as she could. "It became a game to tell a Mississippi accent from a Georgian one."

He tilted his head. "Then let me congratulate you on your ear, Mrs. Smythe. Many of my own countrymen can't tell us apart."

"I think all of you sound very odd," Lucy Whittaker said. "Especially you Scots."

Glynis's smile trembled but she pulled it back into place, remembering the innumerable rules she'd learned. *One must always allow for the idiosyncratic be-*

havior of those who do not share our culture. Of course, Richard had been talking about representatives from the African continent, not an Englishwoman, but she decided to use the advice anyway.

Lucy's air of superiority reminded her of the haughtiest of grande dames of Washington, none of whom she'd kowtowed to.

She folded her hands around her reticule, ignored Lucy's frown, and complimented Charlotte on the decor. A lie of politeness, but one pleasing Charlotte, if her smile was any indication.

A green patterned upholstery covered the many chairs and settee, but the color was not quite the same as the bright emerald silk wallpaper. The three ottomans were upholstered in a green stripe, yet another shade of the color. She felt trapped inside a bilious plant, one growing smaller and more compressed as the minutes ticked by.

Charlotte's green gown clashed horribly with her furnishings.

Bric-a-brac filled every available flat surface along with potpourri jars, each giving off a scent of sandalwood and something pungent, making her want to scratch her nose.

She glanced at Lennox. He was dressed in black, his snowy white shirt decorated with pin tucks and silver buttons.

She clenched her hands in the folds of her skirt, released them, and stared at the painting of Charlotte and her husband mounted over the fireplace. Paintings of all the MacNamara children were arranged on the wall opposite her, and she focused on them. Each child bore a resemblance to their parents, especially in their round faces and pursed mouths.

"Will you be returning to Washington, Mrs. Smythe?"

She turned her head to address Mr. Whittaker again. The warm look in his eyes matched his boyish and charming smile. She had the impression that while Mr. Whittaker might appear to be disarming and unsophisticated, he should not be underestimated.

"I won't be leaving Scotland again, Mr. Whittaker," she said. "I find I've less tolerance for travel than I once had. And you? Will you be returning to America soon?"

"Soon, Mrs. Smythe," he said, his smiling glance including Lennox. "I like Scotland well enough but I've things to do at home."

Such as being a Confederate captain.

Mr. MacNamara chose the moment to ask a question of his own. "Have you been troubled by the fires along the Clyde, Lennox?"

Lennox shook his head.

"Fires?" she asked.

"Arson," he said in a clipped voice. "An attempt to destroy the ships we're building."

"Two of them were destroyed, I understand," Mr. MacNamara said. "Burned right down to the waterline."

Lennox's face was stone, his eyes flat. He didn't comment. If she didn't know him so well she would have thought him unaffected.

Lennox, however, was angry. Why, because Mr. MacNamara had shared the news? Or because he was worried about the ships Cameron and Company were building?

"There's been talk of murders, too," Charlotte added in a shocked whisper, her eyes shining with excitement. Charlotte had always had a bloodthirsty nature. She loved gossip and tales of misadventure.

"It's why I'm so grateful for my walking stick," Gavin said. By pushing a small, concealed button, the handle came free, revealing a long knife.

"You don't think to need to use that, surely, Mr. Whittaker?" Archibald said.

"You never know, sir. We live in dangerous times."

But murder wasn't a subject for a dinner party, so the topic changed a moment later, leaving Glynis to consider the subject silently.

Was Baumann desperate enough to be an arsonist? Or a murderer, if Charlotte had been correct?

She looked up to find Lennox staring at her.

His gaze had always been piercing. Although she'd been stared at by some daunting people in the last seven years, something about Lennox's look made her glance away.

Her cheeks felt warm. Even the tips of her ears felt hot. She massaged her earlobe, caught herself, and placed her hands back in her lap.

"Have you been in Scotland long?" she asked of Mr. Whittaker.

"A matter of months," he said, glancing at his wife. "I met my wife in London," he added, "just before coming here."

"How do you find Glasgow?" she asked, wondering if he would launch into a diatribe similar to his wife's.

To her surprise, he smiled at her. "I like it just fine, Mrs. Smythe, once I figured out how y'all talk."

She smiled back at him, wondering if he knew how odd he probably sounded to her fellow Glaswegians.

Her ear was attuned to accents, especially since Richard had tried to expunge any tinge of Scotland in her voice. Only when she was tired did her R's start to roll or a hint of her native tongue emerge. Normally she sounded English, as proper as an attaché's wife should be.

"The weather here is horrid," Lucy said. "It's always raining."

"In Washington it was very soggy," she said, annoyed by the woman's constant complaints. "Humid in the summer and too wet in spring."

"While London has its share of fog," Lennox offered.

She glanced at him. Was he goading Lucy or her?

Charlotte came and joined them on the settee.

"How long has it been since we were all together like this? Too long I say." She spared a grin for Mr. Whittaker. "We were all the best of friends as children."

Lucy's mouth twisted downward as her gaze flitted around the room. Lennox's mouth curved in a half smile. Mr. Whittaker adopted an interested air, leaning forward and addressing his hostess.

"Surely not that long ago, Mrs. MacNamara."

Charlotte pinkened, her hands fluttering in the air.

Men from the South had the ability to flatter outrageously, a skill they were probably taught from the cradle.

She caught Lennox's eye again and looked away. She was not going to let him know she still remembered their kiss.

She'd grown adept at ignoring the difficult or uncomfortable.

When a maid appeared in the doorway, Charlotte stood, waving her hands toward another part of the house.

"Now then, let's away to the dining room, shall we?"

If the rest of Charlotte's house could be considered cluttered, the dining room was even more so. Two breakfronts occupied a space designed for one, both pieces of furniture chock full of silver and crystal showing through their glass doors. The rose marble mantel on the fireplace at the end of the room was filled with a selection of porcelain shepherdesses and sheep. Glynis counted nine figurines before being led to her seat opposite Lennox.

The dining table, the largest she'd ever seen in a private home, was a long rectangle with curlicues, flowers, and animals carved on the enormous legs, each taking up the same room as one of the thronelike chairs.

Mr. Whittaker murmured something complimentary about the table, and Charlotte said, "My Archibald had it made especially for me."

The top of the table could have been the same rich mahogany as the legs, but Glynis couldn't see it for the lace table runner and the accumulation of silver from the three candelabra, bowls, pitchers, and individual salt and pepper cellars. Each place setting had a charger, a bread and butter plate, and another dish she assumed was a dessert plate, although she had never seen one set out before the dinner began. In addition, each place setting had three goblets, a spoon rest, a fork rest, a cup, saucer, and finger bowl.

She'd never seen anything like it, short of a royal dinner.

The windows no doubt looked out over the front of the house, but the crimson draperies—at least they weren't green—were closed against the night. The carpet beneath her feet was red as well, and woven with the same type of flowers carved into the table legs.

Charlotte stood at the end of the table, her quick glance at each of her guests almost expectant, as if she were waiting for compliments.

For the sake of their childhood friendship, if not empathy, Glynis provided them to her.

"It's an exquisite table, Charlotte," she said.

To her relief, the rest of the guests joined in with compliments, even Lucy.

Mr. MacNamara sat to her right at the head of the table and proved to be a voluble conversationalist. She needn't contribute more than a nod from time to time.

Dinner started with a fish soup, followed by a pork chop stuffed with Stornoway black pudding and sage.

She concentrated on her meal, ignoring everyone at the table, in violation of all the rules of etiquette she'd learned. When she did speak, she complimented Charlotte on her cook. After a while, however, one could only say so much about wilted greens and mustard cream sauce. To her surprise, the maids served two more courses, the last haggis with clapshot and onion gravy.

She let the conversation flow over her, trying not to respond to Lennox's glances or Lucy's petulant silence. The woman pushed her food around on her plate in an insulting manner. Even if she disliked the menu, she could have eaten a few bites to salve Charlotte's feelings.

Gavin Whittaker appeared to be enjoying himself. Not only did he comment heartily about the meal, but he engaged Mr. MacNamara in a spirited discussion of Scottish history versus that of America.

The dinner reminded her of Washington from a linguistic perspective. Mr. Whittaker had the broad vowels of his southern United States origin, while his wife sounded like a Londoner. The MacNamaras were Glaswegians. She was a hybrid, a Glasgow native trained to speak with a British accent. Even Lennox might be considered the same, enunciating some words with a Russian flair and some with French, since he spoke both languages.

He didn't talk much, however, being content to stare at her.

Had she something between her teeth? Had she suddenly grown a wart at the end of her nose?

The meal was taking on an almost humorous bent. Lennox was staring at her, while Lucy was glowering at the two of them. Mr. Whittaker was alternately conversing with Charlotte or her husband, the three of them blissfully unaware of any undercurrents at the table.

She hadn't been so uncomfortable in a long time. At least Baumann wasn't there giving her significant glances. Wouldn't that be a horror?

Why was Lucy frowning at her in such an off-putting fashion? What had she done to the woman other than endure her rudeness?

Weren't they due to leave Scotland soon?

She should ask Lennox, but if she did he'd probably join Lucy in frowning at her. He was remarkably reticent when it came to his ship, but she could understand why.

Was he in any danger? Would he take care? He'd always been a little foolhardy. Or maybe not foolhardy as much as determined. If he truly thought he could do something or achieve some milestone, he went after it with an intensity that was awe-inspiring.

She had a sudden disturbing thought. His glance hadn't left her all evening. He smiled when their eyes met and the expression was one of daring.

Taking a sip of her punch, she tried to calm her heartbeat.

She had the feeling she was witnessing Lennox in the midst of pursuing a goal: her.

Chapter 16

Lennox didn't have any idea what he was eating. Nor did he care. He tried to maintain some interest in the conversations swirling around him, but what he really wanted to do was sit and watch Glynis.

As a child, Glynis had been difficult to contain, as wild as the wind and as fierce as her ancestors. The MacIains had come down from the Highlands to make their mark in the world. Somehow she'd inherited every bit of pride and rebelliousness from them.

Eleanor and Hamish sometimes looked at her as if surprised to find this beautiful, untamed creature in their midst.

On her return to Glasgow, Lennox had the impression she'd been pressed into a mold, shaped and trimmed until she represented the essence of propriety.

At least until she'd kissed him.

In his mind's eye he'd always seen her as she had been in the anteroom, young and beautiful, poised on the edge of her life. He had no idea that the past seven years would give her a wariness she'd never before had. Even her mannerisms were smaller, as if she were afraid to call attention to herself. She didn't reveal her emotions easily. Yet beneath the veneer she was still Glynis, still capable of surprising him.

The kiss had reaffirmed it.

WHEN DESSERT ARRIVED—lemon posset served with shortbread—Glynis almost sang hosannas because it meant she might be able to leave within the hour.

Charlotte had other ideas.

They stood up from the dinner table, but instead of returning to the parlor, Charlotte insisted on showing them the large lantern-lit patio and the hillside view of Glasgow.

Glynis murmured the appropriate niceties at the shrouded plants, escaping back into the house when she could.

In the parlor, she stood in front of the cold fireplace, staring down at the brass andirons. When someone entered the room, she glanced up, to find Lennox striding toward her.

He was like those steamships he built, proud, dominating, the equal of anything on the oceans. Perhaps he gave part of himself to his creation, like a painter imbues a painting with his essence of himself or a writer gives over part of his soul to his work.

She really shouldn't be alone with him. Last night she'd kissed him. What would she do now? Throw herself down on the settee and demand to be taken?

What on earth would Charlotte do if she witnessed a scene like that? Scream? She could just imagine the other woman's expression.

"Why are you smiling?" Lennox asked.

She was definitely not going to tell him. Instead, she asked, "Did you admire the gardens?"

"Admired, praised, admired and praised some more. I also thanked her for the dinner and threw in a bit more praise about the meal."

They exchanged a glance and she was the first to look away.

Her mouth was suddenly dry. He really mustn't have an effect on her.

"I've met Mr. Lincoln, you know," she said. "He's an exceptionally kind man. He wanted to know where I was brought up and what Scotland was like."

"While I'm not exceptionally kind, is that the point?"

"I haven't heard anyone say anything bad about you," she said. "In fact, people normally praise you in my company. You pay your workers more than the other shipbuilders. You donate to a great many causes. I daresay you even feed the poor, albeit anonymously. You are a paragon of virtue, Lennox, and the rest of us have no choice but to be in awe of you."

"Everyone but you, that is," he said, nodding once at her. "Not with your experience of meeting the important people of the world. How I must pale in comparison."

"On the contrary," she said, "you don't pale at all. In fact, I would say, of all the people I met, you might rank as one of the most memorable."

Should she have really admitted that?

No, she shouldn't, because his eyes warmed. With that look, he created a hollow space in her chest, made her realize how foolish she was in his company.

She went to sit on the settee and he joined her. He really should have sat on the chair opposite her, or farther down the settee. He was close enough to touch. Close enough that if he leaned over just a little, they might be able to kiss.

She closed her eyes, took a deep breath, and tried to regain her poise.

"I would say the same about you, Glynis MacIain. You're one of the most memorable women I've ever known. Perhaps you're at the very top of my list."

Her eyes flew open. He shouldn't have the ability to twist her into knots with a few words.

Thankfully, Mr. Whittaker chose that moment to stroll into the parlor.

"I imagine the garden is nice in the daylight. I can't tell a rose from the nasturtium, though. My Lucy says her gardens at home are more impressive."

They chatted about plants for a few minutes before Mr. Whittaker moved away, admiring the collection of music boxes in the corner.

"Is she truly that miserable a person?" Glynis asked in a low voice. "Or am I simply not seeing her attributes? Mr. Whittaker seems to adore her."

"Men are sometimes blind that way," he said. "Especially about the women they adore."

Her eyes met his.

Had he adored Rose? If so, why had he broken their engagement? The gossips of Glasgow had probably spent months talking about it. Had he minded?

"Now I have a little surprise for you," Charlotte said, bustling into the room followed by four children, two of whom looked to be the same age.

To Glynis's dismay, Charlotte had an entertainment planned by her offspring. The smallest didn't want to perform and whined through the entire performance conducted by Archie, with Charlotte beaming with pride.

In Washington the evenings were more formal. The children of the elite were often neither seen nor heard. She'd known women months before she discovered they were also mothers.

She clapped when the off-pitch warblings of the MacNamara clan were done, both in appreciation of their parents' determination and the fact that the children were finished.

Charlotte had other ideas.

"He has memorized a poem," she said before stepping back to allow her eldest son to be the focus of attention.

For the sake of Charlotte's friendship, she kept her

face impassive. She'd endured many an opera diva's recital in Washington. The last entertainment she'd attended, a day before Richard died, featured a soprano's performance of war tunes. The woman's high-pitched rendition of "Battle Hymn of the Republic" had been painful to hear.

Now Charlotte's poor child had to be prompted through the last part of the poem and looked ready to cry.

She caught Lennox's look. She suspected he was wondering how soon he could make his escape. His lips quirked as if he caught her thoughts.

After they applauded, the children were led away to be tucked into bed. In his wife's absence, Archibald moved to the sideboard, helped by a maid. Mr. Whittaker and Lennox were speaking, something to do with the *Raven*. Lucy chose that moment to lean close to her.

"You're not what you seem to be, Mrs. Smythe," Lucy said.

The woman's eyes were narrowed, her mouth pursed. Any prettiness she possessed disappeared, replaced by a venomous look.

"I beg your pardon?"

"Everyone thinks you're sweet and proper but you're neither."

She stared at Lucy. What did she know? Nothing. She couldn't know anything unless she'd talked to Baumann, and she doubted the man would confide in the wife of a Confederate captain.

"I saw you. You were kissing him."

Lucy glanced at Lennox, still involved in a discussion with Mr. Whittaker.

"You and Lennox in the garden. I saw you."

The maid's sudden appearance prevented her from responding. She thrust a tray of MacNamara Candies in front of her. Since Archibald was beaming in her direction, she had no choice but to take one. The chocolate was so sweet she felt it in her front teeth, but she managed a polite comment all the same.

She deliberately avoided looking in Lucy's direction. With any luck the woman would leave Glasgow within a few days. The sooner, the better.

Just when she was thinking of plausible excuses to shorten the evening, Lennox stood, extending his apologies for having to leave.

"Oh, dear Lennox, I do understand," Charlotte said. "You're so busy nowadays. I'm so grateful the three of you could join us if only for a little while."

"Well, we need to skedaddle, too," Mr. Whittaker said, holding out his hand for his wife. "We thank you for the dinner. And for the entertainment from the little ones."

Lucy sent one last frown toward her, then stood, accompanied by the two men.

An unwritten rule in polite circles was that after the first guest departed, the second guest had to allow sufficient time to pass before also leaving. Otherwise, it gave the hostess the impression that all her guests were disappearing en masse.

Lennox glanced in her direction, his small smile telling her that he knew he'd succeeded in trapping her here with the MacNamaras for a little while longer.

After he and the Whittakers left, the house felt strangely empty. She accepted another cup of tea, listened to Archie pontificate about the ruin of the family caused by the love of alcohol and discussed Charlotte's children.

All the while she wondered about Lucy. If a kiss had scandalized the woman, it was a good thing it hadn't gone further.

She was fool enough to lay down in the garden if

Lennox had wanted to love her, an admission that should have shamed her but strangely didn't.

Evidently, the nineteen-year-old Glynis hadn't disappeared entirely.

Chapter 17

"Do you think Duncan will be successful in London?" Eleanor asked.

Glynis shared a look with her mother, thought about answering honestly, then padded the truth.

"I'm sure he will," she said.

"I hate that the land must be sold, but these are difficult times."

Glynis nodded. She thought her brother was doing something other than selling their property, but Duncan hadn't confided in her.

The hour was early but she hadn't been able to sleep, slipping downstairs to make herself a cup of tea, only to discover her mother and Mabel had the same idea.

Now she sat with her mother at the kitchen table listing the economies they could implement. Mabel worked in the background, the smell of scones perfuming the air.

They could start with eating less beef, only baking bread once a week, and reducing their clothing expenses.

"I have a new dress on order," Eleanor said. "I'll cancel it."

"I doubt you need to do that. But perhaps no new garments for a while after that one?"

Her mother nodded.

"We have to keep Mary. If we don't, heaven knows what will happen to the poor girl. She's no family, and being with child and all . . ." Eleanor's voice trailed away.

Nor would her mother think of getting rid of Mabel and Lily. They were no longer simply servants. Now they were friends.

If only Duncan had agreed to take a loan from Lennox, they wouldn't be in this predicament. She should have been more forceful in her attempts to convince Lennox. Perhaps she should have offered him something in exchange.

I'll bed you if you help save the mill.

What would he have said to that?

Shame should have warmed her at the thought, but it wasn't shame racing through her body, it was excitement.

Would he have taken her offer? Would he have been interested? Would he be now?

It wouldn't be a sacrifice loving Lennox, not when she'd imagined it for most of the last seven years. What would it be like having his hands skim over her body? Having him kiss her everywhere?

She pressed the back of her hand against her hot cheek. She needed to stop thinking of Lennox.

When Mabel passed a plate of raisin scones to her, she smiled and took one.

"I think you make the best scones in the whole world," she told the cook. "I could eat a dozen every day."

"You're a bit thin, Miss Glynis. You could do with that many or more."

Both her mother and Mabel smiled at her. She was not going to tell them she nearly starved in the last months in Washington. She'd do anything to prevent them from having to suffer the same fate.

Last night Lennox had been charming, fascinating, and too alluring.

I would say the same about you, Glynis MacIain.

What had that meant?

No, she would not think about him. He didn't exist.

She would have all the windows painted black to obscure the view of Hillshead. She would wear earplugs to deafen herself to the sound of his name. She would implore her mother and Duncan to treat the man as if he were a leper. Maybe they'd even ring a bell when he approached.

Unclean! Unclean!

She'd lived for years without the sight of him. Perhaps she thought about him periodically, but only when homesick. Or when a bit of music made her heart swell. Or when she was achy and wanting to cry. Or when the dawn broke over Washington and streaks of pink and blue reminded her of a Scottish sky. Or at times in a crowded room when she was surrounded by others but curiously felt alone on a silent island.

He rarely entered her mind otherwise.

She couldn't stop herself from recalling his smile, the way his eyes gleamed when amused, and the sound of his voice.

Why had he smelled of pine trees the night before?

She wanted him to laugh again. This time she'd put her hand against his chest to feel the echo of his laughter and the reassuring beat of his heart. She wanted to charm him, delight him, and make him smile.

Most of all, she wanted to kiss him again.

She could imagine what Lucy Whittaker would have said if she'd kissed Lennox more than once.

No, she would not think of Lennox. She must apply herself to the task at hand, ensuring the household could function more frugally.

She showed her list to her mother, along with the

sums she'd totaled. If they practiced a few economies in purchasing food, sold one of the carriages and two of the horses, they could save twenty-five percent of the monthly budget.

Eleanor sent a quick glance in Mabel's direction.

"We wouldn't have to make any staff changes?" she asked in a low voice.

"Not now."

If things didn't change, however, they'd have to let everyone go. Either that or all starve genteelly together.

Her mother nodded and sighed.

"It isn't Duncan's fault," she said, compelled to defend her brother.

Her mother patted her hand. "Of course it isn't, dear. I know. I wish there was something more I could do."

She wondered what her mother would have said if she confessed the same. Or told her she was more than prepared to act the harlot in order to save the mill.

How altruistic she sounded, when it was anything but the truth. She wanted Lennox to love her, toss her on the ground, and end all the years of curiosity and wondering. With him, physical love wouldn't be abhorrent. If he touched her, she wouldn't want to scrub her skin for hours.

When the knocker at the front door sounded she looked at her mother.

"Are you expecting anyone?"

"Not this early," Eleanor said, shaking her head.

Rather than send Lily, Glynis stood and walked down the hall. She swung the door open, staring at the man standing between the Grecian columns, and felt her stomach fall to her toes.

"What do you want?" she asked Matthew Baumann.

LENNOX'S DAY had begun at dawn, which was not unusual. The list of tasks to be done before turning over the *Raven* to Gavin tomorrow had grown exponentially over the last few days.

He made his way downstairs, encountering Hillshead's cook as he passed through to the stables.

"What is it, Peggy?" he asked.

Their cook was a diminutive woman with a shock of white hair she kept wound in a braid at the back of her head. Tendrils of hair always managed to escape, surrounding her wrinkled face and giving her a halo.

She surprised him today by turning to him with tears in her eyes.

"It's Garrison, sir. He has a cough something awful," she said. "I've tried me mam's recipe and he goes on coughing."

"I'll send my doctor over to see him," he said.

She sighed. "I've been told there's an English syrup that'll help."

"Let's see what the doctor says first."

She nodded.

Her husband had worked for Cameron and Company for years before retiring a few months ago. Garrison was a talented woodcarver who'd been responsible for the balusters surrounding the deck of their ships, the decorative trim of the captain's wheel, and other details in the captain's cabin. When he was a boy, the old man had carved him small animals, each one a perfect miniature. He still had them, carefully stored in a trunk in the attic.

"I'll send my doctor over to see him. Don't worry."

Peggy nodded, her smile tremulous.

He patted her awkwardly on the shoulder, then made his way to his carriage.

The day was humid, the threat of a storm graying the sky. The rain wouldn't slow up the finishing touches on the *Raven*. All the painting had already

been done and had a few days to dry so the excess
moisture in the air wouldn't bubble the finish.

Nothing was going to delay turning over the ship to
the Confederacy.

"Where to first, sir?" his driver asked, standing at
the open door.

"The MacIain home."

Tim nodded.

Duncan's problems continued to bother him.
Lennox knew enough about the mill to know that if
maintenance of the Lancashire looms wasn't being
performed, there would be even more problems when
they were finally put back into service.

He doubted Duncan had the money to perform the
necessary work, just as he suspected his friend was
using his personal funds to support the mill.

Duncan's pride was a wall between them, one he
intended to knock down. He was early enough that
he could intercept Duncan before he went to the mill.

A few minutes later the carriage slowed before the
house. He frowned as he saw Glynis standing at the
front door.

What the hell was Baumann doing here? Even more
importantly, why was she talking to a man she pro-
fessed to despise?

"YOU'RE NOT welcome here," Glynis said.

"My feelings would be hurt, Glynis, if I thought
you were serious." He peered beyond her. "Aren't you
going to invite me inside?"

"No."

"What a pity. I didn't get a chance to meet your
mother."

"Go away, Baumann. Away from my house. Away
from Glasgow. Away from Scotland."

His smile dipped only for an instant. His mustache

was almost a living thing, quirking with his smile, leveling out when he was serious. She'd often found herself staring at it as if to gauge his mood.

"A very prosperous city, your Glasgow. Nothing like London or Paris, however, but it has its charm."

"Perhaps you would feel more comfortable at home in London or Paris, Baumann. I, for one, would be more than happy if you were to take yourself off."

"And deprive me of the opportunity to see you?"

His smile gnawed at her restraint.

"Why are you here?"

"To get information. You know about my quest for information."

"No."

He didn't look the least bit unsettled by her refusal.

"This isn't Washington," she said. "I don't owe you anything."

"Our relationship was never about debts, Glynis. Instead, it was a reciprocal one."

She laughed mirthlessly. "Is that what you tell yourself, Baumann? Do you believe it? If so, you're a fool. I had to keep providing you information or you threatened to tell the British Legation why I'd come to you in the first place."

"Were you afraid of being sent back home in disgrace? Your husband should have been, Glynis, you know that as well as I."

"I have no intention of talking to you anymore, Baumann," she said, stepping back.

He slapped his hand against the door when she would have closed it in his face.

"I need information about Cameron and Company."

She looked at him, feigning a calm she didn't feel.

"And you think I'll assist you?"

"I graduated from West Point, Glynis. Have you heard of it?" When she shook her head, he continued.

"It's a university for the military. I expected to get my own regiment and prepared to go to war. Instead, my superiors sent me to Washington, for a different kind of war."

"Are there different kinds of war?"

That comment garnered a laugh from him. "You should know more than most women," he said. "There is the war of ideas, of the need to keep a country together. There's the subterranean war, with one side trying to figure out what the other is doing before it's done."

"So you're here involved in a subterranean war," she said. "Trying to figure out what the Confederacy is doing?"

"I know what the Confederacy is doing, Glynis. I know what Cameron and Company is doing as well. My brother is a ship's captain, Glynis. Cameron is providing ships to the Confederacy, putting him and others in the Union in jeopardy. Extending the war, too."

She studied him, limned by the morning sun. Why did he explain himself? Did he think she cared? He'd never before tried to justify his actions and it was too late now. She knew him too well. He charmed when he wished but he threatened when it served him. He was not unlike a spider, patiently waiting for something to fall into his web.

"There are a great many people who believe in your cause in Scotland, Baumann," she said. "Just as there are many who believe in the cause of the Confederacy."

"You don't need to help me. Unless, of course, you want your friends and family to know you helped me in Washington. What would that make you, Glynis? Oh, yes, a spy. Just imagine their reaction."

She didn't have to imagine. She knew. Duncan would look at her as if she'd grown another pair of arms. Her mother would find some way to justify Glynis's actions but her eyes would be filled with disappointment. And Lennox? She couldn't bear to think what Lennox would say.

"What do you want to know?"

He extracted a piece of paper from his inside pocket and handed it to her.

"My address," he said. "I want to know everything you can discover about the newest ship in their yard. The *Raven*. They're due to turn it over to the Confederates soon."

Her affinity for numbers had served her well in Washington. She remembered details easily, especially measurements.

Did he plan on sabotage? She suspected he did, because his next question had to do with security for the ship. How many watchmen were assigned? Where were their posts?

He bent close to her, much too close for propriety's sake.

"Oh," he said softly. "You're wearing the perfume I love. It smells so much of you, Glynis. Earthy and mysterious all at once."

She held herself still, the practice of the last seven years coming to her aid.

"Step away, Baumann," she said.

To her surprise, he did as she asked.

"I can't do this," she said.

"But you must. We have a bargain, you and I."

"And what's my part in this bargain?"

"Peace," he said instantly. "Once my duty here is done, I'll leave Scotland, or at least Glasgow. I shan't see you again, my dear."

She didn't believe him. He'd said similar things to her before, words designed to assuage her anxiety, but he'd always reappeared.

Wasn't there a saying about supping with the devil? You needed a long spoon. Whatever he said, or how charmingly he said it, she couldn't afford to believe him.

If she gave in this last time, the ramifications would be more disastrous than any information she'd passed him in Washington.

She couldn't allow him to hurt Lennox.

She tucked the paper into her pocket and said, "I'll do what I can. Give me some time."

His mouth thinned; his face fell into stern lines. "That's the only thing I don't have. I need the information within the next day or two."

Then she would have to act quickly. She nodded, forcing a smile to her lips.

A carriage slowed in front of the house. She knew that carriage with its anchor lights and ebony finish.

She stared back at Lennox as he looked at her from the carriage window, his face revealing nothing.

The seconds stretched thin. Her stomach felt hollow, the moment important and desperate.

She expected him to drive away, but to her surprise he left the carriage, stalking toward her with his expression giving no doubt of his feelings.

Lennox was enraged.

"I would leave if I were you," she said to Baumann, still looking at Lennox.

Baumann didn't look the least distressed, which was only one sign of his foolishness. The other was to turn and smile at Lennox.

She could have predicted what happened next.

Lennox grabbed Baumann by his jacket and hauled the surprised man up against one of the pillars.

She always thought of Baumann as a large man, but next to Lennox he was almost diminutive.

"What the hell are you doing here, Baumann?" he

asked, his words as calm and measured as a parlor meeting.

Baumann was evidently beginning to realize the depth of his danger because his eyes widened.

"Let me go, Cameron."

"Not until you tell me why you're here. Why you're bothering Glynis."

"I'm an old acquaintance."

Lennox glanced over at her. "Did you invite him?"

She shook her head.

"Do you want him to remain?"

"Not particularly, but do let the man go, Lennox. I don't need you to pummel him for me."

Baumann's eyes widened even more. Good, it was about time the man experienced a little discomfort. She almost wanted to beg Lennox to hit him once or twice.

He let go of Baumann enough so the other man slid down the pillar slightly, then managed to straighten his jacket and his dignity.

"What are you doing here?" Lennox demanded.

"None of your concern," Baumann said.

Lennox turned and looked at her.

She only shook her head. If he expected more from her, she couldn't give it.

"I think both of you should leave," she said.

"As you wish." Lennox's tone was clipped and there was an expression in his eyes she couldn't read.

Baumann left first, both of them watching as he followed the path to his carriage. He didn't look back, didn't give her any further instructions, but she knew he expected her to fulfill his request. Otherwise, the whole of Glasgow would know about Washington.

The words almost tumbled from her lips in the moments she and Lennox were alone. The confession, however, would damn her in his eyes. He wouldn't understand. How could anyone? Or he would understand and despise her for her actions. In seconds he was gone, leaving her to stare at his departing carriage.

She shouldn't have come home, but it had been too difficult to stay away. She could always leave Glasgow, but how did she leave herself?

Chapter 18

*L*ucy sat at her vanity and stared at her pale face. In days, only days, she'd be expected to get on that horrid ship and sail halfway across the world.

A wife must go where her husband goes and do so without a word of complaint. Never mind everything she cherished would be left behind. Her own mother had traveled from Cornwall to reside in London, but it wasn't the same, was it? She had been transplanted from London and forced to spend months in this ghastly country.

Gavin would take possession of the *Raven* in days. He couldn't stop talking about that idiotic ship. Her speed . . . her ballast . . . her depth . . . her hold—he talked as if it were alive.

"Ships are female," he said, when she'd asked why he always referred to the *Raven* as a *she*.

He'd come too close, nuzzling her ear and disturbing her arranged hair. She had no maid and she'd wanted one. *When we finally settle in America*, Gavin said. Just one more disappointment she suffered in a dissatisfying marriage.

Gavin's blond attractiveness was pleasant and his voice wasn't as grating on her as a Scottish accent. When she first married him she'd been happy, especially since it was all too evident he worshipped her.

Who else could have charmed her parents into allowing them to marry so quickly? Her mother had adored him. Her father had respected him.

She'd never considered Gavin could love her too much. He always wanted to touch her. Each night when she retired, he forced her to tell him she was indisposed, or he would have been endlessly cuddling up to her.

Gavin was as licentious as Lennox Cameron.

In the future, should anyone mention Cameron and Company to her, she would tell them her husband had gone on and on about the quality of the ships they built but she was unimpressed with the character of the company's owner. Lennox Cameron, to her disappointment, had proven himself to be a man of no morals. He had been almost as satyrlike as her own husband. Imagine, groping a woman in a garden where anyone could see them.

Glynis Smythe was no paragon of virtue, either. She had acquiesced without a protest. In fact, from where she stood, Glynis might have even initiated the kiss.

The people of Glasgow should know about their leading citizens.

Only a few more days and she would be quit of Scotland forever. She would never find another reason to come back to this barbaric place.

She had no knowledge of Nassau, and whenever she asked Gavin, he only told her not to worry—he was sure she'd love it.

While she was very certain she wouldn't.

ONCE HE made it to the yard, Lennox sent Tim to his physician with a request to call on Garrison.

He entered his office, greeting the draftsmen already perched on their stools. One by one he inspected the newest changes to the ship still in the idea stage, answered questions, and praised the efforts of one young man, barely seventeen and new to Cameron and Company.

Allan had been the brunt of jokes ever since being hired a month ago, but he'd gradually stopped blushing and started responding in kind.

Gavin Whittaker was seated at Lennox's desk in the corner. When he approached, the man stood, looking up from the plans.

"I'm damn sorry I won't be here to see you build this ship," he said.

Although he acted like a dilettante with his walking stick and his drawl, Gavin was at his core a seafaring man. He knew ships.

"Will it be the equal of the *Raven*?" Lennox asked, waving the man back to his chair while he took the one beside the desk.

"Nothing will ever equal the *Raven*," Gavin said with the pride of a captain soon to take possession of a Cameron and Company ship.

For a few moments they discussed the plans spread out on the desk. Lennox took note of Gavin's comments on the slope of the deck and the placement of the forecastle.

He had orders for two more blockade runners, vessels that would not only outrun the Union ships but carry eighteen hundred bales of cotton on the outbound journey. Inbound? He could just imagine the cargo the *Raven* could carry. Ammunition and guns, foodstuffs, and all the other necessities of life becoming scarce in the South.

He moved to stand at the window, staring down at the *Raven*. She'd passed her sea trials with no corrections or reservations. The boilers and side wheels had been inspected and the vessel's seaworthiness wasn't in doubt.

Tomorrow he would turn over the ship to Gavin.

In a few days he'd watch as Gavin piloted the *Raven* down the Clyde and out to sea. He'd be relieved to say good-bye to Lucy Whittaker but couldn't say the same about Gavin.

There had been too many deaths along the Clyde in the last six months. Even the smaller shipbuilders were feeling the tension, as if the Americans were fighting their war up and down the river.

A Union colonel, ostensibly employed by a company in London, had been killed a week ago, the news relayed to him a few days earlier. Evidently, the victim had fallen from a ship, struck his head and drowned. The fact no one had seen the accident was suspicious. Nor was the man supposed to have been aboard the *Mary Anne*.

That made four Americans to perish near Glasgow in the last year.

Had the dead man been an associate of Baumann's? The question brought him full circle.

Why was Glynis involved in conversation with a Union spy?

According to her own words, she didn't want to see the man again. Then why was Baumann at her home?

Perhaps the most important question was: what did he do about this feeling of betrayal?

Was she working with the man? Was Glynis a Union operative? If so, was he her assignment? Was she supposed to seduce him? Confuse him? Confound him until he was incapable of speech, let alone building ships? Was that what the kiss in the garden was all about?

Was it her intention to ensnare him? If so, she rated a perfect score. He'd been fascinated from the first, watching for the woman who held herself so still to revert to the girl he'd known. At times he thought he'd spied her, but the glimpses lasted only a few seconds. Her eyes would sparkle at him with a dare and then she'd change back into being the proper Mrs. Smythe.

Damned if he knew what he was going to do about Glynis.

Chapter 19

*T*he rain had begun at midnight, with no sign it was going to let up anytime soon. Glynis wanted to pull the covers over her head and tell herself the weather was too awful to venture outside. But that would have been the action of a coward, and after yesterday she had to demonstrate a little more courage.

She had to explain to Lennox.

After dressing, she slipped from the house and made her way to the stables. Once there, she sought out one of the drivers.

"I would like to go to the yard, please, Thomas. To Cameron and Company."

The man only raised one eyebrow, but he didn't move to open the carriage door.

The stable smelled of wax and a hint of kerosene. Did he use both to keep the body of the vehicle shiny?

"It's Sunday," he said, softening the words with a small smile.

She nodded. The one day Lennox would be alone at the shipyard. She wasn't going to be foolish enough to return to Hillshead. Nor did she wish to call on him when he was surrounded by other people.

She had a confession to make and she didn't want any witnesses.

"I've known you since you were a little girl, Miss Glynis. And now you're a woman, well-traveled and all. But I care for my horses and the carriages your family lets me drive. What kind of man would I be if I didn't have the same concern for you? The yard is not a safe place for you in the best of times. On a Sunday it's doubly dangerous."

She had Richard's Derringer, now tucked into her reticule. Beneath her bonnet was a hat pin the size of a dagger. Nor should anyone discount her determination.

"Thomas, I can assure you, I'll be safe."

He shook his head.

"Then I shall walk," she said. "It will only take me an hour or two."

She didn't anticipate walking the distance through the rain, but if she had to do it, she would.

"Aye," he said. "You'd do it, wouldn't you? A stubborn little thing, ever since you were a girl."

That obstinacy had gotten her into trouble more than once. Perhaps this was another example, but she had to talk to Lennox. Her conscience gnawed at her. For good or ill, he had to know the truth.

Thomas sighed heavily. "It's dull we were around here without you, Miss Glynis." He grinned at her and she couldn't help but smile in return.

At last count there were more than twenty shipyards near Glasgow. Although the yards were downriver, the foundries supplying the material were located in the city itself. Each day they spit out copper and brass fittings, boilers and engines, all components for the new iron-hulled ships. Consequently, the air hanging over Glasgow always smelled of smoke.

The farther downriver they traveled, the clearer the air.

The shipyards were unworldly in the silence of a rainy Sunday. On this dark afternoon the shop lights on the wharf were reflected on the wet cobblestones.

The air carried the scent of the rain and the Clyde, the smell of home and one she'd forgotten for so many years.

Thomas pulled up before the sprawling building housing the Cameron and Company offices.

"I'll come with you, shall I?" he asked, opening the door for her.

That wouldn't do at all, would it? She didn't want a witness to this particular confession.

She opened her umbrella and smiled at him. "Thank you, Thomas. I'll be fine."

He only shook his head at her and climbed back onto the seat.

She'd not come here often, but she knew the only entrance to the office was on the dock side.

A carriage was parked not far away, reassuring her that Lennox was there. With the rain dividing its time between a torrent and a mist, she made her way to the office.

Please, don't let him hate me.

She had been without Lennox's good opinion of her for seven years. Why did it seem to matter so much now? Was it because he was the only person who truly knew her?

He'd witnessed most of the embarrassing scenes of her childhood. He'd helped her up when she'd been knocked from her horse, laughed at her when she was drenched in mud, and looked away when she'd fallen from a tree and torn her dress.

Yet he'd never seen her in all of her finery in Washington, with her hair arranged by an expert at the task. He never witnessed her making an entrance into a Washington ballroom, conscious of men's admiring glances. Not once had he heard all the fulsome compliments paid to her.

Or if he does hate me, let it be of short duration. Or, if that cannot be arranged, then help me not to care. Let me consider his good opinion of me as worthless as Richard's had been.

Every time Richard had approved of her, he was really congratulating himself for picking her as his wife. He'd created a poised puppet who could enter any room filled with important people and hold her own in a variety of conversations. She could converse with a lecherous German, a fawning Frenchman, and discuss history with a Greek.

If Lennox did hate her, she would have to bear it somehow.

The rain drummed on the street in a heavy rhythm, then light, like a child making too much noise and cautioned by his parent. A moment later the sound would increase again, then slow to a patter.

Despite her umbrella, droplets found a home in the back of her collar, ran down her face, and soaked her stockings. She sneezed once, shivered with a summer chill, and drew her elbows close to her body. The wet wind carried a cooler layer beneath it, a hint of winter not far away, a caution to enjoy these days of warmth before they disappeared.

The afternoon was now almost as dark as night. She wished the lamps along the quay would light or the docks wouldn't be as deserted. The silence unnerved her, made her feel as if she were the only person there.

Thomas was right. This was a man's world where women weren't welcome.

She stood surveying the docks belonging to Cameron and Company. Spires of masts clouded the air, blocking the view of most of the Clyde.

Drawing in the pong of dead fish and the warm, thick, almost caramel scent of varnish, she climbed the steps to the office and knocked on the door. When

Lennox didn't answer, she peered into the window. Nothing but blackness met her eyes. The day was dark. If anyone had been inside they would have lit the lamps.

He wasn't there.

Relief and regret surged through her. She wouldn't have to tell him about Washington just yet. But she would have to soon. Delaying meant she'd worry longer.

Should she wait?

The wind gusted hard, rain beading her face as she turned then stopped and stared in wonder.

That long, low, gray iron ship had to be the *Raven*. She blended into the dim light of the watery day so perfectly she might be part of the elements.

Glynis recalled the talk about the thirty-five-hundred mile blockade. A Confederate captain had two hopes to make it to a southern port. Slip undetected through the fog and the night. Or be faster than any Union ship.

The *Raven* looked as if she could do both.

The ship was a beauty, her lines making her appear restless, waiting for the challenge of the next wave despite being moored to the dock. She looked like she wanted to race the wind and feel the power of the seas beneath her hull.

After descending the steps, Glynis moved to the gangplank. She'd never been aboard a Cameron and Company ship before, unless she counted Lennox's boyhood boat.

By going on board she would be flaunting a superstition. Women weren't allowed on a ship unless they were married and accompanying their husbands.

"What about figureheads?" she'd once asked Lennox. "Why are they women?"

"That's different," he said, his cheeks bronzing.

She'd waited but he'd never explained. Only later, and she couldn't remember from whom the information had come, she'd been told a figurehead's bare bosom was supposed to quell the sea into obeying while its eyes looked out for danger.

A human woman, however, brought about storms and disaster.

Sailors were a superstitious bunch, another comment Lennox made. Everything she'd learned about ships and the sea had come from him. On her voyage to Cairo and to America, she'd made note of several things aboard ship she wanted to discuss with him, before she remembered Lennox was part of her past, not her present or future.

She crossed the gangplank and over the wet deck, taking care as her footing slipped several times. She expected to feel the gentle swell of the ocean lapping at her hull but the *Raven* was as sturdy as a brick building, a match for any wave.

Great ships were built on the Clyde. Some had been transported to America in crates to be unpacked and put together on the Mississippi. Clyde ships sailed the globe, bearing names synonymous with grace, speed, and workmanship.

She had a feeling the *Raven* was among the greatest of all these and yet she'd been built for war.

The heavens opened up, the growl of thunder timed to the slash of lightning.

This was not a tranquil storm but a fierce Scottish one, sent to bathe the earth and wash it clean. The wind whipped over the deck and whistled through the rigging. Rain slashed across her face as thunder rumbled, announcing its arrival like the Queen's trumpeters.

She turned away from the wind, stopped and stared.

The hand holding the umbrella dropped to her side. Her pulse escalated as her mind screamed at her.

She calmly took a step back and remembered to breathe.

Fear climbed her spine with sharp claws as she stared at the sight at her feet. For a heart-stopping second she thought it was Lennox, but details rushed in to fill her with hope. This man's hair was blond.

She forced herself to look at him.

He lay on the deck, eyes open and staring at the black clouds above. His legs were spread, his arms at his sides, one hand stretched out as if to reach for something.

Blood, diluted by the rain, pooled beneath his body and ran in rivulets over the deck.

Was he dead? He looked dead. But what if he wasn't? If he was dying, she needed to get him help or do something.

In Washington there had been calls for matrons to volunteer as nurses. She had been grateful, God help her, for her status. Being married to a member of the British Legation prevented her from volunteering because of their neutrality. She needn't see the wounded or witness the gore of war.

Now she had no excuse. She had to do something.

Time slowed, became a pudding of air, a gelatinous mixture not unlike Mabel's tomato aspic. She hated the dish, an odd thought to have now as she stared at the man on the deck.

Forcing herself, she walked to his side and sank to her knees, staring at the cane handle protruding from his chest. He looked mildly surprised, as if Death had tapped him on the shoulder, startling him.

His eyes stared up at the rain falling into them. He couldn't be alive, but she reached out and shook his shoulder gently. No, that wasn't going to do anything. She felt for a pulse, her fingers trembling against his neck, feeling cold when she expected him to be warm.

There was no pulse.

She pulled her hand back to find her fingers coated with blood.

Nausea roared up through her.

She wiped her hands on her skirt. The hem was saturated with blood, the material wicking it upward.

Tears ripped out of her, the constriction in her throat making it difficult to breathe. She struggled to stand.

Gavin Whittaker, husband, Confederate, and captain, lay dead at her feet.

"Glynis?"

She turned with a sense of inevitability.

The rain subsided to a drizzle as Lennox stood on the gangplank unprotected. The wind blew his hair askew, and she wanted to freeze this picture of him: powerful, commanding, and a little mussed.

"Is that blood?" he asked, striding toward her.

She stepped aside so he had a view of Gavin's body.

He abruptly stopped, stared at the dead man, then at her.

"What happened?"

"I don't know. I found him here."

He sent her a quick look before kneeling at Gavin's side to test for a pulse, just as she had.

Gavin Whittaker was well and truly dead, and wishing him alive didn't make it so.

"What are you doing here?" he asked. He turned his head, his eyes shining in the dim light.

"I saw the ship," she said. "I wanted to see more of her."

She couldn't look down any longer. She thought she might be sick at the sight of all that blood.

He glanced around. "Where are the guards?"

"I haven't seen anyone since I arrived."

"That's odd. Unless Gavin dismissed them." He stood. "Are you certain you don't know anything about this, Glynis?"

She shook her head.

"Yet you were talking to Baumann a few days ago. What about?"

She wrapped her arms around her waist, staring at him. "Do you think I'm a Union spy and my mission was to kill Gavin? Do you honestly believe I could kill another human being?"

"No, I don't," he said. "But I also think you know something you're not telling."

The expression on his face didn't soften. Nor did his eyes warm.

She folded her arms in front of her, almost like a barrier. Her trembling worsened and the chill from the wind was slicing through her. Her stomach quivered, her lips felt numb, and her knees threatened to refuse to support her.

She'd experienced the same sensations when the police had arrived to tell her about Richard's accident. That night, too, had been rain-filled, thunder accentuating the policeman's words.

I'm sorry, Mrs. Smythe, nothing could be done. The driver said he didn't see your husband until too late. With all the rain, we can see how it would be possible.

"You need to tell Lucy," she said now. "Someone murdered her husband." She frowned at him. "Not me, Lennox."

"You still haven't explained what you were doing here, Glynis."

She shook her head. She couldn't tell him now, not with Gavin dead at their feet. Was he another man whose death she'd have on her conscience? Had Baumann done this?

He reached out and touched her hair. Only then did she realize it had come loose from its careful bun. He pulled the wet tendrils free from her face, the tenderness of his touch making her close her eyes.

She willed herself to another place. Somewhere death didn't hover nearby, where she didn't have a secret, and Lennox didn't suspect her.

"Glynis."

Glynis, mind your manners. Glynis, you can't say such things to me. Glynis, do you know how shocking you are? How many times had he said something similar to her?

She opened her eyes and stepped away. How foolish she was to long for him at this moment. A man lay dead only feet from them. A murderer could be nearby.

She'd returned to Scotland much wiser, yet his touch stripped her of any wisdom or sense.

"I didn't kill him, Lennox."

"I didn't think you did. Did you see anything or anyone?"

She shook her head.

"Are you working for Baumann?"

"No," she said, grateful it was the truth.

"Why are you here, Glynis?"

"I told you. I wanted to see the ship."

He shook his head. "Why did you come to the yard?"

"I came to talk to you," she said.

There, a tinge of the truth.

"Why?"

She looked away.

Why had she said that? Words were a net to trap her, and she felt like a fish gasping for air.

"It doesn't matter," she said, looking away from the rivulets of blood-tainted rain spreading on the deck.

Was the *Raven* cursed now, because she'd known murder? Would the sailors who manned her think the ship unlucky?

She glanced up at him to find Lennox still studying her intently. She had no other explanation to give him.

How had this situation become so terrible? She'd started off with such great intentions. But it was a Scottish poet who'd said the best laid plans of mice and men often go astray.

Burns certainly had it right.

Chapter 20

Lennox sent his driver to summon the police. Until they arrived he suggested they wait upstairs.

The last time she'd been here, his office had been a series of small rooms, one leading to the other until the place was a warren. Now the walls had been knocked down until there was only one large, rectangular space.

A massive desk with three visitor chairs, two in front and one on the side, sat in the corner. Six drafting tables were arranged in three rows in the middle of the room, each table covered with a drawing.

She stopped at the closest table, studying the sheet of paper, but couldn't understand what she was seeing.

"It's the structural plans for a new hull," he said.

She glanced around at the other tables. "Are they all different ships?"

"Two of them are. The others are different types of plans for the same vessel."

"How many ships do you work on at a time?"

"The *Raven* occupied most of our resources. Normally, we're working on three to four ships at once."

That many? Cameron and Company had indeed expanded.

A wall of windows looked out over the quay and at either side of the door. Sunlight would flood the room and warm it well in winter. From here Lennox could see most of the docks and who was approaching the office on the land side.

She could picture him sitting on one of the tall stools, intent on the drawing before him. Hours would go by and he wouldn't notice. Nor would he care as long as he created something from a thought in his mind.

In her childhood she'd often found him scrawling something on a piece of paper. When she wanted to see, he would reluctantly show her a sketch of a ship or a hull.

She left the tables, walking to the white painted shelves occupying both of the remaining walls. In each compartment rested a small rendition of a ship, so flawless in execution she stared in amazement.

"May I pick it up?" she asked.

He nodded.

Putting her umbrella on the floor, she reached out with both hands, cupping them around the delicate ship. The name was painted in tiny Cyrillic letters on the stern.

"It's Russian?"

He nodded again.

From the smokestacks to the captain at the bridge everything was crafted in perfect miniature. She traced a finger across the hull.

"Who did these?" she asked. Had Lennox learned yet another skill?

"Garrison McPherson," he said. "He worked at the yard for years."

"Such a talented man."

He didn't respond, merely folded his arms, leaning against one of the tables.

She gently replaced the model and retrieved her umbrella, continuing her walk.

"Are these all the ships Cameron and Company has built?"

"We haven't built all of them. But most of them, yes. Here and in Russia."

"Why did your father ever decide to construct a shipyard in Russia?"

"He was asked to," he said. "I guess you go where you're wanted."

There were a dozen things she could say to that, but decided silence was the best recourse.

"Does he miss Russia after he sold the yard there?"

"Why the interest, Glynis?"

She glanced at him, surprised. Didn't he know she'd always been fascinated in everything about him?

"People who think Scottish winters are bad have never spent one in St. Petersburg."

She strolled across the room to the opposite wall, with its empty compartments. Lennox planned ahead.

"Where is the *Raven*'s model?"

"It hasn't been built," he said.

She glanced at him, wondering at the change in his voice.

Her attention was caught by another ship, one reminding her of the *Raven*. It leaned forward like it raced the wind, wanting to outsail anything on the water.

"The *Vixen*?"

"One of those ships never constructed," Lennox said. "It doesn't have a practical purpose. Nowadays a vessel has to be worth building."

"It looks like a swan settling over the waves. A steamship with all the grace of a clipper."

"Have you studied ships?"

Once she had, with the intent of impressing him with her knowledge.

"I designed her after you left for London," he said, coming to her side.

He named the ship *Vixen*. Had he named it for

her? Is that what he thought of her? She didn't know whether to be annoyed or pleased.

"Do you want to sit down?"

"No."

She would be better off moving, keeping active, anything but think of Gavin's death.

She should have dissolved into tears or fainted. Perhaps she should wave her handkerchief in the air and claim the vapors overwhelmed her.

Was she being unwomanly by not acting fragile? Was that why Lennox studied her, a V forming on his brow?

The moments ticked by in silence. Now was the time to tell him what she'd come to the yard to explain. The whole horrible story could have tumbled from her lips for him to accept or reject.

The door opened and the moment was lost.

"Mr. Cameron?"

One of the men came forward, introduced himself and his companion as members of the Glasgow police.

The two looked like yard workers, both broad of shoulder and chest, each walking in the curious rolling gait of a man used to the rhythm of the ocean. Had they once been sailors and changed their vocation?

The younger man had a full beard and mustache, while the older man with touches of silver on his temples only wore a mustache.

Lennox led them to the desk in the corner. She sat on the straight-back chair, grateful she didn't have to perch on one of the tall stools. Lennox sat in the large chair behind the desk while one of the policemen sat in front of him. The older man stood beside the window and addressed Lennox.

"Who is the dead man, Mr. Cameron?"

"Gavin Whittaker," Lennox said. "His employer is Fraser Trenholm & Company out of Liverpool, but he represents the Confederate government. I turned the *Raven* over to him yesterday and expected him to set sail in two days."

One of the men nodded, while the other said, "An American again."

"And you found him, miss?" one of the men asked her.

"It's Missus," Lennox corrected. "Mrs. Smythe. Mrs. Smythe is the widow of the attaché of the British Legation in Washington."

"America, Mrs. Smythe?"

A flush of embarrassment traveled up her spine to settle at the back of her neck. It was never a good idea to be the focus of attention, and right at the moment three sets of male eyes were watching her.

She nodded. "However, I'm a Glaswegian and I've recently come home."

"What were you doing here, Mrs. Smythe, on a Sunday?"

I'd come to confess. I wanted to tell Lennox everything in a way he would understand and possibly forgive.

"I came to see the *Raven*," she said, facing them down. "I knew the ship would be leaving soon and I wanted a glimpse of it."

Almost any situation could be endured with enough pride. She tilted her chin up and refused to look away. Let them believe her or not. She couldn't do anything about their thoughts, but she could alter their impressions in the way she answered their questions.

The policeman glanced at Lennox. "Did you know Mrs. Smythe would be here, sir?"

"I often work on Sunday," he said, deflecting their question. "I would appreciate if you wouldn't tell my minister that."

Both men smiled.

"Was Mr. Whittaker dead when you found him, Mrs. Smythe?"

"Yes," she said, giving stern instructions to her stomach to remain calm. She would somehow have to find a way to block out the memory of all that blood.

"Did you see anyone else aboard the ship?"

"I didn't," she said. "Nor did I hear anything."

The younger man asked, "The weapon was a wicked looking knife. Had you seen it before, Mrs. Smythe?"

"Anyone Gavin met would have," Lennox interjected. "He had a great fondness for demonstrating it. It was part of the walking stick he carried with him everywhere."

She gripped her hands together to still their trembling.

The discussion moved to the guards on the *Raven*. As she listened, she realized how shrewd was Lennox's manipulation of the conversation. He told the men that, in view of the recent arson attacks on the Clyde, three guards had been assigned to the *Raven*. The men must have been dismissed by Gavin, who had the authority to do so.

Glynis had just been unfortunate enough to stumble onto Mr. Whittaker's body. She'd been in the wrong place at the wrong time.

"If that will be all," he said, "I'd like to take Mrs. Smythe home. As you can imagine, the discovery of a murder was a shocking event."

The older policeman moved in front of the desk.

"Thank you, Mr. Cameron," he said, nodding to Lennox. "And you, Mrs. Smythe."

She nodded, replicating a regal expression she'd once seen Mrs. Lincoln use. She remained seated as Lennox escorted the policemen to the door, their conversation continuing.

What did he tell them? What did they ask? Was Baumann's name mentioned?

The hem of her blood-spotted skirt dragged on the floor. She looked away, nausea making her clammy. The rain had seeped into all her garments, even her corset cover. Her skin pebbled and she shivered uncontrollably. She noted her reaction in an absent way and dismissed it.

A man was dead. Her momentary discomfort didn't matter.

"I DON'T require an escort, Lennox," she said, sounding tired.

"Pity." He locked his office door and followed her down the steps. "If you had brought one—say your maid, for example—she might be an alibi for you."

She frowned at him, but he only smiled.

"They almost bowed to you," she said. "Yes, Mr. Cameron. Of course, Mr. Cameron. Why were the police so toadying?"

"Perhaps because they don't think I killed the man?"

"Even if you had, I doubt they would have arrested you. After all, you're Lennox Cameron of Cameron and Company."

"They were as solicitous of you, Glynis."

"That's because of you."

He didn't argue with her reasoning. He'd do anything in his power to protect her.

The police were in the process of taking the body now, which meant one last duty had to be completed.

He stopped to talk to Daniel, the driver who'd brought Gavin to the yard, informing him of what had happened and sending him back to Hillshead. At Glynis's vehicle, he gave instructions for Thomas to follow them, then cupped her elbow and led Glynis to his carriage on the other side of the police van.

"You don't need to escort me home, Lennox. I traveled across the ocean by myself. Surely I can make it a short distance."

"Were you that independent in Washington?"

She smiled, the expression oddly sad. "My life in Washington bears no resemblance to my life here."

"Why not?"

She glanced at him, then away. "I was on stage all the time. My personality changed according to the situation. If I needed to be self-reliant, I was. If it was better for me to appear helpless, I could manage that, too."

"And here?" he asked. "Are you as great an actress?"

She gave him a narrow-eyed look, reminding him of the old Glynis.

"Here I'm just myself."

"Which version of you?" he found himself asking. "The girl I knew or the woman with secrets?"

She didn't answer.

He'd never seen her so miserable. He wanted to put his arms around her, find a blanket and warm her, and wipe clean her memories of the past few hours.

She held herself so stiffly she appeared brittle. Her face, perfectly composed, betrayed none of her feelings. Only her eyes were wild, darting back and forth, unable to settle.

"How did your husband die? Not aboard ship by any chance?"

She sent him a quick look then glanced away. "No," she said.

"I forgot. He died in some sort of accident, didn't he?"

There, she settled on a focal point—him.

"Yes," she said. "Do you really think I killed Gavin, Lennox?"

He knew she hadn't. No one could change that much, but he also suspected Glynis was hiding something.

"You never told me why you were talking to Matthew Baumann," he said, deciding to address the niggling feeling he had.

She wrapped her arms around herself, looked out the carriage window and spoke to it rather than him.

"He came to my house. I told him to go away. I'm not responsible for him being ill mannered. I have no desire to see the man ever again."

"You have no idea why?"

"To get my assignment to kill Gavin Whittaker, of course."

She smiled, but the expression held curiously little humor.

"Do you think it's appropriate to jest about this?"

She stared through the window again. "I've found humor is sometimes the only way to tolerate certain situations."

What situations were those? Would she tell him if he asked?

"I can assure you I don't need you escorting me to the door," she said, once they reached her home.

"No, you probably don't. But I need your mother. If I have to tell Mrs. Whittaker about her husband," he said. "I'd prefer to have your mother with me while I do so."

She only nodded, opened the carriage door, and nearly jumped out. He stared after her, annoyed and more than a little worried.

Chapter 21

"*T*hank you for doing this," he said to Eleanor MacIain.

She smiled and patted him on the arm, in much the same way she had when he was a boy.

Lennox always wished he had a mother like Eleanor. Despite whatever trouble and mischief Duncan got into, no one doubted she loved her son.

"The worst thing," Duncan said once, "is disappointing her. She gets a look in her eyes and you feel lower than a worm knowing you've hurt her somehow."

He was twelve when his own mother left. For years she'd written him one letter around his birthday, but after a while even those stopped. He didn't know whether she was dead or disinterested.

"The poor thing," Eleanor said now. "To be so newly widowed."

"Yes," he said, not mentioning he suspected Lucy Whittaker probably wouldn't mourn her husband all that much. Had Gavin been aware of his own wife's apathy?

"How horrible for Glynis to have seen such a thing. Whatever was she doing there, Lennox?"

"I don't know."

"You don't suspect my Glynis, do you?"

He glanced at her. "Not of murder, Mrs. MacIain. But she knows something and she won't speak of it."

He'd seen her with Baumann. Their meeting troubled him, but not as much as the feeling that Glynis was hiding something. He wanted to gather her up in his arms and comfort her and, at the same time, demand she reveal whatever was making her afraid.

His own emotions were too volatile at the moment. Anger, first of all, that someone had killed Gavin. He put the blame for that squarely on the shoulders of Matthew Baumann, and he'd conveyed that suspicion to the policemen in his office. Sorrow, that a man he was growing to consider a friend had been unjustly killed. Irritation, that Glynis wouldn't be honest with him. She'd been terrified today and it wasn't just because of Gavin's murder.

"She's changed," Mrs. MacIain said, as if privy to his thoughts. "She's not the same. But then, neither are the rest of us, are we?"

"Have you changed much in seven years, Mrs. MacIain?"

She pondered the thought and finally smiled somewhat sadly.

"I think I have, yes. Ever since my dear Hamish died. You go on thinking tomorrow will be easier. First thing in the morning you wake up and you think what a glorious day. Then, it all comes sweeping back to you. He's gone and today will be another day without him."

Her hand clasped his, and he was startled to discover her trembling. Mrs. MacIain never looked discomfited or upset in any way. Now he wished he hadn't asked her to come with him, but the situation was a delicate one, requiring the tact of a mature woman.

"She was married to a terrible man," she said, and it took him a moment to realize she was still talking about Glynis and not Lucy Whittaker. "I've only recently learned how terrible he was. My poor darling girl should never have married such a ghastly person."

When he didn't know what to say, he found refuge in silence.

"I always wished she'd had a child. Children bring such joy in life. But now I'm grateful that Richard Smythe had no progeny."

He wanted to ask what she knew, but it was better if he didn't comment about Glynis's marriage. Or even think about her being married.

"You think she's going to take it badly, don't you?"

Now she was talking about Lucy.

"I do," he said. "And although it may seem unkind of me, I think the best thing would be for her to go to a hotel."

"Nonsense," Eleanor said. "She'll do no such thing. We'll take her home and she can have one of the guest rooms. My house is nowhere near the size of Hillshead, Lennox, but it's big enough for one guest."

He glanced at her. "Are you certain?"

She nodded.

"You're very kind," he said. "I can't tell you how much I appreciate this," he added as the carriage came to a stop before his house.

"I've always considered you a second son, Lennox. Why wouldn't I help you in any way I could?"

Thunder roared around them, sounding the news that the storm hadn't finished with them.

He left the carriage and turned to help Eleanor. Her smile looked a little forced and he wanted to apologize for asking for her assistance.

"Let us go and do this terrible thing," she said.

THE SUITE Lennox had given his guests was the equal of her own at home. Perhaps the rooms were a bit nicer. She didn't have a bathing chamber adjacent to her bedroom, a good thing as it turned out after the pipe break last winter. Nor did she have such an expansive view, this one of the gardens of Hillshead visible through the watery curtain of rain.

The settee and two chairs were upholstered in a pale blue and coral pattern, the padded valance at the top of the windows the same fabric. The curtains were also blue, and touches of coral were visible in the pillows, footstools, and carpet.

Eleanor could only wonder who had decorated the rooms, since the colors had almost a feminine feel.

When they'd knocked on the sitting room door, Lucy had answered, staring first at Lennox, then at her. She remained silent as Eleanor gently took her by the hand and led her to the settee.

After sitting beside the younger woman, she said, "I'm afraid we have bad news. Mr. Whittaker has passed."

Lucy blinked at her, staring at Eleanor as if she'd suddenly grown feathers.

"What do you mean he's passed?" Lucy asked, looking at Lennox.

"He's dead," he said. A rather blunt response, but a direct one.

"Of course he isn't dead."

This was not going well at all. How wise of Lennox to ask her to accompany him, especially since the newly widowed Lucy Whittaker was refusing to accept the reality of the situation.

"I'm afraid it's true," she said.

"Of course it isn't." Lucy turned and frowned at Lennox. "Gavin's at the yard, isn't he? Or he's in your library. He's certainly not dead."

Perhaps they needed to take the poor thing to see her husband's body before she truly understood. Sometimes Death swooped down, picked up a loved one like a hungry hawk, and nothing but gazing on the departed would make the dying real. Her own dear husband had been taken at work, in his office at the mill. At least he hadn't been alone. Duncan had been with him, and brought his father home to her.

Gavin hadn't been alone, either. His murderer had been with him. The thought made her shiver.

Had someone followed him from America? Or had the poor man been robbed?

The authorities would discover soon enough. She didn't need to trouble herself with such things, not when she could help in another way.

"Tomorrow I'm sure you can go and see him, my dear."

Lucy stared at her, evidently not comprehending. Shock took a body like that, sometimes.

"We need to get you settled and comfortable. I have the most delicious bramble tea at home. Once you're all tucked up, I'll bring you a pot, plus some of Mabel's scones. They're the best ones in all of Glasgow."

"I don't understand. I'm not going anywhere."

"Mary and her father aren't here, my dear. It's a bachelor establishment. People are bound to speculate about the situation otherwise. Unfortunately, gossip travels fast in Glasgow. We need to consider your reputation."

"I've just been made a widow and you want me to pack my belongings and leave? Tonight?"

Lucy's voice was so shrill Eleanor felt like a crab crawled up her spine, its pincers nipping at her skin.

Gavin Whittaker looked poorly mourned, even now.

"We would be most happy to have you as our guest," Eleanor continued. "We're not as spacious as Hillshead but we've a lovely guest room. It would be best, all things considered."

"You're concerned about my reputation?"

She nodded, grateful Lucy grasped the situation. Newly made widow or not, Lennox was a very well known man in Glasgow, one of its most prosperous citizens. People would not hesitate to gossip about any facet of his life.

Lucy stared dry-eyed at Eleanor, then at Lennox, her mouth pinched, her eyes narrowed, and twin spots of color on her cheeks.

"We want the best for you, my dear," she said.

"If you care so much about reputation, Mrs. MacIain, what do you think people would say about your daughter kissing Lennox passionately in the garden? She didn't seem to care about her reputation."

For a space of seconds, perhaps minutes, Eleanor couldn't think of a response. Warmth traveled from her heels to her nose.

"I beg your pardon?"

There, at least she'd said something.

"Your daughter was in the garden with Lennox. I wouldn't be surprised if they copulated behind the hedges, Mrs. MacIain. What do you think the whole of Glasgow will say to that?"

The inference being she would share every bit of information she had with anyone who cared to listen.

Eleanor rarely found herself cowed, although Lucy managed to cause her heart to beat fiercely. In the most ghastly situations she maintained a determined cheerfulness. Now she forced a smile to her face and prayed for the right words to answer the woman.

Lennox stood still at her side, but she didn't look at him. The last time she'd done so, he'd been staring at Lucy as if he'd like to immolate her with his gaze.

Lucy stared straight at her, a self-professed paragon of all the virtues, a virago with a vicious tongue.

How could she invite this woman to stay with

them? She could just imagine the first encounter between her and Glynis. Her daughter did not deserve to
be assaulted in her own home.

"Under the circumstances," she said, standing,
"perhaps it would be better if we took you to a hotel. I
hear the Lafayette Hotel is a lovely place."

She glanced at Lennox, who nodded.

"I'm not going anywhere," Lucy said.

Lennox smiled, such a strange expression she felt
her skin chill.

"Yes, you are," he said. "If I have to throw you over
my shoulder and carry you there."

Lucy, who had been dry-eyed until now, chose that
moment to begin to weep.

Chapter 22

$\mathcal{B}$efore her mother left with Lennox, she sent Lily to draw her a bath and Mabel to make a dinner tray. The bath sounded wonderful; Glynis hadn't stopped shivering since leaving the yard. But she didn't know if she would be able to eat.

She made it upstairs to her bedroom, walking carefully and with deliberation. If she paid attention to her steps, she wouldn't be thinking of anything else. Not Lennox's errand to tell Lucy Whitaker her husband was dead. Not the sight of Gavin stretched out on the deck of the *Raven*. Certainly not the memory of all that blood.

She removed her dress, sure the fabric was ruined from the rain. Lily worked miracles, however, so perhaps she could coax it back to life and keep it from acquiring the rusty looking stain of some black fabrics.

At the knock, she grabbed her wrapper, donned it, and opened the door.

"Your bath is ready, Miss Glynis."

Before she could thank her, Mabel appeared at the top of the steps, breathing heavily as she carried the tray into the room and placed it on the bench at the end of the bed.

Had she emptied the larder? The tray boasted a teapot with cup and saucer, along with a bowl of stew, four slices of buttered bread, some greens, and enough desserts to feed everyone in the house.

"I always thought a little bit of sweetness helps on a sour day," the cook said.

Today most definitely qualified as sour.

"You ring now if there's anything you want. Either me or Lily will fetch it for you straight away."

Glynis blinked away her tears. "Thank you, both of you."

The older woman nodded and whispered something to Lily. The two servants left her, and she closed the door, leaning against it.

She pressed her fingers over her eyes, trying to ease the burning from unshed tears.

Gavin Whittaker was dead and his death reminded her of all the other men on her conscience.

In the beginning she'd been like everyone else in Washington, caught up in the excitement of words and emotion. She'd known some handsome men in uniform, wished them well, and kissed one on the cheek for good luck as he marched off to battle.

None of the five men she knew returned.

Over the months, she'd begun to think of the war as a gaping maw, trapping young and not so young men. The gaiety, the frenetic energy, the excitement gripping Washington in the beginning had changed to a dread beginning at dawn and lasting until the end of daylight.

What other battles would be published in the papers? How many more men would die for a cause each side felt right and just?

The British Legation had been required, officially, to be neutral, but their neutrality had made them the repository of secrets. Or as Baumann once said, the legation was a treasure trove of intelligence. They learned of conditions in the Confederacy through English subjects living in the southern states. They received dispatches from attachés throughout the South, each one of them revealing something that could be used in the war.

Baumann had announced, on more than one occasion, that she was his most valuable operative.

She might give a good dinner party and hold occasional teas filled with interesting conversation, but to members of the legation she was deemed insignificant and invisible. People didn't modulate their conversations around her. Richard's reputation as a sycophant helped, too. Surely the wife of the toadying British attaché wouldn't carry tales.

Even careless remarks were valuable. Such as the time she'd overheard news about another attaché living in Georgia. His comments about his lifestyle proved the Confederacy was receiving help from Europe. When the blockade tightened, Baumann told her she'd been instrumental in the decision.

He didn't know she held most of what she learned back. She'd been forced to give him dribs and drabs to keep him satisfied and silent, but she withheld the information she thought would be most damaging.

After Richard's death she refused to help Baumann, and he couldn't do a thing to her. She wasn't part of the inner circle at the legation. She didn't meet with influential women. Nor did she care if she was sent home in disgrace. Let him reveal the whole horrid story to anyone he wished.

Now he had come to Glasgow and threatened her again. The man was a canker, refusing to disappear. This time, however, she refused to be blackmailed.

Yet when she'd been ready to tell the truth, murder stopped her.

THE CARRIAGE ride to the hotel was memorable for its lack of conversation. Lennox couldn't remember being in a more uncomfortable position than sitting opposite two women who didn't deign to look at him.

Eleanor's smile had turned brittle and she studiously avoided glancing in his direction.

Lucy's bout of tears had ended once she realized he was serious about evicting her from Hillshead. Her eyes narrowed and her mouth pursed until her blotchy cheeks were as plump as a squirrel's. Whenever she did glance in his direction, he half expected to be singed by her look.

The Lafayette Hotel was located in the center of Glasgow. The building was a showplace with a lobby filled with soaring arches and a wide set of pink marbled stairs leading to the rooms on the second and third floors.

Lennox arranged for a suite for Lucy, uncaring about its cost. He spoke to the manager, requesting extra deference for Mrs. Whittaker in view of her recent tragedy. The man was accommodating, promising to send a tray from the tea room and reserving the bathing chamber for her use. He also agreed that a porter would go to her suite twice daily to ask if she needed anything.

If the man wondered why Lennox was willing to pay so much for Lucy Whittaker's comfort, he didn't mention it.

Ten minutes later he followed Lucy and Mrs. MacIain up the marble stairs. Behind him, Lucy's bags were being carried by two porters obviously straining with the effort.

Perhaps he should have checked to ensure she hadn't nicked any of his belongings. But if she had, it would have been a small price to pay to rid himself of her.

Once inside the room, Eleanor made a point of pointing out all the amenities.

"Look, there's a wash basin right in your bedroom. And a window with a lovely view of Glasgow." She pressed both hands against the mattress. "The bed seems wonderful."

She straightened. "Not that you'll be sleeping much tonight. The first few weeks after a loss such as you've sustained is the worst."

"I won't be here long," Lucy said. "I'm going home."

He truly wanted to feel a measure of compassion for her. After all, her husband had just died. If she hadn't reacted with grief immediately, perhaps it was due to shock. Who was he to judge how a woman mourned?

"I can understand why you would want to," he said. "But until the inquest is over, you can't leave."

Her cheeks grew florid. She clenched her hands into fists and looked as though she wanted to hit him.

"I hate Scotland," she said. "I hate everything about it. You people don't speak correctly. Nor do you eat anything decent."

He made a mental note to tell the hotel staff to provide her an English breakfast.

"How much longer do I have to stay in this horrible place?"

Did she know he most earnestly desired her absence as much as she wished herself gone?

"Less than a month, I would think."

"A month? I have to stay in this hellish place a month?"

Her voice rose an octave. He anticipated the onslaught of tears at any moment.

"Shall I send one of my staff to keep you company?" Eleanor asked, stepping in front of Lucy. "You'll need someone to run errands for you."

"I need a maid," Lucy said, her voice returning to its normal timbre.

"I have a sweet girl named Lily working for me. I'll

send her by first thing in the morning, shall I?" When Lucy didn't answer, she continued. "You'll need stationery, of course. And you'll want to dispatch a telegram informing your family of the tragedy."

Eleanor turned to him, the first time since leaving Hillshead. "Will you handle notifying Mr. Whittaker's employer, Lennox?"

He nodded.

"I want a new wardrobe," Lucy said. "I have to wear mourning and I won't dye my dresses."

When Eleanor glanced at him, he nodded again.

Why did he feel like he was paying for Lucy's silence? What guarantee did he have she wouldn't tell tales about him and Glynis?

"Go away," Lucy said, not making an effort to mitigate her rudeness. "I've had all I can take of you Scots."

She turned and without another word entered the bedroom, closing the door firmly behind her.

"*THERE'S AN* explanation for what Lucy saw," Lennox said once they were alone in the carriage.

Eleanor smiled. "I'm very certain there is. Just as I'm certain Mrs. Whittaker will do anything in her power to make it sound worse than it is."

"I agree. What do I do?"

She looked away, staring through the window at the rainy night. "A few prayers might not be amiss. Otherwise, there's every possibility she will do her best to ruin your reputation."

He nodded. "I'm not worried about me," he said.

She took a deep breath, closed her eyes and said her own prayer, for patience this time. What was she going to do with the two of them?

She turned back. To his credit, he didn't look away, but met her eyes. Lennox had always been direct, even as a boy, taking responsibility when he was wrong.

He'd grown up to be a devastating man, one who no doubt fascinated all manner of women.

Glynis had adored him. Eleanor thought it a youthful obsession, one that would pass in time. She'd paid for the mistake by losing her daughter for seven years.

She wouldn't be so foolish again.

She suspected her daughter's fascination with Lennox had begun at the very start of Glynis's life. Lennox was seven years old to her two when she began holding out her arms for him, screaming his name in an unintelligible utterance of infant language.

He'd been kind to the little girl, scooping her up and returning her to Eleanor countless times.

Glynis said too much had happened for her to feel the same way about Lennox now. Eleanor didn't believe such nonsense. First of all, Glynis acted differently whenever Lennox's name was mentioned. Her cheeks turned pink; she rarely looked at the speaker but concentrated on the ground or the distance, as if wishing to hide her emotions. Secondly, she'd seen her daughter's expression when asking about Lennox's engagement.

Seven years might have passed, true. Circumstances might have altered, again true. But she knew love when she saw it.

She wasn't that old.

She could also recognize misery, and Glynis was miserable. Even worse, she suspected Glynis had been miserable for seven years.

"Did you kiss my daughter, Lennox?"

"Yes, Mrs. MacIain, I did."

She nodded. She expected as much.

Anyone in their vicinity could feel the tension between them as well as the sparks. They'd been there since Glynis turned seventeen and Lennox had started looking at her differently.

"He needs to keep his mouth shut," Hamish said of Lennox once. "Otherwise, his tongue will fall out and he's going to start to drool."

Glynis had been eighteen and they'd just returned from a trip to Edinburgh. She could still remember the look on Lennox's face when he caught sight of Glynis dressed in a new yellow gown and summer flowers adorning her hair.

What would Hamish say to this situation?

"What did you mean about Smythe?"

She bit back her smile. She'd been waiting for Lennox to ask.

"I wouldn't have said anything unkind about Richard Smythe when he was alive. After all, he was Glynis's husband. Nor is it my tale to tell. You'll need to ask Glynis for the details. But what I have discovered about the man doesn't dispose me to liking him very much."

"Did he hurt her?" His voice sounded like rusty nails.

"No more than any bad husband can hurt a wife." Or vice versa, she thought, her mind on Lucy.

She studied Lennox surreptitiously.

Perhaps now Glynis could find some real happiness. Only if Lennox proved to be less obstinate than her daughter. She'd never seen any two people working so diligently at cross purposes.

What she'd like to do was rap him over the head and say, "Lennox Cameron, I know you love Glynis. It might have taken you a few years to recognize that fact but now is the time for you to step forward. Declare yourself. Don't waste another minute."

She couldn't, of course. Lennox was a grown man, not a boy. She doubted if he would listen to advice from her even about Glynis.

Therefore, she would have to nudge her daughter

first. A little manipulation—for a good cause—was not necessarily a bad thing. Sometimes you needed to start where you were in order to get where you wished to go.

If the two of them married, for example, they'd be forced to communicate with each other. Once the bedroom door closed, all sorts of joining could happen.

She would do what she could and after that it was up to them. In the meantime, they had a rat in the corn.

"For heaven's sake," she said, sighing, "see what you can do to discover who killed her poor husband. The sooner Lucy Whittaker leaves Scotland, the better."

Chapter 23

"*W*hat else did she say?" Glynis asked, avoiding her mother's eyes.

Eleanor sat in her favorite chair in the parlor, sipping her tea placidly. She would occasionally look across the room, study the portrait of her husband painted a few years before his death, smile at Hamish MacIain, nod, then concentrate on her tea once more.

Glynis felt anything but calm at the moment. How was she to know Lucy couldn't wait to tell anyone what she'd seen?

"Isn't that enough, Glynis? She saw you and Lennox kissing. Evidently, it wasn't a peck on the cheek."

Glynis stared down into her own cup, feeling a hot flush of embarrassment shoot through her. Having been a matron for a number of years, it was an odd experience to be chastised by her mother. Equally disturbing to have done something worthy of rebuke.

"I went to Hillshead to ask Lennox to help," she said.

Eleanor's eyes widened. "You did?"

She nodded. "He's probably the wealthiest man in Glasgow right now. I thought he would give Duncan a loan."

"Duncan would never impose on a friend."

She glanced at her mother. Evidently she was the only one in her family willing to sacrifice pride for survival.

"One thing led to another . . ." Her voice trailed away. Surely a further explanation wasn't necessary. Besides, since her errand at Hillshead hadn't been successful, it seemed a little unfair it might result in scandal.

"I would just have you remember two things, my darling daughter. Glasgow is a small village in a lot of ways. Gossip is a fact of life here. You're newly returned and you're still a subject of speculation for Glaswegians."

"And the second?"

"Once, you might have been spared because you were a MacIain. But things have changed. The mill is in trouble and many people have lost their jobs. If anything, people will look at you more harshly than at a stranger."

"She just lost her husband. I'd think she'd be concerned with that, not tattling about Lennox and me."

Eleanor peered at her over the rim of her cup.

"The poor man was left in the rain like a dead animal," Glynis said. She hadn't been able to stop thinking about Gavin's eyes staring into the sky, looking up as the raindrops struck him.

Her mother put her cup down. "Oh, my dear girl. I'm so sorry you had to go through that."

"Do you think people will listen to her? She hasn't made any secret what she thinks about us."

Her mother shrugged. "If Duncan is forced to lay off more workers, public sentiment might turn against you. People will pay attention to what she says."

Glynis leaned forward and picked up her cup from the tray.

"Even if they do, Mother, what would come of it? Gossip doesn't bother me."

"That's ignorance speaking, not your common sense. You have never lived with censure. You've never gone to the market and had people turn their backs on you. Or walked into a room and have people grow silent. Or heard whispers behind your back."

"Have you?" she asked, surprised.

"No," Eleanor said, "but I've seen its effects on other women. I won't have such a thing happen to you. Be more circumspect in your behavior, I beg of you."

Glynis remembered one of their neighbors as a child. The boy had collected insects, and took great delight in showing his trophies to any little girls he could find. Some of them had screamed and run away, but she always made herself stand there and examine them, feeling sympathy for the poor insects still alive and struggling.

She felt exactly like one of those insects right now.

Her mother sighed, leaned her head back, and stared up at the ceiling.

"I can only imagine what your father might say."

She was mired in enough shame and humiliation at the moment without adding the specter of Hamish MacIain.

"Did he hate me? For marrying so quickly?"

Her father had been at her wedding but all he'd done was hug her tightly in parting. Still, Hamish Mac-Iain was a man of strong opinions and would have said what he truly felt to his wife.

"Your father could never hate you," Eleanor said calmly. "He adored you. If anything, he was disappointed. He didn't think Richard good enough for you."

"Maybe Lucy will lose interest," Glynis said. "Or find something else to loathe or complain about."

That comment received another glance from her mother, this one just as sharp.

"What do you suggest I do about it? I doubt Lucy would listen to me."

Her mother shook her head. "Don't even consider going to talk to the woman. It would only make the situation much worse. We must live our lives with our heads up."

"Begging your pardon, Mrs. MacIain, but it's Lily."

They both looked up to find Mabel standing there, a frown furling her brow.

"Lily? I sent her to stay with Mrs. Whittaker for a few days."

"Yes, ma'am," Mabel said, "and she's home again."

"What's wrong?"

Mabel stepped back and pulled Lily forward.

"Oh, ma'am, must I go back?" the maid said. The girl twisted her hands as she came to stand in front of Eleanor.

The poor girl looked as if she'd been caught in the rain and barely dried. Tendrils of hair were plastered to her face. Her skirt was sodden; the white apron that had always appeared stiffly starched was limp and wrinkled.

Lily's eyes filled with tears as she began to speak.

"Mrs. Whittaker isn't pleased with me. I didn't get her tea quick enough and I didn't get her things unpacked the way she wanted." Lily stared down at the carpet, then at Eleanor. "I told her I wasn't no lady's maid, Mrs. MacIain, but she had me do her hair anyways."

She hiccuped, wiped at her eyes with the corner of her apron and continued. "I was sorry for the mess I made of it, but she screamed at me for an hour."

"She weren't no lady," Mabel said.

The tears overflowed, streaming down Lily's flushed face. Mabel moved to stand beside her, stretching her arm around the girl's shoulders.

Eleanor didn't remonstrate with the cook or mention that one should always show charity, even in difficult situations. Evidently, her mother realized defending Lucy was futile.

"Do I have to go back, missus?"

"No, Lily," Eleanor said, shaking her head. "You don't have to return."

The maid bobbed a curtsy, her smile reminding Glynis of sunshine in the middle of rain.

"Thank you, Mrs. MacIain," Mabel said. "If the world was as kind as you, it would be a great place indeed."

Lily nodded emphatically beside her.

"Perhaps the woman is just overwhelmed about her husband's death," Eleanor said.

"She didn't do no crying, ma'am," Lily said. The maid glanced at Glynis. "I don't think she likes you, Miss Glynis. She said some terrible things to anyone who would listen, even the chambermaids. The worst cow in the fold lows the loudest, as my gran used to say."

Lily scrubbed both palms over her reddened cheeks and moved to the door. She picked up something and returned to stand in front of Eleanor.

"I was to throw it away," she said, "but I remembered it were your favorite umbrella."

Eleanor nodded and reached for it.

Lily bobbed another curtsy and the two women left the room.

"Sometimes, a gesture of kindness is overlooked," her mother said, putting the umbrella to the side of the settee. "But I'm sure it will not go wasted."

"I'm afraid I don't share your view, Mother. Some people will never see kindness for what it is. Or they'll take advantage of it."

Eleanor smiled. "Have you become cynical at such a young age, Glynis?"

She'd become a realist, but she didn't say that to her

mother. Instead, she asked, "Why did Lucy have your umbrella?"

Eleanor shook her head. "The rain started as we left Hillshead and she didn't have one. As much as I dislike the woman, I didn't want her to get wet and catch a chill."

"Can you just imagine all her complaints if so? 'It's your Scottish weather. Rain in England is never as wet as Scottish rain.'" Glynis shook her head. Lucy could be difficult in the best of moments. Ill, she would be twice as querulous.

Eleanor sighed. "Let's hope that doesn't happen," she said. "And that the inquest is held quickly and whoever killed poor Mr. Whittaker is soon discovered."

She nodded.

Was Baumann still in Glasgow? It would suit her purposes if he disappeared from Scotland and never returned. Otherwise, he might suddenly become voluble and tell the world about Washington.

She wouldn't have to worry about Lucy Whittaker and her exaggerated tales then. Not when Matthew Baumann knew the truth and it was much worse.

THE MACIAIN MILL, four massive red brick buildings with black roofs and rows of windows, stretched the length of Donegal Street. Several of the windows were open now to let in the summer morning air.

Looms filled the cavernous space, looking like skeletons now, devoid of cotton thread and finished fabric. When he was here last he'd seen throngs of people in the aisles, some of the men holding long poles they used to free blockages from the looms.

On that day cotton fibers floated in the air like a snow storm. Today the air was clear.

He nodded to the employee at the door, signed in

and told him he was there to see Duncan. The other man asked if he knew the way, a sure sign it had been too long since Lennox had been to the mill.

Once, he'd visited as often as Duncan had been at the shipyards. When had that stopped? They'd both been pressed by business, but surely friendship shouldn't lapse because of it.

He climbed the two flights of stairs. Offices ringed the space, allowing a view of the mill floor below. He took the aisle to the office at the far corner, knocked, and when he heard Duncan's voice, entered.

This room, at least, hadn't changed. He suspected Duncan wouldn't allow it to be altered in any way, out of respect for his father and a love of tradition.

"Where have you been?"

"In London," Duncan said, his eyebrows arching. "Am I required to get your permission to leave Glasgow?"

He frowned at his friend. "Of course not. I just wanted to talk to you."

"If it's about a loan, don't bother."

"Have you found a solution, then? Is that why you were in London?"

"None of your concern, Lennox."

Duncan was consistent, at least.

"Let's negotiate a short-term loan, say for a year. Enough to do maintenance on the looms and keep your employees."

Duncan's frown joined flat eyes and thinned lips.

"Because of our friendship I won't kick you down the stairs."

"I'd like to see you bloody try," Lennox said, standing in front of his friend's desk. "How long are you going to be a mule about this?"

"Until my bones turn to ash."

He didn't expect any less. Very well, he'd tried. He'd

said what he'd come to say concerning a loan. Now there was a more important reason for being here.

"You're going to hear some stories about your sister and me," he said.

Duncan stared at him. The seconds ticked by and still his friend didn't speak. He'd rarely been the focal point of Duncan's irritation, and found it an uncomfortable place to be.

"You've already heard."

Duncan nodded once. "Your houseguest is a voluble sort."

"She isn't, thank the good Lord and your mother, staying at Hillshead any longer. She's installed at the Lafayette Hotel."

One of Duncan's eyebrows winged upward. "Is there any truth to the stories about you and Glynis knowing each other in a biblical fashion in the gardens of Hillshead?"

"Bloody hell, is that what she's saying now?"

Duncan nodded.

A week had passed. Only a week, and he'd begun hearing things himself. He'd gotten enough leers in the past seven days to last him for the rest of his life.

Men had winked at him, given him a nod, and smiled. *Good work, lad,* they seemed to be saying, and he was left without recourse. He wanted to punch someone. He'd never struck a woman and he wasn't about to start. But the sooner he could get Lucy Whittaker out of Glasgow, the better.

If he'd heard the gossip, he was certain Glynis had as well. He'd be damned if Lucy Whittaker was going to hurt Glynis.

"Is it true?" Duncan asked.

"That I know Glynis in a biblical manner?"

Duncan sat back, piercing him with a look. "She's my sister, Lennox, I'm not going to use the vernacular."

"No," he said. "It's not true."

"Then what's the gossip about?"

He didn't have the slightest idea how to explain what had happened in the past weeks. Glynis had returned to Glasgow, but her arrival had been accompanied by confusion and deception. Add in a murder, Matthew Baumann, Lucy Whittaker, and the entire situation was out of control.

A little plain speaking wouldn't be amiss at the moment.

"I'm going to marry her," Lennox said. "I just wanted to let you know."

First, he had to convince her, but she'd given him the idea how to do that herself. For once, Duncan's stubbornness would prove an asset.

"No coming to the head of the family and asking for my approval? You're just announcing the fact?"

Lennox stifled his smile and nodded. "Not well done of me, was it? Let me rephrase. I'd like to marry your sister, Duncan. Do I have your approval?"

For a moment Duncan didn't answer. His look was somber, his study intent.

"Why?"

"Why?" he asked. "What do you mean, why?"

"Do you love her?"

He didn't know how to answer that. He wasn't sure he wanted to divulge his feelings right at the moment. If he told anyone, it would be Glynis.

"She's always been in love with you, you know."

"What?" He stared at Duncan.

"At least she was seven years ago. Don't tell me you didn't know."

He felt like the floor was opening up beneath his feet. Sitting heavily, he stared at Duncan.

"No, I didn't know."

Duncan shook his head. "For an intelligent man you're remarkably stupid," he said pleasantly.

"She thought I was going to marry Lidia Bobrova," he said, remembering Glynis's question in the Necropolis. "Did you know that?"

"Not until a few days ago," Duncan said.

He couldn't think. Glynis loved him? Had her feelings changed in the last seven years?

"You're my friend," Duncan said, standing. "I consider you a brother." He rounded the desk just as Lennox stood. Duncan clasped him on the shoulder and for an unguarded moment they studied each other.

"But if you hurt her, Lennox, I'll come after you myself."

DUNCAN GLANCED over at his mother seated in her favorite place on the parlor settee. A half-empty cup of tea sat on the table at her side. She'd been so intent on her task that her tea had grown cold.

If the patterns of the last few years held true, Lily would enter the parlor in a few minutes with fresh, hot tea, making a clucking noise like a mother chicken as she removed the other cup.

Glynis had retired to her room to read, mumbling about the book as she did so. Something about how "the silly woman is too foolish to deserve the prince."

He hadn't asked her for an explanation. Nor had he told her about Lennox's appearance at the mill earlier today. Let Lennox speak in his own time.

His mother bit at the thread, folded the garment she had finished mending and looked at him.

"Is there nothing that can be done? Some accommodation? Could we not petition someone?"

Duncan bit back his smile. "No, I'm afraid not. Diplomacy between us and America is touchy at best right now."

She shook her head. "I don't see why everyone has to suffer. They can't sell their cotton and we can't buy it. What a horrendous situation."

More horrendous than she knew. If the American Civil War didn't end in the next three months, he would be forced to implement his own plan to save the mill. Although risky, it was the only solution he had.

"A great deal can be solved by talking with one another, Duncan. Of course, there are times when there is entirely too much talk."

He glanced at his mother, frowning when she sighed. Reaching for another garment, she examined it intently. He looked away when he realized it was a shift, either belonging to her or Glynis.

"I'm afraid the situation must be addressed soon before it becomes worse," she said, sighing again.

"You're speaking of the gossip," he said.

"You've heard, too?" She placed her hands on the garment and looked at him.

He nodded. The mill was a convention of gossip and had always been. His father had been more adept at silencing the rumors than he was.

"That Whittaker woman is saying the most outlandish things, Duncan. How Glynis seduced Lennox and how he nearly ravished her in the gardens of Hillshead."

He'd already heard a version of the tale, but not to this degree.

"Is that true?"

"I'm afraid they were in the garden, Duncan, and there was some kissing." She glanced over at him. "I'm sure there was nothing else, it being Lennox and Glynis. But, still, the woman seems determined to ruin your sister's name."

"I wouldn't put much credence in it," he said. "Glynis has always been talked about, even when she was a child."

She put her mending down and stared at him. "Duncan MacIain, have you no concern about your sister's reputation?"

"I wouldn't worry about it, Mother. I believe it's all being sorted out."

"What, exactly, does that mean?"

He wasn't going to betray a confidence, but this was his mother. He smiled.

"Let's just say Lennox has a plan."

She blinked at him. "Does he?"

He nodded.

She surprised him in the next moment by smiling brightly.

Chapter 24

"Charlotte is here," Eleanor said, entering Glynis's bedroom.

She put her brush back on the bureau and faced her mother.

"I wasn't expecting her," she said, dread seeping into her bones. "Did you invite her?"

Eleanor shook her head. "I suspect she's heard the rumors and she's come to investigate on her own."

For the last week they'd been visited by more than a dozen of Eleanor's friends and acquaintances. Since her mother insisted she be in attendance every time, Glynis had to endure women staring at her stomach. Would Charlotte do the same, wondering when the baby was due?

She stared at her mother. "What on earth do I tell her?"

Eleanor sighed and came to sit on the edge of the bed.

"Her husband is very well known in Glasgow. Charlotte considers herself an important personage."

A curiosity Glynis had observed in Washington. A woman married to a powerful man had a portion of influence herself. An acquaintance had called it the Power of the Pillow.

"You daren't offend the woman for fear she'll say something to her husband, of course. Slip him a small complaint as they're going to sleep or wake him with tea and a word in his ear."

Charlotte could well be a petty tyrant herself.

"When is the inquest going to be held?" she asked.

"From what I've heard, in two weeks."

"Afterward, will Lucy be allowed to leave Glasgow?"

Eleanor nodded. "I might go to the train station and see her off myself."

She stifled a smile and glanced at her reflection in the mirror. For the last week she'd been too pale. Her eyes looked haunted and there were dark circles beneath them. Between worry about the mill, Lennox, Baumann, and Lucy's gossip, she hadn't slept well.

"Well, there's nothing more to do, is there? I have to see Charlotte. We'll talk about our childhood, not rumors. I'll tell her some stories of Washington." She turned and looked at her mother. "Or I could always ask about her children. She's very proud of them."

How had her life become so complicated? Washington had been a hotbed of rumors and she'd been very careful never to put herself in a situation that might be misconstrued. Yet she'd forgotten the lesson within weeks of returning to Glasgow.

She straightened her bodice, fluffed her skirts, and followed her mother downstairs, ready to do further battle for her reputation.

Her mother veered off from the parlor, mumbling something about refreshments, leaving her alone to face Charlotte.

Entering the parlor with a hard-won smile, she greeted Charlotte.

"How nice to see you again," she said, making no comment about the visit being unexpected—or unwelcome.

Charlotte stood at her entrance. She wasn't attired in green today but a dark blue silk.

Glynis's dress was a dark blue as well, only not silk and not as fulsomely decorated with pin tucks and darts. Charlotte's jewelry looked to be sapphires, not entirely proper for day wear. The rings she flashed had a variety of stones in them. She'd most definitely come up in the world with Archibald's success and was evidently intent on boasting of it in the way she dressed.

"Is it true?" Charlotte said, getting to the heart of the matter. "Have you and Lennox become lovers? Archie is distraught that you would have brought such scandal to our home. If we'd known, of course I wouldn't have invited the both of you. How could you do such a thing to me, Glynis? How could you have ruined the memory of a sweet friendship?"

Which part did she address first?

She sat heavily, staring at her entwined fingers, then made herself look up at Charlotte.

How odd that Glasgow gossip had impacted her life to such an extent. First, rumors of Lennox's wedding had resulted in her decision to marry another man. Now the wagging tongues of her fellow Glaswegians were determined to shame her for an impromptu gesture.

Still, of all her regrets, kissing Lennox was not one of them.

"Lennox and I are not lovers. I'm sorry your husband is upset, but I haven't brought scandal to you. Or to myself, either. I would never have harmed you, Charlotte."

She did wish the woman would at least loosen her bonnet ribbons. They looked too tight, almost strangling her.

"Then why is that Englishwoman saying all sorts of things about you and Lennox?" Charlotte asked, finally sitting.

She shook her head. This was delicate territory.

"I don't know," she said. "Perhaps grief has made her senseless."

Charlotte narrowed her eyes.

"I don't know," she repeated. "You know the woman as well as I do."

"I've only been around her one time, at dinner."

"I don't know," she said for a third time. "Why does anyone gossip or tell tales? Because her own life is disappointing? Because she's jealous of something?"

"She said you and Lennox were naked in the garden."

Her smile came easier now. "No, Lennox and I were never naked in the garden," she said. "I don't know why she would even say such a thing."

"To think I might have contributed to such a scandal."

Was Charlotte more concerned about the rumors or that she might be tied to them?

Thank heavens for her mother's arrival, followed by Lily carrying a tray. In the last week Mabel had been baking every day. Their budget had been decimated but they'd had to have something to offer the scores of visitors. Now the tray was piled high with everything from scones to Scotch tablet to delicate slices of plum pudding, one of her mother's favorites. Normally, it was made in the autumn, but because she liked it, Mabel kept a supply of it in the larder.

In addition there were two pots, one of coffee and one of tea, and three cups—which, thankfully, meant her mother planned to remain in the parlor.

No one had ever had such a loyal defender or probably deserved it less.

"I have been explaining to Glynis," Charlotte said, speaking around a large helping of plum pudding, "that there is talk of her and Lennox."

"Is there?" Eleanor said, as calm as if someone had commented on the weather. "How very odd."

Glynis shared a glance with her mother, then looked away.

"They were seen together," Charlotte said, leaning forward. She ignored another helping of the pudding for a biscuit. "Gamboling through the gardens at Hillshead."

She'd never gamboled through anything in her life. She wasn't sure how one gamboled. Did you have to kick up your heels? Lunge forward with a smile on your face? Leap every few feet or so?

She caught her mother's look before she said anything and bit back her smile.

"Needless to say," Charlotte said, "people are talking."

"Needless," her mother said, slicing a piece of chocolate cake for Charlotte.

"I came to warn Glynis."

Or had she come to get the latest bit of gossip to spread through Archie's chocolate shop? Was it known more for its confections or the tales its proprietors told?

"We appreciate your coming, Charlotte," her mother said. "It's the friendship of people like you that make the world a brighter place."

Her mother could have been a diplomat herself. No one could tell, looking at her, that Eleanor had lied straight-faced. Charlotte lapped it up like a cat with a bowl full of cream.

"Of course, what kind of friend would I be if I didn't let her know people were speaking ill of her?"

Glynis pasted a Washington smile on her face and said, "Indeed."

The single word meant nothing, really, but seemed to mollify Charlotte and reassure her mother she wasn't about to say anything stupid.

She wanted to, however. She wanted to ask Charlotte, oh so nicely, why she listened to gossip at all?

Why hadn't she simply turned and demanded the speaker stop talking about her friend?

That comment would be too direct and almost condemnatory. No doubt Charlotte saw herself in the role of social doyenne. Glynis had had her fill of those women in Washington.

"I cannot imagine how tales like that get started," her mother said. "Or how they continue. It's like a west wind. Once it blows, it seems to carry on for days."

Charlotte paid a great deal of attention to her cake.

"I think it's because I'm rumored to be naked in the latest tale," Glynis said.

Her mother's eyes widened.

"It's not enough that Lennox and I are supposed to be lovers, but I'm dancing through the garden without a stitch of clothes on."

Too much white showed in her mother's eyes. Charlotte had stopped eating, her fork in midair, her eyes nearly as wide as Eleanor's.

"In none of the tales is Lennox naked. Why do you think that is?" She tapped her finger to her chin. "I would imagine that if I have to be naked, he should as well, don't you think? Do you think he's gamboling as well? Or is he leaping about like a goat?"

She smiled brightly and looked directly at Charlotte.

"I think it's a good thing for the gossipmongers it wasn't winter. If I were in the garden naked I would have frozen my arse off."

"Glynis!" her mother said at the same time Charlotte gasped.

"Tell me, are there any rumors about Mr. Whittaker's death?" she asked in the silence. "Or has anyone given any thought to the poor man?"

Charlotte stared at her.

Her mother seemed to have regained her equilibrium because she nodded and asked, "Yes, has anyone been arrested?"

LENNOX LEFT the yard early and headed for the MacIain home.

He could court Glynis in earnest but why waste time? He acted decisively when he knew what he wanted, and he wanted her.

He imagined the scene in his mind and had his answers ready to any of her objections.

We haven't seen each other for seven years.

We've been friends for longer than that. Absence doesn't erase those memories.

I've changed.

So have I. Yet we've remained the same people inside. What do circumstances matter, Glynis?

I love you.

There, that statement would silence her, wouldn't it?

The moment I saw you standing in the ballroom at Hillshead, I knew why I didn't marry Rose. Why I haven't been interested in marrying anyone else. Why I found myself at your home for a chance mention of your name or a reading of your latest letter.

I love you, Glynis.

Be my wife and I'll show you. You'll never lack for anything. I'll protect you. I'll shelter you. Your family will be my family. I'll support the mill until the bricks crumble. I'll give you anything you want from anyplace in the world.

I'll name all my ships for you.

I'll hold you in my arms at night and know myself the most fortunate of men. I'll bring you bliss, I promise.

I'll protect you.

What would she say to that?

She's always been in love with you, you know.

He hadn't been able to forget Duncan's words. Is that why she left for London, thinking he was going to wed Lidia? Is that why she'd kissed him when she was nineteen? Did she feel the same still? The next kiss they shared would be one he initiated.

Life was short, too short not to be surrounded by love, surfeited by it. Drunk in it. The brevity of life screamed for something to offset it: joy, laughter, the soul deep belonging of truly loving one particular person.

He'd wasted seven years of his life. He wasn't going to waste another day. If Glynis no longer loved him, he'd solve that somehow. And if she did, well, he wanted to know. He needed to hear it.

A carriage sat in front of the MacIain home. For a moment he wondered if it belonged to Baumann. If it did, he'd solve that situation today as well. No more mystery. No more secrets.

Today everything was going to change.

"*MRS. MACIAIN*, you've a visitor." Lily said from the doorway.

Oh, heavens, another one? When would the women stop coming?

"Who is it, Lily?" her mother asked, her voice higher than normal.

Before Lily could answer, Lennox was inside the parlor. Lennox, her partner in this drama, the satyr to her nymph.

Her stomach dropped.

"Mrs. MacIain," he said, greeting her mother. "Please forgive my intrusion, but I need to speak with Glynis."

He turned to Charlotte, whose face was rapidly changing hue to match the blowsy crimson flowers on her bonnet.

"Mrs. MacNamara," he said. "How nice to see you again."

"Yes," Charlotte replied, her voice icy.

"Could we go somewhere private?" he asked, turning to her.

Oh, this was horrible. Now Charlotte was going to spread the tale that Lennox called on her and the two of them had adjourned to a private place. What magnification could they invent? She could imagine.

I'm not saying she took off her clothes, mind, but why else would he ask to speak to her privately? When I knew Glynis, she was a God-fearing girl. All that travel changed her to a woman of sin.

She wanted to kick something. She was sick of it all, sick of gossip, sick of people expecting her to be proper and perfect, sick of the look of veiled superiority on Charlotte's face, sick of being afraid, sick of herself.

If they were going to talk about her, she might as well give them something to talk about.

She stood and walked toward Lennox, a bright smile on her face.

"Let's go somewhere we can be alone. Maybe to the garden," she said, stretching out her arms as if to embrace him. "It's such a lovely warm day. I won't get a chill when I remove all my clothes."

She ignored his frown, Charlotte's gasp, and her mother's moan, leaving the room with her head held high.

Chapter 25

"*W*hat was that all about?" Lennox asked, following Glynis out of the parlor.

Instead of the garden, she led Lennox to her father's library.

The room was rarely used even five years after her father's death. Duncan preferred to work in the small parlor rather than here. Yet Lily kept the space perfectly dusted and aired, as if Hamish might walk in any minute, take up his seat in the tufted leather chair, and begin writing at the mahogany desk.

Two bookcases, each filled with her father's favorite books, faced the desk and were framed by twin windows looking out toward the side of the house. There, a flower garden carefully tended by her mother provided a lovely view.

If people were kept alive by speaking of them or thinking of them, her father had been immortalized in this library.

She closed the door and faced him.

"I can't tolerate any more of it, Lennox. Every busybody in Glasgow is saying how I've ruined myself cavorting with you."

"Do you cavort a lot?" he asked, a twinkle in his eye.

She sighed. "I don't cavort at all. I'm as proper as a nun. Why everyone has to ascribe certain behavior to me, I've no idea."

"Maybe they remember you as you were, not as you are."

"Oh, but I'd much rather be the person I was than the person I've become."

She stopped, surprised not only by the admission but that she'd made it so freely to Lennox.

"What made you think I was going to marry Lidia Bobrova?"

Another surprise, that the past was suddenly there in the room with them.

"Is that why you married Smythe?"

He took a step toward her, then another. She should have stepped back. She should have put up her hand to stop him from coming too close, but she did neither.

"Why didn't you say anything?" he asked, his breath on her forehead.

She certainly should have protested when he extended his arms around her waist and gently drew her toward him. Instead, she placed her hands on his chest and stared straight ahead.

"What was I supposed to say?"

"You could have asked."

She shook her head. The child she'd been wasn't brave enough. Asking that kind of question would have revealed a heart ready to break.

How did she tell him that?

In the space of those silent moments she realized something elemental. She was no longer a desperate girl-child. He was no longer her god. They were equals now, the years apart easing their differences, giving her experience. She was at least as well traveled and knowledgeable about the world and the people in it.

She looked up at him. Would she ever get used to the sight of him? He was so handsome he took her breath away. Sometimes she wanted to force him to remain motionless so she could study what it was, exactly, that made him so different from other men.

Even after seven years he still had the capacity to make her heart stutter.

She stepped back and his arms dropped. Turning, she walked to the other side of the room and sat in the lone chair beside the fireplace, leaving Lennox to either sit at her father's desk or remain standing.

Because of her hoop she had to perch on the edge of the chair and sink down into the mound of fabric that was her skirt.

He leaned back against her father's desk, crossed one leg over the other and smiled at her. The way he stood there perfectly at ease would make the unaware think he was relaxed. A muscle flexed in his cheek, however, and his eyes were intent.

"I have a proposition to offer you," he said.

There was no reason for her stomach to clench. Her heart started beating even faster.

"I'll give you all the money you want for the mill if you'll marry me."

Stunned, she stared at him.

At the moment, however, she couldn't think of a thing to say. Not one word, witty or otherwise, came to mind.

"I've marshaled my arguments. Would you like to hear them?"

"Do I have a choice?" she asked.

He grinned at her. "You can just agree to marry me."

"Tell me," she said, looking away.

If she didn't see him, she wouldn't feel so . . . Her thoughts trailed away. Womanly. That was the word, and it startled her, not because it was wrong but because it was so right.

Lennox always made her conscious of being female to his male.

Suddenly he was in front of her, reaching down with both hands on her waist, picking her up and sitting again with her on his lap.

Her hoop bent up toward the ceiling, revealing her undergarments. She slapped her hands down on her skirt and made a squealing sound. Not a sophisticated woman of the world sound but one more like the girl she'd been.

He laughed, which made her frown, then crushed her skirt and the wayward hoop with one hand.

"First," he said, as if she hadn't just shown him her lace pantaloons, "there's the mill. Being married to me would allow Duncan to take a loan or a gift, help him make his payroll, and keep the mill from shutting down. I'd be family and he would have to accept help."

She was still thinking about the fact he'd seen her undergarments, but she nodded.

"Secondly, there's my marital status. People are hinting it's time for me to wed. With the increase in our business, I don't have time to go looking for a bride. I know you. You know me. Marrying you would be a relief. Look at all the time I'll spare myself having to meet someone, establish any kind of relationship, get to know their parents, their family, and finally wed. A good two years."

A relief? Marrying her would be a relief? She stared at him, pushing away the impulse to put her palm against his cheek, even now showing a hint of beard.

She had to stop wanting to touch him constantly. Or noticing he smelled of the sea and of wood, as if sawdust clung to him.

"So marrying me would prevent you from being a spinster?"

His smile broadened.

"In a manner of speaking, yes. Third point," he said. "There's your reputation. Our reputation," he corrected. "All of Glasgow believes you're my mistress, so why not marry?"

Mistress? She'd gone from gamboling in the garden to becoming his mistress? Lucy Whittaker had been busy.

"I never thought you the sacrificial lamb, Lennox."

"While I always thought you obstinate," he said, a small smile curving his lips.

She probably should have taken umbrage at that remark, but it was too close to the truth. She looked away.

"There's another matter," he said, his smile vanishing. "As my wife, you would be safe from Matthew Baumann."

She froze, her gaze on the fireplace. She bit her lip and told herself to keep breathing. Finally, she gathered up her courage and looked at him, though she found it difficult.

"There's something between the two of you, Glynis. Do you deny it?"

How did he know? Her mind flew from one idea to another, coming to rest on the thought that he was guessing.

She should tell him. Right now, before any more time passed, she should tell him about Washington. If she did, he would withdraw his offer. He would smile that cool, polite smile of his, as practiced as any politician, and excuse himself.

"I could always leave Glasgow again," she said. "That way, no one would talk about me. Or, if they did, I wouldn't have to hear it."

"You could try."

He sounded perfectly affable and he looked calm if you ignored the glint in his eye.

"What does that mean?"

"I would come after you. I would hunt you down to the ends of the earth, Glynis."

"Are you that desperate for a bride?"

His lips quirked. "I am."

She would have pulled free if he'd let her. Her hoop, however, decided to slip free of his restraint and pop loose again, pointing at the ceiling.

He laughed again, a sound transporting her to the past when she'd tried to amuse him. She wasn't trying at the moment.

She frowned at him again and slapped both arms down on her skirt.

He had marshaled his arguments well, especially the one about the mill.

Her mother would be spared any further worry. They'd be able to keep the household without losing Mabel, Lily, and the upstairs maid.

"For the love of all that's holy, Glynis, would you just answer?"

She blinked at him, uncertain why he was so suddenly irritated.

Despite all his talk of being pressured to marry, she didn't believe him. In addition, he could as easily give her the money and she'd tell Duncan the amount came from the diplomatic service and they'd been mistaken about Richard's estate.

She didn't make those arguments for one reason: this was Lennox. Who cared if he offered for her out of misguided pity? What difference did it make what the reason was? She'd be Lennox's wife.

But he hadn't listed the one reason that would have tipped the scales. He hadn't said he loved her.

What did he feel about her?

She was his childhood nemesis. She'd trailed after him endlessly as a girl. She'd annoyed, exasperated, and amused him. But she was no longer a child.

Then there was that kiss in the garden.

She wanted him in her bed. She wanted him to hold her and kiss her. She wanted to feel the passion she'd felt that moonlit night at Hillshead. If she were his wife, no one would tell tales. No one would dictate her behavior. She would be Lennox's bride, free to kiss him awake and fall asleep with him holding her close.

How long had she wished for that? How many years had she dreamed of it?

Her cheeks warmed as she nodded, acceptance in a gesture.

He simply watched her. Did he want the words? Very well, she'd give them to him.

"Yes," she said. "Yes, I'll marry you, Lennox."

He kissed her before she could move or even think. Suddenly, his lips were on hers, his arms around her waist.

She was trapped by having to keep her recalcitrant hoop from flying in the air, so she had no choice but to submit to his embrace and his kiss.

She had no choice at all.

His thumbs were pressing against her corset at the base of her breasts while his lips tasted hers. His tongue was entirely too brash, darting into her mouth and out again, forcing her to chase him for a taste.

She wanted to hold his face still, rain kisses over his bristly cheeks and his eyebrows, his ears, his chin, and his lovely throat.

What a pity she couldn't take his shirt off and feel the expanse of his chest.

She pulled back with difficulty, blinked up at him, gratified to see his gaze wasn't as focused as it had been a moment earlier.

Passion had them both in its snare. She was trapped in a web and Lennox was the spider. For once she didn't mind feeling like a fly.

Come and get me.

"When?" she asked.

"When?"

She nodded. How long must she wait until he came to her? How many months until they could be man and wife?

"A week."

"A week?"

Her mother wouldn't understand. Or maybe she would. Still, all of Glasgow would be shocked, but then they already thought she and Lennox were racing through the garden like Adam and Eve, didn't they? Lucy had been their snake and was now doing everything in her power to ensure a scandal.

"Why so soon?" she asked.

"Why not?"

She couldn't think of an objection. If they were going to wed, why not immediately?

"A week," she said. "As long as you don't invite Lucy Whittaker to the wedding."

He frowned at her. "Or Matthew Baumann."

She nodded.

Before she knew what he was going to do, he stood, still clasping her waist with both hands. Her hoop twanged as it assumed its proper shape.

Why were women fitted with all these clothes ensuring they couldn't move easily? One day hoops would be outlawed and she'd cheerfully take hers into the backyard and burn it.

She leaned forward, constrained by the damnable garment, and placed both hands on his chest.

Words didn't come as easily with Lennox as they had at one time. Was it because she had so much more to hide? Or because she felt vulnerable around him?

It was one thing to tell herself she felt nothing for Lennox. Quite another to discover she'd been lying all this time.

She wanted another kiss. She wanted to stay here for hours kissing Lennox. She might even tumble to the floor in front of the cold fireplace with him.

The knock on the door put an end to that idea.

"Glynis," her mother called out, nervousness in her voice. "Charlotte is leaving."

Charlotte.

She bowed her head and sighed.

"I forgot all about Charlotte," she said.

Lennox grabbed her hands, raised both to his lips, and kissed her knuckles.

"She couldn't be here at a better time," he said. Moving past her to the door, he opened it wide.

Her mother stood there flanked by a scowling Charlotte.

Lennox glanced behind him, stretching out his hand for her.

"I hope you'll congratulate me," he said, smiling.

She stepped forward, put her hand in his and stood at his side.

"Glynis has agreed to be my wife."

Her mother took a deep breath, released it, and looked upward.

"Thank the saints," Eleanor said, although she was a good Presbyterian.

Charlotte's eyes just widened. How many times would this story be retold at the confectioner's?

Glynis was certain within hours the tale would be spread about how her engagement occurred after only moments alone with Lennox. No doubt Charlotte—or her husband—would regale their audience with how well-kissed Glynis looked when the door finally opened. How Eleanor MacIain, long despairing of her daughter, looked relieved enough to cry.

At least she was fully dressed.

She blew out a breath, held onto Lennox's hand tightly, and realized it was a great deal easier playing the role of a proper Washington matron than it was being herself.

Chapter 26

$\mathcal{G}$lynis realized her mother was looking up at her.

"Did you hear nothing of what I said, Glynis?"

"I didn't, Mother," she said, feeling her cheeks warm. "I was thinking of other things." She'd been remembering Lennox's kiss and wondering if he was as superb a lover as he was at kissing.

Her mother was seated before her as she stood on a crate. They'd decided to alter one of her mother's dresses to serve as her wedding gown. Although the garment had to be taken in at the waist, let out at the bodice, and hemmed, it was better than marrying in mourning or dark blue.

"I'm so glad you chose this one," Eleanor said, handing a pin to Lily. "The cream color was always too young for me, but it will serve admirably. Of course, it would have been nice to order something new. Time being what it is, we didn't have that option."

"You don't mind it being so soon?" she asked.

Tonight she was going to be married. Tonight she was going to marry Lennox. Tonight Lennox would come to her bed.

The thought was terrifyingly wonderful.

"Of course not, my dear. It's seven years too late, now, isn't it?" Eleanor smiled up at her. "My darling daughter, you've always loved him. To the detriment of your good sense, I think. But love is that way. It grabs hold and shakes your mind until you have no sense left."

She glanced down at her mother, surprised. "Is that how it was with you and Father?"

Her mother's smile held a tinge of sadness. "From the very day I saw him. There he was and I couldn't look away. I made my sister find out who he was but he didn't wait for an introduction. He stepped up to me, proud as you please, and introduced himself as a MacIain."

Glynis had heard the story before but she never tired of listening to it.

"'A MacIain?' I said. 'Aye, from the Highlands.'" Eleanor smiled. "Your father was the most handsome man I ever saw in his kilt." She picked up the hem of the dress and smiled again, this time with more amusement. "I think the women of our family must love deeply and well. That kind of love brings great happiness, but there must always be a trade. You must sacrifice something for it."

"Pride," Glynis said.

Her mother looked surprised. "Perhaps it is pride," she said. "The ability to cast aside anything but love. To give without thought of return. Whatever it is, loving the way we do requires some sacrifice." She smiled. "I'm so glad for this day. You claimed him when you were five years old."

Her mother stared at the hem, sighed and finally spoke.

"I was not adverse to Lucy's talk," she said, surprising Glynis. "I hoped it would lead to just this conclusion. I know it's a terrible thing to admit and I hope you'll forgive me for it. I didn't want you to leave again."

"You were hoping scandal would force us to wed?"

Eleanor smiled. "Nothing is actually forcing you

to wed, Glynis. Scandal is just giving both of you an excuse to lay down your pride."

She didn't know what to say. Was her mother right?

Eleanor stood and embraced her, her perfume a cloud of warm spicy scent.

What if Lennox didn't want her? That was a question she couldn't ask anyone because the answer might be too difficult to hear. What if he only wanted to marry her to protect her? Either by keeping Baumann or the police at bay, or ensuring the mill was still operating.

They hadn't discussed emotions. He hadn't declared his undying love for her. Nor had she confessed she'd always loved him.

She gave Eleanor a kiss on the cheek and smiled at her.

"I wasn't going to leave, Mother. I won't, I promise."

Eleanor held her hand as she stepped down from the crate and walked to the pier glass.

"You are the most beautiful bride, Glynis," her mother said, smiling at her again.

She wasn't altogether sure she looked beautiful. Her face was too pale and there was a blemish forming in the middle of her cheek. Powder covered it, and gave her complexion an even more masklike appearance. She used a rose-colored pomade on her lips an hour ago but it had disappeared.

She blinked at herself, wishing she was as pretty as Lennox was handsome. Her face was a strange shape, almost pixielike, and her bottom lip so full she always looked like she'd been chewing on it. Her eyes commanded attention, and she'd grown accustomed to strangers staring at her because of them.

She was of average height and slender except for her breasts, which seemed to belong to a much larger woman. They'd always been a source of consternation to her mother, who had to order the seamstresses in the past to take in the waist of her garments and let out the bosom.

The cream-colored gown made her look even paler. The style seemed to accentuate her flaws rather than her assets, and those assets were spilling out the top of her dress.

She wanted to be beautiful tonight, and it had never mattered much before. She wanted Lennox to be happy circumstances had forced them together. She wanted him to be glad for their wedding night.

Seven years ago she'd imagined her wedding with the whole of Glasgow attending the ceremony uniting the MacIain daughter to the scion of the Cameron and Company empire.

People would have come from miles around to watch the two of them. Speculation might abound but there would be no doubt in anyone's mind they adored each other, from the rapturous smiles they shared to the longing glances in each other's eyes.

She would have worn something from Worth, per-haps, a gown her father declared was perfect for her. *It doesn't matter what it costs,* he might have said.

Her mother would've spent the weeks before the ceremony inviting people to come and celebrate the most glorious of days, the uniting of the MacIain and Cameron families.

Mr. Cameron would have been there, beaming, proud of the new daughter his son had brought into the family. Mary would've kissed and hugged her, grateful to be getting a sister.

She envisioned the occasion so many times it had achieved the status of a dream. Nothing could hope to measure up to it, certainly not her civil wedding to Richard attended only by her parents, Duncan, her London cousin, and Richard's aged mother.

Now she was dressed in a borrowed gown. Her

father was gone and Mr. Cameron and Mary in Bute. Both households were going to be in attendance for the ceremony, to be officiated by a Presbyterian minister, but there would be none of the pomp and circumstance she'd dreamed about as a girl.

The only time her dream and reality blurred together was in the wedding supper. Her mother had decided the event should be grand. Lennox had offered his staff and larder. The house had been a beehive in the last four days. She couldn't take a breath without smelling the delicious odor of roasting meat and plum pudding, and she could hardly move without encountering a servant from Hillshead.

She knew why she was marrying Lennox—she had always adored him. Her feelings hadn't changed however much she pretended they had. But why was Lennox willing to marry her? Was it only a way to help them financially? Did he simply feel sorry for her?

How horrible to marry because of pity.

Even worse, that she didn't care.

LUCY CLOSED the door on the chambermaid, walked to the reading chair the hotel had finally provided for her and sat staring out at the view of Trongate Street. The thoroughfare looked nothing like civilized London.

Two weeks, they said. Two more weeks before the inquest, and she could go home.

She stretched out her stocking feet, delighting in the freedom from shoes. All in all, being a widow pleased her more than having a husband. Everyone commiserated with her. Even the Scots had been kind and considerate.

Would she like some more cream in her tea? Another currant scone? What about a better light for reading?

She didn't know if the consideration was because Lennox paid her bills and left instructions that she was to be given anything she wanted. Or because people she encountered were genuinely sorry for her. It could be a combination of both.

So far she'd only been able to acquire two black dresses, with promises another would be ready before her departure and the other three to be sent to her. If Lennox was paying for a new wardrobe, why should she skimp?

Tonight he was marrying Glynis in a private ceremony, she'd been told. Most of Glasgow had been invited to the reception. She had not, of course, since it would be a glaring breech of decorum.

She wasn't the least disappointed to miss the event.

Tonight, while Glynis was forced to accept her bridegroom, Lucy would be free to read or eat biscuits in her bed.

Gavin wasn't there to tiptoe up to her or whisper how fetching she looked in her new peignoir.

No more "Lucy, honey, how about a little kiss?" No more "We're married, darlin', it's expected."

Her nights were her own. She needn't pretend to be tired or ask Gavin how many times must he bed her in a week. Her mother had counseled endurance, but how much was a woman supposed to tolerate? Gavin had always been touching her.

She didn't miss him telling her how she must act. No "Lucy, you can't say such things. People won't understand. They like their country, however barbaric it may appear."

Or: "You'll love Georgia, honey, I know you will."

She'd wept for Gavin yesterday at his funeral. Lennox had paid for that, as well, and the vault in the Necropolis. The City of the Dead was a most disturbing place, filled with shadows and swift breezes whining around the mausoleums. She'd been very distressed by it. A good thing she'd never visit it again.

Gavin had been such a handsome, personable man, and so solicitous when they'd first met. All her friends complimented her on his courtliness, his wonderful manners. She would never tell them that he'd been a rutting beast with his mind too focused on carnal acts.

When she returned home, she would be the recipient of the same pitying glances as when she ventured down to the lobby in one of her new black gowns. The porter nearly tripped over his feet to escort her to a banquette in the tea room.

People were probably whispering about her. Dear Lucy, widowed so young. A terrible thing, to lose her poor husband in such a way. Gavin would forever be enshrined in everyone's memory. What a tragedy, for the man to go off and get himself murdered.

She would have to practice looking sad.

LENNOX ROLLED up the plans for the newest ship, added a note to one of his designers, and put it in the satchel that would be taken to the yard.

Carving out time from his schedule was difficult but he had a good staff and they could carry on without him for a few days. Finishing up another set of estimates took an hour, during which he found himself staring out his library window, wondering at his emotions.

She's always been in love with you, you know.

Glynis hadn't said anything, hadn't revealed her emotions. Nor had he, for that matter.

He didn't like this feeling of tricking her into marriage. He'd held out the inducement of helping the mill, and it might have been enough to make her agree. He doubted gossip bothered her. The girl he'd known would have simply ignored the rumors. Or had she?

She'd thought he was going to marry Lidia Bobrova. Perhaps it was fitting that gossip led to their marriage. It had certainly changed their lives seven years ago.

She's always been in love with you, you know.

But was she still that girl?

The Glynis he'd known said what she felt, had been ferociously loyal to her parents, Duncan, and her friends. She went out of her way to be kind to others, but she was often awkward socially, as if she wanted to do everything at once and didn't have time to be polite.

Glynis had been impulsive and reckless, filled with life and laughter. There wasn't anything deceptive about her; each emotion shone through her eyes.

The woman who returned to Scotland made you guess what she was feeling. This Glynis was socially poised and restrained to the point of being expressionless. Yet sometimes there were hints of the younger Glynis in her eyes. A flash of impatience or longing or something fading too quickly for him to decipher it.

It all came down to trust, didn't it? How much did he trust Glynis? Once, he could have answered the question in the space of a heartbeat.

He trusted his father to be the same person, his sister Mary to be Mary. He trusted dawn would come each day. He trusted, mostly, in himself, in his determination and tenacity. If he didn't know something, he would learn it. If he needed help, he'd ask for it.

Did he trust Glynis? Could he love someone he didn't trust?

She hadn't commented when he mentioned Matthew Baumann.

Perhaps it wasn't a case of him trusting her but of getting Glynis to trust him. Maybe then, when Baumann's name was mentioned, she wouldn't turn to stone with a trapped look in her eyes.

Would she ever tell him the truth? What was the truth?

He had too many questions and not enough answers, but he was going to brush them away for now. Somehow he and Glynis were going to have to craft a marriage between them, one bridging the last seven years.

The answer, then, was yes. He could love a woman he wasn't certain he could trust. The rest would have to come in time.

Chapter 27

*T*he wedding of Mrs. Glynis Elizabeth MacIain Smythe to Mr. Lennox Alan Cameron took place on a Thursday evening in the bride's home.

The bride, as it might be reported, was pale. She trembled just the slightest bit, but when she realized it, she steadied her nerves and pasted a Washington smile on her face. No one would know she was both terrified and elated.

This was Lennox. She'd wanted to be in this exact spot for most of her life, saying these exact words and knowing he would be her husband in minutes.

Yet her imagination had never put her in this situation, holding a secret she hoped he never learned. She'd never thought to keep anything from Lennox. Did he withhold anything from her?

If she stopped the ceremony now and demanded to know a secret from him, it would probably be how he'd managed to construct the *Raven* to have so much speed yet be so large.

Or perhaps why he hadn't married Rose.

Her secrets did not consist of good things she'd accomplished, but those acts she never wanted exposed.

She should have told him. She should have divulged everything and seen, then, if he'd wanted to marry her. He wouldn't have, of course, which was why she'd been silent.

Of the two of them, Lennox was the better person. He'd always been kinder, calmer, more understanding. He championed the underdog; he gave to the poor. He was unfailingly loyal, generous, and reasonable.

What had she to recommend her?

In Washington people had gravitated to her because she didn't tell tales and she listened to their concerns. She introduced people to each other if she thought they had common interests. She shared their triumphs but never their tragedies. Some of her acquaintances considered her witty.

She had long slender fingers. She could sing passably well and her legs were pretty. There, enough assets to offset a few of Lennox's attributes.

This ceremony was strangely like her first, being held in a private home rather than a church, even though the officiate on this occasion was a Presbyterian minister.

No one had arrived at her home this morning, demanding to steal her away from Lennox. Duncan had not led a group of tipsy revelers to counter their demands. The closest she'd come to an old fashioned Scottish wedding was her breakfast of oats.

She didn't miss the more traditional wedding. All she cared about was that Lennox was beside her and the union would be official.

His voice held an air of command as he repeated his vows before the minister.

Duncan and her mother stood behind her, flanked by Mrs. Hurst, the housekeeper at Hillshead, and a few men from the yard. There hadn't been enough time to send for Mary and Mr. Cameron. All of the people attending her wedding looked overjoyed to be there. The men, introduced to her just prior to the minister arriving, were all smiling.

Her brother had a twinkle in his eye, which was

more understandable than her mother's tears. She couldn't remember her mother crying at her wedding to Richard.

The tradition in the MacIain family was that the bridegroom always wore a kilt. She would have liked to see Lennox in a kilt again, but he was dressed in black with a snowy white shirt.

Had he worn the same at Gavin Whittaker's funeral the day before? Her mother had attended but she had opted to remain at home. Although she'd liked Gavin Whittaker, she loathed his wife. Nor could she imagine Lucy wanting her to be there.

This way, she'd given Lucy something else to gossip about. Now she could regale all of Glasgow of how rude she was not to attend the funeral of the man whose body she'd discovered. Or perhaps Lucy hadn't missed her, taking the opportunity to complain about something else.

"Glynis," Lennox said.

She blinked up at him, called back to herself and the occasion.

"We're married."

"Oh."

HER MOTHER was having a glorious time entertaining what looked to be the whole of Glasgow. Eleanor greeted each guest with a wide smile, easily conveying to them she approved of the match and even the precipitous nature of it. She supervised every one of the servants from Hillshead with aplomb and such a friendly manner everyone was smiling.

If Lennox hadn't treated his servants well, Glynis would have expected a wholesale exodus from Hillshead to their much smaller home.

Every room able to accommodate a guest was filled. People crowded in the doorways, congregated in the halls, pushed against each other as they craned their necks to get a look at Lennox or her.

Glynis planted a smile on her face and pretended to be comfortable being the center of so much interest. The wedding supper served a dual purpose, an official welcome of her back into the Scottish fold and an acknowledgment she was now a Cameron.

Duncan was smiling so often she studied him for a moment, wondering if it was false cheer. But she heard him laugh as he was talking to Mrs. McGillicuddy, an obnoxious lady in her eighties, and decided he was genuinely happy.

The gossip would have continued if she hadn't married Lennox. But now, whatever transpired between them had been forgiven. If she danced naked in the moonlight it wouldn't matter because she was Glynis Cameron. She was the wife of one of the richest men in Glasgow and to be treated with respect.

She stood beside Lennox in the receiving line, accepting all the congratulations while smiling determinedly through the whole thing. For the first time she was grateful for nights of having to wear an eternal smile when her feet hurt or her corset was too tight.

Some of the women guests insisted on anointing themselves with so much perfume a cloud of it followed them, occasionally clashing with other scents. Washing over everything was the smell of the food from the buffet in the larger parlor, a room they rarely used since it was so drafty. Tonight the size was a blessing and the drafts blew the air clean of roses, lily of the valley, and something smelling like rotting heather.

One of their guests, Mrs. McElweny, who insisted on wearing a black bonnet adorned with grotesque purple and red flowers—blossoms never existing in nature—stopped in front of her. The black bombazine she wore in honor of the husband who'd died twenty years earlier was a little rusty but her voice was as sharp as a newly honed knife.

"I don't expect it's normal nowadays for girls such as you to mourn their dear departed husbands all that long."

Just as Glynis was trying to find some words to respond, the woman startled her by smiling and winking.

"However," she said, leaning forward when Lennox turned to greet another guest, "if it was Lennox Cameron, you are to be excused."

She was left staring after Mrs. McElweny.

Lennox sometimes helped her recall a guest as a girl she'd known from school or a man with whom he did business. Glynis nodded, made a note of their names and kept her smile in place.

The next guest was Mr. Peterson, a shopkeeper she knew from her childhood, along with the man's wife and his three daughters, each one barely glancing at her while studiously examining Lennox.

She'd once done the very same, entranced with the look of him. Standing straight and tall, with a ready smile and twinkling green eyes, he was a glorious sight.

Was there ever a man as handsome as him? Or one as fascinating to women?

Charlotte was there, of course, appearing in the receiving line with Archibald.

"Well, it's glad I am to see this day, Glynis." She leaned forward. "You'll keep the gossips at bay, but for only a little while. They'll be counting on their fingers soon enough."

Now was not the time to declare she and Lennox had been relatively virtuous, but not for lack of wishing on her part. She merely smiled at Charlotte and turned to greet the next person.

Matthew Baumann grinned at her.

Startled, she could only stare at him.

"I thought you left Glasgow," she finally said.

"And miss the occasion of your wedding? Or how lovely you look as a new bride?"

"I didn't realize you were invited," she said.

She knew the instant Lennox realized who she was speaking to, could feel the tension as he turned.

"Your mother invited me. I told her you and I had known each other in Washington. Of course, I didn't tell her the nature of our acquaintance."

Was he going to blurt out their history here and now? She wanted to take a step back or even flee but was anchored to the spot by Lennox's hand at the small of her back.

"Perhaps it's time you left," Lennox said, his voice rough.

Baumann's smile didn't dim. "Ask your bride if she wants me gone, Cameron. Or if it would be better to mollify me at the moment and treat me as if I'm a valued guest. Perhaps you might even pour me some wine."

"The buffet is excellent," she said. "I do hope you try it. And the punch. We've three kinds."

Lennox glanced at her, frowning.

Baumann was right. She would do anything to keep him happy. She didn't want the night ruined by the truth.

"Imagine how surprised I was to find you had married again. I truly hope this union is more pleasant than the last."

She placed her hand on Lennox's arm when he would have advanced on the other man.

Signaling with her right hand, she attracted the attention of one of the maids from Hillshead.

"Take Mr. Baumann to the buffet table," she said. "If he needs anything, let me know."

He grinned at her.

Lennox's arm bunched beneath her hand. She saw the quick flash in his eyes and wished she could say something, anything, to ease his anger. There was nothing to say, nothing but a full explanation. Must she utter it on her wedding night?

Give me one night with Lennox. One night with a bit of laughter, the chance to experience my girlish wishes and dreams.

Her smile was only a rictus of expression as she turned to the next guest. Taking a deep breath and then releasing it didn't ease the tightness in her chest.

Finally, blessedly, they were done with the receiving line.

Lennox moved off to greet someone, leaving her temporarily alone. Was he looking for Baumann? What was she going to do about that situation?

"What's wrong, Glynis?"

She glanced up to see Duncan standing there. He reached out and grabbed her hand, pulling her to a secluded corner in the small parlor.

"What did Baumann want?" he asked.

"How do you know him?"

"He introduced himself to me at Hillshead. He told me he worked for the United States government, which I took to mean the Union. Does he?"

She nodded.

Duncan frowned. "That must not please Lennox."

"No, it doesn't. He can't abide Baumann. It would be wise if they weren't in the same room together."

"Why is he here?" Duncan asked.

"To offer me his felicitations. To bedevil me. To make my life miserable. Probably all of those."

Her emotions were in a whirl, churning in her stomach until she couldn't even think of eating. Perhaps she should have a glass of wine or two until she became tipsy. She wouldn't be so anxious then.

What would Lennox say if his bride was drunk?

"I'll go and tell him to leave."

She shook her head. "No, don't. Just leave him alone."

Duncan frowned at her. "It's your wedding day," he said. "You're supposed to be happy. Overjoyed. You don't look happy or overjoyed."

Then she would have to try harder.

"Nonsense," she said. "I'm very happy. Truly."

He didn't need to know how close she was to tears.

She stood on tiptoe and kissed Duncan on the cheek.

"Thank you for being such a good brother," she said. "Now I'm going to find my husband."

Husband. Lennox was her husband. She shouldn't be thinking of anything but that.

She found him surrounded by a group of people. When she moved to stand beside him, he reached out with one arm and pulled her closer. The gesture would have been unthinkable the day before and now only generated smiles.

For a few minutes conversation rolled over her in waves, but everyone stopped speaking when Lennox called for attention. He put his arm around her shoulders, smiled down at her, then addressed the crowd.

"The recent tragedy has made Glynis and I cognizant of the passing of time. We didn't want to waste another moment until we were wed. Thank you for coming to help us celebrate this day."

Lennox could have had a position in the diplomatic service himself. By his words, he managed to convey their union wasn't unexpected as much as urgently desired. Plus, he also addressed Gavin Whittaker's death.

For the next two hours she glided among the guests,

asking after people she remembered, ensuring they were fed and had a glass of punch. Lennox did the same, their singular efforts linked by an occasional glance across the room.

She had planned to avoid Baumann but to her surprise he'd disappeared. Had Lennox or Duncan told him to leave? She wouldn't put it past either of them. Had his main reason for attending the reception been to unnerve her? If that were the case, he'd succeeded.

Finally, most of the guests left. The only ones remaining were friends of her mother's who sat in the small parlor discussing their own marriages and those of their children.

When she and Lennox entered the room, Eleanor stood, hugged her and kissed her on the cheek. When she pulled back, there were tears in her mother's eyes.

"Be happy, my darling daughter. I know you will be. How I wish your dear father were here."

She turned to Lennox, hugging and kissing him as well.

"Now, off you go," she said.

The other three women smiled at her knowingly. Could this moment be any more embarrassing?

Lennox held out his hand for her and she grabbed it, their fingers entwining.

One of the ladies tittered as they left the room.

Were they going to discuss their own wedding nights the minute they left? If so, she wanted to be gone before the discussion began.

The carriage sat at the front of the house. Lanterns illuminated the drive and the faces of the last guests waving at them.

Lennox opened the door for her and she gathered up her skirts, moving inside. He entered the carriage and sat opposite her.

"Were you and Baumann lovers?"

He hadn't forgotten Baumann's appearance. How foolish of her to hope he would. A flaw of hers, to keep thinking circumstances would improve just because she wished it.

"You've asked me that before," she said.

"You said you weren't, but he treated you like an ex-lover. Like he was jealous."

When she didn't respond, he continued.

"You're my wife."

She stared at him, hearing the echo of that declaration across the years. Richard, too, had said the very same thing in an identical tone.

"Which means I'm a mirror of you, is that it?"

He frowned. "Which means he damn well better not address you in public anymore and certainly not with a leer."

She blinked, surprised at his vehemence.

"I know you had a life, Glynis. I know parts of it were exciting. Glasgow must seem dull for you in comparison."

It was her turn to frown. "Of course it isn't," she said. "It's my home."

"I know things happened to you. I know you were married. I know you have secrets, but you don't have to keep those secrets to yourself. You can share them with me."

How many times had she told herself that? The one time she'd tried to tell him she'd found a dead man.

He didn't say anything else but it was evident he wasn't pleased with her silence. His eyes were stones and his mouth narrowed to a straight line. The smiling bridegroom of a few minutes earlier had disappeared.

She wanted to tell him that the truth was too stark for this night of beginnings. She didn't want to talk about Richard, Washington, or Baumann.

For a little while she wanted to be Glynis MacIain, newly married. She wanted to expunge seven years from her life and pretend they never existed. All the good experiences she'd had she would do without. It didn't matter that she'd met important people—who was she in the grand scheme of world history? It didn't matter she'd amused some dignitaries, flattered others, and been a friend to some.

She'd erase every kind word, every compliment, every adventure, every soaring note of music, every amusing play, every trace of awe to have the years rolled back.

Perhaps she could be like the poor woman she'd heard about in Washington who lost her mind on the deaths of her husband and sons. The poor thing could not remember who she was, so she spent the entire day smiling at other people, looking deeply into their faces as if seeking her own identity in their appearance.

She'd claim the loss of her memory. She'd claim she could remember nothing but her life in Scotland.

Baumann? Who was he? Just a man she might have known once.

Just this night, that's all. She wanted one night.

Suddenly there were at Hillshead, lights illuminating the drive and every window in the house, making it appear like a beehive. But the earnest bees were all standing outside in a long line.

"They're waiting to greet you," he said. "As my wife."

He opened the door, the lantern light falling on his face. His eyes were watchful, his lips pressed together as if to hold back his words.

She wished Baumann to perdition for spoiling this night, for hauling the past into her life and for tainting what should have been a glorious celebration filled with love and laughter.

Extending her hand, she stepped out of the carriage, wondering how she could possibly salvage her wedding night.

The truth wouldn't do it.

Chapter 28

*H*er belongings had been delivered to a guest suite prepared for her at Hillshead. Would she and Lennox share a bed? Would she move into his room?

Questions for which she didn't have answers at the moment.

The suite was lovely, the mahogany furniture upholstered in a pale yellow reminding her of bright summer days. Blue tassels hung on the curtains, and pillows in the same blue color were in the corners of the settee.

She bathed and dressed in a pale pink peignoir set, a gift from her mother.

She'd dreamed of coming to Lennox as a maiden bride, knowing his initiation would be gentle and tender. She was no longer a maiden but a woman with memories. Still, she wouldn't be afraid with Lennox.

Lennox wouldn't tell her she must remain motionless—or would he? Was she wrong in wanting him to touch her?

She stared at herself in the mirror. Why was she pale? She wasn't afraid, or was she? They'd already shared kisses and she loved kissing him.

Would he want the light on? Would he want to see any part of her? Richard never had.

One of her mother's favorite expressions was: comparisons are odious. Nor was it quite fair to compare

Richard to Lennox in any degree. Richard was short, with reddish brown hair, a pale complexion, and features as fine as any woman.

Lennox was handsome and charming. His looks were only a part of who he was, and not the most important part. He was generous and kind, intelligent and thoughtful, one of the best people she'd ever known.

To compare Lennox to Richard was like comparing the sun to one single candle. And maybe that was the problem.

She knew she was Richard's equal or better. She knew she surpassed him in intellect, resolve, poise, and even morality. With Lennox, she felt pushed and prodded to be more than herself, better than she was.

He was going to come to her soon and she would welcome him. Not as she dreaded Richard's visits but as she might have if there'd never been a Richard Smythe in her life.

She wished she could have come to Lennox without a memory of dread.

She didn't know enough despite having been a wife for five years. She wanted to know what would give Lennox delight. What would make his eyes darken with desire? Should she be naked beneath the sheets? Should she be standing in her peignoir and nightgown in front of a lamp, the better to be seen?

Proper wives didn't do such things, did they?

How foolish she'd been in telling herself she felt nothing for Lennox. Something in her nature was inextricably tied to him. Maybe it was memory. Maybe it was because he was the repository of so many of her secrets, how she loved the croaking sound frogs made and the summer rain in her face. He was the only one who knew she'd taken his boat out and sailed on the Clyde in the moonlight. She'd been Glynis to him. Not Mrs. Richard Smythe or the British Legation's senior attaché's wife or a Scot whose accent was being over-written every day.

With him, she wasn't who she'd become but who she was deep inside. A girl who'd been raised in love, nurtured with laughter, given much, and unwisely expected the same treatment from the world.

What had she thought? That all she had to do was snap her fingers and everything she desired would drop, like an overripe plum, in her lap? Perhaps that's why she wasn't critical of the women others called "overindulged" in the diplomatic service. She had been exactly the same. After her marriage to Richard, she'd learned only too quickly that the world had no intention of bowing to her demands.

It was as if God, having realized how immature and selfish she'd been, said to her, "Glynis, you must learn to give up all you hold as dear, all you cherish, and all you love. In return, I shall grant you some measure of wisdom."

A double-edged sword, wisdom, since it could be so easily used to see her own flaws.

From the day of her marriage, she and God had an uneasy truce. She didn't ask Him for anything and He didn't take anything else away from her.

But tonight, this night, this wondrous night she'd never thought would pass, was an answer to a hundred unvoiced prayers.

She strolled through the room, her fingers trailing over the silky wood of the bureau, the writing desk, and the armoire until she halted in front of the vanity and stared at herself in the mirror. Her cheeks were flushed now, her lips pink.

Her feelings hadn't changed. Lennox still made her heart stutter. She wanted his arms around her. She wanted to confide in him, to be herself with him in a way she hadn't been for years.

She didn't want to measure every single word before it came out of her mouth. She wanted to laugh with abandon and love without restraint. She wanted Lennox to know her in a way he had when she was a girl, to reacquaint him with who she truly was, not the woman she'd become. She wanted to return to innocence even though that was an impossible wish.

She wanted to be improvident and reckless, the girl who'd run headlong into disaster and only later realized what she'd done.

Yet she was nervous. No, she wasn't nervous. Perhaps anxious was the best word for what she felt. Or afraid?

No, she wasn't afraid of Lennox, but she might be wary about the situation. Would he change with marriage? Would he want to quell the part of her she'd recently rediscovered? Banish the girl with the courage of the archangels and summon forth the woman with excellent manners and restrained bearing?

He didn't knock on the door, but merely opened it, strolled in, and closed it in one movement.

They stared at each other.

Was there some magical word she was supposed to say? If so, she didn't know the greeting. Instead, she took a step back, closer to the bed.

"You needn't look like I'm about to ravish you, Glynis. I don't have to be here at all if you'd prefer not."

She smiled, pushed into amusement by his irritation. Or, she thought, studying his face, maybe it wasn't irritation at all. Maybe Lennox was feeling a similar vulnerability.

She had fought her own emotions for so long it was a relief to admit them at last. This man held her heart in the palm of his hands and yet he didn't know it.

Her feelings had only grown in the intervening years. They'd matured in absence and escalated with longing. Loneliness had made them sprout shoots until they wound through her heart, each tiny leaf bearing his name.

"We need to talk about Baumann," he said.

She shook her head. "No. Not tonight. Not on our wedding night."

He looked as if he wanted to say something but restrained himself.

"Please, Lennox. Don't let him ruin our wedding night."

She wanted to tell him about Washington. The words wouldn't come. If she did tell him the truth, it wouldn't be a bridge between them but create a wall.

Love me. There, could she say that? Could she demand such a thing of him?

What would he say if she asked, "Can we pretend for a while? You never asked another woman to be your wife and I wasn't married to someone else."

Her imagination could easily create that world. They would be filled with joy, not suspicion. Laughter and kindness and love would fill the room.

Lennox was her husband. Did the past matter right at this moment? Did it matter if they were joined because of gossip or expediency or even pity?

"I've wanted to kiss you for a week," she said. "Seven days have never seemed so long."

One of Lennox's eyebrows winged upward.

"Have you?"

She nodded. "When I was a girl, I envisioned you coming to me on our wedding night. I thought about how it would be."

His eyes seemed to darken.

"And what did you imagine?"

She walked to him slowly, taking her time, watching his face as she did so. His cheeks were bronzed, his eyes holding the slightest edge of wariness.

When she reached him she placed her right hand on his shirted chest. He'd come fully dressed to her. Not in his robe or nightwear, but in a shirt and trousers. Had he expected her to banish him?

"I would be in bed, waiting for you," she said. "My hair would be artfully draped on the pillow. The sheet would be turned down to reveal my white nightgown. Roses would be in vases throughout the room."

"You're wearing pink," he said. "And we've neglected the roses."

"I've decided the imagination of a child doesn't matter. You are the only important part of my daydream."

He bent his head, slowly enough to give her a chance to move away if she wished. Oh, but she didn't wish. When his lips finally touched hers, she sighed in relief.

The kiss was an invitation.

She could barely breathe when he wrapped his arms around her and deepened the kiss.

In that instant she knew a greater truth than any she'd ever known before. Nothing mattered but him. He was her anchor, her lodestone, her faith.

What would she have done if something had happened to him? If he'd had the same kind of accident that had blinded his father? She knew, as he pulled her tighter until not even a breath could separate him, she would have come home to be with him. She would have braved censure and scandal and ruin.

What would she have done if fate had taken him from her? She would've heard the news very calmly, returned to her small house, closed the door of her bedroom and willed herself to die.

But now she wanted to live. She wanted to see the dance of lights behind her eyelids as he kissed her, their tongues dueling, their breaths merging.

His hands were on her bottom, lifting her closer and tighter to him.

She slapped her hands against his chest, pulling on the linen of his shirt, needing to touch him, to feel his skin. She wanted to touch him everywhere, memorize him with her fingers.

The strength of his arms, the firmness of his shoulders, attested to the physical work he did at the yard.

"Take your clothes off," she said. "Now."

His chuckle annoyed her because he wasn't fast enough. She put both hands on either side of the placket of his shirt and pulled, feeling the buttons give. She scratched his skin, stretched her arms around until she felt his back, fingers splayed to feel all of him. It wasn't enough.

Her breasts pressed against the hard planes of his chest as her hands wrapped around his neck.

She blinked open her eyes to find him smiling down at her, his gaze intent.

She only smiled back at him and rained kisses over his chest.

His indrawn breath made her want to laugh. Good, let him feel a fraction of the wildness racing through her.

She grabbed his head and held him still for her kiss, wishing he could erase all the loneliness of the past years. She wanted to pull off his clothes, tear them if she must, do something improper and wanton. She was not herself, but that was a lie, wasn't it?

This was the woman who'd always been tamped down, pushed to the back and ignored. Richard had never seen this creature. The only person who ever really knew her was Lennox.

She wanted him in a way she'd never wanted any other man. He was hers and he had always been hers since she was a child and first saw him.

His clothes were too concealing for this summer night with its warm air and soft scented breeze.

A tide was rushing in to nearly drown her.

She needed her clothes off. She was too hot, too constrained.

If she'd felt any modesty before he arrived, it was gone now, buried beneath a need racing through her like lightning.

His lips on her throat accelerated her pulse even further. She shivered, gripping his shoulders as he unfastened the bow holding her nightgown closed.

Her knees weakened as he pushed the garment open. His fingers danced across her skin, hesitated at the top of her breasts.

"Yes," she whispered. *Yes, oh yes.*

She felt as if she'd never been truly alive until his fingertips skimmed her skin. He thumbed a nipple, then tipped her chin up to place a kiss on her mouth.

Her heart was beating so quickly she felt breathless.

"Did you imagine this, too?" he asked, looking down at her.

Words were impossible.

How could she, when she'd never experienced anything like this passion before tonight?

She wrapped her hands around his neck, her eyes on his face.

Delight and tenderness warred for dominance, and shot through it all was wonder he could do this to her. With a kiss he'd changed her to a woman wild with desire.

He led her to the bed but she didn't care where they were. He could have loved her on the soil of Scotland, the earth a pillow for her head. In a carriage, on one of his ships, in a balloon tethered high in the air: the location didn't matter. Only he mattered. Only Lennox.

When he placed his lips on her breast, her heart

stopped, then thudded to a start again. She heard her nightgown tear but she didn't care. Tear every garment she had, it wasn't important.

She stared up at him, grateful he'd left the lamp lit. A lock of hair fell and she brushed it back with tender fingers. His shirt hung open, and now his trousers were, too. She reached down and cupped him, amazed and thrilled.

"At least you're not wearing a hoop, Glynis," he said. His voice was breathless but held a note of humor.

"And you're still wearing too many clothes, Lennox."

His laughter summoned her own. She had the thought passion should involve all the senses: joy and wonder and perhaps a little trepidation.

His lips were on her breasts again, worshipping them. She lay exposed to him in the lamplight and didn't care. He pulled on one nipple and she could feel the sensation in the core of her. Her hands tightened on his shoulders, her nails probably making a mark. Good, let her claim him as her own.

She wanted to touch him everywhere but she also wanted to be touched. There, where her waist flared to her hips. There, at the base of her neck, and then all the other spots craving his touch. Her breasts, between her thighs, her bottom, all seemed to be sentient parts of her, craving to be stroked and loved and praised.

His hands were suddenly between her thighs, stroking her, learning her intimately. She should've been flustered, nearly virginal. But she widened her legs and pulled on his arms, a wordless encouragement.

Delight shuddered through her.

Chapter 29

*T*his wild woman in his arms was Glynis. The realization made him slow his movements, mark these moments as rare and special.

This was Glynis, and his fingers stroked across her skin, feeling her pebbled response. He cupped her breasts, his thumb smoothing an erect nipple. Hearing her gasp harnessed his own breath, stilled his heart and set it to racing again.

This was Glynis and he'd never forget this night.

Glynis. His wife, his love.

He pressed his lips to her throat, her pulse jumping at his touch. She placed her hands against his chest and he could feel her touch all the way to his heart.

God, the Kirk, and the whole of Scotland applauded this consummation.

She wrapped her arms around his neck, sighed his name against his throat, making him close his eyes in wonder and thanksgiving.

She was perfect. From her pointed chin to her beautiful collarbones to her shoulders to her full breasts with their large areolas and perky nipples to the long line of her legs, Glynis was a woman to fuel his dreams.

His fingers splayed across her concave belly.

She raised up a little at his touch. He smiled, pressed a kiss to her navel, inciting a shiver from her.

He kissed her again and his thoughts simply

stopped, adrift in the sheer physical delight of kissing Glynis.

His right hand trailed from breast to navel, delved lower to play among the curls guarding her mound. She was wet for him, her body readying. Her legs opened as he gently stroked her.

"Lennox," she said, her voice a gasp of sound. Her eyes fluttered open, her glazed look making his heart thud. "Please."

You're mine now, Glynis. Mine.

Words he kept to himself, but a sentiment he tried to express in the tenderness of his touch.

He entered her a second later, every sensation in his body attuned to that slow movement. This was Glynis and she was ensnaring him with her sighs, her gasps, the hitch in her breathing. This was Glynis. When she opened her arms, he lowered his forehead to the pillow, inhaling her scent. This was Glynis. When she shivered and sobbed in his arms, he held her, too, feeling like he'd achieved the greatest feat in the world to bring her satisfaction.

This was Glynis—a last thought before everything grayed and bliss stormed through him.

SHE COULD feel herself flush and knew he was looking at her. The lamp was still lit. Surely she should have demanded it be extinguished. She'd been so hungry for him it hadn't mattered if every freckle, mole, or wrinkle showed.

Now, however, she really should pull up the sheet, shouldn't she? Perhaps demand a bit of privacy, decorum—modesty, if nothing else.

Instead, she lay there with a smile curving her lips, her heart dancing a little jig, her skin pebbling. Delight surged through her, as if every part of her rejoiced in this new sensation.

Passion was a heady drug and she could easily become addicted.

"Did I bring you pleasure, Glynis?"

She felt her cheeks heat. Even the tips of her ears warmed. She really wanted the sheet but she blinked open her eyes and forced herself to face him.

"Are you very experienced, Lennox?"

He smiled but didn't answer her. She wanted to press him but it didn't seem at all proper to ask how many women he'd loved right at the moment.

"I should hire you out to the Americans. They could use you as a weapon in their war. All you have to do is look at the women of America and they'd fall swooning at your feet."

His laugh made her smile.

She took his hand and pressed it against her breast where he could feel the pounding beat of her heart.

The pleasure had splintered her, making her moan aloud.

More than I have ever felt. More than I ever imagined. Until tonight I hadn't known it was possible to feel this way. I had not even dreamed my soul could go spinning among the stars and I would be left here, to be reborn again by the sight of your smile.

How did she say that?

She was so filled with emotion she could barely speak. Why hadn't she seduced him seven years ago?

He was so kissable, she had to cup his face with one hand and move her mouth to his.

The world slid away like a silk chemise.

He tasted wonderful, his tongue moving deep. She opened her mouth wider, welcoming and willing.

Long moments later she pulled back to find Lennox smiling at her.

She moved to her side and he did as well until they faced each other. Although she was naked she felt heated. The warmth must come from him being so near, or that his arm was around her, pulling her close.

She hadn't known anything about lovemaking, had she? She could count how many times she and Richard had conjugal relations, as he called it. She didn't want to recall those nights. Not like now. She'd remember *now* forever.

"I'm not as good as you," she said, sliding her hand across the sheet until their fingertips joined.

"Am I good?" he said.

"I'm not as kind or generous or giving."

His face changed, the easy teasing look in his eyes vanishing.

"Yes, you are. You always have been. You would do anything for your parents or for Duncan."

She would do anything for him. Didn't he know that?

Her fingers reached out, played at the nape of his neck.

"I've always liked your hair," she said. The words came without her volition, as if the nineteen-year-old girl inside her was being urged forward. *Come and say whatever you will. Tell him how he fascinates you. Leave no secret unspoken.*

"I've always liked yours," he said. "I like how it's lighter at your temples."

"And your eyes," she said. "I like how sometimes they look green and sometimes gray."

"I like the dark circle around yours," he said. "It makes your eyes look mysterious."

She rolled over on her back, smiling up at the ceiling.

"I'm not that mysterious," she said, turning her head.

"Yes, you are," he said, his smile vanishing.

She wouldn't allow Baumann to intrude yet. Soon. Soon, she would tell him everything.

Would Lennox regret marrying her? She would have years to change his mind, wouldn't she?

"I'm glad I kissed you," she said. "I'm glad I came to Hillshead and Lucy saw."

"So am I."

"I should have seduced you," she said. "But I suspect you would have been honorable and refused me."

"A man made of stone?"

She smiled.

"If you had succeeded, what would Lucy have said then?"

She shook her head. "No more than she already said."

"But you, independent as you are, were prepared to face down the gossips."

She glanced at him again, considering his words. "Only until you kissed me," she said.

"You agreed before I kissed you."

"Did I? Perhaps I was simply anticipating the kiss."

She forced a smile to her face because she felt suddenly on the verge of tears. How odd to go from bright amusement to confused tears in the space of seconds.

"Why didn't you marry Rose?" she asked.

"She wasn't you."

Her heart sputtered to a stop then started again.

She looked at him, allowing everything she felt to show on her face, in her eyes. She couldn't recall ever feeling as vulnerable as now.

He was her lover. But more, he was her love.

The knock on the bedroom door startled her. In one movement Lennox was up, donning his trousers.

She grabbed the sheet, wrapped it around herself and sat listening.

"Tell him I'll be with him shortly," Lennox said.

"Yes, sir," Mrs. Hurst said.

Lennox closed the door and turned to her, his face stony.

"What's wrong?" she asked.

"The *Raven*. It's on fire."

Chapter 30

*T*he messenger was one of the apprentice designers, a lad he'd hired from Edinburgh who had a love of ships as strong as his own. Henry was tall and gangly still, with a long neck and a prominent Adam's apple. His face was lean almost to the point of being emaciated and his wrists hung out of the sleeves of his shirts.

He'd heard one of the other draftsmen call Henry a stork, and the description seemed apt. But once he had enough to eat, the lad would fill in and not look so scrawny or ill-fitting in his own body.

"Sir," he said, standing when Lennox entered the library.

"What happened, Henry?"

"Sir," Henry said again, turning his hat in his hands and staring down at the floor.

Lennox could handle most problems by remembering two rules: nothing was as desperate as it seemed and little was accomplished overnight.

"Is she gone?"

"No, sir, the extra watchmen you assigned saw it quick enough. They were able to put the fire out. But the wheelhouse is damaged and part of the deck will have to be rebuilt."

"Go on back to the yard," he said now. "Tell Samuel I'll be there as soon as I can."

Henry nodded.

"You'll be rebuilding her, sir?"

"I've spent a year building her, Henry. I'm not about to let a little fire stop me now."

Fraser Trenholm & Company technically owned the *Raven* and had since he'd turned over the ship to Gavin. Ostensibly acting as an agent for the Confederate States of America, the company provided a packet service between Charleston and Liverpool. They also procured ships for the Confederate fleet, a duty not as well-publicized.

Although the bank draft had already been deposited, Gavin's death complicated the situation.

He might not be legally responsible, but he felt morally required to make repairs. The best thing to do was buy back the ship. After she was rebuilt he could either sell it to the Confederacy again or another buyer.

"The men think she's unlucky."

He didn't want to hear that. Sailors might be superstitious but shipbuilders were equally so. If a man got it into his head a ship was unlucky, he'd find a dozen reasons to prove it. When the *Raven* was repaired, she'd have a reputation. Not a good beginning to any ship and one that would make it difficult to sell her to another buyer. Not even the Confederacy was desperate enough to take on a ship thought to be cursed.

"Let's see if we can prove them wrong," he said.

Maybe it was time he went to the authorities and told them what he knew: Matthew Baumann acted for the Union. The man was determined to stop the Confederate navy from acquiring more ships by any means necessary, even if he had to resort to murder and arson.

"*HAS MY* husband returned from the yard, Mrs. Hurst?" Glynis asked casually, only stumbling a little over the word husband.

How odd to call Lennox husband. But they'd only been married a day. Only one day and her life seemed upside down.

She had the oddest need to smile, and she did so to the maid dusting the paintings hanging on the wall beside the staircase, to the maid anxiously bobbing a curtsy at the door of the family dining room, to the maid who'd served her breakfast, and now to the housekeeper, Mrs. Hurst.

Despite the fire on the *Raven,* the world was a grand and glorious place this morning. At least her little corner of the world, bathed in sunshine, scented with roses, and graced with a sweet summer breeze.

"No, Mrs. Cameron, he hasn't," the woman said, inclining her head toward her.

Mrs. Cameron. She caught her breath. She was Mrs. Cameron, wasn't she?

Mrs. McNair had been the housekeeper when she left for London. What had happened to the dear lady? She'd been older, with a bun of red hair and blue eyes always holding a warm expression.

"Have you been at Hillshead long?" she asked.

Mrs. Hurst must have been a beauty when young. Even now the housekeeper was very attractive. Wrinkles crinkled the skin at the outward corners of her eyes and framed her mouth, but there was no mistaking the perfection of her well-formed lips, aquiline nose, and tranquil blue eyes. Her brown hair was laced with gray but she didn't stoop. Nor did her hands have the veined look common in so many older women. Whatever her age, she carried it proudly.

Glynis had not been able to afford a housekeeper in Washington, and Mabel and her mother handled all the duties in their home. How did one treat a housekeeper? She would imagine very respectfully. If not, the woman could make daily life miserable.

"I haven't been, no, Mrs. Cameron. Only two years now."

"I imagine Hillshead keeps you busy. Everything seems to run beautifully."

The woman inclined her head in acceptance of the compliment.

"We have a great many people on staff, Mrs. Cameron. That always makes the upkeep of a large house like Hillshead easier."

"How many people?" she asked. Had any of them once worked at the mill?

"Thirty-two, Mrs. Cameron. Seventeen maids, two scullery maids, two cooks, four gardeners, and seven employed at the stable."

Thirty-two names to memorize and thirty-two people to meet.

"Could you furnish me with a list, Mrs. Hurst, along with their duties?"

The woman looked surprised but she didn't demur.

"Of course, Mrs. Cameron. When would be an acceptable time to go over the menus?"

"Did Mary discuss those with you?"

The housekeeper nodded.

"I think, until I have time to talk with Miss Cameron, it would be best to continue as things are. After that, we can decide who handles what."

The woman only nodded but there was a small smile on her lips. Had she passed some test?

She didn't want to usurp Mary's authority or take over all her duties. That wasn't a good way to start a relationship with a new sister-in-law.

"Would you ask the stablemaster if there's a carriage I can use?"

"We have three carriages, Mrs. Cameron," the woman said proudly, almost as if the question were an insult. "One of them is Mr. Cameron's, of course. I'm certain one of the other two would be available."

"Thank you. I'd like to go to the yard."

The woman's eyebrows nearly disappeared into her hair. "The yard, Mrs. Cameron?"

At her nod, the housekeeper stepped back. "I'll let Mr. McElwee know."

Rising from the breakfast table, she raced up the staircase without a shred of decorum, grabbed her reticule, checked her hair in the mirror, and was down again in less than five minutes. Lennox wouldn't return to Hillshead for hours and she wanted to know about the *Raven*. But the ship's fate paled beneath the need to see him.

As a newlywed, perhaps she was supposed to be a little shy around her husband. But this was Lennox. The anticipation of seeing him again all dressed and proper made her cheeks warm. Would he recall the last time he saw her, naked with not even a sheet to cover her?

She couldn't help but smile.

"*I BEG* your pardon, Mrs. Cameron, but would this be your umbrella?"

Glynis glanced at the stablemaster. A portly man, he reminded her of a bear with his full brown beard and bushy hair, especially standing as he was with his legs braced far apart. His large pawlike hands held out a black umbrella with an intricately carved crook handle.

She shook her head. "No, Mr. McElwee," she said. "It isn't. Could it be my husband's?"

My husband: there was that word again. How strange it had the ability to make her smile now.

"I've already asked him, ma'am. It isn't." He frowned

at the offending article. "I've a dislike of anything not in its proper place, Mrs. Cameron. I'll put it in the lost bay. After a month or so, if no one claims it, one of us will take it home or give it to one of the maids."

"That sounds like the best policy," she said.

She settled into the carriage, arranged her skirts, and placed her hands together on her lap. Outwardly, she was the picture of decorum. Inside, her stomach jumped with excitement. She would see Lennox soon.

At the yard, seabirds clamored overhead, their squawking cries barely heard over the hum of activity on the docks. They passed three sets of Clydesdales pulling wagons piled high with timber.

Once, the rhythm of the cotton mills had punctuated Glasgow's day, with a third of Glasgow's workforce earning their living in the textile industry. Now the shipyards employed more men, dictating the time work began, when lunch was taken, and the end of the work day.

When the carriage halted in front of the Cameron and Company offices, she didn't wait for the driver to open the carriage door but did it herself, hopping out of the vehicle before the steps unfurled.

The scene today differed from the last time she was here. Now dozens of men scrambled over the *Raven* like industrious ants. Their shouting mingled with ringing hammers, the screech of winches, and ropes jerked tight against the weight of timbers being lowered into place. A briny breeze heavy with the sharp odors of paint and varnish made her nose itch. As she neared the office, the stench of smoke grew stronger.

She stood at the base of the steps, hoping the damage to the *Raven* wasn't worse than what she could see from there. Traces of soot still lingered at the base of one of the smokestacks, and most of the forecastle had been dismantled prior to being rebuilt.

After a few minutes she turned and climbed the rest of the steps, opening the door to the office.

All but one of the drafting tables were occupied, four of them by young men looking curiously similar to each other. She guessed their age as below twenty. Each was thinner than he should have been. They glanced up when she entered, returning to their tasks after a quick perusal of her.

Lennox was seated at the desk in the corner, and she walked toward him, her smile blossoming. He stood, walking around the desk, stretching out his hands.

"Glynis," he said. "I didn't expect to see you here."

"I came to see how the *Raven* was faring." And you.

She felt herself warm, looked down at their joined hands, then smiled up at him.

Did he know how young she felt? She might have been reborn. Was that what love did to you? Or was it passion energizing every part of her body until she felt new?

"Are you well?" he asked softly, his voice holding a tender note.

If the office had been empty, she would've stretched up on tiptoe and kissed him. How lonely his mouth seemed at the moment.

"I am," she said. So wonderful her mood colored the day, touched it with magic. *He* was magic.

He led her around to the chair, and she sat, gripping her reticule with one hand. The other rested on the desk, fingers stretched toward him as if she couldn't bear to be parted even now.

"The damage doesn't look bad," she said. "Is it worse than it looks?"

He shook his head. "It didn't get that much of a start before one of the guards saw it. But it will take a few weeks to repair."

"It wasn't an accident, then."

He shook his head. "No, because of where it started. There's no source of heat and we didn't have a storm last night, so lightning is out as a cause."

She didn't ask if he thought Baumann a suspect. Ignoring the man, however, didn't make him vanish.

"I'm glad you're here," he said, pulling open a drawer. "It's a draft," he said, holding out a piece of paper to her. "For the mill."

She took it, her eyes widening at the amount. She'd never seen a check for so much money.

"I didn't really marry you to save the mill," she said, still staring at it. "Or my reputation, for that matter."

She glanced up at him.

"Regardless, I promised," he said.

The joy she felt a minute ago dimmed. Did he really think she married him because he promised to save the mill?

Didn't he know how she felt about him? Did he need her to say the words? Now wasn't the time, not with the young men behind them. Even if she whispered, *I love you, Lennox,* would he believe her?

Had he forgotten about last night and this morning? Was the passion he'd felt not connected to any other emotion? Did he feel nothing more than lust?

The smile she'd so often worn to official Washington functions crept to her mouth and took up its long held place of honor.

"Thank you," she said, tucking the check into her reticule. "I'm certain Duncan will be grateful."

Standing, she fluffed her skirt, concentrating on the fit of the reticule string around her wrist.

"Glynis . . ." he began.

She shook her head at him. *Do not speak now when it will not matter.*

He seemed to know how close she was to tears. Did

he think, on the morning after their wedding night, she had come to him for money? Did he think her so avaricious?

What did he think of her?

She wasn't you.

What had that meant? Why hadn't she asked?

He stood and accompanied her to the door, reaching in front of her to open it. How gallant he was. How honorable a man Lennox Cameron was and how much she adored him.

How very strange to want to kick him in the shin.

LENNOX STARED after his wife as she made her way carefully down the metal steps. He kicked himself mentally. The draft for the mill had just been one more task he had to accomplish. He hadn't considered giving the check to Glynis might have overtones.

He'd come so close to telling her how he'd felt last night, only to be disturbed by the news the *Raven* was ablaze. Now, without even trying, he'd hurt her feelings. He'd altered her mood until her smile turned brittle and she hadn't looked him in the eyes.

The instant joy he'd felt on seeing her was tarnished now with the knowledge he'd made a mistake.

"I'll be back in a few minutes," he said to the men behind him.

More than one of them nodded. Did they know he was going to have to apologize, and do some groveling while he was at it?

SHE GOT to the carriage without succumbing to tears, a good thing as it turned out.

Matthew Baumann leaned against the carriage with his arms folded and an annoying grin plastered on his face.

She wanted to slap it off him.

"The very last person I want to see now or at any time is you," she said, anger boiling up inside her.

She reached past him for the door handle but he blocked her.

"Get out of my way," she said.

"Or you'll do what, Glynis?" He tilted his head and studied her, his mustache twitching. "You're flushed, my dear. Do we have the estimable Mr. Cameron to thank for that?"

"Will you move?"

"Did you think yourself quit of me, Glynis, by marrying him?"

"You set fire to the *Raven*, didn't you?"

His smile broadened. "Have you taken on his causes as your own? A born wife."

Anger burned away the last of the hurt she felt.

"Did you?"

"Do you care so much about the Confederate cause, Glynis? If so, you've changed since leaving Washington. Is it because of Cameron? Has he swayed you somehow?"

"What do you want from me? I'm not going to betray my husband."

"Just as loyal as you were to Smythe. That didn't turn out well, did it?"

"Go away, Baumann."

"You worked for the Union, Glynis. Have you forgotten?"

As if she could. She stared at him, tilted up her chin and wished him to perdition. Between Lennox and Baumann, her day had turned to ashes.

"Step back, Baumann," Lennox said from behind her. "I've half a mind to detain you until the police get here. I'll bet they'd be very interested in your movements around the time Whittaker was murdered. Not to mention what you were doing last night."

Lennox moved to stand slightly in front of her.

"I wasn't in Glasgow when Whittaker was murdered," Baumann said. "And I've already spoken to the police. I'm not your man, Cameron."

"Then what the hell are you doing here now?"

"Talking to your wife? Or is that forbidden now? Are you going to have as short a leash on her as Smythe did?"

She glanced at Lennox. She'd seen that thunderous expression before and it didn't bode well for the recipient.

Baumann smiled. "I'll bet she hasn't told you about Smythe, has she?"

"Get off my property," Lennox said.

"Or you'll what, Cameron?" He made a courtly little bow to Glynis. "Until next time, my dear," he said, smiling. "Somewhere your husband isn't present, I hope."

Baumann walked away, taking his time, turning and waving to them just before he entered his carriage.

"I don't want you seeing that man again," he said.

She had no intention of encountering Matthew Baumann if she could help it. But she wasn't going to allow Lennox to dictate to her.

By the time Richard had died, every slight, every pinprick of annoyance, every tiny cut had magnified until she could barely tolerate being in the same room with him. For years she'd accepted all of his dictates, all of his restrictions, and all of his criticisms.

This marriage was not going to begin with her being treated as a child.

She turned and faced Lennox. "Are you going to provide me with a list of acceptable people with whom I can socialize, Lennox? Are you going to dictate how I act, how I speak, and where I go?"

"When it comes to Matthew Baumann, yes."

"Then you are doomed to disappointment," she said. "Because if I want to meet with the man, I shall. If I want to take tea with the idiot, I will."

Without waiting for his answer, she turned and walked away, annoyed that Baumann had interfered in her marriage once more. She didn't want to champion the man; she had no intention of being in his company again. But the idea of being dictated to by Lennox angered her just as much as Baumann popping up to interfere in her life.

"It isn't safe," Lennox said, following her to the carriage. Before she could reach the latch, he jerked the door open for her. "You don't know what he's capable of."

Oh, she knew. She knew only too well.

"What's this hold he has over you?" Lennox asked. "Why does he keep following you?"

She didn't know how to answer.

"I told myself I should trust you," he said. "But you're not giving me much reason."

She could only stare at him. When he closed the carriage door, she turned and faced forward, feeling a hole open up in her stomach. A block of ice surrounded her along with a sense of despair so deep she knew she might not survive it.

Chapter 31

*L*ennox wasn't home.

Glynis sat at the window, staring out at the dark, willing Lennox to come to her. He hadn't been at dinner, either, but Mrs. Hurst had the maids serve her as if nothing was amiss. Would this be a usual occurrence, her eating alone and wondering at the whereabouts of her husband?

She hadn't asked the housekeeper where Lennox was. Nor had she questioned the maid smiling shyly at her while presenting a strawberry ice as a final course. She'd remained mute when encountering the young girl on the way back to her suite.

The servants at Hillshead were a nice group of people. None of them scowled rather than smiled or complained about their circumstances. She was the only one in the house with a dour attitude.

She hadn't invited Baumann to waylay her. She had no control over Baumann's movements. She couldn't block herself off from the man, hold up her hands and say, "No farther, I beg you." What did Lennox expect her to do? Employ a bodyguard to keep Baumann at bay?

If the man wanted to speak to her, he was going to do so. She knew Baumann well enough to know that. He'd infiltrated almost every single event she attended in Washington. Sometimes, people suspected who he was and kept their distance. Other times, he charmed their hostess into believing he was a man of some importance.

Baumann was a chameleon, becoming anyone he wished to be. He was dangerous, unpredictable, and evidently determined to ruin her marriage.

Why hadn't Lennox come home?

Perhaps he was simply involved in repairing the *Raven*. But he had a history of being considerate to other people. Why hadn't he sent word through a messenger or a note?

Did he expect her to go and apologize for something she couldn't have prevented?

Pride was a terrible thing, both his and hers. His probably kept him at the yard. Hers kept her at Hillshead, confused and uncertain. Yet pride had nearly ruined her life before and she'd learned her lesson. Nor did she want to begin her marriage like this. At the same time, she didn't want to feel inept, lacking in some way, a silly woman who must apologize for every one of her actions.

All she'd done was go to the yard.

The minute Baumann appeared, she'd left no doubt in his mind she wasn't happy to see him. She'd told the man to go away not once but several times. What else was she expected to do?

Tell Lennox the truth.

Tell him.

If her marriage had its peaks and valleys now, what would it be like when she divulged everything? Would there be a chance for happiness after that?

But she had to end it. She had to end it now. Before any more time elapsed. Lennox knew something was wrong. He was curious about her past. Baumann was not going to go away. He wouldn't relinquish his hold over her. If he didn't get what he wanted from her, he was going to ruin her marriage.

Did she want Baumann to tell Lennox the truth before she did?

Baumann had wanted information and she'd given it to him. At first it was only a word here, a word there. She'd told him about other women whose husbands were in greater positions of trust. Before she knew it, she'd provided an entire network to the War Department.

In the morning, when the newspapers came, she forced herself to read the account of the casualties, knowing she bore a share of the burden for each death. The infantryman at Bull Run, the sharpshooter at the Battle of Manassas, could be dead because of her.

Baumann said it was the press of war. "People do things in war they'd never do in peacetime, Glynis." Was that it? Had it been war for her or simply survival? One woman's fate as opposed to that of countless men?

Pride wasn't the reason she couldn't bear to tell Lennox the truth. Shame kept her silent. Not only because of what she'd done, but the why of it.

"*I DON'T* care how much time it takes," Lennox said. "Either she's going to be rebuilt right or not at all. I'll sink her before she leaves the yard less than a hundred percent repaired."

The hapless fitter opened his mouth, but Lennox held up a hand to block whatever the man was about to say.

"Just get it done," he said. "No excuses."

The man nodded and turned, jamming on his hat at the door. He was probably spitting oaths as he descended the stairs.

Lennox didn't give a flying farthing that he hadn't

made any friends today. He was the head of the ship-yard since his father had effectively stepped down. It was up to him to ensure the reputation of Cameron and Company was spotless and the product they produced exemplary. Without the yard, thousands of men would be out of work.

But he didn't have to drive them around the clock. Nor did he have to use his own personal problems to fuel his irritation or bark orders.

He shoved the voice of his conscience away and glared down at the plans in front of him.

What the hell was he doing?

He didn't see the intricate drawings he'd begun over a year ago or the notes added on during the ship's construction.

Instead, the scene with Glynis played out over and over. What the hell had Baumann meant, *somewhere your husband isn't present*?

But the most important question wasn't about Baumann. Why had Glynis looked so afraid?

He knew she hadn't been unfaithful to him. Hell, they'd only been married one day. But she hadn't divulged why Baumann was so intent on her trail.

He was damned if he was going to share his wife with anyone. *His wife*: the words ricocheted in his brain. She was his wife. The irrepressible, wild, intense Glynis MacIain was his wife—and what was he doing? Planning on sleeping on a cot tonight.

"The new load of timber is going to have to wait until morning, Lennox."

He looked up to find his foreman standing in front of the drafting table.

"That's unacceptable."

"Even with the lanterns, it's too dangerous. The winch might fail or slip. Someone might get injured. I'll not take the chance."

"You won't take the chance? When did Cameron and Company become yours?"

"When its owner's head got lodged in his arse," the man said, smiling.

Was it that obvious?

"The same kind of accident blinded your father, Lennox. You don't really mean to put the men in danger, do you?"

"No, damn it," he said, threading his fingers through his hair.

He slapped the plans down on the table in front of him.

"What time is dawn?"

The other man shook his head. "Hell if I know."

"Find out. Tell everyone to go home. We'll start again at dawn."

When the other man left the office, he turned and walked back to his desk in the corner.

He didn't like being played for a fool or having this feeling of uncertainty, one brought about by loving a woman he wasn't certain loved him.

Maybe she had once, but did she now?

Glynis wouldn't hold anything back if she was the same person. She would've been honest with him. But she wasn't, leaving him as torn as he felt right at this moment.

He should summon Baumann to his office and get the truth from him. If she'd had an affair with a man, he wouldn't like it, but it was before they were married. What could he do about it? No, the present concerned him, and the future, neither of which looked particularly pleasant at the moment.

Baumann was going to have to learn things had changed. Somehow he'd get the man banished from Glasgow. At the very least he'd make it clear to Baumann his health was directly tied to leaving Scotland.

He knew enough people in London. Maybe complaining about Baumann through diplomatic channels to the War Department would work.

Anything to keep the man away from Glynis.

He couldn't, however, force himself to go to her as a supplicant. He wouldn't beg, even to Glynis. *Give me any scrap from your table and I'll accept it with gratitude.* A humiliating scenario and one he'd no intention of playing out.

What had Glynis not told him about Smythe? He hadn't wanted to pry into her first marriage, but now he was being slapped in the face with his ignorance.

What had Richard Smythe done to her? What did Baumann know that he didn't?

He hated the idea of Baumann knowing her past when he didn't. What the hell was Glynis hiding? What made her look pale enough to faint? What made her afraid?

He didn't have answers to any of his questions. He wanted to put his arms around Glynis and demand that she tell him all her secrets, all her wants and desires, everything she'd hidden from him.

But one person didn't have the right to demand that from another.

Not even a man in love with his wife.

Chapter 32

*S*leep wouldn't come.

Grabbing her wrapper, she left her suite. As lovely as the rooms were, the walls seemed to be closing in on her. Were the servants still awake? She hoped not, since she didn't want witnesses to her restlessness.

She walked to the head of the stairs. From here the steps twisted like a snake down to the first floor. She placed her hand on the banister, the polished mahogany warming beneath her touch as if the wood were still alive.

She descended the staircase, the steps illuminated by moonlight streaming through the cupola.

In the silence and stillness, she could almost hear the house's heartbeat. The whistling wind was its breath, the pulsing of the boiler its heart, and the surge of water in its pipes its bloodstream. A door creaking, a shutter shivering, were Hillshead's bones settling.

As a girl she hadn't noticed details about the house: the fine weave of the carpets, the plaster alcoves or mahogany wainscoting. Nor had she noted the unique seafaring detail on each of the doors on the second floor. Craftsmen had carved a clipper ship into the upper panel of her bedroom door, repeating the surging waves along the frame.

She'd never thought of Lennox as wealthy. Of course she knew he was, but there were so many more important things about Lennox. He was part of Cameron and Company, its heir and its head. Until she'd come to live here herself, she'd never considered the vast fortune Hillshead represented.

The house was at least a dozen times larger than her own home, and larger than any other in Glasgow. Hillshead was filled with treasures. Besides the statuary—each alcove boasted a marble rendition of a Greek or Roman god—and the gilt-framed paintings of past generations of Camerons, there were porcelain urns and figurines, bejeweled potpourri containers, and medieval-style tapestries hanging on several walls.

It's possible she wouldn't have noticed the touches of wealth had she not lived in so many places.

As she was waiting for passage home, she'd spent the last three months in America living in a boardinghouse, an experience she never wanted to repeat. She'd had to share the facilities with all of the tenants.

Now her bathroom was attached to her bedroom. Strips of cedar sheeted the walls. The bowls and tub were of beige and brown marble as smooth as the inside of a shell. The brass faucets were so polished she could see her face in them. Even the water closet had brass fittings and a wooden handle carved in the shape of a ship.

This was Lennox's home. He'd grown to manhood here. He put his hand on the banister just as she was doing, raced down the stairs she was descending slowly or taken them two at a time.

Had he hesitated in the foyer, staring up at the huge stained-glass ceiling above her? If so, she doubted he'd been overwhelmed by a sudden urge to weep.

She'd nearly ruined her life. Single-handedly she'd taken the advantages she'd been given, the love surrounding her, and opted for something else. Her pride had forced her to choose a life without love, only an exaggerated need for perfection.

She was not going to make the same mistake now. Whatever she'd done wrong she would undo.

The night breeze warned of winter to come, cooled her skin and made her shiver. She clutched her wrapper close to her chest with one hand as she walked.

How many times had she come here with Duncan, unaware of the valuables around her, only interested in Lennox? Laughter had echoed throughout Hillshead in childish disregard of wealth or position.

In Washington she'd often been visited by nostalgia, normally at a recital of sad music. She'd dropped down into her memories, allowing her mind to travel home to Scotland. In those moments, rare as they were, she was Glynis MacIain the girl, once enchanted with Lennox Cameron to the point of madness. The applause from the other guests would call her back to the moment, even though she wished she could remain in that place of memory and longing.

Time couldn't be reversed. As much as she might want to, she couldn't wipe the years clean and begin again.

But she could fix what she'd broken today.

How, though? What should she say? What did she need to do? How did she erase her mistake?

Her thoughts were like mice, scattering at the sound of an open door or a lit lamp.

She found herself in the corridor leading to the library, a place Lennox always used as his office. Shadows embraced her as she slowly pushed open the door.

The last time she'd been here she was eighteen years old and had recently returned from a trip to Edinburgh with her mother. She'd seen a crystal inkwell shaped like a ship in the window of a shop and had instantly been reminded of Lennox.

Lennox had been surprised by her gift but seemed pleased as well, placing the inkwell at the front of his desk. To her surprise it was still there, next to the spyglass his grandfather had given him.

Moonlight streaming in through the open window softly illuminated the library. She drew in the scents of leather and tobacco, faint but still noticeable.

The room was large, but all Hillshead's rooms were oversized. Bookshelves lined the walls, each shelf containing a separate subject. She recalled that the ones closer to the desk were about ships and engineering. Farther away were novels and books on poetry. Some of the volumes had been well-worn, but she doubted Lennox had read them. Probably Mary had, instead. Did she read to her father now?

Lennox's desk took pride of place in the center of the room in front of the windows. She circled it, fingers grazing the tooled leather top, envisioning him working here, signing papers, doing his preliminary sketches. A lamp also sat on the desk, along with a large blotter and a wooden tray filled with paper.

Was he at the yard? Would he stay there all night?

"Glynis?"

Her heart leapt into her throat. She looked up to see a shadow in the doorway.

Before she could speak, he strode to the desk and lit the lamp, banishing the darkness. His hair was mussed either by the wind or his fingers. He looked tired, his eyes bloodshot. His white shirt was loosely tucked into the waistband of his black trousers, as if he'd already begun undressing. His sleeves were rolled up to expose his muscular arms. At the neck, his collarbones showed along with the well at the base of his throat.

A spot she wanted to kiss.

His trousers were tailored, the button fastening off-center, the fabric fitted with darts and tucks capturing her attention before she realized she was staring at his crotch.

Hunger slammed into her. She needed him. Before the night was gone, before dawn greeted the day, before the sun rose or a thousand, million things happened, they had to solve this problem between them.

"What's wrong?" he asked, his frown making a V on his forehead and thinning his lips. "Why are you still awake?"

What's wrong? Everything and nothing, but how did she say that?

"Why didn't you come home?" she asked, plunging into the heart of the matter.

"Are you in love with him? With Matthew Baumann?"

Her eyes widened. "Are you daft? Matthew Baumann? I'd sooner toss the man in the Clyde."

"He doesn't feel that way about you."

"You can't be serious," she said. "If he said such a thing, don't believe him. It's not a good idea to believe anything Baumann says. He's a manipulator. He's always been a manipulator. If he wasn't working for the War Department, he'd be bilking widows and orphans out of their last few coins."

"He's in love with you."

She drew back and stared at him.

"That's not funny," she said. "To even jest about such a thing is an abomination, Lennox."

"I see the way he looks at you. It's not a jest."

"The only person Matthew Baumann loves is himself."

"You haven't seen the look on his face when he's watching you," he said.

She didn't know what was worse, the idea Baumann might have some feelings for her or Lennox's jealousy.

The child she'd been would have rejoiced to see evidence of his jealousy. The adult knew how caustic the emotion could be.

"I have no feelings for him. No," she corrected. "I have one. I loathe the man."

"Then why do I find you in conversation with him so often?"

"I can't stop him from following me."

"The question is why he follows you," he said. He crossed his arms, his feet planted apart, almost like he was prepared to do battle with her.

Perhaps they fought a war, one of thrust and parry with words, gestures, and looks. The prize? Their marriage.

"You think Baumann set fire to your ship," she said.

"I do."

She shook her head. "I don't think so," she said. "He's not like that. He's all about subterfuge and getting other people to do his bidding."

"He doesn't want the *Raven* to sail and he'd be a fool to let her. She's one of the fastest ships I've ever built. She'll slide into any southern port before the Union ships even see her."

She glanced toward the window with its view of the night sky, then back at him where he stood watching her. No one else in her memory had eyes as penetrating as his or a gaze piercing through her defenses. A woman could be ensnared by his look, trapped into confessing all sorts of secrets.

She blew out a breath. "He wants information about the *Raven*," she said.

One of his eyebrows winged upward.

"I haven't told him anything." She backed up against the desk. "I would never do such a thing. On the honor of a MacIain," she said, repeating the oath Duncan made her swear as children. Don't tell Mother. Don't tell Father. The oath was the most sacred bond they had, and only sworn on the most important occasions.

He nodded just once.

"Is that why you stayed away?" she asked. "Because you were jealous?"

"Not jealous," he said. "Angry."

His cheekbones bronzed. His eyes smoldered with unspoken words.

"Are you still angry?"

In Washington, she'd seen her share of emotionless marriages, couples who seemed to barely tolerate one another. An hour would pass and some couples would not speak. She'd also seen loving couples, men who smiled down at their wives with adoration on their faces and women who looked up at their husbands with worship in their eyes.

She'd envied them.

"Why did he think you'd tell him?"

"Because he doesn't know me as well as he thinks he does."

"And how well is that?"

Lennox had unerringly shattered her heart. He threatened to do it again, now. If she were really older and wiser, she'd guard herself, seal off the vulnerable part of her, pretend an icy demeanor and not reveal her true feelings. But she knew instinctively that barricading herself against Lennox would only lead to disaster.

"Not as well as you," she said.

When he didn't answer, she walked to him, placing both her hands on his shirt, feeling his warmth radiating to her fingers.

She lowered her head, took another step, resting her forehead against his chest.

"Never as well as you."

"I love you, damn it."

Her eyes flew up to meet his gaze.

"Nothing matters but that, Glynis."

"I love you, damn it?" she asked, bemused.

"Yes. Should I pretty it up?"

She shook her head, feeling time slow. Her heart beat only half as much as normal. She barely took a breath. Their gazes were locked and she drowned in his look.

"Will you come to my bed? Be my husband?"

His smile speared her heart. "Do I look like a eunuch?" he asked.

He grabbed her hand, turned and pulled her with him. She rushed to keep up with him as they raced through the darkened house and up the stairs.

Chapter 33

*H*e loved her.

Someone laughed belowstairs and the sound traveled upward in a ghostly echo.

Lennox loved her. Bubbles moved through her veins. Excitement danced on her skin. Her stomach was filled with butterflies and champagne. Lennox loved her.

He stopped at the landing and looked at her.

"Have you moved into my suite?"

Before she could answer, he took her hand again and walked to her room. He opened the door, entered the bedroom, glancing at the bureau top filled with her brush and mirror, perfume bottle and silver-lidded jars.

"Why haven't you moved into my suite? It's where you belong."

Until this moment she hadn't known where she belonged, but she decided not to say that. He loved her and it didn't matter where she was as long as it was beside him.

He turned, grabbed her hand again, walking out of the suite and down the corridor, their footsteps muffled by the runner beneath their feet.

The maids had been industrious; she inhaled the smell of lemon oil and beeswax as Lennox opened another door.

He moved inside, lit a lamp, and stood there watching her. She took a hesitant step over the threshold, looking around.

She'd never been here before, even as a girl. This was Lennox's room, a chamber whose location she knew, but one forbidden her.

At first glance it was similar to her guest suite. The furniture was heavily carved mahogany with brass drawer pulls. Instead of pale yellow, however, the settee and chairs were upholstered in dark blue with touches of beige. A masculine room, furnished with pictures of ships at sea. At any other time she might have stopped to admire the large painting over the mantel: a clipper ship at full sail on a frothing ocean. But she was being carried along in Lennox's wake.

In the bedroom he stopped, turning to her.

She pulled her hand from his and put it on his arm, feeling the corded muscles. Had he always been so strong?

He studied her, the glow from the sitting room lamp illuminating his face.

Lennox loved her.

She stepped closer, wrapped her arms around his waist and placed her cheek against his shirt. Her heart expanded, her soul opened up to encompass him. This moment was perfect and rare, a blessing she probably didn't deserve.

Lennox loved her. She blinked back her tears, tightened her arms around him and wanted to stay right here for the rest of her life.

His chest moved as he drew a deep breath.

Could anything be more perfect?

She smiled, then pulled back, beginning to unfasten his shirt. He didn't stop her. Nor did he say a word, merely stood with his arms at his sides as she started to undress him. Once his shirt was unbuttoned, she pushed it open, revealing his chest. She threaded her fingers through his hair, leaned close and inhaled.

"What are you doing?" he asked, his voice a low rumble.

"You always smell like wood to me. Wood and the sea."

"Do I now?"

She shook her head. "No. Now you smell of wood, ink, and smoke."

He bent until his nose was against her throat. He sniffed her, raising his head a moment later.

Her laughter broke free. "What do I smell like?"

"Glynis," he said. "Your perfume and the scent of your skin."

She'd never known passion could be soft and sweet or that it could carry an undertone of laughter and one of tenderness.

Pressing her mouth against his chest, she tasted his skin. Salty. His nipple pebbled at her exploring touch. His indrawn breath made her smile broaden.

She took his hand, turned and led him to the bed. She mounted the small set of steps, sat on the edge of the mattress and patted the space next to her.

He grinned, easily sat beside her, not demurring when she raised up on her knees and pushed him onto his back.

"Are you seducing me?" he asked.

"Yes," she said, intent on finishing unbuttoning his shirt.

"There's no need. Whatever you want of me, it's yours."

She smiled, not explaining she needed to touch him, to allow her fingers and hands to explore as he'd done the night before. She wanted to enthrall, enchant, and pleasure him.

She placed her hands on his naked chest, stroking

her palms upward to the base of his neck and outward to his shoulders. Her eyes followed the actions of her hands, marveling at the size and the beauty of his body.

He was the perfect man.

When she reached for the buttons of his trousers, he encircled her wrists with both hands.

"I need to touch you," she said. Would he understand?

He released her.

To make it fair, she took off her wrapper, revealing her soft pink nightgown. His gaze traveled from her neck down to her breasts visible through the silk.

He lay quiescent as she unbuttoned one button. For his cooperation, she rewarded him with a string of kisses from his waist to his chin. The second button was awarded a nip of his earlobe. The third a necklace of kisses around his throat.

She loved touching him. Her fingers were magical, making his pulse escalate. He watched her with eyes so intent she could feel his gaze.

"I really need you naked," she said.

"Do you?"

She nodded, smiling.

He jumped from the bed and removed his shirt. In seconds his pants and the rest of his clothing were in a pile on the floor. Naked, he joined her again, lying on his side, his head propped up on one hand, a wicked grin curving his lips.

She pushed him to his back. When her hair came loose, she removed the last of the pins, shaking it free until it fell over her shoulder. She might've been a mermaid, trailing the end of one strand across his chest, teasing him.

She dusted his stomach with her fingers. Sitting

back on her haunches, she inspected the growing wonder of him.

Now she wished there was a lamp in the bedroom, one allowing her a full inspection. Her hands would have to give the shadows shape. How large he was, how long and hard and heated against her palms. Her fingers danced along his length, inciting a muffled oath from him. She smiled, delighting in her sudden, unexpected power.

Her thumbs played in the hair at his groin, stretched lower as she felt him tense. Gently she stroked his scrotum, her hands curling behind it to hold his testicles tenderly in her palm.

"Glynis," he said, his voice guttural. "Enough."

"This dictatorial nature of yours is new, Lennox. I don't remember you ordering me about so much seven years ago."

"You didn't hold my balls in your hands seven years ago."

"Pity," she said. "I should have."

She looked up at him. She really should have seduced him all those years ago.

"I like to explore you," she said. "Is that a bad thing?"

"Yes," he said, but his hips left the bed as if seeking her touch.

She placed her hands around his shaft again, marveling at the iron hardness of it. Daring herself, she bent and kissed the mushroom-shaped head.

Lennox tensed, rose up slightly, another oath escaping him.

"Do you hate that? Is it painful?"

"If I said yes would you stop?"

"I don't know," she said, enthralled with the power she was feeling. "If you're really in pain, of course I would. I wouldn't want to be the instrument of your discomfort."

Her right hand cupped his scrotum, her thumb gently brushing across the skin. Her left guided his shaft to her lips where her tongue circled the head slowly.

"Are you very certain it isn't painful?"

"Glynis," he said, his voice low and warning.

She smiled, wondering if he knew how much touching him excited her. Her nipples were so hard they hurt. Her body was weeping, fluid bathing the inside of her thighs.

She pressed her lips to the length of his shaft, licking him from the root all the way to the tip.

His breath left him in a shuddering gasp.

He rolled toward her, and she took the opportunity to grab one well formed round buttock, her nails grazing his skin. He jerked, making her smile again. How very strange she had never realized her effect on him. He reacted to her touch the same way she did to his.

Suddenly she was on her back and he was looming over her.

His arms were hairy, the hair tapering off toward his shoulders, the muscles knotting and bunching under her fingers. She threaded her hands at his nape, her thumbs brushing his ears, tracing the shape of them down to the lobes.

Everything about Lennox was as perfect as she wished it to be, as if God himself had asked: *Glynis, what should his neck be like? Should his shoulders be straight and broad? Shall I make him tall, the better to tower over you? And intelligent, to match your wit?*

Shall I give him character, that he is an honorable man, one who cares for those in his keeping? One who shelters and protects? This man to whom I give you in exchange for seven years of patient misery, would you change anything about him?

"Nothing," she said.

He raised his head. "Nothing what?" he asked, his breath soft against her temple.

"God and I were having a conversation," she said, smiling at herself. "He wanted to know if I would change anything about you and I said nothing."

"Nothing?"

She shook her head. Any further words were impossible because he kissed her, stripping thought and intention from her mind.

God could've spared him intelligence. Lennox hardly needed it when she couldn't think around him.

A laugh escaped, startling her.

"Something amusing, Glynis?" he asked, his smile warming her.

She pulled his head down for a kiss. "Not amusing, Lennox," she said against his lips. "Fascinating."

He raised up. "Fascinating?"

"I love your body. Am I allowed to say that? It's strong and beautiful and responsive."

"I'm not beautiful," he said. "Men aren't. Now you, on the other hand . . ." He reached out and trailed a path around one nipple with a finger.

"You *are* beautiful," she said. "You're the most beautiful man I've ever seen. And I like how your cock trembles when I touch it."

He reared back and stared at her. "I don't tremble."

She sighed, bit back her smile, and shook her head. "Would you like me to show you? You quiver. I stretch out my hand and your cock almost bounces, it's so eager. It's like a puppy."

His bark of laughter made her smile.

"Very well, I quiver around you. Is that what this is, a quest for dominance? Shall I allow you to win, my dearest wife? Shall I surrender to you?"

"Please don't. Not until the battle is fully joined."

"How do you propose we do that?"

She spread her legs, invitation without a word.

"You have to enter me, of course. And attempt to vanquish me with the strength of your sword."

"And if I conquer you? What do I win?"

"Bliss," she said, smiling.

"If you win?"

"Bliss again."

"Ah, then the battle is only for the pleasure of it."

He placed his mouth on the tip of her breast, licked it slowly, drew it in until she felt the sensation deep in the center of her body. She closed her eyes at the feeling.

She grabbed his upper arms with both her hands and pulled him to her. He lowered himself until his penis bobbed against her curls, but wouldn't go further.

"Lennox," she said softly.

She felt a hunger as elemental as that for food or water. She had to have him or die. He had to be inside her, making her whole. Only then would she be complete.

She widened her legs still farther, pushed her hips up to entice him. But he stubbornly refused to move, to enter her, to give her release. The emptiness grew, demanded she fill it.

Lennox moved his hips from side to side, the heated tip of his erection grazing one of her thighs then the other.

She followed his movements, undulating on the bed with him. Whatever he wanted her to do, she would, but only for a moment. After that she would tip him over and mount him and ride him like her pony.

The image of doing that made her smile.

"Amused again, Glynis?"

"I was imagining riding you," she said.

He stilled, staring down at her. "You say the damnedest things," he said.

She hadn't heard that comment in years. Normally she was restrained, circumspect, ladylike to a fault. Here, in his bed, loving him, she was herself.

"At least I didn't imagine having a whip," she said. She punctuated the remark by slapping her hand against one of his buttocks.

She wasn't surprised by his laughter. When he surged into her, she closed her eyes, the sensation overwhelming her.

"I've a whip of my own, my darling wife."

"Yes you do," she said, nearly breathless. Her hands clenched on his shoulders, her nails digging into his skin as heat flashed through her.

Slowly he withdrew, the seconds ticking by with astonishing slowness. With the same unhurried movement, he entered her again, punishing her with gentleness when she wanted anything but.

She dug her heels into the mattress, raised her hips to follow him when he left her again, luring him back. Her arms wrapped around his neck. She breathed against his throat, pleaded with him in sounds more than words.

Her feet trailed from his ankles up to his knees and back down again, glorying in the feel of him, the rough hair brushing her toes, the shape of his muscular legs. She rested her instep against his shins in a spot almost created for her. His buttocks were each the size of a perfect round loaf, shaped for her curving hands. She wanted to knead him, rest on his perfect backside, place her hands on his spine and lower herself until her breasts plumped against him.

The tremors started before she was prepared, her sudden climax taking her by surprise.

She held onto him as he increased his speed, racing

to finish as quickly as she. He was the master, yet in her surrender she also conquered.

In the morning she would have to tell him the truth, but for now they were newly married and newly re-united.

Chapter 34

Mrs. Hurst was standing in the middle of the doorway of the Summer Parlor, a room where Glynis retreated in order to read.

There didn't seem to be much else to do until her duties had been decided. Perhaps Duncan could use some help with the ledgers. She had no place cards to write, no menu to plan for an afternoon gathering, no notes to make for information she would turn over to Baumann. Nothing about her life in Washington translated to Glasgow living.

In those last months in America she'd been in the same situation, but without the wherewithal to afford a lovely place to read or even purchase books. She'd spent the majority of her time preparing her wardrobe to be sold.

"Your mother is here, Mrs. Cameron," the housekeeper said. "Shall I show her in?"

"Please do."

"Shall I bring refreshments?"

She nodded. "That would be lovely. Thank you, Mrs. Hurst."

The housekeeper inclined her head somewhat regally and smiled in response.

She'd had a similar autocratic bearing at one time. The ability to control one's features and responses was a definite asset in Washington. The longer she was home, the more she was reverting to her true self, someone who said what she felt.

"I'm here for two reasons, Glynis," her mother said, startling her as she entered the room wearing a frown. "Normally, I wouldn't visit you so quickly after your wedding, but I feel compelled to do so, and that's reason number one."

She stood, ready to give her mother a welcoming hug. Instead, the other woman stopped feet from her, such a censorious expression on her face Glynis was taken aback.

"I have heard rumors from Mabel that you and Lennox are fighting. I couldn't believe it at first, but Mabel does not lie. Nor did she tell tales, normally. The fact she has heard about it means everyone at Hillshead is talking. And if everyone at Hillshead is talking, it means all of Glasgow will begin chattering about it. You know how gossip travels in this town."

Indeed she did, but she didn't speak, neither to agree nor to muster a defense.

Her mother rolled her eyes, an expression so at variance with her normal equanimity that Glynis stared at her.

"Do not be recalcitrant with me, my dear, darling daughter. You may be a woman of the world, but you are still my child."

Glynis took a step back, motioning to one of the settees in front of the fire. The day was a rainy one and the normally cozy parlor was chilled. Despite being summer, a small blaze in the fireplace warmed the room. The flames were diminutive and almost reticent, as if knowing it was not the season for a fire.

"I'm not being recalcitrant, Mother," she said. "I have no idea what people are saying." Nor how anyone knew she and Lennox had argued. Evidently, the maids had made a note of her solitary dinner.

Life was going to be very interesting at Hillshead if people were watching them this closely.

She waited till her mother sat, then took the settee opposite, clasping her hands together and resting them on her knee.

"I'm afraid Lennox and I did have a bit of a disagreement, but it's over."

Thankfully, her mother didn't ask the subject of the disagreement. She wasn't about to mention Matthew Baumann, because her mother wouldn't understand. Worse, her mother would ask questions she didn't want to answer right now.

Mrs. Hurst entered the room followed by two of the maids. The first carried a tray filled with biscuits and cake, plates and silverware. The second maid's tray contained two pots, one of coffee, one of tea, cream and sugar and cups.

The housekeeper didn't need any direction from her.

After the others had gone and they'd served themselves, her mother balanced her plate on her knee, leaned over the table between the two settees and handed a canvas bag to her.

"You left this behind. I do not want such a horrid thing in my house, Glynis. Not that I feel any better bringing it to you. I do wish you would get rid of it, right now."

She took the bag, felt the shape of it, and knew what it was before opening it. She unlaced the neck of the bag, pulled the drawstring free, and withdrew the gun.

Her mother shuddered. "Is there no way I can convince you to toss that horrid thing in the Clyde?"

"I'll take care of it," she said.

"Good." Her mother leaned back, folded her hands together and regarded her solemnly. "Now about your argument with Lennox. Even the best of marriages have their bad times, Glynis. The trick is to devote yourself to your husband."

She had, most assuredly, something else she wasn't going to discuss with her mother. Lennox had gone to the yard early this morning, but not before waking her in a most delightful fashion.

She loved her mother dearly but she was not going to make her a confidante about her marriage.

Instead, she stood and walked to the door.

"I'll be back in a moment," she said, nearly running up the stairs to her room. Once she'd retrieved her reticule, she returned to the Summer Parlor. Sitting next to her mother, she pulled out the draft.

"Would you give this to Duncan, please?"

Her mother unfolded the check and stared at it for several moments without speaking. Finally, she looked at Glynis.

"Oh my dear daughter, is this why you married Lennox?"

She smiled. The success or failure of the MacIain Mill was close to her heart, but it had nothing to do with her decision.

"No," she said. "It isn't. But Duncan will have to accept it now, and if he doesn't I'll simply cash it and deliver the money to his office in a wheelbarrow."

Her mother's lips quirked. "You would, wouldn't you?" She looked at Glynis, her eyes sparkling. "Sometimes I thought the two of you wouldn't survive your childhood, you sniped at each other something terrible. He never got the better of you, though." She cleared her throat. "You make sure nothing does, do you hear?"

She nodded. "Nothing will, Mother, I promise."

Eleanor reached over and smoothed the back of her hand over Glynis's cheek.

"Are you happy, my dear girl?"

"Yes," she said. Lennox loved her. She loved him. Only one thing stopped her from complete happiness and that was Matthew Baumann. She needed to solve that problem now, before the man had a chance to do more damage to her marriage.

"At least Lucy will have no more tales to tell."

"Or Charlotte," she said, an idea occurring to her.

Gossip had changed her life twice. Maybe gossip could work to her advantage for once.

Charlotte might be the answer to a prayer.

I'M NOT sure I can do what you want," Charlotte said, frowning at her.

Sunlight altered the green of the upholstery in Charlotte's parlor to something resembling bile. She tried not to look at it, focusing on Charlotte, instead.

"What would Lennox say? The good book says you should cleave unto your husband, Glynis. By going behind his back, you will only sow discord in your marriage."

She pasted a smile on her face and took a sip of her tea. She hadn't asked for sugar but Charlotte had provided it anyway, along with a plate of MacNamara candies she was required by politeness to sample.

"I'm not going behind his back," she said. "All I want to do is meet with the man."

"Why not at Hillshead?"

Her smile flagged but she pinned it into place. Lennox would be furious if she invited Baumann to their home. Besides, it would defeat the purpose of involving Charlotte.

The woman was an inveterate gossip and had made her life difficult since returning from Washington. But gossips could be useful in certain situations, and this was one of them.

All of Glasgow needed to know exactly who Matthew Baumann was. Only then could he be less free to roam about the city at will, causing havoc. She had no doubt that within moments of this meeting, Charlotte would be spreading tales.

"Matthew Baumann is working for the American War Department. He's a spy for the Union. I believe he may have been responsible for the death of Mr. Whittaker and the sabotage of one of Lennox's ships."

Charlotte's eyes widened.

"If the man is that vicious, wouldn't it be dangerous to meet with him?"

"I knew Matthew in Washington," she said, setting down her cup. "We are not friends but we are acquaintances. He believes I'll provide him information about Cameron and Company. I intend to tell him I'll do no such thing, of course."

Charlotte nodded, her cup still in midair.

In addition to starting the gossip mill about Baumann, she was going to tell the man he was free to say anything he wanted to about her, even the truth if he wished.

She could not remake the past, as much as she might want to. Lennox needed to know who she was, all the way down to her bones. She had already planned on telling him about Washington.

He loved her. She hoped he would forgive her. If he didn't? She'd read a poet in America who'd written words appropriate enough for her thoughts. Whittier had said: "For all sad words of tongue and pen, the saddest are these, 'It might have been.'"

She was not going to allow that to happen. She was going to fight for Lennox as she hadn't seven years ago. The intervening years had toughened her, made a woman of the child.

Lennox was her husband and her love.

"All I need you to do is to send a driver to his lodgings and tell him I need to meet with him. I've heard the Lafayette Hotel has a lovely tea room."

"What about my parlor?" Charlotte asked, surprising her. "What about right here?"

"Here?"

Charlotte nodded. "I will send for Archie, of course, as protection."

That would be even better. Two gossips were better than one.

Charlotte inspected the piece of paper Glynis had given her. "I'll send my driver to find this Mr. Baumann. In the meantime, have some more of Archibald's new concoction, caramel chocolate."

She nodded, watching as Charlotte left the room, wishing she could wait anywhere but in this green horror.

Last night's dinner, something spicy like a stew, lingered in the air and clashed with the lemon potpourri in the parlor.

When Charlotte didn't return, she walked the parlor, examining the portraits, the bric-a-brac, the ornaments on the mantel. Finally, she sat on the emerald settee, amusing herself by watching the clock tick off the minutes.

She folded her hands, willed her stomach to settle, and waited. A quarter hour passed, then half an hour. When forty-five minutes elapsed and Charlotte still hadn't returned, she stood, deciding to leave. Evidently, the errand had failed. Baumann wasn't at his lodgings.

When the door opened, she expected Charlotte to enter the room. She was there, but standing behind Lennox, her eyes sparkling and her cheeks pinked with excitement.

"Archie wouldn't have been happy with me if I invited Mr. Baumann here, Glynis. Besides, you shouldn't do something a man should do."

How like some of the Washington harpies Charlotte was. At least she'd had experience in dealing with such creatures.

She smiled. "It's all right, Charlotte."

Lennox turned, spoke softly to Charlotte, and closed the door.

Chapter 35

*O*nce they were alone, Lennox turned to her.

His frown might have frightened anyone else. So, too, the anger rolling off him. She wasn't cowed.

"Why did you want to see Baumann?" he asked, calmly. "Especially when you gave your word you wouldn't."

"Did I? I thought I explained I had no power over what the man does."

"Are we going to play word games, Glynis?"

"No," she said, returning to the settee.

She'd had weeks to consider this confession. Granted, she'd never considered it would take place in Charlotte's parlor, but then it didn't matter where it was, did it? She'd planned on telling him today, regardless of where they were.

"I wanted to tell him I had no intention of betraying you. And to tell him I was no longer going to be blackmailed. It was time for the truth to come out."

"Blackmailed?"

Something flashed between them, anger and betrayal, hurt and need, feelings conjoined and opposite, hot and cold, wrong and right. She wanted to touch him, to offer an apology beforehand, but words were fragile things and of little use right now.

He joined her on the bile-colored settee.

They sat silent for several moments.

"The story isn't easy to tell," she finally said. "I've rehearsed it a dozen times but it never gets less ugly. But, then, the truth is often ugly."

She stood and went to stand at one of the windows heavily draped in emerald velvet. How could Charlotte bear this suffocating green? She stared out at the front of the house, at the carriages and their inhabitants all with a destination in mind: a shop, a workplace, to call on friends. Did they ever think of what was happening in the houses they passed?

"I didn't like Richard," she said, a confession she'd never before made to anyone. How strange the first time should be to Lennox. "Originally, I tolerated him well enough and I tried to do everything he wanted."

She glanced back at Lennox, unsurprised to see his face still, his eyes shuttered. A stone rendition of Lennox, almost as daunting as Lennox angry.

"I endured our posting to Cairo as well as I could," she said.

Endured, what a strange word for the hell of it. The whole year had been one of lessons, more lessons, and endless criticism coupled with being miserably homesick and then ill for weeks with the flu.

"After a year Richard was posted to Washington, a step up from Cairo but not as elevated as Russia or Spain. But he saw it as his career advancing."

She'd only thought she was traveling farther and farther away from Scotland.

She fingered the drapes, remembering the hope she felt when first arriving in Washington. Maybe her marriage would get easier to tolerate. Maybe she would make friendships, become less heartsick.

The only good thing about Washington was Richard's absence from her bed.

"Richard began spending hours away from home."

She turned and faced him. The time for avoidance and prevarication had passed.

"I wasn't disturbed by that. I should have been, perhaps, but the less I saw of him, the better."

Was Charlotte listening? Was she going to spread the tale about her to the whole of Glasgow? Probably. How odd that it only mattered to her for Lennox's sake, and her family's. She no longer cared. She'd rather stand in the light of truth and be mocked than hide in the shadows clutching a lie.

"But something that had happened in Cairo began to concern me. We went through servants in a record pace. The only ones we seemed to keep were very young girls, hardly old enough to be working. One of them came to me just before we left and told me a tale. One of my husband coming into her room late one night and threatening to dismiss her if she cried out. He raped her."

She took another deep breath. "I opted not to believe her rather than think Richard capable of such an act. But in Washington, the same thing began to happen. The older servants were let go, leaving only girls barely out of the nursery. I questioned one of the girls we employed."

She remembered every second of the interview and each detail the poor girl recounted of the abuse suffered at Richard's hands.

"I went to Richard. He accused me of being provincial. He told me men had interests and I wasn't to interfere with them. I had to be less of a Scot and more sophisticated."

Lennox didn't say a word, but his eyes were steady on her.

"I threatened to tell his superiors about Cairo along with what I'd just learned. That was the day my marriage truly died."

"Where does Baumann fit into all of this?" he asked, his voice sounding like gravel.

"Richard stopped abusing the servants," she said. "I dismissed all the younger girls and only kept mature servants. But I knew him. What's the saying? A leopard doesn't change his spots? Therefore, Matthew Baumann."

She came and sat opposite him.

He occupied the corner of the settee like a pasha on a throne, his knees wide, feet planted firmly on the ghastly green carpet.

He didn't say a word, however, and she'd never possessed the ability to read minds, even his.

The seconds ticked by and she measured each with a heartbeat.

She struggled with how to explain, stumbling over words in her head, hesitating over the right choice, considering what he would think. Disgusted with herself for burrowing into language rather than the truth, she fixed her gaze on him and didn't look away.

"Baumann had a reputation in Washington for being a man who could get things done. I didn't know, at the time, he worked for the War Department. I only knew he could find out what I needed to know. I wanted to know what Richard was doing."

"Whether or not he was unfaithful?"

She shook her head. "I didn't care. I just wondered if he was abusing some poor child."

"Was he?"

She nodded. "He was frequenting a place, a brothel, for lack of a better word. They satisfied his craving for younger and younger girls, sometimes taking them off the street and then giving them a few coins the next day. He liked virgins, I understand. He especially liked raping them."

Nausea coiled in her stomach like a snake.

"Baumann found this out for you?"

Once again she nodded.

"What did he demand in return?"

How intelligent he was.

"He insisted I work for him. At first, all he wanted were the names of women who'd attended a tea. Then what they'd talked about. I've always been good at numbers and details, and it was nothing for me to memorize what I saw and heard."

"You spied for him."

"Yes," she said. "I spied for him." She looked down at her clasped hands. "I told him information I learned at suppers, teas, balls, all the endless social engagements I was expected to attend."

She stood once more, restless. Returning to the window, she saw a bird flying overhead. In Washington, she used to watch as they flew south, wondering if they carried the souls of the war dead aloft, transporting them to their homes.

Tension knotted her shoulders and tightened her throat, but she forced herself to continue.

"When the casualty reports began to come in, I realized some of the information I'd provided had probably led to those deaths. I told Baumann I wouldn't work for him anymore."

She glanced over at Lennox to find his gaze hadn't left her.

"He blackmailed you?"

"Yes." She wasn't surprised he figured that out. "He threatened to tell the British Legation that the wife of their attaché was a Union spy. We would have been sent home in disgrace."

"But Richard was killed," he said. "A stroke of good luck."

Was she going to be speared by a lightning bolt for being glad of a man's death?

"After he died, Baumann had no hold over you."

"None."

"Until he came to Scotland."

She nodded.

"Why didn't you tell me before?"

She came back to the settee. "Because I had been responsible for men dying. Because I'd done things that shame me even now. Because your opinion has always mattered to me. Because I wanted to forget everything about Washington. I still feel sick and dirty about it."

"So you carried the secret around all this time?"

His voice was so tender she wanted to weep, but tears wouldn't wipe away the guilt or the shame.

"I couldn't tell you," she said, focusing her attention on her hands instead of him. "I didn't want you to think badly of me."

"Didn't you realize I never could?"

When she finally looked up, his eyes were so heated she felt scorched.

He stood, extending his hand. She joined him, placing her hand on his arm, and they walked to the door. When he opened it, Charlotte was there, so obviously in the act of listening that Glynis almost smiled.

Part of her plan was working.

Charlotte glanced at Lennox, her hands fluttering in the air.

"Well, then, that's all settled, is it?"

Lennox didn't bother to answer. Neither did she.

Was Charlotte disappointed she and Lennox hadn't come to blows?

She smiled at her onetime friend and knew Charlotte would always belong in the past. Whatever relationship they'd had was buried beneath gossip and perhaps a type of meanness she'd never suspected of the other woman.

"Will you be all right going back to the house by yourself?" Lennox asked.

"You're not coming home?" she asked, surprised.

He shook his head. "No, I've something to attend to."

Or did he just not want to be with her? She was suddenly flooded with misgivings. Had he meant what he said? Or was he finding it difficult to forgive her?

She didn't feel lighter for telling him the truth. Her conscience wasn't suddenly wiped clean. As the years passed, she'd have to come to grips with what she'd done.

She wasn't fool enough to think she was solely responsible for the casualties of war. Yet wasn't each death the result of a long chain of actions? One person after another added his contribution until the finale— a battle won, a city taken, a blockade established. She, too, had contributed her part.

She'd acted like a MacIain loom, placing a thread in the right spot, adjusting another, repeating the process over and over until cloth was produced. The cloth, in this case, being information pieced together from various sources.

Had women been used in other wars? She didn't know, but human nature being what it was, they probably were. This war, however, seemed like a giant spider with a web spreading far beyond America.

She'd thought to come home, to breathe the clean air of Scotland and be away from the stench of war. Instead, it had followed her here in the person of Matthew Baumann and Gavin Whittaker. It had touched her life by starving the mill of raw product, making a titan of Lennox, and spreading the reputation of Cameron and Company throughout the world.

Now it had possibly ruined her marriage.

They left Charlotte's home in silence and walked to the carriage.

"Why didn't you invite Baumann to Hillshead?"

She smiled. "I could imagine your reaction if I'd done that."

He only nodded. "But why Charlotte?"

"She gossips."

He frowned. "And you want her to gossip about you?"

"I want her to gossip about Baumann. The more talk, the better. He operates in secrecy, in fear. The more people know who and what he is, the less power he'll have. He needs to leave Glasgow."

"I don't object to that, but what of your own reputation, Glynis? Charlotte doesn't discriminate in her rumormongering. We both know that."

"I doubt my reputation can be any more sullied than it is, Lennox. I don't want the gossip to hurt you, though. Let's hope people just pity you for your choice of wife."

She entered the carriage and looked back at him. For a moment the world dropped away and it was only her and Lennox. A dozen vignettes flowed into her mind, scenes of her childhood, memories of when she was on the cusp of womanhood.

Seeing Lennox would brighten her day. Talking with him would leave her cheeks pink and her heart fluttery. Just being around him had the power to change her mood to something light and joyous. He'd never stopped having that effect on her.

The time had passed for words and explanations. He would take what she'd told him and make a decision on his own. Their future wouldn't be decided today or tomorrow or even a week from now. But what she'd said—and what she'd done—would be part of the foundation of their marriage.

She felt as if all of her emotions had been tossed to the ground, pavement for the boots of others.

He stepped away and the carriage began to move. She watched him until she couldn't see him any longer.

Only then did she close her eyes, sit back, and try not to cry.

Chapter 36

*H*e wasn't a violent man, but ever since Lennox had learned the truth, he'd entertained thoughts of dismembering Matthew Baumann limb by limb. His ancestors had come from the Highlands. The blood coursing through his veins meant he was a Scot: capable of great pride, prowess in battle, and the ability to cling tightly to that which was precious.

The idea of Glynis being alone in Washington, at the mercy of a husband who cared nothing for her, was not one he easily tolerated. She'd been helpless and desperate, and Baumann had taken advantage of her.

Since she'd been gone, he had tried, very hard, not to think of her at all. But there were times when he was catapulted back into the past by something Duncan said or the sound of female laughter. Instantly the sprite who was Glynis danced through his memory.

Fate, that fickle bastard, had changed the course of his life, bringing her back to him. Now she was his wife. He was damned if he was going to allow Matthew Baumann to hurt her again.

He went to the address Charlotte had given him. The lodgings were run by a very pleasant woman who informed him that Mr. Baumann was not currently home. Did he wish to wait? He did. An hour and a half later he realized that Baumann had probably recognized his carriage and wouldn't return until he left.

He thanked the landlady for her hospitality, the jot of whiskey she'd offered, and her plate of scones, and made his way back to the yard.

There was more than one way to capture a skunk.

"You wanted to see me, sir?"

He nodded, and with a wave of his arm, banished the engineers and draftsmen from the room. He waited until the door closed behind the last of them before motioning James to the chair beside his desk.

James Sinclair was his hull foreman. Not only was the man brawny and capable of taking on any longshoreman who gave him grief, but he had a sharp mind and canny wit.

Full bearded with brown curly hair, James always wore a smile, an expression at odds with his narrowed eyes and suspicious nature. Lennox didn't know much of the man's history, other than he'd come to Glasgow to make his way in the world. He'd been with Cameron and Company for the last three years, advancing up through the ranks and proving himself invaluable.

But it was for James's skill outside work that he'd summoned him to his office. James was a prize fighter, winning bout after bout with hands nearly black from a daily treatment of green vitriol and copperas.

"Makes them hard as iron, sir," James said when questioned. "I'd put it on my face like some of the other men, but I don't intend to get hit in the face all that often."

From his pocket Lennox withdrew the piece of paper Charlotte had given him.

"I'd like you to go to this address," he said. "Find a man by the name of Matthew Baumann and bring him here."

James didn't say anything as he read the address, merely nodded. Another aspect of the man's personality he liked: James didn't ask unnecessary questions.

"He won't want to come with you, of course," Lennox said. "Persuade him."

"By any means necessary?" James asked.

He smiled. The man was going to pay for what he did to Glynis. "By any means necessary."

"BUT MRS. CAMERON, Mr. Cameron told me all of your belongings were to be moved into his suite."

Mrs. Hurst looked worried, her hands fluttering in the air like butterflies.

"He won't be pleased if I don't do as he asked."

"While I assure you, Mrs. Hurst," she said, "he will be grateful you didn't succeed."

In fact, she wouldn't be surprised if Lennox wanted her to move back with her mother.

"Truly, Mrs. Cameron," the housekeeper said, trailing after her, "he was most adamant."

He had meant the move into his suite as a surprise, she was sure. Just like the honeysuckle overflowing several vases in his sitting room. He knew how much she loved the smell of the flowers.

Lennox did things like that.

She turned at the door of the guest suite and faced down the housekeeper.

"Mrs. Hurst, I'm not going to change my mind. I want to sleep here, and here is where I'm going to sleep. Please have my belongings brought back here."

Before the woman could say another word, she entered the suite and shut the door in the housekeeper's face.

When the door opened less than five minutes later, she didn't turn, merely continued staring out the window at the darkened garden.

"I'm certain you're very good at your job, Mrs. Hurst. Right now, however, I must insist. My decision is my decision."

"As is mine," Lennox said.

Startled, she turned and faced him.

"I'm sure you have no objection to me occupying this room, Lennox," she said.

"On the contrary," he said. "I do. As my wife, you should sleep beside me."

She thrust down the emotion bobbing to the surface. Neither hope nor joy had any place in this discussion.

"If you felt that way, you would have moved my things to your suite on our wedding night."

Lennox stared at her. She had the impression she'd just flummoxed him.

"You're right," he said. "Forgive my oversight, Glynis. But I want you there now."

"Have you forgotten what I told you?" she asked.

"Have you forgotten we're married?"

Since this last was said at a near shout, she fisted her hands, planted them on her hips and frowned at him.

"You're angry."

"Damn right I'm angry."

"Well, I'm not in the mood to be shouted at, Lennox, so go away."

"I'm not angry at you, Glynis," he said.

He advanced on her and, in one sweeping movement, gathered her up in his arms.

She'd never been carried by anyone before, even Lennox.

"You're not?"

"I'm angry at the whole damn situation," he said. "I'm angry at Baumann, who seems to have disappeared. I'm angry because someone killed a good man. I'm angry because my ship was damaged. I'm angry at Charlotte for not being a good enough friend to you. I'm angry at Smythe." He stopped, shook his head. "No, that doesn't describe what I'm feeling. I want to dig Smythe up and kill him again."

She stared up at him, bemused as he carried her from the room.

"I've never imprisoned a woman before, Glynis, but I'm almost tempted now. Perhaps a very long chain, one connected to your ankle. So you can't stray farther than Hillshead. No more leaving Glasgow. No more leaving me. There will be no desertions in this marriage."

A thought occurred to her. Had Lennox thought she would leave him like his mother had?

"I wasn't leaving you. I didn't think you would want to be married to me any longer," she said.

He stopped, raised his face as if searching the ceiling of the corridor, and shook his head.

"Are you daft, Glynis? Why, because of what happened in Washington? Baumann took advantage of the situation. He blackmailed you."

"That may be part of it," she said, compelled to give him the truth. "But maybe some of it was I felt needed, valuable in some way."

"Well, you're needed here." He looked down at her. "I need you here. I love you, damn it."

"Do you have to say it like that?"

"Like what?"

"I love you, damn it."

His lips quirked.

"I love you, my darling wife. I love you, Glynis. I love you."

A weight fell off her, as if she'd been carrying a yoke on her shoulders and had just now shrugged it off. She took a breath, feeling somehow lighter than before.

He strode through his sitting room and into the bedroom, dropping her onto the mattress.

Her hoop would not cooperate and insisted on flying upward and exposing her undergarments again. Lennox solved the situation by laying on top of her.

She reached up and placed her hands against his shirt, feeling the fine linen weave.

"You're a Glaswegian," she said. "You should be wearing cotton."

She both felt and heard his laughter.

"And I've no yen to talk about fabrics," he said.

"Oh, and what have you a yen to do, Lennox Cameron?"

"Seduce my wife, Glynis Cameron."

He kissed her slowly, as if they were new to it. Her heart expanded. In a moment she would be buoyant with joy, floating upward toward the ceiling.

What was love? A feeling of belonging? Was love safety? She felt safe with Lennox. She always had. No, love was more; it was the feeling of joy around the other person. The knowledge you could be yourself, share honest thoughts and concerns. Love was freedom. Love was Lennox.

"You have too many clothes on," he said. "And that damnable hoop."

She most certainly agreed.

He got up from the bed, extended his hand and helped her down.

Each of them removed a garment, matching their movements: his shirt to her bodice, his trousers to her skirt, and his shoes to hers.

"The shift and corset should count as one," he said. "Otherwise, you'll still be dressed while I'm naked."

"But then I could study you while I'm undressing."

He put his hands on his hips and grinned at her. "Study, is it?"

"I could stare at you for hours," she said. "You're very impressive."

His grin disappeared but his eyes glowed.

The itchy, warm feeling spread through her, making her breathless.

"You're still dressed," he said.

Fumbling with the tape of her hoop, she sent a near desperate look to him. Lennox came to her, giving up all pretense of patience and tearing the garment.

"I may burn this," he said, nearly snarling.

She giggled, laying her forehead against his chest.

Within seconds she was down to her shift and stockings, and those were dealt with swiftly until they were both naked.

They looked at each other.

Passion, lust, want, need, all blossomed deep inside, warming every part of her. Moisture pooled between her thighs, hunger pricked her skin.

She'd never been aroused by anyone but him. She'd never felt the sensation of being hungry for touch before.

Slowly, she walked to him, placed her hands on his shoulders, curling her fingers against his skin. She stepped closer until her nipples were gently abraded by his chest hair.

His arms went around her, his legs spread apart. They were almost mated standing up, impatient yet unhurried. Each movement, the placement of his hand on her hip and her fingers on his back, was measured in minutes rather than seconds. She moved until her feet trapped one of his. He placed his palm against her buttock.

His breath quickened. Her heartbeat raced.

Resting her forehead against his chin, she breathed in his smell: a faint odor of smoke, varnish, wood, and the sea, but most of all, Lennox. She placed a kiss on his throat, feeling the sound he made beneath her lips.

She stroked her hand over his ribs, his hip bones, the muscular plane of his chest. The sensation of knowing him stunned her.

When he led her to the bed with the delicacy of a

courtier leading her to the dance floor, she followed his lead, her hand clasped in his.

She took the steps, turning and sitting on the edge of the mattress before him. Any modesty she might have had disappeared in the simple *rightness* of this moment.

His hands framed her face, holding her captive for his eyes and then his lips. She sighed into his kiss and wrapped her arms around his waist.

He tumbled her back on the bed and joined her. She watched his face, adrift in wonder. This moment thrummed with tenderness and almost reverence, a coming together of two people who'd searched and finally found each other after years of being apart.

She brushed her knuckles down his arm, marveling at the bulge of muscle. He was so gloriously made.

He mouthed a nipple, gently grazing it with his teeth, summoning her soft moan. She gripped his buttocks, learning their curve. He kissed her beneath her ear, in the sensitive spot at the juncture of neck and shoulder. She undulated beneath him, loving the feel of him hot and hard against her.

Slowly, he entered her, an act of possession executed with tenderness. Tears pricked her eyes.

The girl she'd been must have done something right to have earned Lennox as her husband.

He whispered her name against her temple as he pushed deeper.

Her hands clenched his shoulders with nails biting into his skin. She hurt with need. She whimpered, opened her legs wider, lifted her hips up for his thrusts. She was in a long dark tunnel, heading for somewhere, the destination tantalizingly out of reach.

No, it was a vortex, a whirlpool in which he was her lifeline. Clinging to him, she felt no fear, only exultation. She knew nothing more than Lennox.

Now. Now. Now.

In those moments she lost herself. Breath rushed from her. Sound blurred in her ears, deafened by the thundering of her heart.

He groaned her name and she surrendered, exploding in a shower of stars.

She was his and he was hers, just as he'd always been.

GLYNIS SLIPPED out of bed, grabbed her wrapper and walked to the window.

Down the hill the lights of Glasgow glowed, the city awake even in the depth of night. The river shimmied as if a creature stirred uneasily beneath its surface.

From here the moon appeared to nest in the limbs of a young tree, the faint bluish light illuminating the gardener's cottage and the graveled paths connecting the different sections of the garden.

Something was bothering her. Something she should have noticed before now, like hearing a song and being unable to finish the refrain. Or remembering the first line of a poem and not the rest of the stanza. Whatever it was, she couldn't sleep for trying to remember.

She wasn't surprised Baumann had disappeared. He'd always been a chameleon, capable of becoming anything he wanted to be. As such, he could be in plain sight and you'd overlook him.

She didn't doubt he'd torched the *Raven*. But had he killed Gavin Whittaker? He was a man used to hiding in the shadows, manipulating others to do his bidding. Blackmail, yes. Coercion, yes, he was capable of that and more. Murder by his own hand? It didn't fit what she knew of Baumann.

Maybe she was wrong and he had murdered the Confederate captain. Perhaps he would do anything to achieve victory for the Union.

Why on the deck of the *Raven*? Why that particular Sunday afternoon? Had Gavin encountered Baumann in the act of sabotage? If so, why had the arson happened another day? Had he fled from the scene after killing Gavin?

Baumann wouldn't have fled from the scene.

She glanced back at Lennox, wishing he were awake. Wishing, too, she could confide in him. Would he think she was trying to spare Baumann? Or excuse him somehow?

Perhaps she should talk to the stablemaster herself before mentioning her suspicions.

Lennox moved in his sleep, throwing an arm over her pillow. His fingers spread as if trying to find her.

She stepped to the bed, tossing her wrapper to a chair, grabbing his hand and kissing it.

"I'm here, love," she said, sliding close to him.

Chapter 37

"Do you still have the umbrella, Mr. McElwee? The one you asked me about?"

The stablemaster frowned at Glynis, lowering his brows until they formed one long bushy mass across his forehead. His bulbous nose wrinkled at the effort, and twin lines appeared on either side of his mouth to accentuate his displeasure.

He smelled of garlic and leather, a curious pairing and one making her grateful to have skipped lunch.

"Have you found who it belongs to then, Mrs. Cameron?"

"I'm not sure, Mr. McElwee. Would it be possible to see it?"

He led her to a bay where found items were stored. Standing in the doorway, she scanned the contents. A woman's shoe—how did someone lose one shoe, and an expensive looking one at that? A collection of handkerchiefs, half of them unadorned while the others were trimmed in lace. An apron, not the sort worn by the servants at Hillshead. A lady's tortoiseshell comb, a man's hat, a belt, and a box looking as if it held cigarillos.

"There it is," she said, going to the corner and picking up the umbrella. "Do you know where it was found, Mr. McElwee?"

He shook his head.

"Would it be possible to ask the drivers?"

"Mr. Cameron's driver is gone, ma'am, but Thomas and Daniel are here. Thomas is polishing one of the carriages. Daniel's mending tack."

She followed him out of the bay and down the wide corridor with its packed earth floor.

The stable, constructed of the same red brick as Hillshead, was tucked far enough away that the odors of the horses didn't carry to the house. Bays lined both sides of one corridor while the second held the carriages, pony cart, and Hillshead's two wagons.

A warm breeze blew through the building, bringing with it the scent of hay. The jingle of harness and the soft nicker of the horses accompanied the laughter of the stable boys as they mucked out the bays.

Thomas was a tall, gangly man with a long face and hair the color of the brown paste he was concocting in a pail near the carriage.

She held up the umbrella for him, her eyes watering.

"Have you seen this before, Thomas? I'm looking for its owner."

He shook his head, evidently inhaling the strong odor of turpentine and saddle soap without difficulty.

She could barely breathe.

"No ma'am. Never seen it."

She thanked him and turned away, grateful to leave the area.

Daniel was sitting outside on a wooden bench pushed up against the stable wall. The driver was young, his sandy hair standing on end on the top and left long in the back. His face was pocked with scars and it looked as if he'd tried to hide the worst of them with a scraggly looking beard.

He stood when she approached, but she waved him back down again.

Once more holding up the umbrella, she asked, "Have you seen this before, Daniel?"

"Aye, I have at that," he said, nodding. "Found it in the carriage one day."

"Do you remember when?" she asked.

"I don't recall the day, Mrs. Cameron. But it was right around the time poor Mr. Whittaker was murdered." He stared down at the tack. "If I'd known the man was going to be murdered, I wouldn't have taken him to the yard."

She sank onto the bench beside him.

His hands were those of an older man, scarred with crisscrossed lines and darkened by exposure to the elements. The leather he held was lighter in color than his skin and probably softer.

"You took Mr. Whittaker to the yard?"

Had he been driving the carriage she'd seen when she arrived at Cameron and Company?

"Aye, I did, Mrs. Cameron. Took them both. Lucky, the missus was. If she'd stayed, she might've been murdered, too. Said the motion of the ship made her sick. So I brought her back to Hillshead."

She blinked at him. "You took Mrs. Whittaker to the *Raven* with her husband?"

He nodded.

She hadn't seen Lucy since her husband's death. Had she admitted to being aboard the *Raven* with her husband? Had she told Lennox or her mother? Had they thought to ask?

"But you returned to the yard for Mr. Whittaker," she said.

He nodded again.

"Why didn't you tell anyone she was with Mr. Whittaker on the *Raven*, Daniel?"

He shrugged, went on clamping the pincers on the metal fastenings. "Not my place, Mrs. Cameron. I thought it were a tragedy. She was lucky not to be murdered herself."

She stared at the umbrella in her hands, wishing Lennox or her mother were there. She would have asked them to recount the night they took the news to Lucy that her husband had been killed. Had she been surprised?

Had she seen what happened to her husband? Had she witnessed the murder? If Baumann had murdered Gavin, had he somehow convinced Lucy not to say anything? What inducement had he used? Either fear or money might succeed in silencing the woman, and Baumann wouldn't hesitate to use either.

She tried to put herself in Lucy's situation and realized she couldn't. If Baumann had harmed Lennox, she would have screamed to the heavens for justice to be done. She'd probably still be screaming. Nothing would have stopped her from ensuring Baumann was hanged.

Although she didn't like the woman, she knew how it felt to be trapped in a situation. Maybe she needed to tell Lucy her story. If she did, could she convince the woman to come forward and tell what she knew?

Baumann shouldn't be allowed to manipulate another woman again.

She thanked Daniel and made her way back to the stablemaster's office. Once there, she arranged for a carriage to drive her into the city.

LENNOX STILL appreciated the view of Hillshead with the afternoon sun glinting in the windows. He liked that the house sat on a hill, an oasis of serenity, disturbed by neither the smells nor the noise of Glasgow. He was proud of a heritage he would pass down to his children.

This afternoon, though, he wanted to be home because Glynis was there.

Glynis, who completed his life, filling the yawning

void that had been there ever since she left for London. Glynis, who made his heart ache to think of her fear and abandonment in Washington.

He didn't know how, but he was determined to make her see she'd been a weapon ably wielded by Baumann. She needed to forgive herself. If nothing else, she needed to understand she'd been used by a master manipulator.

Maybe it was a good thing he'd been stymied in finding the man.

He barely waited for the carriage to pull into the drive. After jumping from the vehicle, he signaled his driver to go on to the stables then strode into the house intent on finding his wife.

His wife. He grinned at the words.

She wasn't in their suite, but he hadn't really expected her to be meekly waiting for him.

But she wasn't at Hillshead.

"All I know, sir, is she left an hour or so ago," Mrs. Hurst said.

The day was advanced, the promise of night not too distant. He didn't want her waiting for him at the yard, especially when Baumann was missing. He didn't think the man still remained in Glasgow but he wasn't taking any chances with Glynis's safety.

He walked to the stables, addressed his driver. "I'm afraid I need to go back to the yard."

"Aye, sir," Tim said, buckling the harness he'd just removed from one of the horses.

"We must have passed my wife."

"No, sir," the stablemaster said from behind him.

He turned to face Mr. McElwee.

"Mrs. Cameron had Daniel take her to the Lafayette Hotel."

"The Lafayette Hotel?"

"I think it has to do with the umbrella, sir. Mrs. Cameron thinks it belongs to Mrs. Whittaker."

"And she's gone to return it?"

He was trying to make sense of the stablemaster's words. The less Glynis saw of Lucy Whittaker, the better. Why would she be returning her umbrella? Why not simply send a driver or a maid to do the errand?

"She seemed concerned about the actual day Mrs. Whittaker misplaced it."

Another mystery to join the first. He opened the carriage door, then turned back to the stablemaster.

"When did Mrs. Whittaker lose it?"

The man frowned, the vertical lines between his eyebrows deepening.

"The day of the captain's death, sir."

"Take me to the Lafayette Hotel, Tim."

Worry clawed into his mind. He couldn't put his thoughts into words, but something didn't feel right, and it was enough to add a request to his driver.

"Get there as fast as you can."

Chapter 38

*A*fter introducing herself at the front desk, Glynis was led up the broad marble steps and showed to the second floor by a solicitous porter.

She would have to recommend the Lafayette Hotel to other visitors. The lobby was impressive, with its soaring ceiling and arched doorways. The beautiful stained-glass windows of the cupola tossed blue, yellow, and crimson light onto the marble floor, showering the well-dressed patrons in a rainbow.

Off the lobby was the fabled Tea Room about which she'd heard so much. The glass doors revealed tables filled with women.

At the landing they turned and entered a long hall. A tall window at the end illuminated the crimson runner, ivory wallpaper, and dark wainscoting.

At a door numbered 206, the porter stopped, bowed, and asked, "Shall I bring tea, Mrs. Cameron?"

"I won't be staying that long," she said. "But thank you."

He bowed, glancing at her curiously.

She thanked him again, waiting until he left before knocking.

A moment later Lucy opened the door and just as quickly moved to slam it shut again, but Glynis thrust the umbrella between the door and the jamb.

"I need to talk to you," she said, shouldering her way into the room.

"I don't want to talk to you." Lucy finally released the door, stepping back and scowling at her. "You Scots are devoid of manners."

Glynis ignored the comment and closed the door behind her.

The room was good-sized. In addition to a reading chair and table, it contained a large comfortable-looking bed, an armoire, and a piece of furniture that looked like it might do dual duty as a desk or a vanity. A pitcher and bowl sat atop a small bureau to her left. The rest of the facilities would be at the end of the hall, common enough in most hotels, at least the ones she'd visited in Washington or New York.

"Why didn't you tell anyone you were on board the *Raven* when your husband was killed?"

"Does it matter whether or not I was there?" Lucy said.

"It matters a great deal. You might've seen something." She tapped the end of the umbrella on the floor as if it were a cane. "You left this behind."

"Yes, thank you," Lucy said, turning and reaching for the umbrella.

"Why did you leave it behind?" Glynis asked, pulling it away. "Were you in that much of a hurry? Did you see anyone aboard the *Raven*?"

Lucy shook her head.

"No one at all? Matthew Baumann wasn't there? Did he kill your husband, Lucy, and pay you to keep silent?"

"Who is Matthew Baumann?"

Was it possible Lucy had never met the man? Or was she just a superb liar?

"You don't have to be afraid of him."

"I'm not afraid of anyone and I don't know who you're talking about."

Glynis blew out a breath, feeling foolish. She'd been so certain Lucy had been convinced to remain silent.

She walked to the door, opened it, and turned.

"You didn't see anything? You've no idea who killed your husband?"

Lucy shook her head.

She realized she still held the umbrella. She was extending it to Lucy, but the other woman didn't wait and jerked it out of her hand. Glynis's fingers slid on the handle, accidentally releasing the opening mechanism.

Slowly, the umbrella unfurled, the black fabric stained the color of rust. She stared at it, thinking as she spoke. "If you left the *Raven* before your husband was killed, how did blood get on your umbrella?"

She watched as Lucy's face changed. Gone was the whiner she'd met during their day of shopping and sightseeing. This woman looked older, the lines around her thin lips accentuated and a calculating look in her narrowed eyes.

"Do you know what he wanted me to do? He wanted to take me in the captain's cabin. To christen it, he said. To make sure it knew I was welcome. As if a ship had thoughts and feelings. He cared more about the *Raven* than he did me."

"No one else was there," Glynis said, taking a step back. "You killed Gavin."

"I killed him," Lucy said, her smile eerily pleasant. "I stabbed him with his own stupid knife. It was so incredibly easy, I should have done it earlier. If I had known how quick he would die, or how good I'd be at it, I would have."

Glynis gripped the frame of the door to steady herself. Otherwise, her knees might have given out.

"He loved that cane of his. He was forever showing

it off. He had another one made, you know. A wedding present." She smiled, revealing a great many white, sharp teeth.

She pushed a button Glynis hadn't seen on the umbrella handle, grabbed the crook and pulled it free. At the end was a stiletto, the match of the one she'd seen buried in Gavin's chest.

"I'm going home," Lucy said brightly. "You can't stop me. I'm leaving this horrible country and returning to England. I'll be with my parents and my brothers and sisters and Jasper."

She would be hanged. But Glynis didn't say that. One did not argue with a madwoman.

She took another step back, and Lucy followed her. Yet another step as Lucy's smile grew broader.

Tension hummed through her as she slid her hand in her reticule, feeling a measure of hope once her fingers skimmed the cold metal of the Derringer.

"Shall we see if practice makes perfect?" Lucy asked. "Do you think my aim will be as good with you as it was with Gavin? Will you die as quickly?"

"How are you going to explain me being dead in your room?"

Fear was a narrow ribbon tightening around her chest, harnessing her breath.

For a moment madness left Lucy's eyes and calculation took over. "Thank you, I hadn't thought of that. Perhaps I can simply drag you to one of the empty rooms." Her gaze swept over Glynis. "You don't look like you weigh much. I doubt it will be difficult."

With her thumb, Glynis fumbled for the mechanism to cock the gun. She had never fired the Derringer before and hoped it was as easy as simply pulling the trigger. Why hadn't she checked to see if it had a bullet in it? For that matter, how did she check to see if it was loaded?

Lucy was too close, but wasn't a Derringer a close-range weapon? It was nothing like a rifle for shooting game at a long distance. No, the victim had to be within a few feet.

Nausea zigzagged down her spine at the thought of shooting anyone.

A flash of something caught her attention but she didn't turn her head. Please let it be the porter or someone else, a witness who would summon help.

Terror rooted her to the spot. Fear clamped her insides, making it difficult to breathe.

"Everyone talked about you," Lucy said. "It was sickening. Glynis MacIain, returning to Scotland like a prodigal daughter. That's all I ever wanted to do. I wanted to go home. Do you think I'm going to let you stop me now?"

Lucy lunged. Glynis threw her midsection back, avoiding the knife by a hair. Suddenly, she was grabbed, jerked from the doorway and thrown to the side. Lucy shrieked, raised her arm and launched herself at Glynis.

The sound of the exploding shot deafened her.

She slid to the carpet in a jumble of ill-connected limbs. Nothing was working the way it should. Pain raced through her, making her gasp.

Her hand fell trembling but useless. She hadn't shot Lucy. Looking up, she tried to focus. Where was that pain coming from?

She closed her eyes, then opened them a second later. The tableau had not changed. Matthew Baumann stood there holding a smoking gun. At his feet was Lucy Whittaker, blood spreading from the wound in her stomach.

Had she been shot, too?

She couldn't die now. Not when she'd come home to Lennox. Not when he loved her. Not now.

The smell of gunpowder hung in the corridor. Thundering footsteps made it sound as if a crowd raced toward them, but it was only the porter and the man who'd greeted her at the desk.

Baumann would have to explain. Right now, breathing was all she could do.

Glynis made herself look at Lucy's face, away from the blood and into the madness.

"All I only really wanted," Lucy said weakly, her gaze on Glynis, "was to go home."

Glynis looked away as pain jutted through her, writhing from her arm to her chest. She swallowed against it, clinging to coherence. She thought of Lennox, kept his face in her mind.

She had to be brave because of him. She couldn't die now.

Her feet didn't look damaged. Nor did her legs. She made herself look at her stomach, afraid to find a matching wound to Lucy's. Nothing.

Blood soaked her left sleeve.

Her new dress was ruined. The tear from the knife might be able to be repaired, but the blood would be very difficult to get out of the pale yellow fabric.

Her stomach rebelled, threatening to publicly humiliate her. She closed her eyes. She breathed deeply a few times until she mastered her nausea, then fixed her gaze on Baumann. He was tearing a towel into strips.

"Were you following me?"

"No," he said. "I was watching her."

"Why?"

"I knew I hadn't killed Gavin Whittaker," he said. "That didn't leave too many other suspects."

The porter knelt beside her and tried to put a compress on her arm. She batted him away or at least thought she did, but he clung to her like a tick.

"Please, madam, let me help you."

She reluctantly nodded, hoping she didn't scream, but he was pressing very hard against the wound.

"I even considered you or your husband," Baumann said, taking the rest of the toweling he hadn't given the porter and using it to press against Lucy's wound.

"You thought me capable of murder, Baumann?" she asked, trying to take her mind from the pain.

"I suspect you could do almost anything you wanted to do, Glynis, given enough motivation."

"What was my motivation in your imaginary scenario? Why would I have killed Gavin Whittaker?"

"The better scenario was your husband killing him. Maybe he didn't want to turn over the *Raven* after all."

She shook her head then closed her eyes on a wave of dizziness.

"What a silly thing to think. Lennox wouldn't kill anyone."

Another set of footsteps should have warned her, but she was so faint she wanted to lay down on the floor alongside Lucy.

Of course it was Lennox, and of course he was instantly furious.

"What the hell happened, Baumann?"

"Mrs. Whittaker tried to kill your wife, Cameron. I saved her. I'd appreciate if you didn't look like you're ready to shoot me."

She wished everyone would be quiet and the porter would stop hurting her.

Lennox brushed him away, but his touch was even more forceful.

"That hurts, Lennox."

"I know, love. We have to stop the bleeding."

We? It was her blood, although her blood wasn't as copious as Lucy's. But the porter and the man at the desk were now helping Baumann. How strange to shoot someone and then try to save her life.

"You need to tell Baumann you didn't kill Gavin."

"Later. I'm going to pick you up now."

She blinked at Lennox. She was feeling very, very odd.

"I want you to hold this in place." He guided her hands to the compress, her fingers smooth against the cotton. Was this a MacIain Mills product?

"Glynis, do you understand?"

She nodded, glancing at her arm and instantly wishing she hadn't. What an ugly wound. Her flesh gaped open like a gutted fish, her blood spurting on the floor, the cotton, and her clothing. Even Lennox was bloody.

He gently pulled her into his arms and stood. How very strong he was.

She would have said something, tried to explain the situation, given him an assurance she was fine, just fine, but the air was growing oddly gauzy, like gloaming.

Grayness enveloped her, pain her escort as the world fell away.

WHEN SHE woke, it was in their suite with the drapes open to reveal a bright and sunny day.

Why was she so woozy? And hungry? Her eyes felt gritty, the corners pulled too tight. She blinked, her vision finally clearing. Feeling the pull of his presence, she slowly turned her head.

Lennox was sitting there staring at her as though he wanted to imprint her face in his mind.

Through half-closed eyes she watched him. Sunlight danced on the windowpane as if wanting to get into the room to touch him. The cooing of the doves was almost like a chant, a bright day, a bright day, a bright day refrain, as if giving the other birds a fore-telling of the weather.

How very precious he was to her. She moved the hand closest to him, only to wince in pain. She stared at the impressive bandage on her arm and, in that instant, remembered everything.

"Is she going to live?" she asked.

"The woman tried to kill you, Glynis."

"I know."

Lucy Whittaker was a pathetic creature, one with whom she surprisingly had something in common. Perhaps she would've been as desperate and maddened if she'd been unable to come home to Scotland.

If she hadn't had Lennox, a lodestone for her heart and her dreams, what would have happened to her?

"I don't know how she is," he said. "She's still alive."

Lucy had been shot in the stomach. From what she'd heard in Washington, those were the worst kind of wounds. The poor victim would suffer, sometimes for weeks, before finally succumbing to their injury. Either that or septicemia set in. Perhaps Lucy would be more fortunate than those Civil War combatants and survive.

"And Baumann?"

His face stiffened.

"He saved my life," she said.

"I know, but I don't have to like him."

"No, you don't have to like him."

"He took advantage of you."

She only smiled, knowing better than to defend Baumann in any way.

Baumann was determined to win his own personal war. But she was the one who'd gone to him in the first place. She'd initiated everything.

"I should have figured it out," Lennox said. "She never asked how Gavin died. I should have noticed that, but I didn't."

"Have you much experience with murderers?"

His smile was wry. "Less than you. How did you know it was Lucy?"

"I didn't," she said. "Not until I was in the hotel room and the umbrella opened." In a halting voice she explained what happened.

The encounter had left a residue on her soul, a bit of ash that might disappear with time. Or would it always remain there, a reminder of more naiveté that had been burned away?

"Saving your life is the only decent thing Baumann's done since arriving in Glasgow," he said, his frown an impressive demonstration of irritation. "But how? Was he following you again?"

"He'd been watching Lucy," she said. "He suspected she had something to do with her husband's death."

"It would've been nice if he'd told someone."

She agreed. "But I don't suppose it's reasonable to ask a spy to divulge his secrets."

"The man needs to leave Glasgow, leave Scotland, and stay on his own side of the Atlantic."

Another point on which she agreed.

She didn't need constant reminders of Washington to recall her time there. Those years remained in her mind and her memory. One day, hopefully, she'd be able to replace them with better thoughts and recollections.

"Are there any other secrets in your past?" he asked.

"I've loved you ever since I was a girl," she said. "Now you know my last and greatest secret."

He didn't say anything for a moment, only looked at her.

"And now?"

"I love you still, damn it."

He smiled as he leaned over and gently kissed her.

When she'd been hurt, all she'd thought about was Lennox. She was alive and so was he, sitting beside her with a look of love in his eyes.

She stretched out her right hand over her body and he grabbed it, bent and placed a kiss on her knuckles.

He really shouldn't do things like that. He would bring her to tears, and she felt too close to crying as it was.

If not for the pain, the world would be a perfect place.

Chapter 39

"*I* would have come if you asked," Matthew Baumann said, pulling his sleeve away from James's grasp. "There was no need to send one of your men after me."

Lennox dismissed James with his thanks and sat behind his desk. Once he learned Baumann had taken a room at the Lafayette Hotel, the better to watch Lucy, he simply sent James to retrieve him.

"On the contrary, I think there was every need."

He sat relaxed, his arms bent at the elbows and leaning slightly forward. A deceptive pose since he wanted to march across the room and punch Baumann in the face. If he broke the man's jaw, he wouldn't mind. Perhaps doing so would make it difficult for him to speak or threaten anyone in the future.

Baumann was walking the walls of models, picking one up, putting it back in place. He stopped in front of the Vixen, surveying the model from all sides.

"You're a talented designer, Cameron. Are you building more iron-hulled ships? This one is a beauty."

"I didn't bring you here to discuss my ships."

"No, but you do want to discuss your wife." Baumann turned and faced him, a rakish smile on his face. "How is she?"

"Better," he said. The day after the incident, Glynis refused to stay in bed, insisting on being up and about.

"I have important things to do," she said when he

questioned her. "First, I have to make a list of all the duties Mary and I have to discuss. Who will be in charge of meals and other tasks. Secondly, I have to bury my gun."

"Your gun?" he asked, startled.

She nodded, then shocked him by pulling a Derringer from her reticule.

"It was Richard's. I would have used it on Lucy, but I froze. I wanted to shoot her, but my finger wouldn't move."

"And after you bury the gun?" he asked. "What will you do then?"

"Look over the household ledgers," she said. "We could practice some economies. There's a great deal of waste at Hillshead."

A surge of warmth almost knocked him back on his heels. Not simply desire this time but another emotion, love coupled with joy.

"Then have at it," he said. "My life and my ledgers are open to you."

For now, however, he was facing down Baumann, and ensuring the man knew he was no longer welcome in Glasgow.

"What do you want to ask me? Go ahead, as far as Glynis is concerned I have no more secrets."

"I would reassess the statement if I were you," Lennox said. "That's my wife you're talking about. She's not your operative any longer."

The other man's eyes widened. "I'm surprised she told you."

"She's my wife."

"As you've said." Baumann shrugged. "I don't go around telling people who I employ, or don't, for that matter."

"I suggest you not try to employ anyone else in Glasgow."

Baumann startled him by laughing. "I doubt I could. I've been the recipient of more than one strange glance, let me tell you."

"I'll thank you for saving Glynis, but it's little enough payment for taking advantage of her."

"Did I? War makes people think differently than they would in peacetime, Cameron. All sorts of things that were once meaningful no longer are, like chivalry."

"Or honor?"

Baumann's mustache tilted. "Honor is defined according to which side you're on, Cameron. Am I honorable to the War Department? Most assuredly. But to a Confederate? I'm the epitome of a slimy snake." With the last two words his voice altered, took on a southern drawl. "A friend of mine has a saying. 'War is hell.' Sherman fights in the trenches. My battlefields were in the ballrooms and at the dining tables of Washington."

"Using women as your foil."

"Using anyone," he said unapologetically. "Anyone who could suit my purposes, Cameron."

"You might not have murdered Whittaker, but were you involved in any of the other murders along the Clyde?"

Baumann sauntered to his desk, took the chair at his side and crossed his legs, looking supremely unconcerned at the question.

"I think, if you'll check, you'll find the majority of the murders happened before I was in your country."

"Except for one. A Union colonel, I believe. Was he one of your men?"

Baumann's face took on the appearance of granite. "You'll understand if I don't answer that."

"Why, exactly, are you in Scotland?"

Baumann smiled. "The scenery? The fresh air? You

know why I'm here, Cameron. To investigate your firm."

He waited, but Baumann didn't say anything else. What did he expect the man to do, launch into a fevered confession that he was desperately in love with Glynis?

"Did you set fire to the *Raven*?"

Baumann tipped his head back and laughed.

"Come now, you don't expect me to answer that, do you? I imagine you have a policeman stationed somewhere, waiting for me to make such an improvident confession. Even if I did, why would I would tell you?"

"I've posted enough guards around the ship to prevent you from doing it again. Just a fair warning."

"Oh, but there are plenty of men who are unemployed, Cameron, who'd be willing to do almost anything for the right amount of money. Maybe swim to the side and plant a bomb on the hull. Or toss a bottle filled with kerosene and a lit rag onto a dock. Can you guard your ship against the whole of Glasgow?"

"Yes, dammit, I can."

"Your mother told me you were a stubborn man."

He held himself still with an effort.

"I should have listened to her," Baumann said, watching him intently.

Did the man expect him to explode in questions? Is that why Baumann was taunting him?

"I'm going to break one of my rules, Cameron. She's one of my operatives. One of my best ones. She lives in the South, you know."

"Get out." He pushed the words past numb lips. "Get the hell out of my office, Baumann. And off my yard. And out of Glasgow."

"You look a great deal like your mother, you know. Did no one ever tell you?"

Baumann stood, smiling down at him. "Olivia is a

lovely creature with thick black hair and green eyes like yours. She has a mole near her mouth. The years have not altered her accent. When she's angry, I can barely understand what she says."

"I don't believe you."

"I told her I was coming to Glasgow and she wanted to relay a message. To you and your sister. Mary, isn't it?"

He didn't respond.

"She wanted to know if you could forgive her. She didn't desert you; she just changed her life."

He wasn't going to respond to Baumann's words or his goading smile.

"Very well, Cameron. Since I have some fondness for your mother, I'll tell her you conveyed your warm wishes. Now about Glynis. Treat her well, Cameron. Or I might have to return to Scotland."

"And do what you did to Smythe?"

Baumann's smile slipped. "You figured that out, did you? A tragic accident. A despicable man with a penchant for near children, a dark night, and a runaway carriage. A recipe for disaster, don't you think?"

Lennox only stared after the man long after the door closed.

FOR DAYS, Lennox treated her like she was a precious glass ornament, some objet d'art he rescued from Russia and now cherished as priceless. In addition, he'd summoned her mother, who, on learning of the injury, insisted on clucking over her like a chick who'd wandered too far from the nest. Between Lennox, her mother, Lily, and Mrs. Hurst—who proved to be an exceptional gatekeeper—she was swaddled and cosseted and prevented from doing anything. She couldn't even cough without one of them rushing to her side, asking if she was all right.

She slept beside Lennox at night, and when she was restless with pain, he woke and was at her beck and call. Did she need some of the laudanum the doctor had prescribed? No, thank you. A jot of whiskey, a glass of wine? No, thank you again. Nor did she want something to eat or a book to read. She wanted only to lay there beside him and watch him as he slept, experiencing the joy.

She spent the time healing, each day better than the next, until one morning, she was certain, she would wake and not even notice her arm. She would have a scar, an ugly one preventing her from wearing certain evening dresses, but did it matter?

Eleanor was convinced to leave and take Lily with her when Mary and Mr. Cameron arrived home. Glynis had never seen her new sister-in-law looking so beautiful. She almost glowed with good health and happiness. Even Mr. Cameron appeared wonderfully fit. Her father-in-law hugged and kissed her.

"It's about time the two of you wed," he said to her surprise.

She and Lennox only smiled at each other.

Lennox was finally persuaded to go back to the yard. She doubted, however, if anything would make Mrs. Hurst stop watching her so closely.

To escape the housekeeper's eagle eye, she took to walking in the gardens. Today was another glorious day. Hillshead's perch on the top of its hill made the house impervious to the smoke of Glasgow. Brisk breezes carried it far away, freshening the air and making her feel as if she lived in an enchanted place indeed.

She was dressed in one of her new dresses, the feat accomplished by a dressmaker with nearly as much skill as the woman she'd employed in Washington.

With only one set of measurements, the seamstresses had provided a wardrobe fitting for the wife of one of the wealthiest men in Glasgow.

A man only slightly less wealthy, thanks to his generosity. Duncan had not refused Lennox's draft. To do so would be stupid, revealing an excess of pride. She'd already demonstrated how foolish a MacIain could be. Let there only be one idiot in the family.

She'd told Lennox about Washington. Instead of condemning her, he'd urged her to forgive herself.

Would that be possible? Or was she going to have this stain on her soul forever? Would she always have to deal with what she'd done? She suspected she was, just as it would probably be the right penance. She'd never considered that what she was doing would have ramifications far beyond the moment. Just as she'd never thought marrying so precipitously would affect other people.

Perhaps every person had a worn spot on their soul. A place where a bad deed, an inconsiderate remark, a bit of cruelty, burned away the goodness. Could you ever patch those threadbare spots? Could you ever make up for those mistakes?

If regrets were ships, she'd have enough to fill the Clyde. Yet she had love as well. On balance, she had more love than regrets. She loved her mother, Duncan, Lily, and Mabel. They were all her family and would always have a spot in her heart. She adored Lennox. She always had. She knew she always would.

The sun faded behind Glasgow as if embarrassed, leaving a blushing sky behind. The Clyde reddened, mirroring the sky, bustling with activity as day turned into night: a barge belched upstream, a ship slid out of dock. Slowly, ships became shadows and spires in the darkness.

Stars blinked hazily in the sky as if rousing from sleep as the moon tucked itself behind the riffling clouds.

The air was warm, scented with roses and mint. A soft breeze caressed her cheek and danced up her skirt. Lights began to shine in Hillshead's windows. She heard a frog's low-pitched bellow, the chirping of an insect, the rustle of something in the taller grass just beyond the garden.

How long had it been since she'd taken the time to simply hear the world around her? Not the chatter of people or the hum of voices. Not the clatter of wheels on cobblestones or the drone of engines, but the sound of nothing but life.

The beating of her heart in her chest, the indrawn breath and exhaled sigh, the clench of her fingers against the hewn wood of the bench, were all signs of her own life. The temporary permanence of it, the proof of her existence.

In this instance, in this moment, in this exact time, she felt strangely more Scot than she ever had. She was as elemental as her ancestors, all those proud women who'd marched over the craigs and through the glens of the Highlands, determined to aid their men in protecting their homes. They'd done so clad in plaids and almost nothing else, and here she was in a new dress, sitting outside a magnificent home built by one of their descendants.

If they could have seen through the mists of time, what would the Camerons have thought about Lennox? For that matter, what would the MacIains, proud Highlanders themselves, have thought of her?

Would they have uttered words of caution to the heedless Glynis? Or would they have had any measure of compassion for her?

She heard him coming, his feet crunching on the

gravel. When Lennox sat beside her, his shoes dug into the path, making runnels in the shells. She let the silence build between them until it was a third participant in their nonconversation.

Darkness enshrouded them, creating a perfect place, an island in the world. They were far away from murder, war, revenge, or drama. Here only the echoes of a joyous childhood intruded, scenes of her racing along the paths or climbing one of Hillshead's great oak trees. Lennox shouting at her to stop, he'd catch up with her soon enough. Or telling her she was going to fall, which is exactly what she'd done.

Most of her sweetest memories included him, and now, some of her worst.

She turned to him, wishing the moon would emerge from behind a cloud and illuminate him.

"Why didn't you tell me what you felt all those years?" he asked.

"I tried," she said, looking away.

"When?"

"The night you were entertaining the Russians. When Lidia Bobrova couldn't walk without hanging onto you."

"Just before you disappeared."

She turned to look at him. "What would you have said if I'd managed to tell you?"

"I don't know," he said. "I would have been shocked, but then I was already feeling a little odd. You had just kissed me, you see." He reached over and placed his arm around her shoulders. "I wasn't able to forget that kiss for a very long time."

"I should have seduced you," she said. "You would have had to marry me."

He laughed. "If Duncan hadn't shot me."

"When did you know you loved me?"

"It began the night we kissed. But before I knew it,

you were married and here I was, feeling as if I'd been hit by a cannonball. In all those years I told myself to forget you. To go on with my life. I met a nice sensible woman I discovered I couldn't marry because she wasn't you."

She sighed and put her head on his shoulder.

"I can't be sorry, Lennox," she said. "If you'd married her we wouldn't be here now."

"In the garden with my wife."

My wife. She loved the sound of that. *Mrs. Cameron.* That, too.

"When you came home you were Glynis, but all grown up. Everything crystallized in that moment."

"I tried to forget you," she said. "I tried, truly. But every time I turned around and saw a man with black hair, I was reminded of you. Every time the wind blew the scent of the sea to me, I thought about you."

"Every day's a new day, Glynis. A new start. We shouldn't carry around the past like sacks of coal. We're married and we've the rest of our lives together. Let's not waste time regretting what happened."

Could she do that? Could she simply accept her good fortune and turn her face to the future? She was going to try.

"We'll shock the gossips of Glasgow with how happy we are," she said. "Still, I imagine they'll carry on for a while with tales of me. Mrs. Cameron, involved in a shooting in the Lafayette Hotel. Or Mrs. Cameron, knifed by a madwoman."

"Mrs. Cameron, solving a murder."

"There was that, I suppose," she said.

"Mrs. Cameron, adored by her husband."

Her toes curled.

She glanced up at him, his face limned by moonlight. He was her best friend and always had been.

Now they were lovers with a thrumming need stretching between them.

"And I want you, Lennox. I have for a very long time." When he bent and kissed her softly, her breath left her on a gasp.

She tilted her head and looked at him.

"Lennox," she said softly. "Are you trying to seduce me in the garden?"

He bent until his lips hovered just over hers. "Now that's an idea, Glynis Cameron. Would you dare to be so brazen?"

He stood and pulled her up to him. His mouth landed on hers, crushing her lips. His hand slid around her neck, cupping her head as his mouth opened, demanding surrender. His tongue slid between her lips, inciting her moan as she dropped her head back into his palm.

His body fitted against hers as if they were designed for each other. He kneed her legs apart, his thigh rubbing against her, the friction almost unbearable.

Her hands scrabbled inside his shirt, desperate to feel him, to taste him. Heat sizzled through her, danced with fiery feet up her spine and back down, settling in her abdomen.

Suddenly, they were on a grassy spot near the intersection of garden paths. To her left was the kitchen garden. To her right was the path to the flower gardens. And Lennox's fingers deftly unfastening the buttons of her bodice.

"I've noticed you've no hoop," he said, his moonlight grin charming her.

"I'm at home. I'm only wearing a petticoat."

"Good, as long as it doesn't spring up and hit me, we'll manage fine."

She didn't have a chance to ask him how, exactly,

they would manage before he'd freed her breasts, leaving them exposed to the moonlight and his seeking lips.

He yanked her close, her back arching, his mouth branding her with his touch. Her hands gripped his arms as he lifted her and just as gently deposited her on the grass.

She realized he had no intention of removing her clothing at all, not with his hand insistent beneath her skirt. All she could do was reciprocate, but he was placing kisses all over her breasts, driving every thought from her head.

"Take your trousers off," she managed to say to his answering chuckle.

"I've no wish to be bare-assed naked, my darling Glynis."

"I don't know why," she said. "It's a beautiful ass."

Laughter added another spice to passion. The sensation flooded through her body to puddle low in her stomach.

She wanted him now and needed him forever.

The moonlight accentuated the planes and shadows of his face. He was the most beautiful creature she'd ever seen, monochromatic, alluring, and hers.

Her breath left her on a groan when he found her with his fingers.

"Ah, Glynis, you've spoilt me for any other woman." He levered himself over her. "No one else will ever love me like you do, my darling girl."

Pushing her skirts aside, he found the open slit in her pantaloons and entered her.

"They won't make the top of my head explode. Or make me feel like I'm out on the ocean with a new ship surging beneath me."

"Are you calling me a ship?" she asked, feeling an exultation she'd never before experienced. She wanted to laugh and shout at the same time.

"You're my ship, Glynis. Mine."

Words were beyond her. All she felt was delight and need and tears and joy and a wanting deep in her bones.

He withdrew, entered, and withdrew again, a movement like the endless tide. She toed off her shoes, wrapped her legs around his, her heart racing and her breath sawing in her lungs.

His talented mouth drugged her with his kisses, teased her nipples until they were erect and begging.

She could see the moon over his shoulder bathing them in a bluish light. Pagans in the garden, loving on the good earth of Scotland, mating in hunger and near desperation.

The explosion of feeling caught her unaware, forced a startled cry from her, one silenced by Lennox's kiss. Then he joined her in bliss, the moment frozen in time, a recollection she'd use to replace other memories not so dear.

When she came back to herself she was lying on the ground with her skirt still thrown up around her waist and her breasts bare to the night breeze.

"I've lost one of my shoes," she said dazedly, re-membering the bay in the stable. Now, at least, she knew how a shoe could be lost.

Had the estimable Mrs. Hurst engaged in a passion-ate interlude with the bearish stablemaster? They were both unmarried and of a similar age. She pondered the thought until Lennox spoke.

"It's over there in the flower bed," Lennox said. A moment later he abruptly sat up. "I forgot about your arm," he said.

"So did I. I'm fine." The wound ached a little, but that was a small price to pay for the bliss the rest of her was experiencing.

She fiddled with her skirt, pushing it over her bent knees.

"Are you certain?"

She placed her hand on his bristly cheek. Her heart expanded in a futile effort to hold all her happiness.

"I'm very certain, Lennox," she said softly.

He arranged himself next to her, his arm a pillow for her head. She stared up at the sky and its panorama of swiftly moving clouds and stars. The moon seemed to wink at her as if promising not to speak of what he'd witnessed. Somewhere not far away, an animal scampered through the grass, no doubt to tell the tale of what he'd seen to his interested brethren.

"We have gamboled in the garden," she said.

"That we have."

She really should be more horrified but she only felt wonderful, her body still echoing with satisfaction.

"Do you think we were seen?" she asked, looking up at the windows.

"I sincerely hope not," he said. "If so, we've certainly given the servants enough fodder for gossip. And my father and sister."

Oh good heavens, she'd forgotten they'd returned. Sitting up, she stretched out her arm and grabbed her shoe.

"It's all your fault," she said. "You seduced me."

"Or you seduced me."

"Perhaps we seduced each other," she countered. "Mr. and Mrs. Cameron frolicking in the garden as we were once accused of doing. Adam and Eve cavorting among the flowers and the vegetables."

He laughed and she joined him.

If anyone saw them, she simply didn't care.

"I love you," she said, glancing over her shoulder at him. "I love you so much, Lennox. I'll love you forever."

"And I love you, Glynis. With my whole heart. *Byde weill, betyde weill.*"

She smiled at the Scottish saying: everything comes to him who waits.

Tossing her shoe down, she leaned closer for another kiss.

Author's Notes

If you've ever walked through Glasgow, you know the Glaswegian accent is difficult to decipher without practice.

Glasgow, the largest city in Scotland, is a wonderful place to explore. The Necropolis, begun around 1831, is the site of beautiful monuments by Scottish architects.

Scotland's main contribution to the Industrial Revolution was the building of steel-hulled ships. By 1864 more than twenty shipyards existed along the Clyde and at least twenty thousand vessels were built there in the past two hundred years.

Few archival records remain relating to shipyard employment, so I took an educated guess at how many men might have been employed at Cameron and Company.

"Clyde built" has come to mean excellence and reliability. Cunard liners (such as the Queens) were Clyde-built ships. So, too, some of the paddle wheelers that traverse the Mississippi.

Something I never realized until my research on Clydeside shipyards: the Clydesdale horse was bred to haul lumber and various supplies along the Clyde.

William Cameron's career was modeled after an amalgam of shipbuilders who had yards both in Russia and Scotland. Charles Mitchell, a Scottish shipbuilder, was decorated with the Imperial Order of St.

Stanislaus, Second Class (awarded to foreign nationals) for his work in St. Petersburg.

Glasgow's police force, sometimes described as the first municipal police force, did more than just policing. Like the older city watchmen, they also called the hours, swept the streets, and fought fires.

Continue reading for a sneak peek
at *New York Times* bestselling author
Karen Ranney's breathtaking second
installment in the MacIain series

Scotsman of My Dreams

Coming August 2015

Chapter 1

London
July, 1862

Three hours past noon on a muggy July day, Minerva Todd got into her carriage, jerked her gloves on, retied her bonnet ribbons, and stared straight ahead as if to speed the vehicle to its destination.

The day, although already well advanced, was shy on sunlight. Pewter-colored clouds moved in from the east, bringing with them a sodden breeze and the scent of rain.

She inserted a gloved finger between her cheek and the bonnet ribbon, wishing the fabric wasn't irritating. Anything new was bound to chafe, at least until a certain familiarity had been achieved.

The dress was not new, however. Instead, she wore one of her serviceable dark-blue day dresses. She'd had half a dozen of the dresses made so she could detach the white collar and cuffs when she was working. Otherwise, she wore her most favorite garment, a divided skirt much like trousers.

Today she had to appear garbed like a proper woman of London, at least until this ghastly errand was finished.

As much as she would have liked to be on an expedition, the wet spring and early-summer weather had prevented it. Yet, even if she'd been blessed with sunshine in Scotland she wouldn't have left London. Not until she had an answer about Neville.

Where was her brother?

The earl had not answered her five letters, the latest only three days ago.

She had no choice but to call on the man.

She'd heard stories about Dalton MacIain. The man had a foolish soubriquet—the Rake of London—and was rumored to have once had a royal lover, one of the cousins of the Queen herself.

The fact that he'd broken off the arrangement was scandalous enough, but he'd also recounted certain personal facts to a gathering of men no better than himself. Namely, that the woman in question liked the color red. To please her, he'd had his undergarments dyed crimson. He'd flaunted his Scottish heritage by parading around her rooms attired in nothing more than a swath of crimson and black tartan.

The Queen had not been pleased by the tales of her cousin's licentiousness. The poor woman had been shipped off to Australia to tour sheep farms. No doubt she'd been told to mend her ways if she ever wanted to appear at court again.

Wayward women were never applauded in society.

The Rake of London, however, was a perennial darling. People laughed at his escapades. They excused his excesses. They allowed—no, encouraged—his complete disregard of the most basic tenets of civilization.

He was, in a word, a reprobate, a miscreant, and a libertine. And now he was an earl. A complete and total waste of a proper title.

When the carriage stopped in front of the large townhouse belonging to the man, she stared through the window at the broad steps, her eyes traveling upward to encompass the three stories of the structure. How like MacIain not to simply live in a fashionable square, but in a house that took up one whole corner of it. The structure seemed to proclaim itself a royal residence. At the very least, it was a home for someone filled with his own consequence.

From what she'd heard, the man was attractive. Looks faded. Intelligence didn't. The earl was, from his actions, a very stupid man. What did she care how attractive the apple if the fruit within was rotten?

Besides, overuse of the sexual member prompted disease, a few of them quite ghastly. At their meeting she would keep her distance, check to see if his limbs trembled, or if he had a certain type of rash.

Had he been gentlemanly enough to respond to any of her letters, she would've opened each with great care. Perhaps she would have worn her gloves and spread the paper flat on some scrubbable surface. Once she had the information she needed, she would have transcribed everything and burned his original letter, the better to protect herself from any of his many contaminations.

She had quite a wealth of correspondence from various men across the continent. The topic had not been as important as her missives to the Earl of Rathsmere, but each man had been kind enough to answer her letters.

Yet the earl had not seen fit to respond to her inquiries, and he was the only one with the information she was desperate to obtain.

Her driver dismounted, came around and opened the door for her.

"Are you very certain you wish to do this, Minerva?"

She smiled at Hugh. He was the perfect example of attractiveness, intelligence, and character.

"I see no other recourse," she said. "He hasn't answered my letters. What else can I do?"

"He may refuse to see you."

She nodded, placing her hand on Hugh's arm, allowing him to assist her from the carriage.

"He may," she said. "If he won't see me today, he'll see

me tomorrow. If he won't see me tomorrow, he'll see me the day after. And a thousand days if necessary, Hugh."

Hugh's mouth was as expressive as words. Now it quirked in a smile.

Very well, perhaps she was a tiny bit stubborn in certain situations. She was a woman who toiled in a man's world. She couldn't afford to be perceived as soft and demure. That was for women who rarely left their parlors or used fans, for the love of all that was holy. She couldn't imagine using a fan to flirt with a man. She'd feel like a fool.

Shaking her skirts free, she did a quick perusal of herself. Of course she looked nothing like the scores of women who'd probably made their way up these broad white steps.

She was simply Minerva Todd, whose assets were not those of figure or face.

At the top of the steps she took a deep breath, squared her shoulders, and stared at the black painted door with its whimsical brass knocker. Why a mushroom, of all things?

She raised the knocker and let it fall, hearing the soft echo in the foyer. Her heart galloped in her chest, tightening her breath. Despite having donned her gloves, her fingertips were cold.

He must see her. He must tell her.

Even if it was the worst possible news, she must know.

When no one answered the door, she let the knocker fall twice more.

The front windows were clean and sparkling. The stoop had been swept. No debris of any sort was on the steps. Yet she had the feeling the house was deserted.

Taking a step back, she looked up at the windows on the second floor. All of them were shielded by curtains. No one stood there watching her.

She turned, calling out to Hugh standing beside the carriage.

"Would you go to the stables, Hugh? See if there's a carriage there."

If the earl wasn't home, it would be the reason he hadn't answered her. Did he have a country home? How would she find out where it was?

He nodded and began walking to the corner and around to the back of the townhouse.

Returning to the door, she felt the first droplets of rain. A moment later the heavens opened up and she was drenched, as if a bucket had been upended over her head.

The house had no place where a visitor might stand and be shielded from the elements. An oversight that felt almost as if the earl had designed it.

She let the knocker fall again.

The rain smelled of dust and the London streets. London seemed to be a city that contained odors, holding them in as if jealous they might escape. Now she picked out the scent of honeysuckle and roses, old buildings, manure, dust, and the ever-present and pungent smell of the Thames.

She was fortunate that her home, her parent's house, was located on a square isolated from the foulest stench of sewage, as was this house.

The door opened so suddenly she nearly fell forward.

A tall, thin man greeted her. The sleeves of his shirt were rolled up, revealing muscular arms. His hair was brushed back from a face made stern by a prominent nose and pointed chin.

Sweat dotted his brow and above his lip.

His look of irritation was a little off-putting, but she ventured a smile anyway.

"Yes?"

She had the strangest urge to apologize. No, that would never do. She was here for a reason.

"I'm here to see the earl."

"Are you?"

How very odd to be questioned by a major domo.

She pulled out her calling card and tried to hand it to him. Her hand was outstretched but he wasn't taking it.

"I am. Will you tell him that Minerva Todd is here to see him, please, on account of her brother, Neville."

"He isn't receiving visitors."

"Please tell the earl I shall not take up much of his time. I only have one question to ask."

Had the major domo begun as a footman? His height was impressive. She truly disliked having to look up at him. The stony expression on his hawkish face would have been daunting if she weren't determined to see the earl.

"That won't be possible."

He moved to stand half behind the door, edging it closed with his foot. Minerva deliberately inserted her leg in the opening. She wasn't as tall as the major domo, but she was not excessively short either. She and Neville were of a height.

"Please, I really must see him."

His brown eyes remained flat and unmoved.

"I regret, Miss Todd, that His Lordship is not receiving visitors," he said.

"Can you take him a message, then? I need to know where my brother is. Neville hasn't returned to London."

"I'm afraid I couldn't."

"I shall report you for insolence," she said, annoyed beyond measure.

The man startled her by smiling, such a transformative expression that his entire face softened. The hooked nose lost prominence, the jutting chin didn't seem as sharp. Even his brown eyes bore a twinkle.

"You do that, Miss Todd."

"You're a detestable major domo."

"I'm the earl's secretary, Miss Todd," he said, making a small bow. "Stanley Howington. I suppose I act as major domo as well."

"Do you have no other staff?"

"Is that any of your concern?"

"It is if you leave a visitor standing in the rain."

"It's the housekeeper's half day off and the maids are engaged in other tasks, Miss Todd, not that it's any of your business."

"Did you go to America with the earl, Mr. Howington?"

He shook his head, placed his hand on the latch and started to slowly close the door again.

She waved her card at him and he reluctantly took it.

"Will you ask him about Neville?" she asked, putting her hand on the edge of the door. In order to completely close it, he was going to have to shove her out of the way.

Mr. Howington, for all his rudeness, didn't look the type to brutalize a woman.

"Will you, sir?"

"His Lordship doesn't like to discuss America, Miss Todd."

She told herself that she could be excused her bad manners because of worry. A month of attempting to get the Earl of Rathsmere to answer her was frustrating to the extreme, and having Mr. Howington say he wouldn't see her now was enough of an incitement for rudeness.

She grabbed the edge of the door and pushed it inward.

"I am not talking about America," she said, her voice this side of a shout. "I am talking about my brother. Where is Neville?"

A gust of rain-soaked wind suddenly pushed her toward the railing. She lost her grip on the door and stared up at the secretary.

"I need to find my brother, Mr. Howington. He hasn't returned from America."

Since the door was advancing on her knuckles, and was already pressing against the toe of her shoe, she had every expectation that the Earl of Rathsmere's secretary would toss her from the stoop. So much for not brutalizing a woman.

"Do not force me to be ungentlemanly, Miss Todd. You are getting drenched. Would it not be best for you to retreat to your carriage?"

"At least tell me you will ask the earl."

He considered her for a moment. She had the feeling whatever he said next would be a lie, anything to get rid of her.

"Very well," she said, taking a step back.

Sometimes it was necessary to retreat in order to fight again another day.

Rain had permeated the back of her dress until even her shift was wet. Droplets slid down her spine leaving an icy trail.

Her bonnet emitted a peculiar smell, something reminding her of their neighbor's dog. Frederick loved water and sought it out at every opportunity. At the moment Frederick and her bonnet smelled the same.

She turned, grabbed the wrought-iron railing, descending the steps with hard-won dignity. Hugh stepped in front of her, his hair wetly plastered to his skull.

Nodding to him, she entered the carriage, knowing

her errand had been futile but more determined than ever to succeed in her task.

She had to find Neville, and no secretary, diligent as he was, was going to stop her.

She would see the Earl of Rathsmere. She would.

SIZZLING ROMANCE FROM
USA TODAY BESTSELLING AUTHOR
KAREN RANNEY

The Devil of Clan Sinclair

978-0-06-224244-0

Widowed and penniless unless she produces an heir, Virginia Traylor, Countess of Barrett, embarks on a fateful journey that brings her to the doorstep of the only man she's ever loved. Macrath Sinclair, known as The Devil, was once rejected by Virginia. He knows he should turn her away, but she needs him, and now he wants her more than ever.

The Witch of Clan Sinclair

978-0-06-224246-4

Logan Harrison, the Lord Provost of Edinburgh, needs a conventional and diplomatic wife to help further his political ambitions. He most certainly does not need Mairi Sinclair, the fiery, passionate, fiercely beautiful woman who tries to thwart him at every turn. But if she's so wrong for him, why can't the bewitched lord stop kissing her?

The Virgin of Clan Sinclair

978-0-06-224249-5

Beneath Ellice Traylor's innocent exterior beats a passionate heart, and she has been pouring all of her frustrated virginal fantasies into a scandalous manuscript. When a compromising position forces her to wed the Earl of Gadsden, he discovers Ellie's secret book and can't stop thinking about the fantasies the disarming virgin can dream up.

At Avon Books, we know your passion for romance—once you finish one of our novels, you find yourself wanting more.

May we tempt you with . . .

- **Excerpts** from our upcoming releases.

- Entertaining **extras**, including authors' personal photo albums and book lists.

- Behind-the-scenes **scoop** on your favorite characters and series.

- **Sweepstakes** for the chance to win free books, romantic getaways, and other fun prizes.

- Writing **tips** from our authors and editors.

- **Blog** with our authors and find out why they love to write romance.

- **Exclusive content** that's not contained within the pages of our novels.

Join us at
www.avonbooks.com

An Imprint of HarperCollins*Publishers*
www.avonromance.com